the
Au pair

the
Au pair

janey fraser

arrow books

Published by Arrow Books 2012

2 4 6 8 10 9 7 5 3

Copyright © Janey Fraser, 2012

First published in Great Britain in 2012 by
Arrow Books
Random House, 20 Vauxhall Bridge Road,
London SW1V 2SA

www.randomhouse.co.uk

Addresses for companies within The Random House Group Limited can be
found at: www.randomhouse.co.uk/offices.htm

The Random House Group Limited Reg. No. 954009

A CIP catalogue record for this book
is available from the British Library

ISBN 9780099558187

The Random House Group Limited supports The Forest
Stewardship Council (FSC®), the leading international forest
certification organisation. Our books carrying the FSC label are
printed on FSC® certified paper. FSC is the only forest certification
scheme endorsed by the leading environmental organisations, including
Greenpeace. Our paper procurement policy can be found at:
www.randomhouse.co.uk/environment

Typeset by SX Composting DTP, Rayleigh, Essex
Printed and bound by CPI Group (UK) Ltd, Croydon, CR0 4YY

This book is dedicated to William, Lucy and Giles who,
between them:

Locked a Swiss miss in her room just before the school run;
Preferred to play with 'Collette'* instead of me
(*Not her real name);
Taught unsuitable words to all of them;
Learned unsuitable foreign words in return;
Got through five au pairs in two years (don't even ask).

This book is not dedicated to the au pairs who variously:
Peed in my front garden;
Ran off with a Frenchman whom I'd stupidly
introduced her to;
Refused to vacuum every day because
'we do not do that in my country';
Invited all her friends round during my absence,
to share my chocolate biscuits and Bombay Sapphire.

The Au Pair is also dedicated to my husband
(who isn't allowed to have one) and all good au pairs and
nice families everywhere.
As for the others – you know who you are!

Acknowledgements

Unlimited gratitude to my agent Teresa Chris, my literary Godmother. Also to Gillian Holmes for her magic eye; Sarah Page for her marketing skills; Marissa Cox for her PR expertise and warm emails; and everyone at Arrow. Not forgetting Betty Schwartz and Hilary Johnson whose words encouraged me in the early days. Also the Romantic Novelists' Association.

Finally, a big thanks to all the au pair agencies which helped me with my research. Please note that any similarity to living characters is entirely coincidental.

Chapter 1

'I tell you, Jilly, I'll never have another one again. Never! Antoinette is a nightmare! Absolute nightmare! I specifically asked the agency for a non-smoker but before we'd even got back from the airport, she'd lit up one of those filthy Gauloise things. Then – get this! – it turns out that she's eighteen and not nineteen like the agency told me, *and* the only experience she's had with children is visiting her fifteen-year-old nephew in Lyons once a year.'

Who'd have an au pair? It was simply asking for trouble, thought Jilly as she listened to her friend Paula pouring it all out. Frankly, she couldn't imagine anything worse than a live-in stranger. It was hard enough living with your own family.

'It's like having another child,' raged Paula, march-ing over to her enormous silver American fridge and grabbing a bottle of Pinot Grigio though it wasn't even eleven o'clock yet. 'On her first night, she just sat there at dinner without offering to help as though she was a guest!'

'Perhaps—' Jilly started to say. Too late! Paula was steaming on.

'*Then* she used up all the hot water for an hour-long shower. As for her English, it's a mixture of *Janet and John* meets *Desperate Housewives* with a heavy Woody Allen Parisian accent.'

'But…'

'And when I asked her to take Immy to the nursery summer club – with a map that I'd drawn specially for her – she ended up at the *garden* nursery. Isn't that ridiculous?'

Not really. It was quite a tall order for an au pair to do the nursery run on her first day. Jilly was torn between the desire to be loyal to her friend and also fair to this girl who was doubtless feeling very lonely and unsure in a foreign country. 'You were a bit worried about her introduction letter,' she started to say but Paula waved her hand dismissively.

'She was all I could get at short notice! *And* another thing…'

It was no good! When her friend Paula was in full flow like this, there was no stopping her. Maybe that's why she was so skinny – all that nervous energy.

Lucky her! Jilly, who was constantly fighting the battle against a size 14, was always envious of anyone who could wear drainpipe jeans without looking as though a rugby ball had got stuck halfway down each thigh.

'Maybe it's my fault for getting a French one,' continued Paula, rummaging around the dirty dishwasher for a glass. 'But it's so difficult, isn't it? It's a sort of emotional pick and mix. The Germans are meant to be bossy, the Turkish have BO and the Scandinavians nick your husband.'

Talk about generalisations!

Paula gave a short, sharp, ironic laugh. 'And considering Nigel and I are the one couple in twenty owning up to a sexless marriage – did you read that survey in the *Mail*? – I don't fancy any competition from some nubile teenager. Especially under the same roof. You heard about Mark and Suzy, didn't you? They're having a trial separation. Apparently he's met some nineteen-year-old.'

Really? Suzy from the parents' committee at school? Jilly didn't know them well but they always seemed quite happy together. It just went to show that you never knew what went on behind closed doors. But as for Paula and Nigel…well, surely they were fine? Just as she and David were! Granted, her own marriage wasn't exactly bursting with passion but it had reached that nice, cosy, comfortable stage where the two of them would cuddle up at night, ankles hooked together, secure in their love and the family they had woven around them.

'Of course you don't need to lose weight,' her husband would reassure her, even though her post-twin tummy was still wedged firmly between them. Yes, he loved her used-to-be-blond hair, just the way it was. And no, she wasn't too old to have the same shoulder-length style she'd sported as a teenager.

Even so, Jilly wouldn't fancy having a sultry eighteen-year-old French girl in the house. Why put yourself in the line of fire, as her mother might say. Mum had very firm views on men who strayed, not to mention women who 'gave them the opportunity', as she put it.

'I'm sure Nigel isn't the kind to elope with an au pair,' she started to say but Paula was off again, perched on the edge of her chrome designer breakfast bar stool, still in her sparkly silver leotard after her

Zumbalatesalsa class. In contrast, Jilly was wearing a slightly too tight pair of jeans which had been clean at 6.30 a.m. but now bore an egg stain on one knee and a guilty smear of chocolate ice cream on the other. The first came from the children's breakfast this morning and the second from a comfort-eating binge soon afterwards. The anticipation of the forthcoming school summer holidays with three children to amuse always took its toll on her stomach.

'I thought an au pair would be cheaper than a cleaner and a babysitter!' Paula was getting really upset now, drumming her silicone-gel nails on the black and white kitchen island between them. 'But she's costing me a fortune in petrol, cheese and coffee. And she leaves her towels on the bathroom floor as though this is a hotel.'

That didn't sound good. 'Have you spoken to the agency?'

'Pah!' Paula's face was going pink with indignation. 'When I rang to ask for a swap, there was an answer phone gaily informing me that the agency had closed down.'

That was terrible! 'So what are you meant to do until then?'

'Sit it out, I suppose! I can hardly throw her out on the streets.' Paula took another slug from her glass before offering her the bottle.

'No thanks.' Jilly covered the mug with its MOTHER KNOWS BEST slogan, still half full of the finest decaff. Thanks to Paula's enthusiastic bottle waving, it was now in serious danger of becoming a coffee-spritzer.

Paula frowned disapprovingly. 'Anyway, when I

Googled the agency, I found it doesn't even belong to a professional association. *Then* I discovered through Twitter – get this! – that *anyone* can set up an au pair business round their kitchen table? Isn't that awful!'

Before Jilly had a chance to agree, there was the sound of heavy plodding down the stairs.

'Shhh,' hissed Paula with a horrified look. 'She's coming. Quick. Talk about something else.'

Even as she spoke, a small sullen girl, with dark curls shrouding a heart-shaped face, marched in. If it wasn't for the scowl, she would be gorgeous! But even *with* it, she was still extremely pretty in a gypsy-like fashion. Her skin, noted Jilly, hinted at a Moroccan background. She was wearing a thick black jumper and shivering in an exaggerated fashion as though there was snow on the ground instead of midsummer roses in full bloom. The distinct whiff of BO coupled with cheap-smelling perfume made Jilly feel slightly nauseous.

Until now, she'd thought Paula was behaving like many of the rather slightly spoilt, non-working mothers of Corrywood who lived for the gym and Twitter. But now she was beginning to feel sorry for her friend.

'Madame Paula.' Antoinette's black eyes were harsh and challenging. 'I have changed the shits.'

Jilly did a double-take. Did the au pair just say what she *thought* she had? Paula raised her hand to her forehead in dramatic despair. 'I told you, Antoinette. You have to flush the loo twice in your bathroom. It can be temperamental. Like you.' She added the last two words in a low voice but if Jilly could hear, surely so could the girl...

7

'*Non!*' The au pair's voice was angry, as though she was reprimanding an employee rather than her employer. 'I not talk about difficult toilet that does not rush.'

'Flush,' corrected Paula. 'So...what...are...you... talking...about exactly?' Paula enunciated each word very slowly as though speaking to a small child and at the same time, shooting Jilly a *see-what-I-have-to-put-up-with* look.

Antoinette's eyes were becoming even blacker and harder in a way that sent shivers down Jilly's spine. This girl gave her the creeps! 'I change the shits in the children's rooms like you told me to.'

Paula's face cleared. 'Oh, you mean the *sheets*!' She gave a small cocktail-party shriek of hollow mirth but Jilly could see the relief on her face. For a moment there, both women had had visions of the au pair leaving...well...something rather nasty upstairs. 'In England, Antoinette, we say "sheeeets" instead of... instead of "shits".'

Another frown. Another scowl. 'That is what I inform you.'

Poor Paula began to look very uncomfortable. Jilly's heart went out to her! On the surface, her friend seemed to have it all: lovely home, children and a husband. But when you got to know Nigel better, he was (quite frankly) a bit of a lech who would hold your hands in greeting for much longer than necessary and then follow it up with a wet kiss on both sides of the cheek in an over-familiar fashion. He was also a bore, convinced that his opinions were the only correct ones. Neither Jilly nor David could stand him, although, for her friend's sake, they had to put up with him socially.

'This is my friend Mrs Collins, by the way,' continued Paula, flushing, clearly trying to change the subject.

Keen to help, Jilly put out her hand. 'Nice to meet you, Antoinette.'

The girl made no attempt to respond but simply gave her the same sullen look she had just given her employer. Oh dear!

'Could you please go into the garden and look after Immy?' said Paula as though she was asking an enormous favour. 'She's on the swing.'

Antoinette shivered again. 'But I am so frizzing.'

'Then put on your coat!' trilled Paula in an over-bright voice. 'In England, we are great believers in fresh air.'

It was like trying to persuade one of the children to go out and play! Surely the whole point of having an au pair was to have some help instead of adding to your work load?

'OK.' Antoinette rolled her eyes. 'But I put her in her poshchair.'

'Her what?'

Those black eyes glittered with irritation. 'Her *posh*chair.'

'Do you think,' intervened Jilly quietly, 'that she means "pushchair"?'

Antoinette scowled. 'That's what I inform you before.'

'I see! Well no, actually I don't want her in her pushchair. Immy needs to let off steam or else she won't sleep tonight.'

9

Antoinette's eyes were fixed on her employer. 'I do not understand.'

'I think you do,' muttered Paula. She waved her hand towards the garden. 'Out, please. No pushchair. Comprendez?'

Sullenly, Antoinette took her shiny pink coat, which was hanging on a peg by the back door, and stomped outside.

'Wow,' breathed Jilly. 'I see what you mean. It can't make for a very pleasant atmosphere.'

'It's not!' Paula was pouring herself another slug of Pinot. 'I'm almost glad when she's out. In fact, that's another thing. She hasn't been here for half a minute but already she's slinking off to English classes at the college.'

'But isn't that why she's here?' Jilly enquired. 'To improve her English?'

'Not,' said Paula, glaring at her for siding with the enemy, 'if she goes straight to bed after the nursery run, claiming that she can't do any work because it is "the time of the month". Then she managed to block the pipes with continental tampons and guess who had to get them out?'

Ugh!

'I haven't even had a chance to show her where the Dyson's hibernating. *And* she wants her seventy pounds a week pocket money in advance. It's outrageous!'

Jilly had known Paula for years, ever since they'd met at antenatal. She'd been expecting the twins and Paula her eldest, William. They'd rubbed each other's backs during mock labour role play. Swapped tips over stretch creams. Asked the other to be godmother to their respective children. Gone to baby signing classes together. And then moved on to Puddleducks, the lovely pre-school round the corner run by that kind but competent Gemma Merryfield who was now Mrs Balls.

Paula's little Immy was still there, although William, along with her own HarryandAlfie (somehow their names always came out as one), had progressed to Corrybanks, the local primary. But never, in all this time, had Jilly known Paula to be so worked up. If this is what an au pair did to you, you'd be better off without one, surely?

'What's she doing now?' Paula nudged her. 'I can't look myself or it will seem as though I'm spying.'

Jilly tried to glance casually out of the kitchen window, which faced a beautiful lawn, leading down to a copse with a wooden swing and slide ensemble from the Indulged Kids Company. (Her twins had to make do with a plank of wood suspended by a rope from their old gnarled apple tree. Still, they seemed to love it.)

Meanwhile, three-year-old Immy – short for Imogen – was sitting at the top of the expensive slide, waving her stubby little arms at Antoinette, who was now perched on the white designer garden bench, huddled over her mobile and puffing madly on one of the forbidden Gauloises, oblivious of her charge's pre - dicament. Dear little Immy, who was stoutly built in the manner of her father, was always getting stuck in places. Last year it had been a small gap in the park railings and a twenty-minute wait for the fire brigade.

'I think you might want to…' began Jilly. No! Too late. Immy had somehow released her squat little bottom from the constraints of the slide and launched herself down on to the ground. Although it was difficult to hear any yells from that distance, she appeared unhurt. No thanks to the shivering shape in the bright pink raincoat who was still attached to her mobile and hadn't even bothered looking up. She was walking back up to the house now without so much as a glance back.

'But she doesn't like William,' continued Paula. 'He calls her 'Ant' and keeps asking if she's really an insect, which gets her really mad. He went into her room the other day. Absolutely disgusting! The bed was unmade. There were clothes all over the floor. Everything stank of sweat and…'

Her voice tailed off as the back door opened. Uh-oh. From the look on the new girl's face, her English, not to mention her hearing, might just be better than her hostess gave her credit for.

'Your son venture into *ma chambre*?' repeated Antoinette, chewing yellow gum at the same time as speaking. 'My room is Pry Vate! It says so in the book that the agency gave me.' As if on cue, she whipped out a leaflet and handed it to Jilly as though she was the judge in all this. 'Look!' she repeated.

Jilly, thanks to her pre-children days in HR where she'd been used to scanning staff contracts, was a quick reader. It did indeed say that an au pair was entitled to her own room and that this should be considered private – or 'Pry Vate' as Antoinette had put it. There were also a host of other regulations which, so it seemed, were heavily weighted in favour of the au pair rather than the employer.

Paula's face, meanwhile, had gone rather red. 'I'm sorry,' she stuttered. 'I actually asked William to go in. I thought the window needed opening to let in some air.'

'Hair?' Antoinette shivered, pulling her pink raincoat around her as though to protect herself from interfering Englishwomen and nippy summer weather. 'There is too much frizzing hair in your country.' Her eyes moistened. 'It is not like home.'

Poor kid! Jilly felt a jerk of sympathy for her as big, fat tears rolled down the girl's face. Paula was really kind at heart but did have a sharp tongue which had been known to loose itself occasionally at PTA meetings.

'I'm sorry, Antoinette,' Paula said. 'I really am. Is there anything that would make you feel better?'

Instantly the tears stopped. 'I like to see my friends.'

'Your friends? I didn't know you had any.'

'My new friends.' Antoinette's tone had changed to one of hair-tossing defiance. 'The friends I create at school.'

Paula was nodding eagerly as though keen to make up for her earlier crime. 'Well, I know I asked you to babysit tonight but if you want, you could have an evening off.'

'No.'

For a minute, Jilly thought Antoinette had said 'Non' but then she realised, as the doorbell rang, that she had said 'Now'. Suddenly that phone call in the garden became clear! The little monkey had put on a

13

display of homesick tears – helped by Paula's admission that ten-year-old William had invaded her room – and now, judging from the stream of foreign voices coming into the house, had invited round the local au pair mafia.

'Paula,' she began but her friend merely shrugged, mouthing, 'What can I do?'

'*Tu veux du café?*' Antoinette was saying to a tall, skinny, blonde girl with a picture of a red heart next to the Eiffel Tower on her skinny T-shirt which clearly didn't have a bra underneath. '*C'est* decaff. Very good.'

'I feel as though this isn't my own home any more,' whispered Paula as another girl wandered in, wearing a pair of frayed denim shorts over black tights and a pale lilac pashmina elegantly twisted round her neck. The effect, odd as it was, was incredibly stylish and exuded so much more confidence than Jilly had had herself at that age.

'All I needed was another pair of hands but now I seem to have inherited a busload of foreigners in search of an adventure at my expense!' Suddenly she stopped, clasping her hand to her mouth. 'Oh my God, where's Immy?'

Jilly pointed through the window to the top of the slide where a small pair of fists were flailing furiously. 'Looks like she's stuck again.' She glanced at Antoinette who was now handing round the biscuit tin to her new friends, two of whom were actually sitting on top of Paula's marble island, long legs crossed provocatively. 'You look after this lot and I'll sort her out.'

*

14

Poor Paula, thought Jilly, driving home. What a dreadful situation! Apparently, Antoinette and her friends were going clubbing tonight. What would happen if she didn't get back safely? Such a responsibility!

Was this what lay in store for *her* as a parent, Jilly thought suddenly. She had started her family comparatively young. How terrifying to think that Nick, her eldest, was only three years younger than eighteen-year-old Antoinette! So far, touch wood, he'd been reasonably easy apart from the usual arguments about Facebook and loud music. He didn't stay out late. He hadn't had a girlfriend to distract him from homework. And he didn't smoke, which was more than she could have said about her brother at that age!

On the whole, she thought slightly smugly to herself as she pulled into the drive of their deceptively spacious 1930s semi, her little family was ticking along quite nicely. All right, the house wasn't as tidy as she would like it – just look at that pile of football kit that Nick had dumped on the floor, and the trail of muddy footprints going up the stairs. But it was home! *Their* home.

Frankly, she thought, bending down to pick up a postcard from her parents, she'd much rather live in semi-chaos (was there any *other* way with three children?) than share their personal space with a hostile stranger like the surly black-eyed Antoinette.

Yet so many mothers did it! In fact, it was quite rare here in Corrywood *not* to have a cleaner or an au pair. One of the parents at Puddleducks – Johnnie's mum – had gone one further and had a string of Swedish male 'mothers' helps' who had made pick-up time quite exciting.

Maybe that's what she needed. A sexy Swede to boost her self-confidence and be a firm hand with the boys if she ever went back to work. Jilly felt a tremor of unease as she began to gather up Nick's football stuff. 'When are you going back?' was one of those subjects she and Paula discussed every now and then, if only to convince themselves that it was still a possibility.

Jilly's mind went back to uni where she had met David during freshers week. They'd been inseparable and it had seemed perfectly natural to get married straight after graduation. The fact that she landed her dream job in HR at the same time was an added bonus! But not long after, she had fallen unexpectedly pregnant with Nick.

Both she and David had had high-flying career mothers and because David was doing well, they agreed she should be a full-time mum, especially as it would make sense to have another baby soon. But that just didn't happen! No particular reason, said the doctor. It can be like that sometimes. Yet ironically, just as Nick started school and Jilly began polishing up her CV, she found she was pregnant with the twins.

Wonderful as it was, part of her had felt rather deflated that she wasn't going back to work after all. But as David said, it didn't make sense with three children to bring up. Yet all the way through the nappies and the sleepless nights and the homework arguments and the long, sometimes tedious school holidays, she secretly played the going-back game in her head, as though persuading herself that she wasn't 'just a mum'.

Who was she kidding? Not only had her confidence sunk but HR had moved on so fast that all her skills were out of date. Besides, David wasn't keen. 'What's the point of having children if you're not around for them,' he always said firmly. 'How would you manage during the holidays or if the kids were ill or when I'm away?'

He had a point. Take today. Jilly glanced at her watch. Only an hour to go before it was time to collect the twins from after-school cricket practice. Then there would be the usual squabbles and arguments over tea (everyone wanted something different), not to mention Bruno who needed walking.

Not for the first time, she wished her parents hadn't taken on this small wiry terrier from a rescue centre. Bruno spent more time with them than with Mum and Dad thanks to their new-found passion for cruises.

'You don't mind dogsitting for us, do you, darling?' her mother was constantly saying. 'It's very good for the children to have him around, don't you think? Teaches little Bruno to share!'

Talking of the dog, where was he? And where was Nick? The messy football kit indicated he'd got back earlier from school than usual.

'Anyone there?' she yelled up the stairs. No answer. No one ever answered in this house unless they wanted something.

Surprise, surprise! Her son was lying stomach down on his bedroom carpet, glued to Facebook. It was a wonder there wasn't an umbilical cord between her eldest and the screen. Meanwhile, Bruno was growling in the corner with a pile of dirty underwear around him. Honestly! Why couldn't he just grab shoes like other dogs instead of having a fetish for underwear?

'Nick. NICK!'

Still no answer. There was only one way to deal with this!

An angry face with a mop of blond hair glared up at her. 'Oy, Mum. What are you doing?'

'Pulling out the plug so you'll listen. You were meant to have tidied up the kitchen.'

Nick rolled his eyes. 'I forgot.'

'Then can you do it now?'

'Give me a break, Mum. I'm listening to Great Cynics.'

'Then you won't get your allowance.'

'Fine.' He turned over on to his stomach again, picking up a packet of salt and vinegar crisps even though it was almost lunchtime. 'There's nothing to spend it on anyway. This town's crap. I'm bored.'

'Then you can stop being bored and tidy up instead! Besides, there's only two weeks until we go away.'

'Camping in France?' Nick gave her a pitying look. 'That's so sad.'

'No it's not. It will be fun. Look, I'll do a deal. If you take Bruno for a walk, I'll sort out the kitchen.'

Nick groaned. 'In a minute.'

'No, Nick. I said NOW.'

As she spoke, there was the sound of the front door slamming. Looking out of the window, Jilly saw to her surprise that David's grey BMW was in the drive. That was odd! He was never usually back before eight or often nine at night. And wasn't he meant to be in Manchester tonight?

18

'David?' She flew down the stairs and into the sitting room where her husband was pouring himself a large gin and tonic from the drinks cupboard. David didn't drink at lunchtime! Not during the week, anyway. 'What's going on?'

His face looked uncertain. Troubled even. 'Sit down, Jilly.' He led her to the sofa, a nice squashy comfortable Sanderson with a floral blue and yellow print that Mum had given them when she was 'downsizing'. 'I've something to tell you.'

Oh God no. Her mouth went dry and her throat tightened. Was he ill? Had something happened to Mum or Dad on the cruise?

'What?' she croaked. 'Quick, tell me.'

David looked away and she felt a lurch of panic. 'Please,' she repeated, grabbing his jacket, 'what is it?'

He looked in her direction but his eyes couldn't meet hers. 'I'm ashamed,' he said quietly; so quietly that she could hardly hear him.

Jilly felt a trickle of sweat running down her back and her hands go clammy. To think she had been secretly smug just now at Paula's about her own love life. How could she have been that naive? She knew enough women at school who'd been through this. Women whose husbands suddenly, out of the blue, announced they were having an affair and were leaving; usually for some predatory bitch in the office.

'For God's sake, tell me what you've done!'

His eyes continued to wander. 'It's not what I've done, Jilly. It's what they've done to me. I don't have a job any more. Well, I do, but it's not the same.' He sighed. 'I should have told you but I didn't want to worry you. They've been making cuts at work all over the place. Then my boss called me in this morning and said that they were closing the new division.'

'But that was your baby!' Jilly tried to think straight. David had been brought into the insurance firm because of his financial experience. He'd set up a series of new proposals which, until the credit crisis, had been profitable. She'd known it wasn't doing that well but she hadn't realised things were that bad.

David laughed shortly. 'That's why they're mad at me.' He shook his head as though he was cross with himself. 'There's no easy way to say this. I took a bit of a gamble with something and, well, it hasn't paid off.'

'What kind of a gamble?'

He stood up, walked to the fireplace with its mock gas fire beneath – 'very realistic', everyone always said – and looked up at the silver-framed photographs on the mantelpiece. Nick at his christening in a much younger Jilly's arms when she hadn't needed to highlight her hair. A grinning David with a twin in each arm. Mum and Dad in front of a huge cruise liner on their thirtieth wedding anniversary.

'I persuaded them to offer a new kind of insurance package. But it's bombed. Made them lose money. Quite a lot of it.'

'So they've sacked you?' she managed to say.

'No,' continued David in a voice that didn't sound like his. 'But they're offering me another job in the company instead.'

Thank goodness for that!

'It's still not good,' he said quietly, observing her

face. 'It's the same basic salary but it doesn't have a commission structure.'

But they needed that in order to...

'Pay the mortgage.' He completed her sentence for her in the way he was always able to. Jilly drew her husband towards her, showering him with little kisses. The fact that he wasn't having an affair – absurd idea really, given how much they loved each other – made her feel giddy with relief.

'I've always said,' she murmured into his jacket, 'as long as we're all together and healthy, it doesn't matter what happens in life.'

'Yes.' David's voice wavered. 'But how will we manage?'

'We'll cancel the holiday for a start. We'll make cutbacks. And I'll get a job!' It seemed so easy to say that she almost believed it.

David shook his head. 'But we've talked about this. Both of us have said how difficult it would be for you to go back to work *and* look after the children.' He ran his hands through his dark hair which had tiny flecks of grey at the side. Flecks which, she suddenly realised, hadn't been there a few weeks ago. 'I feel so guilty that I've put us in this situation!'

Jilly clutched David's jacket even more tightly as though scared he might slip away. 'You were only doing your best. I'll think of something. Something that I can do *and* look after the children.'

But what? Avon? Door-to-door selling? Market research? Then, suddenly, a picture of the sulky Antoinette in the garden, puffing away at her Gauloise, came into her head. What was it that Paula had said?

Anyone could set up an au pair agency business round the kitchen table! It wouldn't have to take long. Just a couple of ads on the net and the local paper. Word of mouth would help too...

'In fact,' she said, feeling an unexpected thrill of self-worth and excitement shooting through her, 'I think I might just have an idea...'

JILLY'S AU PAIR AGENCY

SMALL, FRIENDLY, HANDS-ON BUSINESS,
ONE HOUR FROM LONDON.
SPECIALISES IN PLACING RELIABLE AU PAIRS
IN LOCAL FAMILIES.
REASONABLE RATES.
VETTING ASSURED.

Chapter 2

'There's something in the post for you,' said her mother. 'Look! It is from *Angleterre*.' She pronounced the last word with an emphasis that suggested extreme danger mixed with lethal curiosity.

Marie-France stiffened as Maman pushed the letter with the airmail stamp across the kitchen table towards her, with an expression which she'd learned to read over the years. It meant: *what is going on?*

Collette Dubonne always liked to know what was going on. So, too, did Marie-France. When you were so similar – they shared the same long dark wavy hair, trim but voluptuous figure and the dubious ability to dive in without looking – it was bound to lead to arguments. In such cases, distraction was a good idea.

'*Tu veux du café, Maman?*'

'No, Marie-France,' retorted her mother sharply. 'I do not want any coffee, thank you. I want to know what is going on. Now are you going to tell me or shall I find out for myself?'

Her mother put her head on one side coquettishly as though her daughter was one of her many admirers and gave her a knowing look. With only three years to go before her fortieth birthday, she was still a lovely woman with that wide smile and full mouth, which was never without its veneer of gloss. Her impeccably plucked eyebrows arching slightly at the ends indicated a woman who was not to be messed around. Indeed, she was far more beautiful and youthful than most of Marie-France's friends' mothers, which was why people often mistook them for sisters. Sometimes when she looked at pictures of her mother at her age, it was like looking in the mirror.

The only difference was that Marie-France was more level-headed, mainly because she didn't drink as much as her mother. Not that her mother was an alcoholic, but she did like her half a bottle a night and that sometimes made her tearful or melodramatic. Now, however, she was in her sharp, on-the-ball mood.

'Don't play with me, Marie-France. I want to know why you have received a letter from England. *Qu'est-ce passe*? And don't look at me like that. Give me some respect.' She sighed. 'When I was your age, we did what our parents told us.'

Marie-France made a 'pah' sound. 'You know that's not true – at least not in your case.'

Her mother held up a beautifully manicured hand. 'Don't think you can change the subject like that. Who is that letter from?' She examined the postmark, frowning because it was too faint to read the name of the town.

Very well, Marie-France told herself. She had to face the music at some point so she might as well get it over with now. 'Because I am going to work over there as an au pair.'

'WHAT?'

Honestly! Her mother should have been an opera star. She certainly had the dramatics to go with it, not to mention the well-developed pout. Collette Dubonne had a reputation in the village as a force to be reckoned with. Just as well that one of the few people who could match her was her daughter.

'This is all because of our little chat the other month, isn't it, *ma fille*? Because you made me tell you something that I had not wished to.'

'*Made* you?' Marie-France couldn't help laughing. 'No one can make you do anything, Maman. You said *you* wanted to tell *me* something so don't start distorting the facts the way you always do. You should have been a lawyer.'

'Distort the facts?'

It was always the same! Whenever she put her mother on the spot, she would repeat a phrase to give herself more time. It was a clever trick and one which Marie-France herself had adopted over the years.

'You exaggerate, Maman. Come on. You know you do and that's why you're – usually – such fun to be with. My friends love you because you're different from their mothers.'

It was true, even if the friends' mothers didn't trust Collette with their husbands. Still, the compliment had done something to mollify the initial anger in her mother's face.

'The letter is from an English au pair agency,' continued Marie-France firmly, popping on her sun-glasses even though they were in the kitchen with its old range and the view out of the window towards the rundown chateau in the distance. Wearing sunglasses indoors was another of her mother's old tricks she had picked up. It hid your eyes so it was easier to tell a fib. Or two.

'I've applied for a job.' She raised her chin defiantly. 'It's only for six months.'

'Six months?' Her mother stood up, gripped the side of the kitchen table and then sank down again, moaning as though in a Greek tragedy. Marie-France leaned across and took her mother's hands. They were incredibly small, belying her mother's mental strength, yet also brown from the warm summer sunshine that they enjoyed in this part of France, so close to the Swiss border. Lovingly, she stroked them, as though calming the pulse which was beating furiously.

'I just don't want to see you hurt, that is all,' murmured her mother.

Bon! When her mother reached the tearful, plaintive stage, it usually meant she had given in. 'I'm not going to be,' she replied with a strength that she didn't feel inside.

There was a shaking of those dark curls, which mirrored her own. 'Ever since you were a little girl, Marie-France, you have put that wall of steel up around yourself. I understand why. But you cannot keep it up for ever. Trust me, I know.'

Her eyes moistened and for one awful moment, Marie-France feared the tears were genuine. But then her mother, in one swift deft move, ripped open the envelope which she had foolishly left on the table unattended.

'*Jilly's Au Pair Agency,*' her mother read out loud. Then she frowned as she took in the address at the top of the letter. 'Corrywood? *Mon Dieu*! I do not believe it. You are going to *Corrywood*?'

Marie-France's heart began to thump again as she recalled how she had trawled through every ad online to search for one as near to the place as possible. When she'd found an agency that was actually based in the town, she hadn't been able to believe her luck. 'That was a coincidence. I just found it on the net.'

'Coincidence!' Her mother leaped out of her chair again, knocking a plate of warm croissants on to the floor, snorting and waving the envelope in the air as though it was a headless trophy. 'You expect me to believe that! There are hundreds of au pair agencies in England. I know what you have done. You have chosen to go back to the same place where—'

'Please don't be upset.' Kneeling down to pick up the croissants – a good dusting would soon put them right – she spoke soothingly; something she'd learned to do as a child to minimise her only parent's juvenile and often erratic behaviour.

'The person – people – in question might not even be there.' She waved her hand in a dismissive gesture towards the magnificent magnolia tree outside. As a little girl, she used to sit under it and catch the petals as they fell, imagining that they were velvet slippers. 'They might have moved away.'

'And if they *haven't*? What happens then?'

Marie-France felt a thud of excitement in her throat. 'Then they will get to know the truth, won't they?'

Her mother shook her head vigorously so that her tumbling curls quivered in sympathy. 'I don't think you're doing the right thing, *petite*.' Her voice dropped. 'You could break up a family.'

'So what?' Marie-France felt her voice come out in

a low growl. 'I do not care. They hurt you. They need to pay.'

Her mother reached for the packet of cigarettes which she had promised to give up on her next birthday. 'And what about your place at the Sorbonne?'

Marie-France looked away. For as long as she could remember, she had wanted to read psychology and when she had achieved her grades, she'd been so excited. But then had come that long conversation just before her birthday and suddenly all her priorities had changed. 'I have asked them to defer it for a year and they agreed.'

Her mother spluttered. 'You did all this without telling me?'

'It's *my* life! No one else's.'

'*Tu es impossible.*' She stubbed out her cigarette in her bowl even though she'd only just lit it up and turned her attention to the letter. 'I just hope you will not dig up any worms, as the English say. What kind of home are you going to?'

'I don't know yet. That's why the agency has posted me this letter. It contains details of the families on her books who have expressed interest in me.'

Her mother sighed. 'Then I suppose, if you are determined, we will have to take a look.'

We? Already her mother was scanning a photograph of two parents and three children, grouped around an assortment of sparkling new-looking bicycles. Marie-France's heart lurched with jealousy. Look at that kid in front, grinning like that. Bet she hadn't been bullied at school for not having a father or a new bike.

'Three children are too much,' said her mother firmly. 'You would not have a moment to yourself. Besides, look at the circles under the woman's eyes. It is what you get when you have a big family.'

Marie-France knew this was her cue to compliment Maman on her own complexion. The irony was that she knew, all too well, that her mother would swap her exquisite looks in a second for a more conventional lifestyle with a husband and more children.

The two of them spent the next hour going through the forms that the agency had sent in reply to her application. Just as well it was a Sunday morning, otherwise her mother would be working at the chic little dress shop in the nearest town of Sevingy. She had climbed her way up to the position of manageress from sales assistant since Marie-France had started school. During the holidays, the owner – who sympathised with her employee's situation – allowed her to bring her daughter in and Marie-France would sit for hours in the back room, fingering the beautiful silks and linens reverently. Sometimes, English tourists would come in and she would marvel at how well her *maman* spoke the language. Perhaps it was because of that that she concentrated so hard on her English at school so that she achieved a high mark in her *baccalauréat*.

'I rather like this one,' said Marie-France, handing her mother a family introduction letter together with a photograph of a sharp-featured woman with two children sitting primly on a sofa.

Her mother gave a dismissive wave of the hand. 'A teacher? Too bossy.'

30

Marie-France glared across the old dark pine table. 'Who's going there? You or me?'

'But her dress is like a sack. And she wants you to work two evenings a week!'

'That's standard.'

'Not in my day.' Her mother sighed dreamily. 'We had a wonderful time! All those parties! All those young handsome Englishmen.'

'I thought,' said Marie-France cutting in, 'that's where you went wrong.'

Her mother's eyes fixed on hers soulfully. 'You might look *gentille*, Marie-France, but you have a heart of stone at times.'

She stared hard back. 'Just like you? And before you start muttering about respect, remind yourself that you were the one who taught me to stand up for myself.'

There was another deep, dramatic sigh. Standing up, her mother flounced towards the back door, lighting up another cigarette. 'There aren't that many to choose from. I don't think much of your agency.'

'It's small.' Marie-France felt almost defensive of it. 'I don't want a big one that just puts you anywhere and doesn't keep an eye on you.'

'Rubbish.' Her mother was puffing furiously now, blowing smoke out into the garden towards the mountains in the distance. 'You just like it because of where it is situated.' She picked up another picture; this time of a very skinny woman standing next to a good-looking man with swept-back dark hair. In front of them grinned two children. The girl looked rather cute.

'*Regarde*, Marie-France! This one already has a cook and a gardener and a driver and a ten-bedroom house!

31

She wants someone to look after the children in the holidays and then amuse them after school.' Her mother's eyes glinted! 'There is a swimming pool. *Fantastique!* This is the one for you. There will be no work for you and you can have a holiday at the same time. Trust me, Marie-France. I have an instinct for this sort of thing!'

Marie-France knew all about her mother's instincts. It was instinct that had made her move out of Paris all those years ago when her daughter was a baby and bury herself, far from her disapproving family, in this tiny village. It was instinct that made her push her daughter into extra English lessons and get a job in a Swiss hotel during the holidays, 'in order to improve your prospects, *chérie*'. And it was instinct that made her mother disapprove of Thierry Baccall.

Marie-France had met Thierry at school and, for some years, he had been just a friend. No more than that, she used to warn herself, although there had always been a dangerous spark between them. They were in the same class for many subjects and when she lent him a pencil (he was always losing his) or crib notes for a test (for which he was invariably unprepared), there were times when his hand brushed hers and she felt a thrill passing through her.

Of course, he was not the right boy for her; not with that slightly greasy lock of hair which flopped over his eyes and the noisy motorbike which he drove too fast. When he began dating one of her friends, Marie-France felt sick with jealousy followed by relief when the romance ended after a few months. Then last year, on her seventeenth birthday, when she had had a party in the village hall, he had come up to her without speaking and drawn her to him during a slow dance. After that, they had not looked back, despite her mother.

'He is not right for you,' she would say. 'He is a labourer! Such dirty hands! How can you think of making your future with a man who has no intention of going to university?'

Marie-France, hurt by the barbs, would reply that Thierry was a mechanic; a good one whom she admired for his skills.

'Both in the bedroom as well as the work shed, you mean,' her mother would retort and Marie-France would turn on her heels, making no attempt to deny something that was true, and then for a few days there would be a coolness between the two women until they made up.

Now, nearly three weeks after the first batch of family photographs and details, Dawn Green with the handsome husband and swimming pool had sent her a welcome letter, together with a waxy crayon drawing of a daisy ('The children made this for you!') as a formal acceptance. Hopefully she had made the right choice but even if she hadn't, what did it matter?

All she needed was a base for her investigations. Marie-France shivered and not just from the thought of her task ahead. It was also because it was finally time to break the news to Thierry. Until now, she'd kept it quiet from him in case he tried to make her change her mind. So she waited until the following weekend when he arrived as usual on his motorbike to collect her.

'Would you mind,' she said after he had kissed her with the same passion and fervour that he had done on that first night on the dance floor, 'if we just drove somewhere to talk instead of going out to dinner?'

He raised his handsome eyebrows – solid and dark – and glanced at the window behind her. 'Somewhere where your mother will not spy on us, you mean?'

Marie-France turned to follow his gaze just in time to catch a flash of her mother moving away. *'Absolutment!'*

Laughing, she put on the spare blue and silver helmet that he had brought for her and climbed up on the bike, clutching the back of his leather jacket and feeling moist the way she always did when their bodies were close. I am going to miss this, she told herself. I am going to miss him so much.

They drove up the winding narrow lane that led towards the mountains, stopping at a high point just above the village but below the snowy peaks. In the distance, she could see the lake which the English referred to as Lake Geneva but which the French called Léman. Gently, he removed her helmet, his thick rough fingers stumbling over the catch, before cupping her chin with his hands and looking down at her. 'You have something to tell me?'

Her body melted the way it always did when he touched her. Silently, she nodded.

'Would this have anything to do with the rumours that are flying around the village?'

Rumours? But her mother had promised not to tell anyone the news until she, herself, had told Thierry!

'Rumours,' he continued, brushing her cheek with

34

his lips, 'that you are leaving us to go to England?'

She nodded. 'I have to. Because...' She stopped. 'You know why.'

He nodded. Thierry was the only person she had spoken to about her mother's revelation and he'd been incredibly comforting. But it hadn't been enough.

'I love you, Thierry. I really do. But I have to do this before I get on with the rest of my life.'

He nodded again, pulling her towards him. The cold leather of his jacket helped to cool down her cheeks, which were burning. Then he stepped back. 'You will come back to me?' Suddenly, his eyes flickered in self-doubt. 'You will not fall in love with a rich English lord?'

She laughed. 'Of course not. It's you, Thierry.' Her hands began to unbutton his jacket. 'You know it's always been you.'

His hands held her breasts, tracing the outline of her nipples with thick, tender fingers. Usually, this worked for Marie-France. But for some reason, she couldn't relax. Instead, her mind kept going back to the scene with her mother, a couple of months earlier.

In the early part of her life, Marie-France had thought it was quite normal not to have a father. It was not as though she needed anyone else: she had her mother. Her mad, infuriating but amazing mother who could dance around the kitchen and sing songs with her one minute, and then, with a look, send her to bed without supper if she spoke out of turn.

But when she started school, it all changed. 'My *maman* says I am not to play with you because you do

35

not have a father,' announced one of her classmates.

Marie-France had pretended not to care but when she went back home that night, she repeated the conversation to her mother. Collette's brow had darkened and the following morning, she had marched down to the small school with her daughter – much to Marie-France's embarrassment – and demanded to see the headmaster. But the teasing continued so Collette had visited the girl's mother. Quite what was said, no one knew, but suffice it to say that no one tormented her again.

When Marie-France herself dared to ask why she was the only child in the village not to have a papa apart from one other girl whose father had been accidentally killed during an army exercise, her mother gave her the same tragic dark look she had doubtless given the headmaster and the girl's mother. 'He left us,' she said. 'Before you were born. I do not know where he is and I do not care.' Her eyes filled with tears. 'He hurt me so much, chérie, that it pains me to talk about it. Please do not raise the subject again.'

So Marie-France had respected her wishes, although it didn't stop her fantasising about her father. Maybe he was very rich and his family had not wanted him to marry an ordinary working-class girl from Paris? Perhaps he had changed his mind and was now looking for them? She spent hours in her room, working out different scenarios in her head. When she was old enough, she decided, she would try and find him somehow. Then, on the eve of her eighteenth birthday, her mother brought up the topic, completely out of the blue.

'It is time,' Collette had announced, as though it was time for dinner; a meal which usually consisted of a simple bowl of soup in winter or an omelette with salad. Beautiful women like them, her mother had always warned, had a duty not to get fat.

Marie-France had looked up from the floor of the small, snug sitting room with its real log fire where she had been trawling through an exercise book for a test the next day. 'Time for what?'

Her mother had put down the magazine she was flicking through. 'Time that you knew about your father, of course.'

Marie-France felt a quickening in her chest as she settled herself at her mother's feet, not daring to say a word in case she changed her mind. 'I was a young girl in England.' Her mother's voice took on a dreamy tone. 'I was only eighteen and I fell in love. But afterwards, he – and his family – they do not want to know.'

Then she stopped. 'That is all.'

'All?' Marie-France could have wept with disappointment. 'How can that be all? What was his name?'

Her mother shrugged. 'That one is difficult.'

'That is ridiculous! Don't play games with me. You must have known his name unless... *Mon Dieu*. Please do not tell me it was a one-night stand.'

'What do you think I am?' Her mother had glared at her. 'If you must know, his name was... it was John Smith.'

So her father was English! Marie-France's mind began to race. Her mother was going to close the subject. She could tell the signs! It was essential that

37

she got in one more question fast if she was ever going to track down her father. 'Where in England? Where did he live?'

The question seemed to take her mother by surprise because the name of the town slipped out of her mouth more easily than Marie-France had dared to hope. 'Corrywood.' She said it dismissively. 'It is a small place. Not exciting like London.'

'*Corrywood*,' repeated Marie-France. 'But why did you not marry him? Did you turn him down like you've turned down Maurice?'

'That is enough.' Collette stood up and put on her coat. 'I do not want to answer any more questions.' Her mother was taking out her lipstick from her bag and outlining her lips. 'I am tired of the subject, *chérie*. I wish now that you had never brought it up.'

'*You* mentioned it. Not me.' She touched her mother's arm. 'Please, Maman. It is my history.'

'No.' Collette turned and she could see tears in her eyes. Real ones this time. 'It is not your history. It is mine. But there was at least one good thing to come out of it.'

There was a silence punctuated only by the clock. 'You, *chérie*,' she said softly, drawing her daughter to her for a brief hug before turning on her heel imperiously. '*You* came out of it. And now I am going out. Maurice is taking me somewhere special. Do not wait up.' She winked. 'I will be late.'

The following day, Marie-France had emailed the Sorbonne to defer her entry for a year and, with the aid of a map, began scouring the net for an au pair agency in England. As close to Corrywood as possible.

Now, she had just a week to get ready. The days passed in a flurry of packing ('L'Angleterre, it is always cold and rainy,' warned her mother ominously) and saying goodbye to her friends. Yes, of course she would email and text. There was Facebook too!

'I'll be back for Christmas,' she had reassured Thierry and her mother. For once, they had been thrown together in an uneasy truce, neither happy about her going but, at the same time, unable to stand in her way.

'Christmas? I hope so,' said Thierry, who had come to say a final goodbye. He had sprayed on too much cologne for the occasion, which added to her pre-travel nausea. 'It's not as though I can get time off work to come over to you. Not like your uni friends.'

Marie-France chose to ignore the last remark. He'd been making a few of those recently; sly digs at her classmates who had decided to go on to further education instead of turning to honest toil, as Thierry put it, and a weekly salary in the back pocket of his jeans along with dirty fingernails and muscles that rippled when he peeled his shirt off.

Meanwhile, Maman was still fussing over her luggage in a bid, Marie-France suspected, to hide her feelings. 'I have bought a present for your family as the agency suggested!'

'Thank you.' She opened the bag and frowned. Anti-wrinkle cream with a reduction sticker on it?

Her mother smirked. 'It might help with that frown on Madame Green's face, do you not think?'

More likely to make her new 'boss' take it as the

insult it was intended! Just as well that Marie-France had bought a book about France which might keep the children amused.

'I'd better be off then,' said Thierry, pulling up his collar even though it was a beautiful warm day. 'Let you two get on to the airport.'

There was a short silence before her mother spoke. 'If you want to come with us,' she said grudgingly, 'there is room in the car.' She gestured to the cases. 'You can make yourself useful by carrying my daughter's luggage. It is full of nice things for when she goes out in the evening.'

Thierry's face fell just as her mother had intended.

'I'm not going there to have fun. I'm going to . . .' She stopped, aware that two sets of eyes were on her. 'I'm going to find myself.'

There was another silence. Thankfully, Thierry broke it first. 'Right. On we go then.'

Suddenly, the enormity of what she was doing hit her. She was leaving everything she had ever known! The small but impeccably kept house where she had lived since she was a toddler thanks to her mother working so hard to pay the rent. Thierry, who was always being ogled by other girls in the street. Her mother, who drove her mad at times but who was her rock. Not to mention her place at the Sorbonne, which, true, was only being deferred but which, right at this moment, seemed much more appealing than a strange family in a cold, windy country where, according to her mother, they went to bed at ten and failed to appreciate cheese, wine or romance – in that order.

Conversation was stilted in the car with Marie-

France unable to talk in case she burst into tears and her boyfriend and mother making awkward attempts to jolly up the atmosphere. 'Just think,' said Thierry, 'you will be able to mount Big Ben.'

Her mother rolled her eyes. 'You don't *climb* it. They stopped people going up it years ago. *Mais, ma petite*, you will be able to fly on the London Eye.'

By the time they reached the airport, she was almost ready to go back home again. 'It will be all right,' said Thierry gruffly, hugging her to him and almost crushing the guitar slung around her left shoulder.

'*Excuse-moi.*' Her mother was virtually stamping her feet in her impatience to step in. '*Ma chérie!*' She kissed Marie-France on top of her forehead with a loud smack. 'You will write, will you not? It is so much nicer than those horrid emails.'

She nodded, still not trusting herself to speak. Both Thierry and her mother were fading into a blur of tears. 'You will be all right when you are there!' called out Thierry as she gave him one final hug before going through security.

'*Prends soin de toi!*' called out her mother.

Then Marie-France, choked with a curious mixture of excitement and homesickness (already!) rounded the corner to join the long queue at security. As she looked back, she realised with a pang that she could see neither Thierry nor her mother any more.

She was alone. Completely alone.

HOST FAMILY APPLICATION FORM

NAME: *Matthew Evans.*

MARITAL STATUS: *Widowed.*

CHILDREN: *Lottie, aged 8.*

PLEASE OUTLINE THE DUTIES YOU WOULD LIKE YOUR AU PAIR TO UNDERTAKE: *Cook, clean and look after my daughter while I am at work.*

DESCRIBE ACCOMMODATION AVAILABLE: *Single room with shared bathroom.*

DESCRIBE YOUR LOCATION: *Pleasant market town, fifty minutes from central London (on fast train).*

IS THERE A COLLEGE NEARBY OFFERING SUMMER LANGUAGE TUITION? *Yes.*

WILL YOU ACCEPT A SMOKER? *No.*

ARE YOU LOOKING FOR AN AU PAIR WITH A DRIVING LICENCE? *Yes.*

DO YOU HAVE ANY PETS? *One lizard.*

ANY OTHER STIPULATIONS? *Applicants should be mature and speak reasonable English. They should also have previous experience with children.*

Chapter 3

Damn. He was late! Matthew drummed his fingers on the steering wheel impatiently as he sat in the heavy traffic on the M25 into Heathrow. He could have left earlier if Lottie hadn't had lost one of her new brown lace-ups which had finally turned up in the understairs cupboard.

'Did you hide it, princess?' he'd asked quietly and eight-year-old Lottie had shaken her head, her blond plaits flying furiously.

'Course not, Daddy.'

Yet somehow he had known that was exactly what she'd done. Anything rather than go to school. Lottie hated being apart from him and that was probably his fault. Ever since Sally had died, his daughter had started to act rather childishly and speaking more like a four-or five-year-old. For his part, he'd been too clingy. Too over-protective. Too ready to let her get away with things...

The van in front began to move and Matthew released a sigh of relief. If this hold-up – due to roadworks, he could now see – began to clear, he might just be only a few minutes late for the new au pair.

'Why do we have to have someone living with us?' Lottie had asked on the way to school that morning. It had not been the first time and his answer was always the same. Maybe the repetition was comforting, as her bereavement counsellor had said.

'Because I've got to go back to work now,' Matthew had said in the most reassuring tone that he could muster.

Lottie's voice from the back seat was high with indignation, as though they hadn't been through this before. 'Why?'

Often, said the counsellor, the simplest words were the best such as 'Mummy got sick and died' and 'That doesn't mean that Daddy is going to die too.'

Matthew had taken another breath. 'Because Daddy's friends at work gave him nine months off after Mummy went to heaven but now they want him back. So Daddy has found a nice girl from a country called Bulgaria to look after you when you're not at school.'

'But I don't want someone from Vulgaria,' Lottie had said in her whiny I'm-about-to-cry-unless-you-do-what-I-want voice. 'I want Daddy.'

So he'd had to stop the car then and comfort her which had made her miss assembly at school and now he was going to be late for Sozzy which sounded horribly like 'sozzled' even though she had put 'non-drinker' on her form. Matthew's lips twitched with amusement and then stopped. He always felt guilty when something seemed mildly funny as though he had no right to make or enjoy a joke after Sally. Cancer was no laughing matter.

What, wondered Matthew as he put his foot down, would his wife have thought of him having an au pair? James, his fellow partner at their architectural practice, had been incredibly understanding about giving him extended compassionate leave but it couldn't go on for ever.

It had been Christina, his own counsellor – recommended by their understanding GP – who had suggested that maybe now was the time to go back. 'You've done a great job, Matthew,' she had said, leaning back in her chair on the other side of the coffee table which lent a deceptive air of informality to her little office, 'but you admit you miss the buzz of work. It could be healthier for Lottie too if you weren't around all the time; it will make her more independent and less clingy.'

'But who's going to be there when she gets back from school?' he had pointed out.

'Have you thought about an au pair? I had one myself when my daughter was younger.'

Then had come the call from James to say that they had just landed a big commission and that they could really do with Matthew's creative skills on board. If not, maybe they should 'reconsider' his future at the practice.

Somehow, this seemed like a wake-up call. It was true, thought Matthew as he glanced in the car mirror, observing with irritation his slightly frayed blue and yellow shirt collar. He *did* miss work! Missed the excitement of getting the brief and then coming up with ideas to transform someone's conservatory or build a house with wheelchair access or design a school extension. He'd been doing some work from home but there was a limit to what you could achieve when you weren't in the office.

Even so, he would give up tomorrow if he had to

choose between it and his daughter but Christina's words played on his mind. There was, as his counsellor had added, such a thing as being over-protective of your children. A vision of an adult Lottie – independent, happy and confident, just like her mother – flashed into his head.

So Matthew had applied to an au pair agency he'd seen advertised in a magazine. It had been going for years and was a member of a professional organisation, which was always a good thing. 'Naturally, my girls all come with references and have been checked medically and for criminal records,' the woman at the other end of the phone had said when he'd rung for details.

That had reassured him although he'd felt slightly sleazy when she'd emailed photographs to look at. It had been a bit like sorting through applicants for an online dating site! Eventually, with Lottie's help, he had selected a girl who had already taken a degree in mathematics and wanted a year off. What really swung it for him was her age – twenty-two, which compared favourably with the plethora of eighteen-year-olds he'd been sent – and the fact that she came from a large family so would hopefully be maternal.

'I want to cut my hair like that one day!' trilled Lottie, pointing at the girl's urchin crop.

Matthew felt a lurch of loss at the fact that his wife would never again be able to style their daughter's long hair. 'Maybe your new au pair will help you do some pretty things with yours.'

That idea seemed to have appeased his daughter slightly – until this morning with the lost-shoe scenario, which, he was now convinced, had been a ploy to make them late for school and the airport. Still, he thought, making a quick left off the motorway, he was only fifteen minutes behind schedule, which, all things considered, wasn't too bad really. Now all he had to do was find somewhere to park.

By the time he'd found a space in the multi-storey, grabbed a parking ticket and dashed across to Arrivals, weaving his way through trolleys with that mixture of airport perplexity, panic and excitement, he couldn't see anyone that looked remotely like Sozzy's picture.

Maybe she'd spot him first? He'd sent her a snapshot of him and Lottie that Sally had taken during one of their last family days out together. His short dark hair hadn't gone prematurely grey round his ears then, as it was now, and he'd been a bit thinner: grief had since made him put on weight rather than lose it and he could have done with a bit more height to carry it off. Lottie, in the picture, had had a gap between her teeth. She had another tooth growing in its place now. Something else Sally would miss out on.

Uncomfortably, he remembered his promise in his last email to Sozzy. 'I'll be carrying a notice with your name on it,' he had said but somehow, in the rush to get Lottie off to school, he had forgotten to do so. Feverishly he searched his pockets for a pen and scrap of paper.

Suddenly, the awesome responsibility of losing a stray foreigner – who had never, according to her letter, been abroad before – dawned on him. This was utter negligence on his part! Supposing someone did

47

this to his Lottie when she was twenty-two? He'd kill them!

Just then his phone began to ring inside his back pocket. Please don't let it be school, telling him that Lottie was playing up again! Last week, she had hidden another child's jacket behind her own, which had caused problems at playtime. Attention-seeking, her teacher had said kindly.

'Mr Evans?' The voice at the other end of the phone was slightly crisp and irritated. 'This is Janine from the au pair agency.'

'I'm so sorry I'm late!' Matthew found himself babbling apologetically. 'I got delayed but I'm here now.' He looked wildly round the Arrivals Hall where another planeload was decanting. 'The thing is, I can't see her.'

There was an exasperated noise at the other end. 'I'm afraid there's been a bit of a problem at immigration. The silly girl left her accession worker card behind – all au pairs from Bulgaria need one to show that they are going to a proper job in the UK. You'll have to find the Immigration Office so you can vouch for her. I'm so sorry.' She sighed. 'This has never happened to me before.'

It would be *him*, wouldn't it? Somehow, Matthew managed to find an official who directed him along a warren of corridors and into another room. Sitting moodily on a chair was a short, plump, boyish-looking figure with cropped hair and orange roots.

'Sozzy?' She looked so harsh compared to her picture! Her grubby denim jacket had a crudely sewn-on 'Bad Girl' badge and she had a clutch of silver nose rings in her right nostril. Those eyes, which had been half closed when he came into the room, were now focused on him challengingly. Go on, they seemed to say, admit it. I'm not what you ordered.

Matthew's heart sank. Then she looked away, making to adjust one of her large white plug earrings and, for a brief second, he caught a flash of vulnerability (almost self-loathing) which hadn't been there before.

'Mr Evans?' said another official. 'Could you please confirm that this young lady is an au pair, coming to live and work in your family for the next nine months.'

Matthew's hand had already closed over the copy of the welcome letter he had sent to Sozzy and which the agency had, fortunately, advised him to bring to the airport 'just in case'. He nodded. For a minute, he considered pushing it back in his pocket but then he noticed the girl's feet. They looked so small in those open-toed heavy sandals. Almost like a child's. It must be awful for her, sitting here in Immigration, in a strange country, not knowing what was going to happen to her all because she couldn't find a docu-ment. Let's face it, that happened to everyone at times, didn't it?

'Yes,' he said heavily. 'I have a copy of our work contract here.' He gave the girl what he hoped was a reassuring smile. 'Hello, Sozzy. Welcome to the UK.'

It was difficult to make conversation in the car on the way back. He asked if she'd had a good journey (silly question really) but Sozzy had merely shrugged. Apart from that, she had hardly said anything. When he glanced across at her, she just seemed to be looking out of the window as though taking it all in.

'Don't worry too much about leaving your card behind,' he said in what was meant to be a reassuring voice. 'We all make mistakes.'

Another shrug. He tried again, desperate to show that he was human too. 'In fact, I was late at the airport. Before I set off, my daughter lost a shoe and so we had to spend ages looking for it before I could take her to school.'

'I do not worry.' Her voice was surprisingly deep. She reached into her bag and pulled out a piece of paper. 'I find the document now. So it is all right.'

No apology? Matthew got a horrible sinking feeling. She wasn't upset as he'd first thought. Just rude. Or maybe it was a cultural thing.

'It will take us about thirty minutes to get back,' he said in an attempt to relieve the atmosphere. 'My daughter Lottie is being brought back from school in the afternoon by a neighbour. I thought it would give you a chance to see your room and unpack first.'

She nodded. 'How enormous is Corrywood?'

A question at last! 'It's hardly enormous.' He laughed but then saw that she was very serious. 'Enormous in English means very large but our town is, well, medium-sized – although it's very picturesque with a canal nearby. My wife...my wife and I moved out of London to start a family there but then she fell ill.'

He stopped. Usually people started saying how sorry they were when he mentioned Sally. They might tell him they knew exactly how he felt because their aunt had died of cancer too, or their next-door neighbour. But this girl's face was scarily impassive. Maybe she hadn't understood what he was saying, despite stating on her form that her English was of 'medium level'.

'My wife has been dead now for just under a year,' he said quietly.

The girl nodded. 'I *know*,' she replied, accentuating the word 'know' in such a way that he almost felt reprimanded for stating the obvious. 'The agency, she tell me.'

Not one hint of compassion in her voice! Still, Matthew told himself as he joined the motorway, maybe it was the accent that made her sound so... well, almost robot-like. He mustn't judge her. Every - one was different. They drove for another ten minutes in silence until he couldn't bear it any longer. Reaching across, he turned on the radio. 'A childminder is due to be sentenced today for shaking a two-year-old so badly that the child will need constant round-the-clock care,' announced the presenter in a sombre tone.

Matthew froze. This was exactly the sort of thing he had been worried about! Nervously, he glanced across at Sozzy's bulky figure. She had her iPod earphones in now and was furiously texting away on her mobile. Was she the kind of girl who might get up in the night and knife them in their beds? No, that was ridiculous. Yet things like that happened all the time. You only had to listen to the news.

It was a relief when they approached Corrywood. 'This is our town.' He glanced across at Sozzy, who still had her iPod in. Goodness, the music was so loud that he could hear it from where he was sitting. 'I said this is our town,' he repeated.

Still no response! He could hardly reach across and touch her on the arm in case she took it the wrong way, yet he still felt obliged to carry on talking out of politeness. 'There are several coffee shops as you can see and there's a cinema on the corner. Further down, there's a gym where Sally and I used to belong. It's good fun. You might like to join.'

She turned round, jerking out her earplugs, her black eyes accusing. 'You are saying I need to go to gym? You think I am fat?'

'No, no.' Matthew felt himself going horribly red. 'Of course not. I just thought you might meet some friends there.'

'I meet friends at school.' She was putting away her iPod now in a small black case which still had a plastic security tag on it, bearing the name of a duty-free shop. The uncomfortable thought crossed his mind that she might have stolen it. Then again, if she was guilty of shoplifting, how could she have charged it? Matthew immediately felt bad for thinking the worst of a girl he hardly knew.

Those black beady eyes were on him still as he swung into their road. 'When do I start?'

'No rush.' He was trying to be as nice as possible in order to make up for the gym gaffe. 'I thought that Lottie and I would show you around town tomorrow.'

'No.' Those eyes were unsmiling. 'When do I start school?'

'Do you mean your language classes?'

She nodded emphatically.

'I thought you were booking those yourself.'

'The agency say the host family is responsible for finding out about classes.'

Matthew was confused. 'I did. I emailed details to the agency but I assumed it was up to you to book.'

'No!' A short, squat brown finger stabbed at the third paragraph on the sheet. 'It says here that family pay cost of school.'

What? He pulled up in the small parking space outside the house and had a look. *Your family may, in certain cases, be prepared to contribute towards the cost of language classes but this is a matter which you must discuss with them.*

'We need to talk about this later,' he said weakly. The last thing he wanted was an argument before the girl had even got into the house. 'We're here now.' He gestured at the honey-bricked Victorian terraced house which he and Sally had bought when the wisteria was in full bloom. Before the thought of illness, let alone death, had occurred to either of them.

'Why don't we go in and I'll make us a cup of tea before Lottie gets back from school?' He paused, wondering if she could understand all this. If not, that might explain her brusqueness. 'Paula, one of the mums at school, is bringing her back. It's half-day today because they're finishing early for the summer holidays.'

She shook her head. 'I do not drink tea. Just beer.' She pointed to a bottle poking out of her bag.

Matthew gulped. 'Right. Well, I'll just get your case out and we'll go inside.'

One of the neighbours – a woman he was only on nodding terms with – was staring through her curtains.

Matthew hoped she didn't think that this was a girl-friend. Not so soon after Sally. As quickly as he could, he ushered Sozzy inside.

'I'll show you your room, shall I?' he said, wishing, too late, that he'd asked his sister down from Edinburgh to supervise all this. There was something rather tricky about showing a strange woman up the stairs!

She shrugged. Bending down, he picked up her ruck-sack. Heavens, it was heavy. 'I take it,' she said, grabbing it from him and swinging it on the back of her shoulders.

'If you're sure.' Now he felt like a drip. She was certainly strong! 'It's first on the right.'

He waited, letting her go in first and hovering awkwardly outside because there wasn't a great deal of room for two people inside. He'd spent some time getting the small spare room ready. It hadn't been easy; not because of the physical effort needed to clean it but the mental. This had been Sally's little study; her sanctuary, she used to joke.

Now he was wondering if it was big enough. *The au pair's room does not need to be spacious*, the agency guidelines had said, *but it must be clean and com-fortable. There should be a desk, if possible, so your au pair can do her studies.*

'Vot is this?'

What was she saying? It sounded like 'What is this?' but it had come out in such a guttural fashion that it might have been something in her own native language. Perhaps he ought to buy a *Teach Yourself Bulgarian* book.

54

Sozzy was coming out now, her face red with anger. 'My bedroom! It is not fit for a dog.' She was pushing him into her room now. 'Look!'

Appalled, he stared at the chaos in front of him. Last night, he had stayed up late to make sure that Sozzy's room was just as he hoped a twenty-two-year-old would like it. He had put a striped bedspread on the bed; it had been at the back of the linen cupboard and he remembered buying it with Sally when she had been expecting Lottie. He'd found a clean set of pale blue guest towels for the new occupant and he had rehung the curtains so they sat more neatly on the rail.

Now it looked as though someone had broken in and ransacked it. The vase of flowers was lying on its side and there was a damp, dark water stain on the carpet below. The bed was dishevelled with dirty footprints all over the pillow. The curtains had been ripped off the rail so the pelmets were hanging like lonely floral fringes. And there was a horrible smell coming from somewhere that he couldn't quite place.

But the worst thing of all – the thing that over-whelmed him with embarrassment and disbelief – was the childish note on the desk in large printed letters.

GO HOME. WE DON'T WANT YOU HERE!

'I am so sorry.' He was still staring, taking it all in. 'That's my daughter's writing.' He picked up the piece of yellow paper, which he recognised as having come from the diary he'd given her for Christmas – another of the counsellor's ideas.

'She wants me to go home?' Sozzy's eyes were even blacker, if that was possible, and she spat out each word so he could see the chewing gum in her mouth. 'Your daughter, she does not want me here?'

'I didn't realise she felt like this.' He was beginning to babble again, not knowing how to explain. 'It's been so hard for her, this last year. I suppose she's got used to me being here with her and she doesn't like the idea of me going back to work.'

The girl was already dialling a number on her mobile. 'I ring agency,' she said accusingly. 'I inform it what you have done.'

As she spoke, there was the noise of a car pulling up outside and footsteps running towards the house, followed by furious banging on the door. 'It's Lottie,' said Matthew, feeling the perspiration trickle down from under his arms.

'The agency has answerphone on!' Sozzy stared at him as though this was his fault.

'Look, please, just wait a minute before you leave a message,' he said desperately. 'We haven't really given each other a chance yet and this is as strange for us as it is for you.'

There was the sound of small footsteps calling out from the hall. 'Daddy,' sang out a voice. 'Is the oh pear gone now?'

Matthew flew down the stairs towards his small daughter, who was standing at the open door, smiling at him sweetly. 'Why would you think that, Lottie?'

Her eyes widened in the way they had done this morning when she had declared she had no idea where her other shoe had gone. 'I don't know.'

'I think you do, Lottie. I don't think it was very kind to mess up our guest's room, do you?'

A dark red flush swept over her face. 'But I don't want her here, Daddy. I just want you and me.' Her eyes were pleading. 'Please. Pretty please!'

He mustn't let her wind him round her little finger like that! But before he could say anything, something tumbled down the stairs. It was Sozzy's filthy rucksack followed by Sozzy herself, clumping down in those sandals, leaving dirty footprints on the carpet.

'I exit!' She was lighting a roll-up as she stomped, even though Matthew had specifically put *non-smoker* on his application form.

'I leave message for agency and tell them you are no good family.'

'But where will you go?' Matthew suddenly felt horribly responsible for the girl. 'You don't know anyone.'

'Yes.' Sozzy was nodding emphatically. 'I have a friend in London. Goodbye.'

Chapter 4

'That's crazy!' said Jilly, cupping the phone between her ear and shoulder while ploughing through her inbox at the same time. 'Are you sure?'

'Quite sure,' clipped the voice on the other end from the Association for Au Pairs and Families. 'You can't be a full member of our organisation until your agency has been running for more than a year.'

'So I can't be listed on your register?'

'No.'

'Then how will clients find me?'

The voice sounded as though she'd been through this one before. 'You could try advertising in local papers and of course on the net.'

Crash! There was an ominous sound from upstairs, suggesting that something had got broken somewhere. Oh dear! She'd let the boys lie in late this morning – it was the summer holidays, after all – so she could fit this phone call in. Please don't come rushing in, making a noise, Jilly prayed silently. It would look so unprofessional. Just as well that the person at the other end couldn't see her sitting at the kitchen table, still in her dressing gown without so much as a dab of foundation on her nose.

'But...' she began to say.

Oh God. There was another crash followed by a yell. It wasn't a he's-going-to-kill-me yell or a he's-broken-my-arm-again scream, thank heavens. Just the sort of normal ear-splitting vocal horseplay that went on from the minute that the boys woke up. Some twins were joined at the hip. Others, like HarryandAlfie, took sibling rivalry to a new level. Like potential homicide.

'MUM! MUM!'

Jilly felt a wave of panic. Setting up an au pair agency had seemed such a brilliant idea at the time. You can do it round the kitchen table, her friend Paula had said. But in four weeks, she'd only managed to get one placement and that was sheer luck because a French girl from a small village near the Swiss border happened to have spotted her website.

Success! Jilly had matched her up with Dawn Green, a mother from school. In fact, she thought, glancing at her watch, Marie-France should be arriving at Heathrow about now!

But apart from her, there was no one. How was she going to help out with the family finances at this rate? The mortgage payment would be coming out next week and that would leave precious little for bills, food and the other myriad expenses needed to run a growing family of five. HarryandAlfie both had feet that grew overnight which meant they needed new shoes *again*! At sixty-odd pounds a pair, that was no joke.

She picked up the phone and moved to the window overlooking the garden in an attempt to get away from the noise, which was now stomping its way down the stairs. 'Do you have any tips for people like me who are setting up?'

The woman from the association sighed sympathetically. 'My advice, to be honest, is to decide whether you want to go national or specialise in your local area.'

'MUM! MUM!'

'Definitely the latter. I want to make it one of my selling points.'

Jilly could hear her voice rising excitedly, just as it had when she'd outlined her 'business plan' to David. 'I've lived in this town ever since we moved out of London. I know lots of families here and I've pledged, on my website, that I will personally check each one rather than simply pass on contacts.'

'That's always a good idea.' The voice was encouragingly approving.

'MUM, ALFIE'S NICKED MY COMPUTER GAME!'

'IT WAS MINE.'

'NO IT WASN'T!'

'YES IT WAS!'

'But my problem,' continued Jilly, moving into the downstairs cloakroom and locking the door behind her so she could continue the conversation, 'is that I haven't had many hits.'

'Try getting in touch with foreign agencies. They can introduce you – for a fee, of course – to girls in their own countries who want to work in the UK.' She sighed. 'All the details *are* on our website.'

Oh God. Harry (or was it Alfie?) was now rattling the door handle. 'MUM, OPEN UP!'

'But I've approached a few already and because I'm not registered with you, they're not interested,' continued Jilly desperately. 'It's a catch-22 situation.'

'Not easy, I'm afraid. Goodness, what is that dreadful noise?'

The door was going to come off its hinges at this rate! Jilly crouched down into a corner of the loo next to the Harpic, cupping the phone with her hand to try and reduce the sound of HarryandAlfie, who were now banging fiercely on the door from the other side. 'Noise? What noise?'

As she spoke, there was the deafening sound of glass shattering! Oh my God, had they hurt themselves? Jilly stared in horror at the small face on the other side of the broken pane in the door. Harry was yelling now and Alfie was jumping on top of him but there wasn't any blood, which was usually a good sign.

'Is everything all right?' enquired the voice at the other end of the phone.

In Jilly's experience, the louder the yell, the more optimistic the prognosis. It was usually when one of them went horribly quiet – like last Christmas when Harry had kicked Alfie off the sofa and given him concussion – that you had to worry.

'Yes thanks. My, er, my au pair is meant to be look - ing after the children but she doesn't seem to be around.'

'What oh pear, Mum?'

Harry crawled out from under Alfie, triumphantly waving their jointly owned PSP, which had caused the FAD, otherwise known as First Argument of the Day.

His small square face – a mirror image of his brother's and so like their father's with those dark brown eyes and mop of chestnut hair – scowled at her.

'You said you'd never have an oh pear cos you didn't want a stranger looking after us.'

Why couldn't her kids be as inarticulate as the national average? Their arguing-back skills were second to none. Still, maybe they could become barristers and look after her and David in their old age...

'Sounds like you've got your hands full,' said the voice at the other end. 'I wish you luck with your agency. Goodbye.'

Jilly's hand shook as she took in the fractured spiderweb glass on the door and Alfie who was now pinning his brother to the ground. There was only one thing for it.

'OK, everyone. Who wants an ice cream in front of a DVD?'

Both boys stopped immediately. 'Ice cream? Before breakfast?'

Why not? It would buy time to ring their local handyman who virtually had a season ticket here, thanks to the twins' capacity for home-wrecking. She could also email a few more agencies abroad to see if they would place their girls with Jilly's unregistered Au Pair Agency.

'Only,' she added as they returned to the kitchen, 'if you don't make a noise while I'm on the phone. You know I'm working.'

Alfie shot her a disbelieving look. 'But you don't go out to an office like Dad.'

'No, but I have an office here instead so I can look after you as well.' She glanced over at the small round kitchen table which was stacked with files marked MUST DO and CHASE UP.

Ideally, she'd like to use the spare bedroom upstairs as an office but it was full of 'stuff' that she needed to keep, ranging from old files to baby clothes that she couldn't bear to throw away. 'Are we really having an oh pear?' demanded Harry.

She felt a twinge of compassion. Harry, the youngest by twenty minutes, was the worrier of the two. He was the one who fretted on the few occasions she left them to visit her parents in Surrey or to go up to London for the day. Sometimes she thought it was because they'd had to spend weeks in the prem. baby unit. For weeks, she and David had been allowed only to see them in the incubator instead of cuddling them as they had yearned to.

Her heart contracted when she thought of that time. They'd been so tiny and so vulnerable! Who would have guessed that they'd grow into such big hulking boys who couldn't keep their fists off each other?

'No.' She began spooning out the ice cream, wishing she could add a slosh of tranquilliser to it. Someone could make a real fortune out of that flavour. 'I wouldn't inflict you two on anyone.'

Alfie frowned. 'What does "in flict" mean?'

'It means that I don't want anyone I don't know living with us. It wouldn't be fair on you or on them.'

'Why?' Alfie seemed to have forgotten about the PSP, which Jilly had managed to hide in the fridge to avoid further arguments.

'Just because. That's all. Now here's your ice cream. After I've made my phone calls, we'll go out.'

'Where?' asked Harry suspiciously.

Nowhere exciting. Just the supermarket. The fridge

was completely empty apart from one solitary fish finger clinging for dear life to a block of ice at the back because she'd forgotten to defrost again. *And* she'd run out of bags for the Hoover as well as wipes for the kitchen surfaces.

'Can we go roller-skating?' piped up Alfie.

'Maybe later if you give me some peace for half an hour.' She raised a hand in a high five. 'Deal?'

Too late. They'd already scarpered, leaving a trail of chocolate ice cream behind them. Not just on the carpet but on the walls as well, judging from the brown handprints. One more cleaning job to do before David got back. But in the meantime, she could get on.

She hadn't realised what a big business this au pair lark was. It might have helped if they'd had one themselves but Mum had always declared that anyone who chose to leave their offspring with a stream of French or German or Swiss girls was 'asking for trouble with one's husband'. Instead, Mum had chosen to send her and her younger brother Jeremy away to boarding school. She'd loved it. He hadn't.

In the holidays, they'd been dragged into Mum's office and told to 'do some drawing' or, when they were older, to amuse themselves at home.

'You ought to send the twins away,' declared her mother every now and then, waving her hands as though they were a pair of nuisance flies.

'I want to be there for them, Mum.'

'Are you saying that I wasn't for you?'

The conversation would inevitably end there with Jilly not wanting to hurt her mother. For the truth was that Mum *hadn't* been there for them, thanks to her fashion-design business, which had become hugely successful over the years. And now she had children of her own, she could see that she and Jeremy had missed out on cosy after-school chats with Marmite fingers. Instead they'd had stilted how-are-you conversations after six weeks away.

Two years ago, her mother had sold her business – at a really good price – and joined the cruise set. 'You meet all kinds of interesting people,' Mum had declared. 'Honestly, I don't know how we managed before. You really ought to socialise a bit more, you two. Beats marriage counselling any day.'

Socialise? All David wanted to do when he got home was to slump on the sofa in front of the evening news. When they did go out – about once a month – it was always on a Saturday and usually round to Paula and Nigel for a takeout curry while the girl next door babysat. On alternate months, their friends would come to them. It might seem tame to her parents but it suited David and her.

The sound of laughter from the boys next door indicated they were having a ceasefire. Thank heavens! She could now get on with the stack of paperwork and take another look at the website, which she'd managed to set up herself. Not bad really, even though she could do with a section called SATISFIED CUSTOMERS. Hopefully it wouldn't be long before she could add one.

Half an hour later, Jilly's stomach rumbled as a reminder that she hadn't had breakfast. But Europe was an hour ahead and if she didn't get a move on with more calls and emails, she'd be in trouble. Blast. There went the phone again. Maybe she ought to get a business line so she could tell if it was work or personal. But that would be *another* cost...

'Jilly? It's me.'

Paula always announced herself as 'me', assuming everyone knew who it was.

'Look, Antoinette has taken Immy to toddler gym so I thought we might have a coffee. Shall I come round?'

It was tempting! But she had to be disciplined if she wanted to make this agency work. 'Sorry, Paula. I'm working.'

'Can't you have a break?'

Paula sounded like a child who wanted another to come out to play.

'I'd love to. Really I would, but I've got to give this a chance. You know things are difficult...'

'David's still finding it tough then?'

'Yes, but don't mention it to him. His ego's rather fragile at the moment.'

'Poor you. Still, you've placed an au pair with Dawn, haven't you?'

'I owe you for that. Thanks.'

Jilly felt a wave of gratitude towards Paula, who had discovered that Dawn, another school mum and a member of Paula's Tai Chi class, was looking for help. Dawn, they all agreed, was rolling in it. Not only did she have a driver, a gardener and a cook, but she also lived in a beautiful house at the top of Laburnum Hill, considered one of the best areas in Corrywood. The girl from the small village near the Swiss border had really landed on her feet there!

'Look, I'm sorry but my mobile is going. Must dash. Call you later.'

'Hi. This is Dawn.'

Oh no. Had she changed her mind?

'MUM! MUM! HE WON'T LET ME WATCH MY PROGRAMME!'

'IT'S MY TURN TO CHOOSE!'

'NO IT'S NOT!'

'YES IT IS!'

'Hi!' Jilly fought to raise her professional voice above the noise. 'Is everything all right?'

'No. I'm afraid it's not.'

She knew it!

'I'd forgotten I've got a lunch appointment which I can't get out of and our driver's got the day off . So I can't meet Mary-France at the airport. I've tried to text her to say get a cab but her phone is off.'

'MUM! MUM!'

'That's probably because she's still going through customs,' said Jilly tightly. 'And it's Marie-France, not Mary-France, by the way.'

'Whatever. Look, you couldn't do me a really big favour, could you?'

'MUM!'

'Can you pick her up for me? Otherwise she'll just have to wait there until evening.'

What did Dawn think this was? The Marks & Spencer collection service? 'Marie-France has never been abroad before, Dawn. She's going to be worried if she's left there for hours.'

'MUM!'

'I'd be well grateful.' Every now and then Dawn's

south London roots came out although she did her best to hide them with a rather fake-sounding accent that was a cross between *Geordie Shore* and *The Only Way Is Essex*. 'I'm paying you a fairly hefty agency fee after all, aren't I?'

Hefty! It was on the tip of Jilly's tongue to point out that it was actually far more competitive than many other agency rates but stopped just in time. David had warned her that it might not be easy to do business with other mums at school. It wouldn't do to fall out with anyone. Not yet, anyway.

Crash.

'MUM! HE'S BROKEN SOMETHING.'

'IT WAS HIM, NOT ME.'

'NO IT WASN'T.'

My God. The kids were becoming virtually feral through parental neglect. 'OK,' said Jilly resignedly, switching off her laptop. 'But there *will* be someone at your place, won't there, when I bring her back?'

JILLY'S AU PAIR AGENCY:
GUIDELINES FOR AU PAIRS

Before arriving in the UK, you are bound to be nervous about meeting your new family. This is normal! Before long, this apprehension will disappear and you will feel at home!

Chapter 5

Marie-France felt almost sick with excitement from the second that the plane left the ground to the moment it thudded down on the tarmac. *Incroyable!* She had finally flown for the very first time in her life and now, here she was in *Angleterre*!

Hoisting her large pink suitcase off the luggage carousel, she made her way through the Green Nothing To Declare channel, searching the sea of faces waiting expectantly by the barrier.

'I will wave a piece of paper with your name on it,' Madame Green had promised in her email. But she could see neither her new family nor a sign.

Marie-France suddenly felt very small inside. Awkwardly she reached the bottom of the walkway, put on her sunglasses to hide her concern and sat on her suitcase, trying to look as though this was normal.

Remember, she told herself firmly, why you are here. Any number of these men milling around might actually be her father! It could be that one over there, wearing a white shirt under a smart blue jacket but without a tie. He was the right sort of age. Or it might be that other man waiting by a coffee shop, with slightly long brown hair curling on to his collar and dark shades. Such coincidences happened, did they not? It was perfectly possible that her father was, by chance, at one of the busiest airports in the world on business. He might well spot her in the crowd and see that she looked exactly like her mother!

The thought sent excited tingles of apprehension running down her spine just as they had when her mother had said it was time 'to tell you something' on the eve of her eighteenth birthday. Then, finally, it had all made sense! She'd always felt a natural affinity with *Angleterre* even though she had never been here before.

Once, when she had been fourteen, an enterprising teacher at her school had organised an exchange with a school in London. But when she'd pleaded with her mother to allow her to go, Maman had simply said she didn't have enough money for the air fare. So that had been that. Instead, she'd had to content herself with being top in her class for *Anglais*.

'You are a natural,' her teacher would say admiringly, and that had made Marie-France feel really good about herself. Now at last she could see why! English was in her blood!

These excited flights of fantasy distracted her for a while but an hour later, there was still no sign of anyone coming up to claim her. Right. Enough was enough. She would call Madame Green at once. Fishing for her mobile in her handbag, she felt a small lump of sick forming at the bottom of her throat. By mistake, she must have left her phone on silent instead of switching it off on the plane, which meant the battery was now dead.

Marie-France looked around. Arrivals had got even busier yet there was still no sign of anyone approach - ing. There was nothing to do but wait. If no one turned up by the evening, she'd book into a hotel with the emergency money she'd brought with her in crisp euro notes from the bank.

'Marie-France!'

Enfin! A medium-height slightly plumpish woman in jeans and flats with shoulder-length mousy blonde hair – nothing like the photo in the welcome letter! – was heading towards her, clutching a piece of paper that had her name in black spidery writing. Her warm, jolly smile set Marie-France's mind immediately at rest.

'Madame Green?'

Relief made her kiss the woman enthusiastically on both cheeks but the surprise on her hostess's face reminded her of her mother's warning. 'The English do not kiss when greeting each other. They shake hands. *C'est tres sale.* Make sure you wash your hands well, *ma petite!*'

'Actually, I'm Jilly from the agency.' She flashed a different kind of smile. An apologetic one. 'Dawn was delayed so she asked me to collect you. Did you have a good flight? Yes? Great. Is this your luggage? Right. Let's get it into the car. I've got to be quick. I've left the boys inside.'

What was she saying? Marie-France tried hard to concentrate on the flood of words coming out. It was all so different from her English lessons at school where the teacher had spoken more slowly and written words up on the whiteboard.

Still, she understood enough to know that, for some reason, Madame Jilly was here instead of Madame Green. Eagerly, she followed her rescuer to a big airport lift where several others squeezed in with them along with their cases.

'Right,' said Jilly brightly in a voice that reminded Marie-France of Maman's when she was making the best out of a tricky situation. 'The car's over there. It won't take us long to get back and then...'

'Excuse me, madam.' A large man with very short hair and an orange jacket was blocking their way. 'Afraid this entrance is closed. There's been a bit of an incident.'

Beside her, Jilly stared straight ahead as though she had just noticed something and emitted a short shrill scream that reminded Marie-France of the cockerel in the village at home. 'Oh my God. The boys! I knew I shouldn't have left them!'

Confused, Marie-France saw Madame Jilly slip past the official and race towards a rather dirty-looking white car which had somehow slipped down the slope and crashed into the one in front. An angry-looking man with a briefcase was waving his fists. *Mon Dieu!*

Now what was happening? A small boy was climbing out of the front of the dirty white car and Madame Jilly was shouting at him with a face that looked very different from the one she had shown to Marie-France.

'I told you, Alfie, to sit still. You were meant to stay in the back, not let off the handbrake. Now look what you've done!'

The handbrake? That word sounded familiar from a vocabulary exercise at school. It was something to do with cars, *n'est-ce-pas?*

'Harry dared me to drive!' Alfie was snivelling, tears streaming down his face. He was a cutie, thought

Marie-France, with those brown freckles. In the back of the car, she could see an identical face peering out worriedly. So Madame Jilly had twins! And there was even a small brown dog in the back, paws pressed up against the window. So sweet!

'Please,' she said quietly. When her mother was ranting and raving, it was always best to speak softly to calm her down. 'I will care for your boys while you rearrange your problems.'

'Thank you.' Madame Jilly had tears in her eyes too. 'I am so sorry about this.'

'So am I.' The man's angry voice cut in. 'I need your insurance details and your name and address. Frankly, I also ought to report you for neglect.'

Neglect? What was neglect? Marie-France resolved to look it up in her dictionary later but for the time being, it was clear that Madame Jilly needed her help. At least neither car looked badly damaged. She opened the front passenger door before realising it was the driver's. Of course! In England they did things the wrong way round.

'*Bonjour!*' She opened the rear door and held out her hand to the two small boys in the back. '*Je m'appelle Marie-France.*'

Two identical faces stared at her with suspicion. 'What does that mean?'

'You do not learn French?'

'Sort of.' One of the faces screwed itself up as though it had just tasted something he didn't like very much. 'But we're not very good at it.'

Marie-France was reminded of the summer camp she had worked at last summer in Geneva. Maman had been right when she'd accused her daughter of not liking babies. So vulnerable and needy! But she had got on well with the nine- and ten-year olds in the children's club at the Swiss hotel and the twins looked as though they were a similar age.

'Not very good at French? We will change that with my magic song. But first please deposit the dog on the front seat as it makes me sneeze.' She clapped her hands. 'Right. Now sing this after me! *Frère Jacques*, *Frère Jacques*...'

It was ages before Madame Jilly got back into the car. Her face looked red and flushed. Poor woman!

'Thank you so much, Marie-France.' Turning round, she smiled gratefully. 'I don't know what I'd have done without you. Bruno, DOWN.' She shook her head. 'I know I shouldn't have left the boys but I was so worried about being late for you and I thought it would be quicker if I just dashed in without them.'

'Mum, Mum, we can speak French now! Sea voo play means "please". And mare sea means "thank you".'

Marie-France laughed. 'You have learned some new words, *vraiment*!'

'Mum, Mum. Can Marie-France live with us instead of going to Tom and Tatty Arna?'

'I'm afraid not.' Madame Jilly was swinging out of the car park into a road past huge billboards advertising exotic destinations. 'But you might see her during the holidays perhaps.'

'Tom's really spoilt.' This was the small boy on her right. 'You're always saying so, Mum.'

'I don't think I actually said that—'

'Yes you did! When he had a monkey at his birthday party, you said it was extra arrogant.'

'Extravagant, actually . . .'

'*And* you said Tatty Arna was really rude when she came to tea cos she got down before we'd finished.'

Marie-France could recognise certain words. Arrogant? Rude? This didn't sound very promising.

'They live in this GI-NORMOUS house,' said the small boy on her left, stretching out his hands to make the point.

'And they've got a swimming pool!' bubbled the other one.

'I've told you before, boys,' said Madame Jilly's voice from the front. 'It's not the houses that people live in that matters. It's what the people are like.'

'Yes, but you said that Tom's mum was noo vo reesh.'

Nouveau riche? What was wrong with new money? She and Maman had spent so many years of being careful that any kind of money was welcome.

They were turning on to a busy road now and Marie-France stared out of the window, taking it all in. So many buildings! Not one green field in sight! Meanwhile the boys' constant chatter made the journey pass surprisingly fast.

'Have you climbed the Eyeful Tower?'

'Do you have a French Queen?'

'Does everyone in France speak English?'

'Can we sing that funny song again?'

By the time they turned left into a road where the houses were, as the boys had said, really enormous,

Marie-France felt as though she would really rather go home with the twins. They were so sweet and, even though pet hair made her sneeze, she quite liked the little dog, who clearly felt the same about her, judging from the way he had taken up residence on her lap. Achoo!

'Bless you,' said Madame Jilly, winding down her window. 'OK. We're here.'

'Can I press it?'

'No. Me!'

There was a wild scramble as both boys flung themselves past her, pushing their heads through their mother's side window in a competition to press the security pad on the gate.

'Hello?' The voice sounded a bit slurred.

'It's me, Jilly.'

'Who?'

'Jilly. I've got Marie-France for you.'

'Oh. Right. Come on up.'

The drive ahead of them was so long that she couldn't even see the house at first but then it loomed up in front. *Mon Dieu!* Look at those huge glass windows in front from the ground right up to an arch like a church. She wouldn't want to clean those. It would take all week.

Harry – or was it Alfie – was elbowing her excitedly. 'There's the pool. Look! And Tom is in it! Can we stay, Mum. Please. Please!'

'No.' Madame Jilly's voice was firm. 'We haven't been asked to play. We've come to drop off Marie-France.'

'But you said it wasn't really our job, Mum! You

said that on the way. You said that if Tom's mum had got her act together, she'd—'

'That's enough.'

The car had stopped and Madame Jilly was leaning into the boot to get her luggage out. Meanwhile, the front door was opening and a very petite woman with short dark hair and a frown – just like the picture – was standing there, champagne flute in her hand. She wore pale pink sparkly jeans and a flowing jacket which made her look as though she belonged on those exotic billboards outside the airport.

'Jilly! I can't tell you what a day I've had! After that lunch I told you about, I had to dash down to get my nails done and now we've got an extra two people for dinner tonight which makes fifteen!'

Her eye fell on Marie-France. 'Hi. Your room is sixth on the right at the top of the stairs. But come down as soon as you can. I need you to look after the kids in the pool while I have my massage.'

Marie-France suddenly began to feel very tired.

Madame Green's eyes narrowed. 'You do speak English, don't you? That's what it said on the form.'

She nodded.

'Good. Otherwise you'd have to go back. Now I've just got one teeny little problem. Our cook's not feeling very well. She's made the main course but there're still the hors d'oeuvres and the afters. You French are good at cooking, aren't you? So I wondered if you could help me out?'

'Actually,' said Jilly tightly, 'Marie-France has had rather a long day. It might be an idea to let her relax for a bit.'

The dark woman's eyes narrowed and Marie-France remembered her mother's words. 'Be as helpful as you can at the beginning, *chérie*. First impressions count. Then you can start to make your own rules.'

'It's fine,' she said quickly. 'I like to help and I embrace cooking.'

She remembered this time to hold out her hand to Jilly instead of kissing her on both cheeks. 'Thank you for arriving me.'

'Actually, we say "bringing me" but it's a pleasure.' This time, it was Madame Jilly who gave her a brief hug, slightly to her surprise. 'Say goodbye to Marie-France, boys.'

The twins began waving madly from the car and, once more, Marie-France wished she could stay with them. '*Au revoir!*' she called out. '*Au revoir!*'

'Right!' Her new boss turned smartly on her high heels, waving towards a huge glass staircase in front of them with a balcony that went round at the top like a modern chateau. 'See you in five minutes. OK?'

Marie-France made her way up the stairs and along the corridor. Sixth on the right? The house seemed to go on for ages! Glancing behind her to check no one was looking, she turned the handle of the fourth on the right out of curiosity and peeked in. If challenged, she could always say she'd made a mistake! There was a huge four-poster bed shrouded in a turquoise blue drape in front of her and a large sunken bath in the corner. Wow! She couldn't wait to see her own room!

Pausing outside the fifth on the right, she listened. Nothing. Again, she opened the door. This one was a carbon copy of the other except that the four-poster was in a canary-yellow design. Her heart quickened with excitement as she then turned the handle of the sixth room...

Merde! Surely there must be some mistake? This was a cupboard! There was only just room for a single bed under the eaves and instead of a proper wardrobe, there was a hanging rail. Crushed with disappointment, she put down her case and looked out of the window. What a view! A line of black plastic dustbins. Ugh. She could smell the garbage from here.

Marie-France's first thought was that she should march downstairs and demand better accommodation but then common sense prevailed. No. She would make herself indispensable first to this rude Madame Dawn. She would look after the children in such a way that her new boss would not be able to manage without her. She would cook such a meal tonight that they would regard her as a national treasure. And then she would start making her demands. After all, as she and Maman had agreed, the English owed them one.

Within an hour of arriving, she had made a pear tarte Tatin in Madame Green's enormous kitchen, which was as big as her own home. For an appetiser, she had created a salmon soufflé. Mmmm. Marie-France licked her finger. Not bad, if she said so herself!

But her employer merely glanced at her efforts without remark. 'You can give the children their dinner now. By the way, they only eat peanut butter on toast with raspberry jam. Then you can get them to bed.'

It took ages to get them ready! 'Let's see who can do it fastest,' she'd suggested to chivvy them up.

'I won, I won,' said Tatty Arna. She was a spitting image of her mother but with a gap between her teeth.

'No, I did.' Tom pushed his sister against the wall of her bedroom, which had a picture of a fairy castle on it.

'He's hurt me, he's hurt me!'

These two fought as badly as Madame Jilly's twins but in a much more vicious unkind way. There didn't appear to be any love between them.

'You two are getting on my nerve!'

Tom made a rude face. 'It's *nerves*, silly, cos there are lots of them.'

Marie-France gave him a stern look. This one, if she wasn't mistaken, would try and get away with everything, including lack of respect. 'That's what I say. I am thinking it is time for you to retire to bed now and read a story.'

'*Read?*' Tatty Arna's voice rose to a high shriek. 'It's the holidays! We don't have to read now we're not at school. We're allowed to watch television instead for as long as we want!'

As she spoke, the little girl picked up a remote control from the side of her bed and aimed it at the wall opposite. There was a click and part of the wall slid open to reveal a giant screen. Wow!

'I've got a bigger one in my room,' yelled Tom, jumping up and down.

Spoilt little brats. Still, there were only so many changes she could make on her first day. Besides, it was nearly time for the party! 'OK. Then watch it while I get ready for dinner.'

Au pairs will be invited to eat meals with the family,

the agency guidelines had said. Quickly, Marie-France ran along to her own room and slipped into a simple silk shift dress which her mother had bought for her in the sale at her dress shop. The colour – a striking cerise – looked good against her dark hair, or at least so Thierry had told her before taking it off in the woods on her last night. The thought made her chest wobble a bit but then she heard voices downstairs. How exciting! The guests were arriving. Marie-France felt a tingle of pleasure both at the compliments which would surely come her way from the food and also – more importantly – at the possibility that one of the guests might help her in her quest.

'Talk to as many people as you can,' Thierry had suggested when they'd discussed ways of tracking down her father. 'There must be someone there who knows where he is.' Maybe in a small town, but Corrywood was so much bigger than she had imagined!

Marie-France had just got to the bottom of the staircase when she spotted Madame Dawn who was wearing a very short skirt in a similar colour to her own. She looked up at Marie-France. 'Is there a problem?'

'No. I complete my work so I descend now.'

'Descend?' Madame Dawn looked bemused. 'But we have guests tonight. You'll need to stay in your room, I'm afraid, in case the kids wake up. You can help yourself to something from the kitchen and take it back up with you.'

'But the agency, she say that au pairs should eat meals with the family!'

'Not dinner parties,' Dawn snapped back. 'Use your head.'

Use her head? How very rude! Dumbstruck, Marie-France watched Dawn march off to greet guests at the door, wearing a 'polite face'.

'I'm so glad you could come. Guess what? I've made your favourite. Pear tart. It's a new recipe. And I've got a really neat starter too. Of course it's home-made.' She laughed gaily. 'It's a brand-new recipe!'

But that was *her* pear tart!

For a minute or two, Marie-France eyeballed her employer from the back, anger rising in her chest. Then clicking her heels on the ground to make her point, she wove her way through the guests towards the kitchen. Leaning against the fridge was a tall, handsome man with an aquiline nose and a darkish complexion. He was wearing a pink-striped shirt in formal contrast to his pale blue jeans and he was opening a bottle of white wine. He looked up expectantly.

'Hi! You must be Marie-France. The new au pair. Good to meet you. I'm Phillip, Dawn's husband. I hope you're making yourself at home here.'

What a lovely friendly smile! So much nicer than his wife! Marie-France glanced at the pear tart and the soufflé on the side and wondered whether to tell him the truth. Maybe later when she'd established a better relationship with him.

'Yes, thank you. Your wife, she instructs me to take my food upstairs to my room.'

'Did she now?' He frowned. 'Sounds a bit like Cinderella to me but then again, who am I to contra - dict Dawn?' He laughed and took a swig straight out of the wine bottle. 'Would you like a glass? From another bottle, of course?'

She nodded gratefully. '*Merci*.'

'Now let's see what we've got to go with it. Cheese? Pâté? Fruit?' He handed her a plate, brushing her hand accidentally as he did so. 'Anything else?'

She nodded, wondering if it was too soon to ask. Still, nothing ventured, nothing gained, as her English teacher used to say at school. 'Just one small thing, if that is possible.'

A few minutes later, Marie-France was sitting happily on her bed listening to the sound of laughter through the window from the terrace outside. Her cheese – tasteless compared with the *fromage* at home – and the glass of too-sharp wine lay untouched by the side of her bed. The children were quiet, which meant they were still watching TV or had fallen asleep. That gave her a chance to do what she really wanted. To look through the local telephone directory that Phillip had lent her.

Mon Dieu! There were so many Smiths! Marie-France's eye ran down the page in mounting concern. Still, she could make a start. After all, she had the name. She had the dates. All she had to do was ring each one and politely enquire whether they had lived in Corrywood at the same time as her mother.

Easy!

USEFUL BRITISH IDIOMS FOR AU PAIRS

In hot water (In trouble)

In the dog house (As above)

Two ticks (In a short time)

In a jiffy (As above)

You've lost your marbles (You're crazy)

Sugar daddy (Older man with money)

Chapter 6

Matthew watched Sozzy's short, defiant figure march off down the street with her grey rucksack studded with safety pins slung over her shoulder. 'Wait,' he called out, 'please wait!'

But she didn't even look back. If it wasn't for Lottie, he'd have given chase, but he didn't like to leave her alone in the house. That look on his daughter's face when he'd introduced them hadn't just been dislike. It had been fear! He couldn't impose a stranger on her, yet at the same time, he needed to go back to work – and sooner rather than later if he was to keep his job.

Now what was he going to do? Walking back to the house, he noticed the nosy neighbour's curtains twitching. She probably thought he'd had some kind of lover's tiff!

'Lottie,' he began as he went back into the house, 'that was a very naughty thing to do, messing up Sozzy's bedroom and leaving such an unkind note.' There was no answer. His heart began to quicken. Dear God, don't say she had run off too? 'Lottie?' he tried again.

'In the kitchen, Daddy!' she called out gaily in a voice that suggested nothing had happened. 'I'm making you a cup of tea and I've opened a tin of alphabet spaghetti.'

She put her head round the door, smiling winsomely

up at him, her plaits flopping over her shoulder. 'I'm getting your dinner ready, just like Mummy used to.' Then she flew towards him, burying her face in his stomach. 'We don't need anyone else to look after us, Daddy. I can do it. You'll see!'

His heart contracted in a mixture of pain and pride. Were *all* eight-year-olds mature one minute and childish the next, depending on how they wanted to play it? Christina had warned her about this. There was a name for it apparently, when children tried to look after the bereaved parent to make up for the absent one. There was a danger, too, of the parent accepting this help out of loneliness or sheer misery. Before long, the two became mutually exclusive and over-reliant on the other.

'It isn't really fair,' Christina had said in that cool, calming office of hers with pale green curtains that fluttered in the breeze, 'because it doesn't give either of you the chance to make independent relationships in the future.'

As her words came back to him, Matthew knew he had to stand firm.

'Lottie.' He sank down to her height, holding her hands so she had to stand a little further away from him and looking into her eyes. 'I understand that you weren't very keen on Sozzy.' He hesitated. 'She wasn't exactly what I had expected either. But Daddy has to...' He stopped again, reminding himself that he must stop referring to himself in the third person. He'd fallen into the habit when Sally was ill and he'd been trying to comfort his little girl. But she wasn't that any more. She was growing up and if he didn't start to treat her like an eight-year-old, she wouldn't act like one. 'I mean I've got to go back to work soon and I need someone to look after you now the summer holidays have started and also later in the autumn when the new term starts. So I'm going to ring the agency and see if they can find someone else.'

'But, Daddy...'

'I'm sorry, princess. But we've got to be practical. However, you can do me a big favour.'

Her eyes – so like Sally's – were fixed on him warily.

'You can make me that lovely cup of tea you promised. Just be careful you don't burn yourself.'

She nodded. 'I won't, Daddy. I won't.'

He rang the agency as soon as she was out of earshot, explaining exactly what had happened. Janine, at the other end, was surprisingly understanding and Matthew wondered if this sort of thing had happened before.

'Sometimes,' she said, 'we do get the odd girl who just uses the job as an excuse to get into the country and then disappears. It's unfortunate.'

Unfortunate? 'It's really left me in the lurch!'

'I am sorry for that, Mr Evans, but your daughter's behaviour was not exactly welcoming, was it? From what you tell me, it was a contributing factor to Sozzy's departure. I'm not very happy about the fact that a twenty-two-year-old has just disappeared. We will have to inform her family and possibly the police if she doesn't turn up soon.' Her voice had a worried edge to it. 'They usually do surface within a day or so in my experience.'

But what if she didn't? He hadn't thought of that.

Suddenly the idea of his own daughter disappearing into the bowels of Bulgaria made him sweat with fear.

'However, you are in luck,' continued Janine brightly. 'We happen to have a Swiss-German girl in this country who is looking for a job. She was with another family in Dulwich but there was, shall we say, a clash of personalities.'

That didn't sound hopeful. 'Haven't we had one of those already?'

'Mr Evans.' The voice grew severe. 'All au pairs are different personalities just like you and me. It would be unrealistic to expect everyone in the world to get on with each other, don't you think? My job is to find the right match between au pairs and families.' There was a short almost flirtatious laugh. 'Rather like finding the right partner in life.'

Matthew thought of Sally and how he had thought that she was the perfect woman for him as soon as he had caught sight of her, coolly making her way through a crowded wine bar all those years ago.

'The good thing about Berenice is that because she's already in the UK, her paperwork is all up to date. So she could start immediately. I can send her over tomorrow for an interview if you like.'

Fair enough. 'Does she speak good English?'

'Excellent. She also comes from a very nice family.' Janine sounded as though he ought to be grateful for that. 'I believe her father works in the diplomatic world. Shall we say three o'clock then?'

Matthew had had quite a strong word with Lottie beforehand about the need to give Berenice a fair chance. 'Shall we buy her a cake?' he suggested.

Lottie had frowned. 'Mummy used to *make* hers. Don't you remember?'

Why, he wondered, did he always manage to say the wrong thing? He seemed to be doing more and more of that recently. Maybe it was because the anniversary of Sally's death was approaching. Was Lottie aware of that too and was that why she was being so difficult about having an au pair?

The doorbell rang at precisely three o'clock. Matthew was impressed. He'd suggested picking up the girl at the station but the agency had said she would rather make her own way to the house so she could take a good look at Corrywood en route to 'see if she liked it'.

'Do you want to answer the door with me?' he now asked Lottie, who was scowling in front of the television that he had tried, in vain, to get her to turn off.

There was no answer. The doorbell rang again, more insistently this time. 'Just coming,' he called out, leaving Lottie and making his way hastily through the small hallway, wishing too late that he had tidied up the collection of shoes by the front door.

Wow. His first thought was that the agency had sent a model! In front of him stood a tall, very slim, extremely elegant blonde with the kind of hairstyle that seemed to be shorter at the back and went down in little pointy bits to just above her shoulders. She was wearing a pale blue dress with a matching jacket and high heels. On her shoulder was a pale blue leather handbag. In contrast, the girl wore a very bright glossy lipstick, which matched Sally's geraniums in the pots outside. The whole effect was disturbingly attractive.

'Meester Evans?' She held out her hand. 'I am very pleased to meet you.'

'Likewise.' He felt his tongue slipping as he spoke so that it came out like 'lyth-wise'. 'Please come in.'

As he shut the door behind her, Matthew glanced next door. There they were! The twitching curtains! His neighbour probably thought he was inviting a string of girls in as 'entertainment'. Matthew couldn't help thinking that Sally might just think this was a huge joke.

'Berenice.' He gestured towards his daughter, who was squatting in front of the television. 'This is Lottie. Come and say hello, darling.'

Grudgingly, she turned round and Matthew saw her eyes widening, taking in Berenice's glamorous outfit and those brown bits round her eyes that made her look like an Egyptian cat. 'Is your hair real?' she asked breathlessly.

'Lottie! That's rude.'

Berenice smiled. A nice wide, open smile with lots of glossy stuff on it. 'Not at all. Your daughter is very astute. In fact, they are extensions.' She knelt down next to Lottie and took her hand. 'See? If you run your finger like this along my head, you can just feel where they join on.'

'Wow!' Lottie's eyes were even wider. 'May I have extensions too, Daddy?'

Matthew felt his heart lifting. His daughter *liked* Berenice! Just as important, she seemed to like Lottie.

'Why don't you turn off the television, Daddy?'

Lottie gave him a little warning smile. 'Mummy always turned if off when we had guests unless she wanted me to amuse myself.' She turned to their visitor. 'Would you like a cup of tea? Daddy and I bought a cake, especially for you. '

They spent over an hour talking in the sitting room with Matthew outlining the basic duties that he would expect of her if she wanted to take the job. 'It would be very helpful if you could do some housework like hoovering.'

He glanced at the carpet, which looked a bit grubby, and the silver-framed photographs of Sally on the pine mantelpiece, which needed dusting, as did the glass-topped coffee table in front of them.

Berenice tilted her head questioningly. ''Oovering? Who is 'Oovering?'

'It's the vacuum cleaner.' He flushed. 'We use it to clean carpets.'

'Ah!' Her face lightened and they both laughed politely. She was perched on the edge of the sofa, her legs (in those shiny kind of tights which his wife had sometimes worn on special occasions) close together in a pose that could have come straight out of a Sunday supplement.

'And you might need to help Lottie clean out Eddie, her lizard.'

Her eyes brightened. 'Eddie Izzard? I enjoy him too.'

'Er no, not like the comedian. Eddie is a pet lizard.'

She frowned. 'I am sorry, Meester Evans. I do not do pets. Now, I have more questions! Is there a language school in town?'

'Yes.' He had done his homework on that this time. 'I've already rung and they do have a spare place.'

She bent her head to one side as though considering the idea. 'And will you expect me to work two evenings a week?'

That's what the guidelines had suggested in the agency notes but he didn't need an evening babysitter. 'No. I simply want to be with my daughter when I get back home. So you can have every evening off.'

Another slight bend of the head, this time to the left. Matthew felt a rush of anxiety now in case she turned him down.

'And my weekends, they are free?'

'Absolutely.'

'Then I will accept the job.' She bent her head graciously for a third time as she spoke, as though accepting some kind of honour or award.

Matthew wanted to hug her. 'Thank you.' He glanced across to Lottie, who had sidled up admiringly next to their visitor, twiddling the ends of her hair. 'What do you think, Lottie? Would you like Berenice to be your new au pair?'

Lottie was nodding madly. If she did that any more, she'd lose that wobbly tooth at the front which had been promising to fall out for ages. 'Yes. I'll make your room really nice this time.' She gave Matthew a shy smile. 'Promise.'

Berenice moved in the following day so Matthew could show her how everything worked in the house. He planned to spend the last few days of his com-passionate leave at home, to help her learn the ropes.

But he'd also, Matthew told himself, go out for a couple of hours every day, just to make sure the new au pair could manage on her own. It was a terrifying thought. How could he allow a stranger to look after Lottie? Then again, he didn't have much choice.

'I've signed Lottie up for an afternoon summer activity course in the local hall,' he explained. 'When I start work again, I won't be back until early evening.'

He stopped. Even though Janine from the agency had told Berenice he was a widower, they hadn't really discussed it yet. Perhaps now was the time to do so. 'My wife died almost a year ago.'

Berenice bent her head graciously in that odd manner of hers, as though absorbing small talk at a dinner party. He was getting used to the movement now. Maybe it was something she'd picked up in diplomatic circles.

'It hasn't been easy for Lottie.'

Another nod.

'She's been seeing a bereavement counsellor.' No need, he told himself, to mention that *he* was seeing one too. 'On the surface, she seems all right but there are times when she does something... well, out of character.' He thought of the room she'd messed up for Sozzy. He ought to check with the agency about her. Find out if she'd got in touch. Presumably she was all right or else he'd have heard something.

Now those cool grey eyes in front of him lifted up to his. 'I will take care of her, Mr Evans. Do not worry.'

'I'm sure you will.' He tried to look as though he was perfectly happy with a strange woman moving in.

'Thought I might go out this afternoon so you could have a dry run.'

She raised her eyebrows. 'Dry run? What is she?'

Matthew felt his lips twitching. 'It means trying something new first. Now are you all right to look after Lottie while I do a supermarket shop?'

'Ah! Shops!' Her head nodded enthusiastically.

Clearly this *was* a word she was familiar with. It ought to have been higher up his list of priorities too. He really wasn't much of a cook. Since Sally's death, he and Lottie had lived too much on tins and takeaways. But now with Berenice around, this would all change.

When he got back, laden with supermarket bags, Lottie was stirring something in a pan with Berenice standing next to her. She was wearing, he saw with a pang, one of Sally's aprons – the floral National Trust one he'd given her one Christmas.

'I am teaching Lottie to cook,' she announced. 'Dinner will be ready in ten minutes. You will be ready then, yes?'

It was almost like being in someone else's house as a guest but, hell, he was tired and there was something rather nice about coming downstairs and tucking into, what he had to admit, was an amazing fish dish with vegetables in a hollandaise sauce. Pudding was apple strudel. 'I made it, Daddy, with Berenice's help! We went down the road to get the ingredients. I lent her my pocket money.'

But he'd just *been* shopping!

'We tidied up the kitchen too!'

Lottie's face was gleaming. Indeed they had. Part of

Matthew felt Berenice should have asked his permission before moving the pink and green china plates on the dresser which Sally had always had in a certain order. Then again, it seemed slightly petty to make a fuss. As long as Lottie was happy, it was all right. That night, Matthew slept better than he had done for a long time.

'So it's working out?'

Christina was sitting opposite him in a matching beige-flecked chair. They were having one of his monthly sessions which the GP had arranged.

He nodded. 'It's been just over a week now and our new au pair – she's called Berenice – seems to get on very well with Lottie. She bosses me around, though. And rearranges things.' He laughed, trying to make a joke out of it in case she thought he was making a fuss. 'Strikes me as being a bit of a control freak.'

Christina's eyebrows raised slightly. She wasn't a pretty woman, he had sometimes thought. More a handsome one with pale blond hair tied in a knot at the back and a very straight back. But she had a lovely voice and a kind face (framed by rather trendy purple-framed glasses) that could make you feel relaxed about telling her anything. Well, almost.

Although Christina wore a thin gold band on her left hand, she never mentioned her own personal life. In a way, she reminded him of a kindly but sensible prefect. Sally, on the other hand, had been more like a naughty sixth-former. Once, shortly after they had got married, she had taken the kitchen scissors to a new dress and slashed it – right in front of him – before taking it back to the shop and claiming it was damaged! She'd then demanded her money back and compensation to boot.

Matthew had been shocked by that. In fact, it had been one of the first danger signals. He couldn't, he thought, bringing his attention back to Christina, imagine his counsellor doing anything like that. Still, you never knew. People could be deceptive.

'You need to set the boundaries clearly.'

Matthew's mind, which seemed to be going all over the place at the moment, went back to yesterday when he had come home from a long aimless walk to find the house immaculately clean and hoovered. 'Plis. Remove your shoes,' Berenice had told him in a rather clipped, precise voice. 'I do not want any mess on the floor.'

So much for boundaries! 'I do try. But Lottie seems happy – although a bit tired – and that's the main thing.'

'And what about you?' Christina glanced at her notes. 'It's nearly a year, isn't it?'

He nodded. Suddenly a huge lump came up into his throat and he felt the tears before he could stop them. 'I've started walking, like you suggested,' he managed to say in a tight voice, 'but it can't obliterate every - thing. Maybe it will be better when I go back to work and have to think of other things.'

'I think you're right.' Christina pushed the box of tissues towards him just in time.

'Sorry,' he tried to say.

She shook her head. 'Don't be. It's part of the healing process. In fact, it's a good sign.'

'You know,' he said, the tears pouring out now, 'I still wear the aftershave cologne she gave me last Christmas. Only a little bit every day because I'm worried how I'll manage when it's empty. Then I'll feel she's really gone.'

Christina's eyes filled with sympathy. 'That's normal too. I once had a client whose husband gave her a box of chocolates before he was killed suddenly in a car crash. She made a promise to herself that she would eat one on their anniversary every year.'

He'd stopped weeping now. 'But didn't they go stale eventually?'

She nodded. 'Exactly.'

After the counselling session, he went back to the house. It was only five o'clock and his spirits felt a bit lighter. Christina had been right. Crying had made him feel better even though he felt an idiot for having broken down in her office. Still, he was home now. Maybe, if Berenice hadn't started to make supper yet, they'd all go out to eat and...

What was this? Lottie was bending over a kitchen cupboard on her hands and knees scrubbing the inside. 'Poppet. What are you doing?'

His daughter glanced around, looking scared. 'Shh, Dad, or she'll hear. Berenice told me that if I didn't get this cupboard clean before you got back, I couldn't have lunch tomorrow.'

No!

Lottie's eyes filled with tears. 'She makes me do all the housework, Dad. It's why I've been so tired.'

The old tightening feeling in his chest returned. 'Is this another of your stories, princess?'

She shook her head wildly. Suddenly he realised that something was different.

'What happened to your hair?'

Another tear rolled down his daughter's cheek. 'The oh pear cut my fringe. She said it would look better this way.'

This was outrageous!

Lottie dropped her voice to a whisper. 'She said that if I told you, she'd say I was making everything up. But go upstairs into your bedroom and you'll see.'

His bedroom? Quietly, he tiptoed up the stairs and pushed open the door.

'Monsieur Evans!'

Almost unable to believe his eyes, he stared at Berenice. The girl was standing in front of Sally's full-length mirror wearing her beautiful black backless slinky evening dress!

'What do you think you are doing?'

She gazed at him coolly. 'I was just trying it on. It is a waste, do you not think, for the clothes to stay in the wardrobe?' Coolly, she flicked some clothes along the rail. 'Some of them, it is true, are not worth wearing but I rather like this.'

'Get out.' Matthew heard his voice rise. 'Get out of my house. How dare you chop off my daughter's hair, treat her like a slave and wear my wife's clothes.'

Berenice bent her head to one side. 'Your daughter is spoilt. She does no work. Besides, I think her hair looks better like this.'

This was outrageous! Matthew thundered down the stairs, fumbling in his pocket for his mobile. 'Janine? This is Matthew Evans.' He slipped into the sitting room, shutting the door behind him so no one else could hear. How awful, he thought, to have to hide away in his own house to get some privacy!

'I am afraid that Berenice is not suitable for us.' His voice rose in anger. 'She cut my daughter's hair without asking permission and had the nerve to try on my dead wife's clothes so I have asked her to leave immediately...A fortnight's notice? You want me to give her a fortnight's notice after *this*?'

The thought of living with this woman who had taken such liberties was impossible!

'I will go early if you pay me two hundred and fifty pounds,' said a cool voice on the other side of the door.

Matthew flung it open. Had she no shame, eavesdropping on him like that? Matthew threw her a disdainful look. 'She says she is happy to leave early if I pay her two hundred and fifty pounds. I think that says it all, don't you? However, I am prepared to do so. And frankly, Janine, if this is the best you can do, I won't be needing your services any more.'

Then he put down the phone next to Sally laughing at him from the silver frame and wondered what exactly he ought to do next.

Dear Jilly's Au Pair Agency,

My name is Fatima and I find you on the internet. I live in Wapping, London, but I am not happy. My family, he is not kind to me. I like to work in the countryside. Do you have a place for me?

Yours expectantly,

Fatima Mamid

Chapter 7

'So you see, Jilly, I just can't keep Fatima. I really can't! When I speak to her, she seems to understand, but if my husband asks her to do something, she shoots him a filthy look and says, "I do not understand."'

Susan Wright lowered her voice. 'I've a funny feeling that Fatima doesn't like men! Whenever a male presenter or actor comes on TV, she switches channels immediately.'

Jilly listened with a sinking heart. When Fatima's email had popped up on screen, desperate to swap Wapping for Corrywood, it had seemed too good to be true. Susan Wright, who lived in a lovely part of town by the park, had recently collared her in the library, asking if she could find her an au pair just for the summer holidays 'as soon as possible before I go mad!'.

So after interviewing Fatima over the phone (the girl had sounded pleasant enough), she'd put the two in touch. An au pair agency was rather like fishing. You sent girls out to families, hoping for a bite. Sometimes it happened. Sometimes it didn't.

Perhaps she should have sounded out Fatima in person. But she'd been up to her eyes in looking after her own lot now the school holidays had started.

'Maybe there's some cultural reason for her behaviour,' Jilly now suggested to the very disgruntled

Susan Wright. 'But if you'd like to look through the other girls I sent you, I'll do an exchange. I'm afraid none are actually in this country at the moment so it might take a few weeks until they get here.'

'By then the school holidays will be nearly over and I won't need anyone!' The voice at the other end dramatically altered from friendly to cool. 'Forget it. I'll go through another agency. Naturally, you'll refund the placement fee.'

Hand back money she'd already spent on the week's shopping? Jilly felt her mouth go dry. That would be really difficult. 'But my terms make it clear it's non-returnable.'

'Jilly! You have provided a service which is not up to standard. Do you want me to take this further? To the ombudsman perhaps?'

She could have argued with her but it would have caused bad feeling and, in a small town, she couldn't afford that. Especially not with another school mum. So reluctantly she sent the deposit back and explained to a tearful Fatima on the phone that she'd try to find another family to place her with.

'But where am I to live?'

Jilly felt like saying it wasn't her problem but that wouldn't be very kind. 'How about a hostel? Or maybe a cheap hotel?'

It wasn't very satisfactory but what else could she do? 'It's the girl I feel sorry for,' she tried to explain to David later.

He ran his hand over his chin ruefully as he always did when musing over a problem. Usually she found the gesture endearing but now it worried her. David had warned her that setting up an au pair agency was bound to be fraught with difficulties. And if her husband had one fault, it was that he *did* like to be right...

'I can see what you mean, Jilly, but you've got to set emotional boundaries. Now, has Dawn given you that petrol money for picking up the French girl from the airport the other week, like she promised?'

'I don't like to nag her any more. She's a friend – well, sort of.'

He sighed. 'You can't let that get in the way, Jilly. Not when you're running a business.'

'I'm only doing this because I'm trying to help.'

His face tightened and, too late, she wished she hadn't said that. David, who was usually so even-tempered, had become increasingly uptight since the problems had started at work. 'Thank you for reminding me, Jilly.' He stood up, moving away from her, hurt written all over his face. '*You* were the one who always said you wished you'd worked a bit longer before having the boys.'

The argument resulted in a distinctly frosty atmosphere between the two of them for the next few days. Her husband's words rankled, not least because there was some truth in them. Then, a couple of days later, an email popped up from one of the many European agencies she'd contacted, in a bid to find more would-be au pairs. It was in German! Oh dear...

'MUM, MUM!'

Oh God. The boys were awake already even though it was only ten in the morning. Since the summer holidays had started, she'd given up the you-will-go-to-bed-on-time struggle and taken to letting them stay up late in bed with their computer games. The upside was that they were so tired, they woke up later than usual in the morning. The extra breathing space gave her time to get on with advertising her business and building up a network of contacts. Guiltily, Jilly wondered if that made her an awful mother.

'Please. I'm trying to concentrate.'

'IT WASN'T ME, MUM. HE DID IT FIRST.'

Did what? Alfie staggered sleepily into the kitchen, clutching his PSP. In her day, it used to be a teddy.

Harry followed, with an exaggerated limp, wearing a T-shirt that said *It was him*. Their uncle had brought it back from the States last summer (Alfie had an identical one) and she had to admit that the slogan said it all.

'Did what?' she groaned.

'Bruised my knee. Look! He whacked me with the computer mouse.'

There was indeed a rather nasty green and yellow map forming on his leg although there was an identical one on Alfie's.

'*And* we're starving,' Harry added indignantly as if this was related to the injury. Ah. Until a few weeks ago, she'd have had breakfast ready and waiting with placemats out and the table already laid. But there was no time for niceties. Not if she was going to help keep the family solvent.

'Here.' Guiltily, Jilly shoved a bowl of cereal into their hands. 'You can eat that in front of the telly.'

'Really?' Alfie's eyes lit up with surprise. Usually

meals in front of the television were a no-no. 'Cool.'

Right. Now she could get on with trying to work out what the email meant. Maybe – that was a thought! – Paula could translate. Hadn't she read modern languages at Oxford in the years BC (before children)?

Swiping the files out of the way so she could retrieve the handset from a puddle of spilled soya milk, she dialled her friend's number. 'Hi! It's me. Look, I'm sorry to bother you but could you possibly come over? I've got this email from a German agency that I don't understand and…hang on, my mobile is going. Can you get here as soon as you can?'

Dropping the handset so that – shit – it broke on the floor, sending the batteries scattering, she grabbed her mobile. It was an unknown number. 'Hello?'

'Is that Jilly's Au Pair Agency,' asked a voice doubtfully.

Whoops! She must remember to answer more professionally now she had a business.

'Yes it is. How can I help you?'

'This is Caroline Thomas. You sent me details of a Norwegian girl called Margit.'

'That's right.' Jilly felt her hopes rising. Did she want her? Please! Please! It was like waiting for an exam result!

'We would like to take her on but only for the summer holidays.'

YES!

Jilly was scrabbling for the right file. There it was! Jammed up against the muesli packet and – what? – a final demand for the gas bill. Shit. She'd thought David had paid that.

'MUM, MUM. HE WON'T LET ME HAVE MY PROGRAMME!'

'IT'S MY TURN TO CHOOSE. YOU SAID SO.'

'Can you hold on a minute, please?' Jilly shut the kitchen door between her and the boys and held the mobile between her ear and shoulder while leafing through Margit's file. No! The kitchen door was bursting open.

'MUM!'

Gesticulating madly at the boys to indicate they should be quiet on pain of death (in other words, 'no television ever again'), she scooted past them and into the downstairs loo, clutching both file and mobile. 'Er, sorry to keep you there. Let's see. Ah that's right. Actually, Margit is looking for a nine-month placement.'

Mrs Thomas sounded annoyed. 'I'm not prepared to take on someone for that long until I know her better. If I am happy with her performance, I might consider it.'

Oh God. Mrs Thomas sounded like the kind of mother who kept spare batteries for emergencies and did her Christmas shopping by October half-term. 'I can ask the Norwegian agency who put me in touch with her,' said Jilly doubtfully.

'Thank you. And by the way, I want her to start next week.'

'MUM, MUM!'

How many more knocks could the downstairs loo door take? She might as well move her office in here permanently.

'Sorry about the noise but I'm in a sort of meeting.

I'm afraid I must go but I'll back to you as soon as possible.'

'MUM!'

Unlocking the door, she stormed out. 'Alfie! Don't ever make a noise like that when I'm on the phone.'

A small face stared up at her. 'It's not Alfie, Mum. It's Harry.'

What was wrong with her that she couldn't even tell her own boys apart? Harry's right ear was slightly smaller than his left and always had been. Until now, Jilly had always prided herself on being able to tell her virtually identical twins apart. If this was what work did for you, was she doing the right thing?

Then a picture of that unpaid gas bill swam into her head. Frankly, she had no choice. Because if this didn't work, she'd need to get out and do a proper paid job and then who would look after the kids?

'Hello?' said a clipped voice. 'Are you still there?'

Shit! Horrified, Jilly stared down at the phone. She'd forgotten to turn it off. 'Sorry, Mrs Thomas. I think we had a crossed line there. As I said, I'll get back to you as soon as I've spoken to Margit. Thank you for your call.'

And with that, she ended the conversation before she could make an even bigger fool of herself.

'I *think*,' said Paula, rereading the email doubtfully, 'that this means the German agency is prepared to work with you if you split the placement fee sixty-forty. In *their* favour.'

'Shouldn't it be fifty-fifty?'

'You'd think so.'

'Can you email them back for me and say I'd like half-half?'

'I could but...hang on, there's a clause here that says – well, I think it does – that they can send you an immediate list of names if you agree.'

'I've got a list of English families who want help for the summer.' Jilly moved the jar of discounted decaff to create a bit more space. 'It's here somewhere. There we are. My ad in the local paper brought in loads of enquiries – did I tell you that I'd managed to place Fatima again with a family from Puddleducks? – but everyone wants short-term au pairs for the summer instead of the usual six to nine months.'

Paula gave a short laugh. 'I could have told you that. The last thing you want is to be landed with someone whom you don't really like for that length of time. That reminds me. Antoinette has signed up for a language course every morning which is *exactly* when I need her for my lot.' She sighed. 'Still, she's getting on a bit better with Immy. Frankly, I don't know how you manage without any help.'

Jilly felt a twinge of guilt. 'I'm afraid I've just given my lot a bumper bag of crisps and another DVD from the library. That's why they're so quiet.'

'Great!' Paula gave a conspiratorial smile. 'You're learning. You know, until you started your agency, I thought you were a bit too good to be true. Always doing stuff with your kids: taking them to museums and that boat in Portsmouth, the what's-its-name...'

'The *Mary Rose*.'

'That's it! God, my kids have done my brain cells in.

Of course, you had a big age gap between Nick and the twins. That must have helped.'

'You're kidding! Try having twins at the same time as a hormonal teenager! I'm beginning to think I've bitten off more than I can chew.'

'Nonsense.' Paula, bless her, was already emailing the German agency. 'You're superwoman. We've always said so. Perfect Jilly who can make a soufflé rise every time and whose kids always have neatly labelled school uniform.'

That might have been the case in the past but it wasn't now. Since she'd started working from home, everything seemed to have gone to pot. Paula's comments made Jilly resolve to tidy up those files, get the kids dressed and away from the telly.

'*Send*!' Paula sat back with an air of satisfaction. 'You've got another email here. Look.'

Wow! It was from the Norwegian agency. That was fast. And it was written in English, thank heavens. 'Fantastic! Margit is prepared to work until the end of the summer holidays and will extend it if she is needed. She can also fly out this week!' Jilly hugged Paula. 'The placement fee is only a hundred and fifty but it will pay the gas bill.'

Paula looked at her pityingly. 'I didn't realise things were that bad.'

She nodded. 'If David doesn't find a different job soon, we're going to fall behind with the mortgage. Now do you mind keeping an eye on the kids? I've got to fill in the insurance form.'

'Insurance?'

'Every au pair agency has to be insured in case our

111

girls supply false information or hurt the kids or do any of the other zillion things that could go wrong.'

'Hurt the kids? That wouldn't happen, surely.' Paula waved her hand towards the window and the leafy lanes of Corrywood. 'Maybe in south London but not round here.'

Jilly dropped her voice. 'To be honest, I didn't realise I had to be insured myself until I was reading up about it on the net last night. I've already placed one girl – the French one – with the Greens without being insured but don't tell anyone.'

'Right,' said Paula uncertainly. 'Look, you've got another email. It's the Germans. Blimey, they're efficient, aren't they? Don't like the look of that one, do you? I wouldn't trust my husband within a yard of her. Looks like that gorgeous model Heidi thingamajig.'

Jilly ran her eye down the list of names and mug shots alongside them. 'What does the blurb say?'

'Let's see.' Paula sat down, put on her glasses and took on a rather smug expression as she proceeded to translate. 'Clara, aged eighteen is a non-smoker. She's lactose intolerant, vegan and she doesn't drive.'

'No good.' Jilly was going through her printed-out list of families with a Coco Pops stain on the front page. 'Everyone wants a driver.'

'Not surprised with all the activity clubs the kids need to get to. How about this one? Brigitte is twenty – that's better – but she's a smoker.'

'That's a no no then.'

'Well, at least she's admitted it. Antoinette *said* she'd given up but is now on two packs a day. She's also

112

developed this strange allergy to dust since arriving so can't do any polishing.'

How convenient!

'Wait, this one looks a bit better.' Paula stabbed a finger at the screen. 'Grette is twenty-one. She's got a driving licence *and* has experience of children. Wow. Can I have her instead of Antoinette, do you think?'

'No!' Jilly giggled. 'This isn't the swap shop.' Then she grew more serious. 'These are real lives at stake. Finding the right match is an art.'

'Ooooh! Just listen to you!'

'MUM! MUM! IMMY'S STUCK BEHIND THE SOFA!'

Paula groaned.

'I'll sort her out,' promised Jilly, jumping to her feet, 'if you don't mind translating that last one's details so I can send it off to one of my English families.' She gave Paula a big hug. 'Thanks. I really owe you one.'

By the end of the following week, Jilly had placed the Norwegian girl *and* the German one with two local families. She'd also managed to build up a link with the German agency, thanks to Paula, as well as a Parisian one, although she hoped Paula's German was better than her own rusty schoolgirl French.

Meanwhile, the twins had spent most days slobbing in front of the television in their boxer shorts and T-shirts while Nick moped around the house, declaring he was 'bored'. At fifteen, he was too young to get a summer job apart from his paper round and too old to want to hang out with his younger brothers. Before working, as Paula had reminded her, she'd have taken them out on a trip. They used to go everywhere! Legoland. Woburn. The Natural History Museum. But this summer, they'd done absolutely nothing.

Still, maybe now she'd got some clients – and a few cheques coming in – she could make up for it. Just as long as it didn't involve any expense.

'Come on, you lot,' she announced, after Paula had left for her salsabellylates class. 'We're going out.'

'Can we get a new computer game?' asked Harry hopefully.

'No. We're meant to be saving money, not spending it. So we're going to get some nice fresh air.'

'Bor-ing,' groaned Alfie.

'I thought we might go to the park and feed the ducks.'

'Double bor-ing.'

'We're not babies any more, Mum.'

They were right! What was it Mum had said the other month before dashing off on her latest cruise? 'These early years can slip past faster than you realise. You need to make the most of each day.'

'We could take your skateboards,' she suggested hopefully.

'I need new pig wheels on mine.'

'And mine.'

Jilly was shocked. Not even a *please*! Had she and David spoilt the kids in the days when they'd been able to do so? 'I'm afraid we're going to have to manage with the ones you've got.'

'Why?'

'Why?'

'Because they're expensive and—'

Oh no, not the phone again! Just as she was finally giving the kids some attention.

'Hello!' she trilled, forcing herself to sound professional. 'Jilly's Au Pair Agency!'

Why was it that those words always made her feel like a fraud? It *was* her agency, yet somehow running it from the kitchen table made it feel as though it was a hobby rather than a business.

'This is Mrs Thomas. Have you got my email yet?'

'No, but…'

'I sent it a good four minutes ago. Margit isn't working out. I made it quite plain that I didn't want a smoker but there's a distinct smell of cigarettes in her room. I want my money back and I'm going to lodge a complaint against you. In my view, you've acted under false pretences.'

False pretences? 'Actually, Mrs Thomas, I'm afraid we can only act in good faith over matters like this. If an au pair tells us that she isn't a smoker, we have to believe her unless proved to the contrary.'

'MUM! YOU SAID WE WERE GOING SKATEBOARDING!'

'However, I will obviously have a word with Margit and—'

'MUM! HARRY HIT ME!'

Waving madly at the boys to indicate they needed to keep quiet, she ran upstairs into the bathroom, locking the door behind her. 'And if she won't stop smoking inside the house, we will find you someone else.'

Quite how, she had no idea; the promise had just slipped out of her mouth in a bid to appease her client.

'MUM! OPEN UP, MUM, SOMEONE'S RINGING THE DOORBELL.'

'Mrs Collins! This is really very unsatisfactory. I have to say that I thought I was dealing with a proper agency here but it is obvious, from the sounds at your end, that this is a sideline of yours. If you do not sort out this matter, I will report you. And it goes without saying that I expect my registration fee back.'

'MUM! ALFIE'S OPENING THE FRONT DOOR AND IT MIGHT BE A STRANGER!'

Dropping the phone, Jilly tore down the stairs just in time to see that Alfie was, indeed, standing on tiptoes to unlock the door. There, in front of her, stood a small, rounded figure with spotty brown skin and a mass of dark hair with yellow and red beading in it. For a minute, Jilly thought she was one of those door sellers from whom she sometimes purchased a duster, out of pity.

'Mees-is Collins.' The girl's face pleaded up at her, revealing a gap in the middle of her teeth. 'I is Fatima. I follow your address. My family, she has thrown me out. I have nowhere to go.'

Too late, Jilly remembered one of the pieces of advice she'd read from another au pair agency's guidelines. *The danger with taking on au pairs who are already here is that it's not always easy to send them back. You might end up giving them temporary accommodation yourself until something can be sorted out.*

Well, there was no way they could do that!

'Fatima,' she began as the girl waddled in before she could stop her, carrying a plastic supermarket bag stuffed with a black hoody and a wet-looking striped towel. 'Why have they thrown you out?'

Fatima patted her stomach. 'I is expecting.' Her eyes filled with tears. 'It is why I come to your country. My dad, he would execute me if he know.'

She looked around the hall, peering round the corner into the sitting room, her eyes widening as though she was looking at Dawn Green's opulent nine-bedroom house instead of her own, more modest home.

'So I can live on the sofa? Yes?' She clutched at Jilly's hands. 'Please. I am very hard worker. I will help you. You will not be regretful!'

USEFUL PHRASES FOR AU PAIRS
To help your pronunciation,
some words are spelt phonetically.

I have sis tight iss

I am allergic to deodorant

I am late

I desire to visit Buckingham Castle

Your husband sleepwalks

Please may I borrow your rase er

Extract from the *Useless Guide for Foreigners*

Chapter 8

Marie-France woke early. As always, her first thought was her father. She'd been here for nearly a month now yet was still no nearer to finding him. The telephone directory hadn't helped at all. Several people had simply slammed the phone down, declaring that they didn't take 'cold calls'.

It was all so frustrating! She could be getting ready for the Sorbonne now. Then again, this might be her only chance to find her roots. She had to succeed. She simply *had* to!

Slipping out of bed, Marie-France performed her morning stretching exercises and then looked out of the window. How strange! Sometimes she still expected to see the glorious sight of a chateau in the distance. Today, there was a small bird with a red chest on top of one of the dustbins below, pecking insistently at a piece of 'cab itch' on top.

Recently, Madame Dawn had put everyone on the family on a 'cab itch' diet. Everyone apart from Tom, that was. The joke was that no one else needed it. They were as skinny as rakes. As for Tom, all he needed to do was take more exercise instead of lying on the floor with his computer games.

Children in England were so spoilt! Then again, everything in this country was so different. It wasn't just that they drove on the wrong side of the road. It was their custom of taking milk in tea. Shops which were open on Sunday so that each day of the week was the same as the others. The cold wind even though it was summer. And the way they wrote the dates with the day before the month. Boring clothes in shops where grey seemed the favourite colour. The obsession with something called steak and kidney pie. Strange phrases like 'use your loaf' which, when she'd looked it up, had nothing to do with bread. The list was endless!

'Marie-France!'

It was Tatty Arna's voice. Marie-France opened the door, still in her chemise. '*Oui, ma petite?*'

When she'd first arrived, she had put Tom and Tatty Arna down as a pair of spoilt brats. But over the last few weeks, Marie-France had learned to feel rather sorry for the little girl. She and her brother had every - thing they could possibly want in the way of material possessions but the one thing they didn't have was their mother. Madame Dawn was always out!

If it wasn't a lunch, it was coaching at the tennis club or a shopping trip or a dinner party or a pilates lesson or maybe t'ai chi. 'You don't mind doing extra hours, do you?' their mother had asked and Marie-France had once more nodded quietly and said that was fine pro - vided she was paid extra and maybe given time off in lieu.

Now, as Tatty Arna's little face gazed up at her, Marie-France knelt down and gave her a cuddle. Funny really. She'd never considered herself to be the maternal type before. But Tatty Arna with her sleepy eyes and pyjamas that smelt of that funny English washing powder reminded her of herself at that age.

'Tom woke me up.' The little girl rubbed her eyes. 'He jumped on me because he said I'd taken his new television.'

Marie-France's mind went back to yesterday when Madame Dawn had returned from an extra long lunch, carrying two yellow bags with the name *Selfridges* on each. 'They're mini-tellies for the kids,' she'd announced. 'Might keep them quiet for a bit. All the celebrities' brats have them apparently. Will save you the need to read a bedtime story.'

Now Marie-France knelt down next to the little girl. 'And did you take it?' She gave her an understanding squeeze. 'Just to annoy him?'

'No!' There was a big sob. 'I don't know where it is. And I can't go back into my room because he's waiting there for me.'

Tom was such a bully! Always hurting his sister and then declaring that she had started it. Marie-France didn't care for him; she could see exactly what kind of man he would grow up into. 'Come with me, *chérie*.' She slipped into her jeans and white T-shirt. Her shower would have to wait until later. 'We two can make croissants in *la cuisine*!'

'It's *us* two, not *we* too!' Tatty Arna giggled. 'You do speak funny English but I like it! I like cooking too but Mummy never lets me. She says there isn't any point because we have people to do that kind of thing for us.'

'Nonsense.' Marie-France shut the door behind her, wishing that she had a lock to keep her things private. 'Cooking is an enormous pleasure in life. But you know what is even better?'

The little girl, whose hand was now in hers, shook her head. 'No?'

'Tasting!' Marie-France ran her lips around her mouth in an exaggerated way. 'And if you are good, you can try out the first croissant!'

They spent a happy half-hour or so in the kitchen – with Cook jealously looking on – while Tatty Arna, under Marie-France's instructions, rolled out the puff pastry. '*Fantastique!* Now we spoon dollops of melted chocolate on top – see? – and roll them up before popping them into the oven.'

When they came out, all crisp and golden, even Cook's mouth was watering.

'*Vous en voulez?*' Marie-France offered with a friendly smile.

The cook, a stout woman with a wedding ring that looked far too tight for her bulging white finger, glared at her suspiciously.

'What's she saying?' she asked Tatty Arna as though Marie-France was some kind of alien.

'She wants to know if you'd like one.'

Marie-France gave a nod of approval. She'd been trying to teach the children a few phrases of French since she'd arrived and although Tom refused to listen, little Tatty Arna was a quick learner.

The cook eyed them hungrily. 'Might as well.' She took a bite. 'Blimey. They're hot.' She waved it around in the air and then took another bite so that chocolate was smeared all over her mouth. 'Not bad, I suppose, for something that's French.'

Marie-France nodded with approval. Maybe now was the time to ask Cook that question she'd been burning to ask. 'I know you have inhabited this area for many years,' she began.

Cook stopped, mid-mouthful. 'What's that to you?'

'I was imagining,' continued Marie-France, hoping that the cook could understand her English, 'if you are acquainted with a family called—'

'That smells very good!'

Biting back her disappointment at the interruption, Marie-France swivelled round. Monsieur Phillip lounged against the doorway wearing a grey suit and a crisp white shirt slightly open at the neck, revealing dark curly hairs underneath. How handsome he looked!

'We've been making choir sounds,' chirped Tatty Arna.

Marie-France laughed. '*Croissants, ma chérie.*' She sang it out loud to show her how the first part of the letter went up the scale and then dropped.

Monsieur Phillip eyed the tray hungrily. 'Any chance of a spare one before I hit the road?'

'*Naturellement!* But you must have some strong coffee to go with them or else they do not taste the same.'

Somehow, they all found themselves sitting round the table – even Cook – with Tatty Arna looking much happier. Maybe now was the time to make more enquiries about her father.

'I want to ask something plis,' she continued, handing the plate around. 'I tell you before that I look for old family friend of my mother. She was au pair in this town many years ago and she—'

'*What the hell is going on?*'

123

Madame Dawn strode in, wearing a grey designer tracksuit with sparkly bits. It made her look like a baddy in a sci-fi film, thought Marie-France. She had clearly been for her morning run and she wasn't wearing make-up, which made her face look pale and lined and her eyes like a little piggy's. Now she was staring straight at her!

'I asked you to make those croissants for a charity breakfast party. I've been angling for an invitation for months. Now you've gone and scoffed them all so what the hell am I going to take instead?' Her eyes fell on Tatty Arna. 'How many has she had? You know she's on a diet. She's fat enough as it is.'

Marie-France gasped. Fat! There was hardly anything to the child; she was all skin and bones, unlike podgy Tom who couldn't do anything wrong in his mother's eyes. Now little Tatty was crying and no wonder.

'Sweetheart,' began Phillip.

Madame's eyes flashed. 'Don't *sweetheart* me. I spend hours killing myself to look good for you and then I come down and find you lot having a tea party.' She glared at Marie-France. 'Clear this mess up now. And then go and get Tom up. He's in a right state because his new telly has gone missing. After that, you can start the dusting. The cleaner is on holiday this week so you'll need to muck in like the rest of us.'

'But I commence my class today,' began Marie-France.

'Too bad.'

'*Dawn.*' This time, Phillip's voice was much firmer. 'I believe that the agency said we were meant to allow our au pair time off for language classes.'

Her boss's thin red lips tightened and Marie-France felt a twang of anxiety. The last thing she wanted was to be sacked. If she was to find her father, the best place to be was Corrywood and if that meant acting as a maid, so be it.

'It ees OK. I can ignore my class.'

A slow, triumphant smile crossed Dawn's face. 'If you are sure.'

'Nonsense.' Phillip was looking cross now. 'I insist that you go.'

Don't do this, Marie-France wanted to say. You are making it worse. 'Perhaps,' she said quickly, 'I prepare *les enfants* for their activity course today *and* I do some cleaning before I go. That is all right? Yes?'

Dawn glanced at her husband, her eyes narrowing. She really was, thought Marie-France, one of those women who should never, ever, get out of bed without eyeliner in place. 'I suppose so. But make sure you're back in time to prepare dinner. We've got some people coming round and I want you to make another of your pear tartes Tatins.'

'Suck up all you like to that woman,' Cook muttered as Madame Dawn swept out of the kitchen, closely followed by her husband, 'but you won't last. Why do you think the last au pair left and the one before that and the nanny before that one and the nanny before that? I'm only here meself until I can find something better and if you've got any sense, you'll do the same.'

The language school was held at the local school, Corrybanks Primary. Jilly had emailed details in advance so Marie-France could book up.

'I've had to wait ages for a place,' moaned a girl from Lithuania as they filed into the classroom, which was lined with pictures of the Kings and Queens of England from what looked like a class project. 'When I arrive, it is full.'

She said all this in a very broken accent which Marie-France could barely understand. In fact, her own English was much better than any of the others. Amazing how she had picked up words from the family in just a few weeks.

'Me too,' hissed a girl in a rather common Parisian accent. She wore a tacky silver chain round her neck, bearing the name *Antoinette*. 'My family is more interested in me looking after their kids than helping me to learn the language.' She plonked her mock Yves Saint Laurent handbag down on the desk. 'Now they want me to look after another family's *enfant* as well.'

'That doesn't sound very fair,' agreed the Lithuanian girl.

'*Exactement*. So I have *three* kids in my hands! I say they must give me extra money and more time off. That is fair, *n'est-ce pas*?'

Antoinette broke off as the language teacher came in. To her delight, Marie-France discovered the woman was French and had been living in England for five years.

'I fell in love with an Englishman,' she confided, sitting on the desk and revealing a shapely pair of legs which were almost as good, Marie-France noted, as her own and Maman's. 'Yes, it is true!' She blushed. 'Are any of you looking for someone special?'

Antoinette, next to her, shook her head vigorously. 'I don't believe in long-term relationships,' she retorted.

'I want to have fun while I'm here.'

The class laughed.

'Be careful,' warned their teacher. 'There are some gentlemen in England but just as in your own countries, there are some unsavoury characters too. What about you?' Her eyes had turned to Marie-France. 'Are you looking for a man? Please reply in English!'

Marie-France almost laughed at the irony. 'Certainly I am,' she retorted. 'Is not everyone?' There was a laugh, especially from Antoinette. It was clear from the way she spoke and from her low-cut red T-shirt that she was what the English called a tart. 'But when I do discover him, it is not for a one-night stand.'

There was an uneasy titter.

The girl on Marie-France's left, who was secretly rolling up a cigarette under the desk, spoke up. 'I do not understand.' She spoke in a guttural Scandinavian accent. 'What is a one-night stand?'

'It is an affair which lasts as long as a bottle of Beaujolais,' shot back Marie-France.

'Bravo!' The teacher was already standing up and writing something on the board. 'Today we are going to have a lesson on love and also tackle our tenses at the same time. *Regardez! I love. I loved: I will love.* And please, Margit, put away that roll-up. We do not allow smoking in the class.'

The lesson lasted nearly two hours. Afterwards, Antoinette invited them all back to her house for coffee. 'Madame is at the gym, thank God.' Her eyes rolled as they walked along the high street, past shop windows which seemed so dull compared with French boutiques. That dress back there was little more than

127

a black sack! Maman would have a fit if she saw that!

'But soon we are going on holiday,' she continued boastfully. 'My family is taking me to a place called Ork Knee.'

'They're taking you *with* them?' enquired a German girl whose French was almost fluent. 'Then make sure they give you some time off. Mine took me to Disneyland at Easter and I ended up looking after the kids all the time. They said that they expected me to pull my weight as they were taking me to a nice hotel. But it was crap! I had to share a room with the kids. Can you believe that?'

Antoinette shrugged. 'Then maybe I say I will not go. I stay here instead.'

'My family, they is having their vacation in the bath,' said one of the new Italian au pairs. 'The English, they are very strange, are they not?'

Marie-France hadn't thought of asking about holidays with her family although she had overheard Phillip saying something the other night about the Cayman Islands. Would they expect her to go with them or would they allow her to stay at home to 'house-sit' so she could get on with tracking down her father? She hoped it would be the latter.

'Right, this is it.' Antoinette tossed her dark curls and strode up a horseshoe-shaped gravel drive towards a detached house with a grey roof and roses climbing round the door. *Très jolie!* She fished in her bag. 'I'm sure I had the key in here somewhere. *Merde*. Never mind. I know where my family keeps the spare.'

Turning over a large grey stone by the side of the front door, she unearthed a key. 'I should have set the alarm before I went out but I couldn't be bothered,' she said as they all poured in. 'Right, everyone. The kitchen's this way.'

Marie-France watched aghast as Antoinette put on the kettle and opened a packet of chocolate biscuits, scattering crumbs on the floor. She would never be so familiar in someone else's house but then again, Antoinette wasn't the kind of girl she would have been friendly with in France. Meanwhile, a couple of the other girls had moved through to the sitting room where they were putting their dirty feet up on the white sofas. The Scandinavian – Margit – was now lighting her roll-up right next to her. 'Want a puff?'

Marie-France wrinkled her nose disapprovingly. 'Not for me. Especially not that kind of cigarette.'

Margit shook her shoulders. 'Suit yourself. This is my only chance. I told my agency I did not smoke because I thought it would be easier to find a family. Then she finds out and I am in a dog's house.'

Marie-France moved away towards the window. Outside was a wooden swing and slide and at the top, sitting crying, was a small girl. 'Antoinette,' she hissed in French. 'Your family is at home. Look?'

Antoinette waved her hand dismissively. 'That is just Immy. She is OK.'

Marie-France frowned. 'Who is looking after her?'

'I am.'

'But you were at school all morning?'

'So?'

She was beginning to understand now. 'Your family thought you were looking after the little girl but you left her here. Alone?'

'Why not?' Antoinette's eyes were flashing. 'The mother lives at her gym. If she cared so much, she should look after her own kid. Besides, Immy likes playing in the garden and it is quite safe.'

'She's crying!' Marie-France rushed past. 'Where's the back door? I'll look after her.'

'Suit yourself! She's only...*Merde*. Someone's coming in!'

There was indeed the sound of voices coming from the front door. 'So I told her that...'

Marie-France stared in horror as a small, dark-haired, skinny woman walked in along with Jilly – Jilly from the au pair agency.

'What is going on?'

The skinny woman's voice rose as she surveyed the coffee cups everywhere and the stumped-out cigarette ends on plates.

'I ask my friends to my house.' Antoinette was speaking in a defiant voice instead of one which sounded sorry. 'You give me permission!'

'Yes, but I also said I didn't want anyone smoking indoors.' The dark-haired woman looked around, her eyes darting from one side of the room to the other. 'Where is Immy?'

'In the garden,' said Antoinette quickly. 'I come in to get her some juice.'

'She's crying,' said Jilly, moving to the window. 'Looks like she's stuck again.' Her eyes fell on Marie-France reproachfully as though she had participated in this mess. 'Don't worry. I'll get her.'

Marie-France had wanted to explain that none of this

had been her fault but there wasn't a chance. 'I like to stay and tidy up,' she offered while helping to put some of the coffee cups in the dishwasher, 'but I must return to my work.'

Jilly, who was playing with a now-comforted Immy, gave her another reproachful look. 'Are you happy with your family, Marie-France?'

Now was not the time to admit how badly Dawn was treating her or she might find herself out of a job. '*Oui, madame.*'

The skinny woman opened a bottle of wine even though it wasn't yet lunchtime. 'Probably living the life of Riley there, I should imagine, with that pool and all those servants.'

Riley? What was that? Marie-France made a mental note to check it out. Meanwhile, she really had to go. She'd been hoping to pop into the library on the way back and if she didn't get a move on, there wouldn't be time.

'Well,' said the tall thin man at the library when she'd explained she was trying to find someone who had lived in Corrywood nineteen years ago, 'Your best bet is to look on the electoral roll but you need an address for that.'

That was no good then! Her mother insisted, before she left, that she 'couldn't remember' it. So what, wondered Marie-France as she made her way back up the hill to Dawn's place, should she do now?

Reaching the gates, she pressed in the security code Madame Dawn had taught her ('It changes every month so make sure you remember') and walked up to

131

the enormous front door with those huge pillars.

Before she could find her key, the door swung open. A furious Madame Dawn was standing there with a small television in her hand. 'What do you call this?'

Bon! She had found it. 'That is the television you search for before!'

'So you admit it then?'

'I do not understand.'

'Of course you do. We found this in your room. You stole it.' Her eyes flashed. 'You're no more than a common thief! Now don't move because I'm going to call the police!'

'The police?' A deep voice sounded from behind her. 'What's all this about?'

'Tom found his television in that girl's room!' hissed Dawn.

'And what was he doing there in the first place?'

Just what she was about to ask!

Dawn looked embarrassed. 'He was exploring.'

'Tom!' The child was standing at the top of the stairs, grinning, with defiance flashing from those piggy eyes. 'Come down here. Your mother says you found the television in Marie-France's room. Is that true?'

The boy nodded.

'If it is there, it is because someone places it there,' spat Marie-France. 'If you tell lies, Tom, the police will put *you* in prison! Not me!'

Tom burst into loud tears. '*She's* the liar. Not me!'

'You will go to your room, Marie-France,' hissed Dawn. 'Now. And stay there until I say you can come down. Got it?'

CONFUSING ENGLISH IDIOMS FOR AU PAIRS

Give someone a leg-up (Helping someone)

Raining cats and dogs (Intensive rain)

Letting the cat out of the bag (Revealing a secret)

Eating someone out of house and home (Being greedy)

Driving someone round the bend (Annoying someone)

Tearing your hair out (Feeling very frustrated)

Cold as brass monkeys (Freezing)

Lend an ear (Listen)

Chapter 9

Thank goodness for Paula! Without her help, Matthew told himself, he couldn't have gone back to work. As it was, James had been very understanding. If he hadn't been a partner, he'd never have got so much time off.

'Of course Lottie can come to us during the day for a week or so,' Paula had said when he'd rung round Sally's friends for emergency help. There hadn't been that many, to be honest. His wife hadn't been the kind of woman who'd had lots of friends. 'Poor you! It sounds as though you've had some really bad luck. My own au pair isn't great, to be honest, but we're still together.' She made a sympathetic noise. 'Almost sounds like a relationship, doesn't it? But that's what it is, really. Immy, don't do that or you'll get stuck again. Sorry. Antoinette – that's my girl – is out at the moment so I'm struggling with my lot. Anyway, just drop Lottie off on your way to work and we'll hang on to her until you're back.'

So he'd taken her at her word, even though Lottie hadn't been very keen and had protested all the way that 'Immy is a baby' and that Paula's son William, who had been at Puddleducks with her, wasn't her 'friend' any more.

It had almost broken his heart to leave her and drive off while she stood at the doorstep next to Paula, who'd put her arm around her in a motherly fashion when it should have been Sally doing the same thing. In fact, he'd had to pull in at a lay-by on the way to the office and actually have a bit of a weep, which was, Christina had been saying for months, exactly what he needed to do instead of bottling it all in. It just wasn't great timing when he was due in the office by eight thirty.

How odd, he shivered as he pulled into the car park and found his 'usual' space. He hadn't parked here since the week before Sally had finally died. Now he was back here, in his suit which he'd had dry cleaned and his shirt which he hadn't pressed particularly well and the navy striped tie which Sally had given him two birthdays ago. It was almost as though he'd never been away.

But no. Judging from the look on Karen's face as she got out of the little blue sports car which had pulled up next to his, there wasn't going to be any chance that he could pretend anything was still the same.

'Matthew, how *are* you?' His PA, with that rather irritating little-girl voice, was approaching him now with both arms outstretched and her wide generous mouth positively homing in on each check. She paused slightly but long enough for him to take in her trade - mark perfume that always made him sneeze.

'We've all been thinking of you.' She was standing a short distance away from him now but still somehow clasping both his hands as though dragging him out of a deep stretch of water, determined not to let go. 'You poor, poor thing! What a dreadful ordeal to go through. And so young too! You did get the flowers I sent, didn't you? I wanted to send my own, although of course I contributed to the general office collection. But I felt that, having met Sally twice, I knew her, Matthew. I really did! And although I don't have children of my own – well, not yet, at any rate – I *felt* for you with your dear little daughter.'

By now they were walking towards the entrance and the name plate *James Matthew Architects* was gleam - ing at him. He and James had started it nearly four years ago when they'd both found themselves working for a company that they didn't particularly care for. Amazingly, in the recession, it wasn't doing too badly.

'Now, it's bound to feel a bit strange on your first day.' Karen sounded like a mother at the school gates. 'But everyone knows what you've been through, of course, so they'll all make allowances. If there's *anything* I can do for you, aside from the usual things, of course, all you have to do is let me know.'

'Thanks.' Matthew was beginning to feel suffocated. Karen had always been over-solicitous but now she was simply making everything worse. Much worse. He turned to face her before they got as far as the reception desk. 'There *is* one thing, actually.'

Those loose soft blond curls bobbed energetically and her low-cut blouse imitated the movement. 'Anything, Matthew. Anything.'

'I don't want to talk about Sally.' His words came out sharper than he'd meant them to and her fallen face made him feel a heel. 'I just want everything to be normal again. OK?'

The curls and cleavage nodded disappointedly. 'I understand, Matthew. I really do.'

Right. Now he had to walk past everyone else's desks to get to his own office at the end. Matthew braced himself for the embarrassed faces but found to his relief that, on the whole, everyone seemed quite normal.

'Hi, Matthew,' said someone.

'Good to see you back, mate,' said another.

He and James had agreed they wouldn't stand on ceremony with their employees. Nice to see that hadn't changed.

'We've got a new sandwich service,' someone else called out, 'so bung in your order before eleven a.m. or you'll be left with tuna.'

It was feeling better already!

'Matthew!' James was coming out of his office, giving him a quick hug. Someone wolf-whistled across the floor. 'Cheeky buggers,' grinned James, stepping back.

After Sally's death, James had rung him every now and then to see how he was. Occasionally, he had invited him out for a beer. But Matthew had turned him down, not wanting to leave his daughter. Privately, he felt hurt that his friend and his wife hadn't asked him and Lottie over for a meal together.

Now it seemed as though James was trying to over-compensate. 'Come on through.' He ran his hands through his hair which, Matthew noticed, had got considerably thinner over the last year. 'I can tell you, I'm glad you're back. We've got a few big deals in the last couple of months and I need your input badly.'

*

'You'll feel better when you go back to work,' Christina had said during one of their recent sessions. 'It will distract you.'

She'd been right. By lunchtime, Matthew's head was full of designs for the new shopping centre which James, amazingly, had won the tender for. It was a huge project and part of him was ashamed that his partner had had to do all the hard work in securing it.

'I felt you had enough to cope with,' his friend said as they munched their cheese granary sandwiches over the outline plan. 'How's Lottie doing?'

Matthew felt a pang, thinking back to her anxious little face when he'd dropped her off at Paula's this morning.

'Not great. She misses her mother badly of course and she's still getting the occasional nightmare.' He could hear his own voice trembling and had to force himself to look out of the window and concentrate on his car down below in order to steady himself.

'I know. I'm sorry. Charlie sends her love, by the way, and says that if there's anything she can do, to let her know.'

Charlie had been with James for years but neither seemed to want kids so how could they know what he and Lottie were going through? 'Thanks. I will.'

'Who's looking after her now?'

Matthew groaned. 'It's a long story. It was meant to be a girl from Bulgaria, or Vulgaria as Lottie insisted on calling it. Then there was Berenice but neither of them worked out – don't even ask why – so a friend of Sally's is having Lottie until I can find another au pair.'

James grinned. 'I saw a film about au pairs once when I was a teenager. It was part of my adolescent passage.'

Matthew felt uncomfortable. 'Yes, well today's girls aren't like that. At least the two I had weren't. In fact, you won't believe—'

'That your mobile?' James nodded at the small black phone on the desk. 'It's OK. You get it. We need a bit of a break anyway.'

Caller withheld? Matthew felt a twinge of unease. Who was it? Paula? Had she been trying to get hold of him because Lottie was sick? His imagination ran riot. Maybe she was lost. Or hurt. Dear God, please may she be all right. He should have stayed at home to look after her himself.

'Mr Evans?'

'Speaking.'

'This is Janine from the agency.'

Relief shot through him. Lottie was all right after all. Still, he didn't like the sound of the woman's voice which was in direct contrast to last week when she had sounded very contrite.

'I've just interviewed Berenice, Mr Evans, about the unfortunate hair incident and it appears that there is more to this than we had thought.'

A cold feeling passed through him. 'I don't understand.'

'Berenice claims that your daughter *insisted* that she cut her fringe. In fact, she wanted her to cut off much more. She said she wanted to look like one of the other au pairs you had before.'

Sozzy? Matthew vaguely recalled that her daughter

had indeed admired her spiky style but that had just been a silly whim. She hadn't meant it, surely?

'Lottie also suggested that Berenice tried on your wife's clothes. Your daughter said that you had left instructions that Berenice should go through them before you gave them away.'

'That's preposterous!'

'Are you sure, Mr Evans? Lottie also apparently asked if she could help with the housework instead of being forced to do it as you said.' The voice was a bit softer now. 'Forgive me for speaking out of turn but grief can do strange things to people, especially children. Berenice said that Lottie was always making stories up. There's something else too. Your daughter claimed that you often smacked her for losing her shoes.'

'That's an utter lie!'

Matthew heard his own voice rise just as Karen walked past the office, glancing in with undisguised curiosity.

'She also claimed that her mother wasn't dead at all but that she comes to visit her every night when she is asleep.'

Matthew felt his mouth going dry. That part was certainly true. Lottie did keep saying that but, on the doctor's advice, he didn't contradict her.

'I'm not suggesting you take Berenice back, Mr Evans. I think the damage has been done on both sides. But I do feel that before you take on another au pair from an alternative agency, you might want to have a word with your daughter first. I'm a mother myself and I can't help feeling that Lottie is deliberately seeing off any strangers in the house because she doesn't want anyone else there.'

He could feel the panic rising in his throat. 'But how am I going to be able to work if I don't have some help?'

There was a sympathetic sound at the other end. 'That's a question which only you can answer. Good luck, Mr Evans.'

James gave a little I-couldn't-help-overhearing cough as he came off the phone. 'Everything all right?'

He nodded. A small tell-tale pulse began to throb in his right temple the way it had ever since that day when Sally's first lot of tests had come back. 'Fine. Everything's just fine.' He reached across the desk to pick up the plans. 'Let's get back to this, shall we? I don't know what you think but in my view, this bit over here is crying out for another window '

Matthew forced himself to concentrate on work until it was a reasonably decent time for him to pick up his jacket. Usually he stayed later than this but he didn't want to impose on Paula any more than was necessary. So this was how single mums felt! He'd always thought that the word 'juggling' was a cliché but now he could see that it summed up his dilemma perfectly. It really was a balancing act; trying to make sure that you did your bit at work but were a responsible parent at the same time. Add a large gallon or two of grief and that might just about give someone the tail end of the picture.

Still, he told himself as he made the forty-minute-or-so drive back to Corrywood, at least he had his job! Those few hours at his desk when he had refused to allow himself to dwell on Lottie and Berenice and who was or wasn't telling the truth had helped to block everything out. But now it was time to ask some tough questions.

Paula's house was one of those easy-on-the-eye homes with a horseshoe gravel drive which had been built in the 1930s. It sang out security and safety and those sponge cakes in the kitchen which Sally used to make on her two days off a week from the lawyer's office in London where she had worked as a part-time legal secretary. He and Sal had both liked the look of these houses, which were in a better part of town than they were. 'One day,' she had said dreamily at the stage when there had still been the possibility of a 'one day', 'I'd love a home like that.'

Why was it, Matthew asked himself as he knocked on the front door, that some people had everything? Paula's husband worked away during the week in Brussels to pay for all this but when he came back, he had his wife and his kids and the Sunday night drama on television which he could watch without wincing if one of the characters died of cancer.

Odd. No one was coming. Matthew knocked again, more urgently this time and his heart began to beat faster. Ever since Sally, he had become convinced that something else would go wrong. If Sally could be taken, so could Lottie. Christina said it was part of the natural grieving process but the explanation didn't make the symptoms any easier to deal with.

At last! A shape loomed up through the glass.

'Yes?'

The dark, sultry girl standing in front of him,

barefoot in skinny denims and a T-shirt which dipped in the front, eyed him suspiciously as though he had interrupted her from something.

'Hi! I'm Lottie's father. Are you Antoinette?'

'Yes.' This was said in precisely the same tone as the first word. She nodded dismissively. 'Plis. Enter.'

He did as he was told, looking around for his daughter. There was the sound of laughter from the room on the right. Lottie was sitting on the floor cross-legged, laughing at one of the idiotic children's presenters on television. During his time at home with Lottie, he'd decided that the level of intelligence in children's programmes had seriously dipped since he'd been a child. By her side was a half-eaten bowl of pasta. On the sofa were Paula's children. Paula herself was nowhere to be seen.

'Daddy!' Lottie turned round when she saw him and jumped into his arms. Her expression immediately changed and now she was burying her head in his chest, hanging on to his shirt lapels as she had apparently hung on to Sally when she'd started play-group as a toddler. 'I missed you, Daddy. I missed you.'

A large lump formed in his chest. 'I missed you too, princess. Let's go and find Paula to thank her for having you.'

The moody girl cut in: 'Paula is performing her Zeeep-o class.'

Zeeep-o?

'It's a fitness class, Dad.' Lottie turned her wet eyes up to his. 'Mum used to go.'

Did she?

She pressed her tear-stained cheeks against his. 'Can we go home now?'

He nodded. 'Please say thank you to Paula for me and thank you also for having my daughter.'

The girl nodded.

'We'll see you tomorrow then?'

She nodded again but was now focusing on her phone.

Well, thought Matthew as he insisted that Lottie strapped herself in the car ('Do I have to, Daddy?'), she wasn't the most talkative of au pairs! Or the most polite. But she had looked after his daughter well enough or so it seemed and it wasn't as though she'd been eating a packet of crisps for tea. That pasta had looked quite healthy with that green broccoli.

'Daddy.' Lottie's plaintive little voice rose from the back. 'Daddy, do I have to go back to Ant In Net's again?'

'It's Antoinette, darling.'

'I don't like her, Daddy. She smells.'

That was true enough. The stench of BO had been overwhelming.

'It's just for a bit, darling, until I can find another au pair.'

'But I don't want any more oh pears.'

They'd been through this so many times that it was becoming a chant. Repetition, Christina had said, was comforting for small children. You only had to look at their reading books to see that.

'It's just for the summer holidays until you go back to school.'

'No it's not. You said we'd still need an oh pear then

144

so there was someone to look after me when I got home from school.'

'Let's see what happens, shall we?'

'No.' Lottie began to whimper in the back. 'Mummy used to say that and look what happened to her.'

Matthew bit his lip. 'Lottie.' He glanced in the driving mirror. 'Did you tell Berenice that she could try on Mummy's clothes?'

'No, Daddy!'

Her tone was so shocked that he knew, immediately, she was telling the truth.

'OK. I knew you hadn't. Now how about a little treat on the way back. An ice cream perhaps?'

The following week didn't go too badly really. He and Lottie managed to get themselves, somehow, into a sort of routine. He'd set the alarm for 6.30 a.m to give himself time to iron her clothes for the day and get her up. Breakfast was a slow affair. He remembered now Sally telling him how Lottie always dawdled. How hard it was getting her out of the house to school on time. Perhaps he should have shown more sympathy.

In the end, he took to buying those breakfast cereal bars and letting her eat them in the back of the car to Paula's, often wearing different coloured socks and, once, odd shoes. When he got to work, he threw himself into it, blocking everything else out so that by the end of the day, he was drained. Then it was back to Paula's, pick up a subdued Lottie and somehow persuade her to go to bed before him. Often in the night she would wake screaming for Sally and he would lie down next to her, singing the nursery rhymes from her babyhood, so that she eventually nodded off.

It would be better, he told himself, when the new au pair arrived and Lottie could spend the days in her own familiar surroundings. This time, he had signed up with a different agency and had been far more careful when filling in the forms. He wanted a girl over twenty-five (the more mature the better, although apparently there was a cut-off age of twenty-seven) who didn't smoke and who had been to England before. That way, he reckoned, the culture shock might not be too great.

The following morning, Matthew wasn't surprised to find that Lottie was very quiet. Today was the day he'd been dreading for months. The anniversary of Sally's death. A whole year. Sometimes it seemed much longer. Sometimes like the other week.

'Daddy,' lisped Lottie with that little girl voice she put on when she wanted something. 'I've got a tummy ache. I don't want to go to Ant In Net's again.'

Did she know the significance of the date? Would it be best – as Christina had suggested – to be open about it? Maybe. Matthew knelt down beside his daughter. 'Is it because today is Mummy's special day?'

She hesitated.

'The day she died a year ago?' continued Matthew.

Lottie nodded solemnly although from the slightly surprised expression in her eyes, he had a feeling that she hadn't twigged before but was now using this as a calculated excuse. An uneasy sense crawled through him. Had she taken after her mother who'd been so clever at deceiving him?

'Mummy's been away for too long now. Do you think she'll come back soon?'

Matthew fought with the lump in his throat. 'I've told you before, princess. Mummy had to go to...to another world. Now we must get going or I'll be late for work.'

Her eyes widened and at the same time, filled with tears. God this was difficult.

'Can't you take me with you?'

Matthew hesitated. Would James understand? If the tummy ache got worse, he could take her to the doctor.

'OK. Let's get you dressed and then you can come with me.'

Her eyes lit up. 'Thank you, Daddy!'

She didn't look so poorly now. Was she trying it on? 'But you've got to be good, Lottie. Really good.'

'I will, Daddy. I will. I'll take my crayons in with me and my play tapes.'

By the time they got into work, Lottie's 'tummy ache' had miraculously disappeared. Meanwhile, everyone was fussing over her!

'Let's find you a place next to me,' cooed Karen, pulling up a chair. He'd quietly briefed her on the sig-nificance of the day and she was being brilliant. Kind but not over-fussy to either of them. 'Here's some computer paper. Now would you like to do me a nice picture?'

Someone else had nipped out and bought her a packet of chocolate buttons which went down faster than the fizzy drink that someone else had given her.

'Poor little lamb,' whispered Karen softly. 'Maybe she just didn't want to stay at home.' Her voice dropped. 'I used to do that when I was her age, you know.'

Matthew felt an unexpected flash of sympathy for a small, slightly dumpy Karen in school uniform.

'Not, of course, that I would dream of doing that at work,' she added hastily.

Matthew laughed. 'I know you wouldn't.' He glared over at his daughter whose blond plaits were flopping over her drawing. 'Thanks for looking after her. I'll be out of my meeting by lunchtime.'

'No rush. If you're not, I'll take her out with me and the girls for a sandwich.'

'That's so kind.'

He made his way back to his own office with its precious door which, nowadays, in this world of open-plan offices, was a rare privilege. Thanks to Karen, he could catch up with his emails. Maybe have a glance at *The Times Online*.

What was this?

An unnamed woman, believed to be about 20 years of age and from an Eastern European country, was found last night strangled in Hyde Park.

She had a nose ring and was wearing scruffy jeans and a denim jacket with the words 'Bad Girl' sewn on the front. If anyone has any information, they are urged to contact the police on…

Matthew felt a globule of bile rising into his mouth. Bad Girl? Nose ring? Oh my God.

Numbly, he picked up the phone and rang the number given in the paper. 'My name is Matthew Evans,' he heard himself say. 'I've got a horrible feeling that I might be able to help you.'

SURVEY BY *CHARISMA* MAGAZINE

Nearly 65 per cent of au pairs claim that their English families treat them badly!

Complaints included:

Not talking to them enough

Expecting them to stay in their rooms in the evening

Giving them too many jobs

Not paying them on time

Chapter 10

What had she done? Jilly asked herself. Invited a complete stranger into her house, that's what! Even though she'd always said she couldn't stand the idea. But Jilly just hadn't had the heart to turn away this tearful, pregnant girl who had nowhere else to go. The twins would just have to share. They were always in and out of each other's rooms anyway.

David, being a man, didn't quite see it that way. 'We can't take in a lame dog,' said her husband firmly when he finally got home from the office, long after the rest of them had eaten. 'We've got enough on our plates.'

The kids, who were still up, thanks to the crisis, immediately started to shout at once. 'Bruno isn't lame,' protested Harry indignantly. 'He's really fast. That's why the window got broken this morning.'

'The window?' Her husband raised his eyes questioningly.

'Don't even ask,' replied Jilly heavily, putting a plate of scorched leftover cottage pie in front of him. 'No one got hurt although I had to fork out over a hundred pounds for the glazier.'

David groaned. 'See what I mean? We can hardly afford to keep ourselves going let alone a complete stranger from Turkey. It's bad enough subsidising the rest of Europe when they get into debt.'

'*Turkey!*' Alfie's eyes were shining. 'We did a poem

about turkeys at school last year. It's all about how you should look after them at Christmas. My teacher says it's why she's a vegetable arian. Can I be one too?'

'No,' sighed Jilly, wondering if the twins' cot was still in the attic. She'd a feeling they'd given it away. 'It's too complicated. Besides, Daddy isn't talking about turkey birds. He's talking about the country where Fat Eema – I mean Fatima – comes from.'

'But they must eat turkeys there, mustn't they?' insisted Alfie. 'Or at least have them as pets. Otherwise, what's the point of calling it that?'

'No, stupid. It's like Bath where Jack's going on holiday. His au pair thought they were going to sit in the bath for two weeks.'

Somehow – as usual! – what had started as a conversation between her and David had developed into one of those crazy, nonsensical arguments with the kids. She only hoped they hadn't woken up Fatima, who had waddled straight into the sitting room and fallen asleep on the sofa while Jilly hastily rearranged bedrooms.

'She's *pregnant*, David,' Jilly hissed. 'That means no one's going to want her as an au pair and if we make her go home, her father will kill her.'

He made a poo-poo expression. 'She's exaggerating.'

'*Is* she? How do we know what he's like? If there's one thing this agency has taught me, it's that we don't know what goes on in other people's homes.'

'So what are you suggesting?'

'I'll take her down to the doctor tomorrow and we'll find out what the score is.' Jilly felt a rush of concern for this poor girl. 'I don't even know if she's had any tests. We'll go from there.'

David had shaken his head but despite his earlier words, she could tell from his eyes that he felt a certain amount of sympathy. 'And in the meantime, we put her up here?'

'What choice do we have?' Jilly gave her husband a hug. 'Thanks. She'll be able to keep an eye on the children while we work.'

Since then, she'd taken Fat Eema – somehow the kids' name had stuck – to her own GP, who booked her in for antenatal care. She was apparently about six months pregnant. Was she intending to stay in the UK long-term? Jilly found herself nodding and saying that she didn't think Fatima had any intention of returning to her own country at the moment.

To be honest, their latest addition to the family wasn't much trouble. Although Jilly didn't like to ask her to do any heavy housework, she was very happy to sit with the boys while they tried to kill each other. In fact, she was rather good at diplomatically sorting out blood-curdling squabbles in her broken English. They no longer yelled at each other as though they were shouting in capital letters. Well, not quite so often, anyway.

But the funny thing was that as soon as Fatima heard the sound of David's key in the lock, she would scoot up the stairs, huffing and puffing, and then shut herself in her room until he went to work the next day. 'Her old family said she didn't like men,' recalled Jilly.

David shrugged. 'Maybe she bats for the other side.'

Jilly shook her head. 'I think she's been hurt. Poor thing.'

He threw her a strange glance. 'You're too soft for this business. Know that?'

Too soft? Maybe he was right. In the meantime, she had returned the deposit to Mrs Thomas and placed Margit with a twenty-a-day family who were quite happy to take one more smoker on board. She only hoped everyone was happy now. This sort of business relied so much on word of mouth. All it took were a few words from unhappy clients and it could do untold damage.

Now as Jilly sat, still in her pyjamas even though it was nearly 10 a.m., she felt sick as she trawled through her admin files. These insurance forms were so complicated! She'd tried to get them sorted at the weekend but David hadn't been very happy about that.

'Don't you want to have some family time?' he had asked after failing to persuade her to sit down and read the Sunday papers.

'Of course,' she'd snapped. 'But I've got work to do which I can't manage when I'm on my own with the kids.'

'There's no need to be tetchy.' He had turned away, picking up his newspaper in a way that suggested he had had enough of this conversation. 'Besides, aren't they at an age when they can look after themselves?'

'Look after themselves?' she'd repeated disbelievingly. 'If it was that simple, why do you think women need help? You have no idea, do you? By the way, I hope that's the Jobs section you're reading.'

'Know what? You've changed since you started this agency of yours.' David threw her a hurt look and stormed out into the garden, leaving her feeling a confused mixture of anger and regret. Since then, he'd been cool and distant. This morning, he had left for work without even saying goodbye. This really wasn't like him – or her. The strain of making ends meet was really getting to both of them.

For the next-half hour or so, Jilly buried herself in admin. It wasn't just her files that needed updating. She also needed to email back some foreign sub-agencies who might be able to supply some girls and a couple of boys too...

What was that? Bruno had heard the noise as well and was pawing at the kitchen door before bounding up towards Nick's bedroom. 'Nick?' She knocked loudly on the door. 'Are you all right?'

The groaning was getting louder and Bruno's scratching was getting desperate. 'Nick?'

Please don't let him be ill, Jilly found herself thinking guiltily. She had too much on today! That insurance form simply had to be sorted and then, in the afternoon, she had to interview a Swiss-German girl who had contacted her through her website.

The door seemed stuck but putting her shoulder against it, she managed to push it open. Nick was lying on his stomach, both hands under his body moving up and down in a rhythmical fashion. The printout of the au pair list together with several mug shots of applicants from a French sub-agency was on his pillow. Oh my God! How awful! Her teenage son was getting turned on by her clients!

'Mum!' His eyes, red and wide with shock, gazed up at her.

'Sorry,' she spurted before dashing out and shutting the door. For a few moments, she stood there, her back against it, trying to take in the implications of what she'd just seen. Her son was masturbating! He was experiencing the kind of adult feelings that she did (not that there was a great deal of action in the bedroom nowadays – they were both always too tired).

But it wasn't just that. It was what was turning him on! Pictures of au pairs whom she was bringing into this country and for whom she was responsible! Jilly returned to her kitchen table, not knowing whether to laugh or cry. What she *did* know was that she definitely needed to have a conversation with Nick when he emerged, no doubt shamefaced and awkward. She'd have to somehow assure him that masturbation was normal while at the same time pointing out that it might be best if he stuck to magazines in future. How embarrassing! In the meantime, she'd give him some time to himself.

But by lunchtime (where did the hours go?) when she went upstairs to investigate, Nick's bedroom was empty. Jilly's heart began to pound as she took in the window, which was wide open. On his bed was the crumpled list of au pairs and the word *Sorry* written at the top. Oh my God. He hadn't jumped, had he?

Hotly pursued by Bruno, she tore down the stairs and out into the garden. The old apple tree outside Nick's room looked as though one of its branches had broken – yes, here it was, lying on the ground – but there was no sign of her eldest son.

'He's gone out!' She looked up as a small figure came running towards her from the garden. It was Harry. 'Nick says he's gone to see some friends cos he had an argument with you.'

'It wasn't an argument,' she began and then stopped. 'Where is Fatima?'

'Asleep again.'

Fatima was always tired at the moment, but then again, that was understandable given her condition.

'And what are you doing outside still in your pj's?'

Harry pointed at her. 'What are you doing in *yours*?'

She'd completely forgotten about getting dressed! What kind of mother was she?

'We're digging for worms.'

Digging for worms?

'Yes.' Harry nodded at her. 'We're going to sell them to the men by the canal for bait so we can give you and Dad some money.'

Alfie's little face looked twisted with worry. 'We heard you arguing cos we don't have enough to pay the bills and we don't want you to worry any more or get divorced like Clemmie's mum.'

Now she really *did* know she was a lousy mother. 'Alfie, darling. And Harry too.' She crouched next to them. 'That's very sweet of you but, honestly, it's all right. Parents do argue sometimes, just like brothers. But it doesn't mean they're going to get divorced.' She stopped, wondering how to phrase the next bit. 'As for the money, well, it's true that things are tight but we can manage. Honestly we can.'

His face brightened. 'Really? Then can we have a laptop each cos everyone else has got one? Tom says he's selling his cos his mum is getting him a state-of-the-tart one.'

'We'll see. Now why don't we all go back into the house, get dressed and have something to eat. I've got a bit of work to finish off and then maybe we'll go out for the afternoon.'

Even as she made her promise, Jilly remembered she had to interview Heidi. More importantly, she needed to find Nick to tell him it was all right. Honestly, how did working mums do it all? Returning to the kitchen, she turned on the radio for some light relief while she tidied up her files.

'The body of the young woman who was found in Hyde Park earlier this week has now been formally identified as Sozzy Psuzki, a twenty-two-year-old au pair from Corrywood in Bedfordshire.'

Jilly's skin began to crawl.

'She had been strangled and sexually assaulted. Police are appealing for witnesses or anyone who can provide any information.'

Shaking, Jilly picked up the phone. 'Paula? Have you heard about that au pair?'

'Awful, isn't it?' Her friend's voice was a mixture of excitement and shock. 'She was meant to be working for one of the dads at school actually; you know, Matthew Evans, whose wife died. Apparently she was only there for a few hours before storming out. In fact, he's been leaving his little girl Lottie with us while he finds another.' She sounded embarrassed. 'I did tell him you'd set up an agency but he wanted one that belonged to a professional organisation. Sorry.'

Jilly was still trying to take all this in. 'So where did this poor au pair come from?'

'An agency in London.'

'I mean which country?'

'Let me think. It reminded me of the Wombles when I was a kid. That was it. Bulgaria! Poor Matthew's in an awful state. He hasn't had much luck with au pairs. After that one, he had another who went through his wife's stuff so that's why we said he could share Antoinette. Sorry. Must dash. I've got my belly-dancing class.'

Jilly leaned for a few minutes against the kitchen counter. Supposing this had happened to her? What if her agency had been responsible for placing that poor murdered girl? She'd feel terrible about it!

After all, she and countless other women throughout the country were finding jobs for thousands of young girls, most of whom had barely left school. They were launching them into a world where they were expected to take on huge responsibilities like looking after young children and yet, at the same time, some of them – maybe like this poor Bulgarian girl – were no more than kids themselves. What had she got herself into? And wasn't this even more of a reason for taking in poor Fat Eema who had nowhere else to go?

'Jee-lee?'

Talk of the devil! Fat Eema, wearing one of her old navy-blue Mothercare dressing gowns, lumbered into the kitchen and sank down on the chair with a groan of relief. 'I feel more restful today!' She grinned, revealing that gap along with a rather black-looking side tooth.

Mentally Jilly added 'Ring dentist' to her list.

'I feel starvation.' She patted her stomach, which seemed larger, if that was possible, than when she'd arrived. 'We eat breakfast now. Yes?'

'But it's already lunchtime,' Jilly began. Then she stopped. Forget it! There were more important things to sort out.

Heidi, who arrived dead on time for the interview, was virtually perfect. She was slightly older than most of the girls on her books and her English was excellent. Her references were glowing. In fact, there was only one drawback. She was stunning. Absolutely stunning with naturally blond hair, or so it seemed, china-blue eyes and a lovely smile. Exactly what the wives of Corrywood *wouldn't* want.

'I am fed up with waitressing in London and I want to look after children now,' Heidi told Jilly as they sat in the sitting room, which she'd hastily cleared up a few minutes earlier, shoving stuff behind cushions. 'I do not want to find a job from the internet because I think it is better to have the personal contact like this. *Ja?*' She beamed, showing flawless teeth. 'Then if anything goes wrong, I have a person to go back to and not an email address which does not answer. *Ja?*'

'I am sure we can find you a family,' Jilly assured her. 'In fact, I have a waiting list. But we need to find the right one for you. If you leave it with me, I will be in touch.' A thought came to her. 'Where are you living at the moment?'

The girl's smile wavered slightly. 'In a hostel in

London. There are six girls to one bathroom.' She made a face. 'Some are not very clean.'

Jilly bit her lip. The news item about that poor Bulgarian au pair had been haunting her all day. Supposing something happened to Heidi before she got a placement? 'Then we will make sure that we find you someone quickly,' she said.

The beaming smile returned. 'Thank you.' She extended her hand.

As she showed Heidi out, Nick and a couple of friends walked up the path in soaking wet jeans, suggesting they'd been swimming in the canal again. She hadn't seen him since the bedroom incident this morning and he was refusing, she noticed, to meet her eyes. Poor kid!

'Heidi, this is Nick my son and some of his friends. Boys, this is Heidi, who is looking for a job as an au pair.'

Three adolescent jaws dropped in front of her. Heidi flashed them another of her smiles. 'Very pleased to join with you, *ja*?'

It should be "meet you", Jilly wanted to say but somehow that would have sounded rude.

Then to Jilly's amazement, she shook hands with each boy. 'Goodbye,' she said, 'I do hope I will see you soon.'

There was a short silence after she left and then one of Nick's friends spoke. 'She's a real babe.' He looked down at his hand. 'I'm never going to wash this hand again. Never.'

Nick was bright red. 'Mum,' he said.

'Mmmm?' Jilly was trying not to laugh.

'I was thinking. Do you think we could get an au pair? Um, like that one?'

Jilly shook her head. 'Sorry. That's why I work from home. So we don't need any extra help.'

'But we've got Fat Eema.'

'Is that the munter you were telling us about, Nick?'

'Boys!' Thank heavens Fatima was asleep again. 'That's rude. Now if you lot are hungry, there's some quiche in the fridge. Help yourself. I've got to make some calls. OK?'

The first two families on her list had already found an au pair through other agencies. However, the third name – Mrs Parks – sounded interested and Jilly arranged for Heidi to visit the following day for an interview. Please may it work out, she thought, catching sight of the unpaid electricity bill. The final reminder would be here shortly.

Then the phone rang. 'Is that Jilly's Au Pair Agency? This is Kitty Banks. One of my friends has just rung to say that you offered her a Swiss-German au pair but that she'd already got one. I'm on your books and I wondered why you hadn't called me.'

Kitty Banks... Jilly ran her finger down her list, propped under the milk that someone hadn't put back in the fridge. She was near the bottom. 'I'm afraid I have to take people in order but—'

'I'll pay extra! I'm quite happy to do that for the right person. I'm absolutely desperate. We can offer someone a very nice standard of living and I promise you that I will make it worth your while. '

Jilly's mind flashed back to the Bankses' house from

161

her home visit. Not too flashy but definitely comfortable and Kitty Banks, she now recalled, was an intelligent if slightly pushy woman with just one child. Quite why she wanted another pair of hands wasn't really any of her business.

'I'm afraid it doesn't work that way—'

'I'll pay you five hundred pounds as a placement fee instead of the original hundred and fifty,' she cut in.

Jilly paused. Five hundred pounds! That would more than pay the electricity *and* gas bill! But on the other hand, she'd just lined up an interview between Heidi and the other family. No. No. This wouldn't be right. But then again, if they fell behind with the electricity, they'd be in trouble.

'Can you hold on a minute?' Jilly dialled Heidi's number on the mobile. 'Heidi, have you caught the train yet? No? Great. I wonder, could you possibly come back? There's a family who wants to meet you for an interview. Yes. This afternoon if that's all right with you.'

The following day, there was a repeat plea on the radio about that poor murdered au pair. No one, it seemed, had come forward with any useful information. It worried her so much that she resolved to take some time out and visit the girls she'd already placed, in order to make sure they were all right. First on her list was Marie-France. Sure, the girl had said, when she'd called. She would be in although Dawn was out having colonic irrigation.

'Is everything going all right?' she asked as they sat by the pool watching Tom and Tatty Arna (as Marie-

162

France called her) chuck water at each other. She'd had to bring the twins with her and they'd dived right in before she could stop them. Oh dear. It wasn't as though they'd been invited round to play.

'Fine.' Marie-France nodded uncertainly.

'Are you sure?'

Marie-France sighed. 'Dawn has accused me of stealing Tom's mini-TV. He lost it and then – or so she says – he found it in my bedroom.'

The old Jilly would have been instantly sympathetic but she was learning now. There were usually two sides to a story. 'And *did* you take it?'

Marie-France's eyes flashed. 'No! Dawn, she say that she will not eject me this time if I cook for her next dinner party. But if it happens again, I am out on my ears.'

Jilly hesitated. During her years in HR, she'd developed what she thought was an intuition for knowing if people were genuine or not. Part of her felt Marie-France was telling the truth but there was also something that wasn't quite right...

'Is there anything else?' She looked at the kids, who were now shrieking at each other at the tops of their voices. Tom had a reputation at school for being 'a live wire'.

'Yes, thank you.' The girl flushed. 'I need some assistance for a research project I am doing.'

'That sounds interesting.'

The girl carried on talking without taking her eyes off Tom and Tatty Arna as they splashed water at each other furiously. That was good, noted Jilly. It showed the girl was responsible. 'It is about the lives of English people about twenty years ago. Do you know anyone who lived in Corrywood then?'

'No.' Jilly was slightly taken aback by the question. She'd expected something about the standard of her room or the kids but not this. Still, Marie-France was one of the more intelligent au pairs. She vaguely remembered from her form that she was going to read psychology at the Sorbonne when she went back. 'I don't. Sorry. We only moved out here five years ago.'

She nodded disappointedly. 'OK. It doesn't matter. Tom, please don't fire that water gun straight at Tatty Arna's face like that. You might destroy her.'

Jilly was impressed. The girl seemed to have the right balance of firmness and kindness. She only hoped the 'theft' incident was a misunderstanding.

'Madame Jilly, there is one more thing I like to tell you. It is about your friend Paula's au pair. Antoinette. She is not one of your girls, no?'

'No. Paula found her through an agency before I'd set mine up. How do you know her?'

'Through school. I do not think she looks after her family very well. The other day, we went back to her house and the little girl, she is in the garden on her own. Antoinette leaves her while she goes to language school. The other day, she left her for two hours when we all went shopping in Knights Bridge.'

Jilly was astounded. 'You are sure of this?'

Marie-France nodded. '*Absolument*.'

That was awful! 'Thank you for telling me. Paula has gone on holiday for a fortnight – without Antoinette – but I'll have a word when she gets back.'

Jilly got to her feet. 'And do be careful when you go up to London. It can be a busy place. '

Marie-France smiled. 'Do not worry. I can look after myself.'

She hoped so. After all, she *was* eighteen. But as she drove back, with the twins scrapping in the back of the car, she couldn't help thinking again about that poor Bulgarian au pair.

'Tom says that the French word for mother is mare but that's a horse, isn't it?' demanded Harry, interrupting her thoughts.

There was an audible dig in the ribs from behind. 'No, it's *not*, stupid. Mare means poo, doesn't it, Mum? William's au pair is always saying it.'

Why did they constantly ask tricky questions when she was trying to concentrate on the road? 'Well, *mère* and, er, *merde* are spelt differently although they sound sort of similar.'

Alfie gasped. 'So that means the French have the same word for poo and mother?'

'Well, phonetically speaking, you could say that.'

'What does phone etic mean?'

Jilly sighed. 'It's how things sound.'

'Like Tom's mini-TV? That makes a really cool noise.'

'Can we have one for Christmas if we're really, really good?'

'No.'

'Is it cos we might do what Tom did?'

Jilly was only half listening. 'What did he do?'

'Hid it in the oh pear's bedroom so everyone would think she'd nicked it.'

What?

'Why would he do that?'

'So he can get another, silly. A bigger one.'

Really? So Marie-France wasn't a thief after all! Thank goodness for that. Oh heck, that meant telling Dawn she was wrong. Something that probably wouldn't go down well. And she also had to warn Paula about Antoinette…

That evening, after leaving a message for Paula on her answerphone, Jilly resisted the temptation to sort out her paperwork and cooked a huge shepherd's pie instead.

Unusually, David was back early enough for them all to eat together. Hastily, she put out two extra chairs to accommodate him and Fat Eema, who started tucking in before the rest of them, as if she hadn't just had a huge lunch three hours earlier.

'That's rude!' said Harry in a shocked voice but Fat Eema just ploughed on through her meal, regardless.

'Can't we eat in front of the telly like we usually do?' whined Alfie.

David shot her a look. 'No. We're going to talk together.'

Nick groaned. 'Bor-ing. Anyway, we can't all talk together because someone here can hardly speak English so that means we can say whatever we want!'

'Now come on,' said Jilly briskly, about to dish up another portion. 'Let's just…'

Not the phone. Again!

'Leave it,' said David sharply.

The voice on the answerphone was so loud that they

could hear it from the hall. 'Jilly, this is Dawn. What the hell do you think you were doing, coming round to my house – uninvited – and letting your kids play in our pool? If I'd checked you out on Google, I wouldn't have used you in the first place.'

David frowned. 'What was that all about?'

Jilly jumped up to turn on her laptop. 'The twins came with me on a home visit, that's all, but I don't know what she meant by Google . . . Oh my God!'

'What is it?' David was behind her now.

'Look! On the comment section right under the reference to my website.'

Feeling sick, she read it out loud. '*WARNING! DO NOT USE THIS AGENCY. I have just been gazumped! Jilly's Au Pair Agency promised me I was next on the list for an au pair but then I found out that she placed her with another family who were prepared to pay more. YOU HAVE BEEN TOLD!*'

MORE USEFUL PHRASES FOR AU PAIRS

I have lost my front door key

I have missed the last train back

I am homesick

I think I have caught nits from your kids

I am eight weeks late

I have blocked the shower

I have put the cat back in the bag

Chapter 11

Dawn, thought Marie-France gratefully, hadn't been too bad since Tom had grudgingly admitted – thanks to Jilly's intervention – that he had planted the mini-television in her room.

'You will lose your allowance for the month,' Phillip had thundered in the horrific row that had ensued. Just as well he hadn't seen the rude face that Tom had made behind his back.

Marie-France had felt both angry and deeply embarrassed. She hadn't come to England to get embroiled in family squabbles or be accused of petty theft. The only reason she was here was to find her father!

The next step, she decided, was to go back through all those Smiths in the telephone directory, and write each one a little note. They might respond to that better than a phone call. But there were seventeen Smiths altogether and even though only a handful had 'J' as an initial, she ought to check them all out just in case.

So she'd pedalled round to every one of them on the expensive eighteen-gear flashy silver bike which Dawn had lent her ('No one else uses it so you might as well'). In her note, she explained she was trying to get in touch with a Mr John Smith but didn't say why, just in case it scared them off. So far, not one person had come back to her even though she'd left Madame Green's landline number *and* her own mobile.

'What would I do if I wanted to trace someone in this country?' she asked Francine, the language-school teacher, one morning after the other girls had streamed out, exchanging cigarettes and chatting loudly. 'You have tried online?'

'Yes,' Marie-France hesitated. 'But I don't really have enough details to get what I need.'

'I think there is a place in London that holds records of births, deaths and marriages. I will ask my husband and let you know.' Francine gave Marie-France a conspiratorial nudge. 'These English – they do things so differently, *n'est-ce pas*?'

That was true enough, thought Marie-France as she walked back from class. She'd never known anyone drink as much tea as this country. And this habit of taking baths was so grotesque! It was simply wallowing in dirty water. Last night, Dawn was in hers for hours! Phillip, she suspected, was much more of a shower man. This morning, when coming down for breakfast, he had smelt of the fresh pine woods where she and Thierry used to walk.

The thought of Thierry made her feel homesick. He'd sent a few texts but they were abbreviated and to the point. The gist was always the same. When was she coming back? What did she do in her spare time?

I told you when I'm returning, she had texted back. *In the spring. As for doing stuff in my spare time, you know I'm trying to find my dad. I'm not here to go clubbing.*

She didn't add that she'd received plenty of

invitations to do so from the other girls in class. They all went to some place called Kings Tun. 'Fantastic!' giggled Heidi excitedly. 'You should come. *Ja?*'

But because she kept making excuses, they stopped asking. Still, she thought as she turned down the long gravel drive to Dawn's house, maybe she should take this opportunity to go up to London alone on her day off. She'd always loved art and there were some fabulous galleries she could visit, according to the guidebook Phillip had thoughtfully lent her.

Sometimes Marie-France wondered if this love of the arts was inherited from her father. It was infuriatingly frustrating to know so little about him! Did he have her nose, which was thin and almost bony? Were his eyes a mixture of blue and green? Did he also like walking in parks – there were some lovely ones in London – and playing the guitar? Why had he left her mother in the lurch like that? So many questions. So few answers…

'YOU'RE NOT OUR FATHER SO YOU CAN'T TELL ME WHAT TO DO!'

She heard Tom's yells before she reached the front door. It sounded as though he was round the back, in the garden. Not wanting to intrude but also unable to contain her curiosity, she hovered by the wrought-iron gate that led down the ivy-covered pathway to the enormous kidney-shaped swimming pool and the sauna cabin beside it.

There, she could just see Tom standing by the pool opposite Phillip, who was wearing smart navy blue chinos and a beige jacket. Of course. He and Dawn were going out. Dawn had specifically asked her to forgo her usual afternoon off so she could 'babysit'. Instead, she had been promised the following day off in lieu.

'I know I'm not your father,' Phillip was saying in a voice that sounded as though he was struggling to stay patient. 'Or Tatiana's. But I *am* married to your mother and that gives me the right to tell you when you are out of order.'

Mon Dieu! So Phillip wasn't the children's father? The knowledge gave Marie-France a funny little tingle down her spine for a reason she didn't like to admit, even to herself. The one thing she could never do would be to break up a family but if these weren't his children . . . no. She pulled herself up. Don't even think like that. Phillip was a good-looking man who had shown her some kindness. That was all.

'Your behaviour, ever since I've known you, Tom, has been outrageous.' Phillip's voice sounded clear and decisive even from where she was standing. 'You won't do your homework. You steal things from people and then pretend someone else has taken them . . . Hey, don't you dare try to push me in!'

Marie-France stared aghast as the boy bent his head again and tried to head-butt Phillip into the water. There was a struggle and then a splash. She almost laughed out loud as the boy toppled in. Served him right! Tom was now splashing about in the water, yelling indignantly. 'I'll tell Mum you pushed me.'

'Go ahead.' Phillip was walking away, brushing his hands as though to rid himself of the child. Help! He was coming her way and it was too late now to go back.

'Marie-France!' His face clearly expressed surprise.

'I am sorry.' She could feel herself going very red. 'I did not mean to listen in. It was just that I heard voices.'

'That's all right.' He pushed open the gate for her and unexpectedly put his hand in the small of her back as though to guide her round the path that led towards the sitting-room French windows. 'I've been wanting to talk to you for some time, actually.' He was striding towards the mini-fridge in the corner, concealed inside a wooden cabinet. 'Would you like a glass of wine?'

She nodded. '*Merci*.'

He poured himself one and clinked it against hers. '*Salut*.'

She was surprised. 'I didn't realise you spoke French. Your accent is very good.'

He nodded modestly as though acknowledging the fact although not in a boastful way. 'I worked for two years in Paris when I was in banking.'

She'd been wondering how he got all this money.

'And you are a banker still?'

'No.' He laughed. 'I moved into security.'

'What kind?'

'All types.' He waved his hand around as though he didn't really want to talk about it. 'Looking after people. Their money. Their houses.' He gestured that she should sit down. 'What I really wanted to ask you, Marie-France, was whether you are managing to survive in this viper's nest?'

'Viper's nest?' She moved uneasily in her chair. 'I don't understand.'

'Oh, I think you do.' He poured himself another glass after offering to top hers up. 'Tom and Tatiana aren't the easiest of kids to deal with. Nor is their mother.'

Marie-France took another sip to hide her embarrassment. Her mother had warned her that Englishmen always said their wives didn't understand them.

'We only got married last year,' continued Phillip moodily. 'That's right, have another drink. And frankly, from the day we exchanged vows, it's as though Dawn is a different woman. She never used to be like this, you know – all demanding and unreasonable.'

Small beads of sweat were appearing on his forehead and his eyes were red and troubled. 'No one else would understand this insane household unless they actually lived here.'

'Tom is horrible,' she conceded, 'but Tatty Arna is rather cute. But I think they must read more. They do not have enough books.'

'Hah!' He drained his glass. 'That's because they're not high up on my wife's priority list. The nearest she gets to books are magazines and that's just the pictures.'

'But Tatty, she has holiday reading to do. I try to force her. It is hard.'

'I know.' He leaned forward. 'They have different dads, you know. Dawn doesn't stay with the same man for long, as I'm beginning to discover. Still, I shouldn't be telling you all this.' Phillip patted her arm lightly and his touch sent an electric shock through her. 'Now is there anything I can do for you in return? Is your bedroom satisfactory? I haven't seen it but Dawn says she gave you the guest room.'

'*Guest room?*' she spluttered. 'It is a cupboard for brooms!'

His face darkened. 'Is that right?' He leaped to his feet. 'May I see it?'

'*Non.*' Common sense told Marie-France that it would not be sensible for Phillip to go to her room. 'It is adequate. I do not want to fuss.'

They were standing now, so close that she could smell that lovely pine scent that seemed to go with him wherever he went. For a few seconds, it looked as though he was going to…

'*Phillip?*' The shriek rang out from the house. 'Where are you? We're going to be late!'

'Looks like I'm being summoned.' His voice was regretful. '*Au revoir.* And let me know if the kids play you up. Remember! I'm on your side!'

The following day, Marie-France went up to London. In return for babysitting, Dawn had given her the whole day off, which meant she had enough time to visit the National Gallery and the Royal Academy, where there was an exhibition of English seaside pictures. So beautiful!

Afterwards, she spent ages walking round, breathing in the excited hustle and bustle of Oxford Circus – you could have fitted her entire village in Top Shop alone! Then she caught the tube to this really long road that led to Buckingham Palace. How amazing to think that the Queen actually lived there! Excitedly, she bought a postcard with a picture of a guard in a bright red uniform to send home. Even if she didn't find her father, it was almost worth coming over to England just to see this!

Then, on her way back, she came across the most wonderful park with trees everywhere. *Incroyable!* An oasis in the middle of London. '*Excusez-moi*,' she asked someone. 'What is this called?'

'Hyde Park,' said the woman walking past quickly.

Hyde Park! Was that because you could hide there? She sat for a time on a bench – it was getting a bit cold now – next to a couple who, oblivious to her presence, began to kiss.

Thierry used to hold the back of her head with both hands like that, she observed enviously. Was he doing the same to someone else now? Marie-France bit her lip. She was taking a chance, she knew, leaving her handsome but headstrong boyfriend back home. But finding her father was something she needed to do. If Thierry really understood her, he'd know that.

Phillip understood her! She could tell that from the look in his eyes. What would *he* be like to kiss?

No. Marie-France pulled herself up again. She must not imagine such a thing! This was exactly the trap her mother had fallen into. She must not, on any account, make the same mistake. Instead, she must stay focused on her search.

Her French teacher had told her that there used to be a place called Somerset House that held the records of births and marriages and deaths. But now – just her luck – it didn't exist any more. Francine thought there might be somewhere else instead and was going to find out more by the next lesson. But maybe now she was in London, she could do her own research.

Leaping up, she made her way back towards the busy road that led to the tube station. 'Excuse me,' she asked the man selling newspapers from a stand, 'but I am trying to trace my father.'

He cackled, revealing a row of uneven teeth. 'Aren't we all?'

'I was told there was somewhere in London that might help.'

How rude! He was completely ignoring her, holding out a grubby hand for someone else's change.

'I couldn't help overhearing what you were saying,' said a soft voice behind her. She turned to see a kindly looking woman holding a toddler by the hand. 'I had to find out about a death myself the other month so I went to a large archives centre in London that stores it all on microfiche. It's in Westminster. Here.' She scribbled down directions on a piece of paper.

Flushed with excitement, Marie-France threaded her way through the evening crowds; someone trod on her foot and someone else elbowed her in his bid to get past. It took ages to get there and by the time she found the building, there was just half an hour until closing.

'Do you have proof of your address?' asked the girl on the desk.

Marie-France hadn't been expecting this. 'I am from France but I am staying with my family.' She fumbled in her handbag. Thank goodness! She had her contract letter from the agency with her, containing Dawn's details.

'Fine. Can you fill in this form?'

Shaking with excitement, Marie-France did as she was told.

'All our information is on microfiche readers.' She pointed to a room which was full of tables and people peering at screens. It looked so daunting! The girl looked kindly at her. 'Would you like me to help you?'

'Please. Thank you.'

Together they sat down at one of the desks. 'I am looking for a John Smith,' said Marie-France breathlessly. This was the place that would help her! She just knew it. Any minute now and she would find out who her father was and then . . .

'Date of birth?'

Marie-France's heart fluttered with uncertainty. 'I do not know exactly but I think he is in his sixties now.'

'Is he married?'

'Possibly.'

'You don't have a date of a marriage then.'

'No.'

'And is it possible that he is dead?'

Her mouth went dry. 'I do not know. I hope not.'

Marie-France could tell from the girl's tone that this wasn't good. 'If you can find out a bit more, we might be able to help. But I'm afraid that John Smith is a very common name in this country.'

It wasn't fair! To have got so close to the answers she needed on those microfiche films but not to have succeeded. If only her mother had known more, she could have found him. She knew it. Instead, the lack of information about her parenthood made her feel cheap – and also angry. Dejected, she made her way back to Marly Bone.

When she finally got out at Corrywood Station, she realised that Antoinette must have been on the same train too. The girl glared at her, revealing a nasty bit of gum in her mouth. '*Arrête*, Marie-France, I want a word with you.' Her eyes narrowed like a cat's. 'I hear you've been snitching on me.'

Marie-France felt herself flush.

'Yes you have. Don't deny it. You told your agency that I left Immy on her own.'

'Well you did.'

'That's none of your business.' Antoinette's eyes were dark and angry; they reminded her of an old woman in the village whom everyone said was a witch. 'Luckily my employer believed me when I told her you made up stories. But I'm going to get you for this. See if I don't!'

Ignoring her, Marie-France stormed off. Girls like that weren't worth arguing with. But nevertheless, she felt uneasy as she made her way up the hill and down Dawn's drive through the security gates. Antoinette was such a bitch! But what, she wondered, as she opened the front door, if everyone believed her lies?

Marie-France was so engrossed in her thoughts that she was taken aback by a flustered-looking Dawn storming out of the study. 'You're back early! I don't need you today. I told you that. You can go to your room. I want some privacy.'

As she spoke, there was a noise from the door behind her. How intriguing! Madame had a visitor and she didn't want her around!

'It's the first on the left,' Dawn tossed over her shoulder.

'*Pardon?*'

'Your new room.' Dawn gave her a nasty look. 'After you went moaning to my husband, he insisted you were moved. Enjoy it. You won't be there for much longer.' Then, turning, she slammed the study door shut and there was the sound of low murmuring.

Not be here much longer? Was Dawn going to sack her wondered Marie-France as she went up the stairs. That would mean she'd have to go home or find another family, which might not be in Corrywood. Then...

Wow! Marie-France's worries flew out of her head as she stared in wonder at her room. There was a beautiful double bed with a blue silk bedspread *and* her own ensuite. Fantastic! But what was this? A note on the bed! In Dawn's terrible, almost unreadable writing.

A Mr John Smith called. Wants you to ring him back. Do not give out our landline number again. Use your own phone.

And below, scrawled in such a way that she wasn't sure if the '5' was really a '3', was a phone number...

JILLY'S AU PAIR AGENCY:
GUIDELINES FOR FAMILIES

It is a good idea to write down your au pair's jobs for the day so she can see exactly what you want her to do.

For example:

Monday. 9 a.m.–12 noon. Clear breakfast. Wash kitchen floor. Vacuum entire house. Tidy children's rooms. Make beds even if children are still in them (only joking!)

Chapter 12

Nothing like this had ever happened to Matthew before! When murder trials were reported in the paper, the murderer often turned out to be someone that the victim knew. So might it be possible that the police suspected *him*?

The whole thing was so awful! According to the police, Sozzy had been killed in a London park only hours after storming out of his house. Yet somehow her body had lain in the undergrowth undiscovered for days. Why had she gone there in the first place?

The police were still 'making inquiries'. In the meantime, the poor girl's parents had apparently been contacted but neither was coming over to the UK, which was astonishing. If anything had happened to Lottie at that age – God forbid! – he'd have been the first on the plane. They hadn't even rung him, as he would have done in their shoes, to find out as much as they could about her last hours.

'Not every parent is as caring as they should be,' one of the police officers had said. You could say that again. But he still couldn't help feeling guilty. If Lottie hadn't left that awful note telling Sozzy to go home and if he had been more welcoming instead of showing shock at the girl's appearance, maybe none of this would have happened.

'You mustn't blame yourself,' said Janine from the agency in a soothing tone that contrasted sharply with their earlier tense conversations. 'It *is* tragic but I'm afraid to say that this isn't the first time I've heard of such a situation.'

He was shocked. 'You mean it's common for au pairs to be murdered?'

'Not murdered, Mr Evans, but...well, other things. When you think about it, young girls are coming over to a country they know little of. They can be very naive; easy targets, if you like.'

'Then surely it's our job to make sure that they are all right?'

'Exactly. But there's only so far we can go.'

He still didn't feel exonerated and later that day, in the office, found himself confiding in his PA. He hadn't meant to but Karen had come in with a very welcome cup of tea and shortbread biscuits not long after the phone call. 'I just can't help wondering who did it. She said she had friends in London but the police say no one has come forward.'

Karen made one of her poor-you faces but somehow it didn't seem quite as annoying as it had done in the past. 'That's terrible, but I do think your agency lady is right. You can't blame yourself and from what you've told me, she sounds – I mean, sounded – quite stroppy.' She sighed. 'They *can* be at that age. I've got a niece who is really rather rude to everyone. No respect, if you know what I mean.'

He knew exactly what she meant.

'It sounds as though you've had some bad luck with your au pairs,' said Karen, pushing the plate of shortbread biscuits towards him. 'The second one didn't work out either, you said.'

'No.' He hesitated. 'I found her trying on some of Sally's things and she cut Lottie's fringe.'

'That's awful!'

'It might have been Lottie's idea, actually.'

'Lottie?'

He felt rather treacherous but he'd said too much now to stop. Besides, there was something about Karen's kind, slightly plump face that made him feel he could talk. Really talk, in a different way from how he spoke to Christina, who was, after all, only listening in a professional capacity.

'Berenice – the second au pair – said Lottie *told* her to. At first, I thought she was lying but I'm beginning to wonder. Lottie hasn't been the same since Sally died.'

Karen nodded, munching her own shortbread finger thoughtfully. 'The poor kid's been through a lot. Where's Berenice now?'

'Gone to a much nicer family in Barnes.' He gave a rueful shrug. 'One that won't wrongly accuse her of things.'

Matthew found himself aware of a warm hand patting his arm lightly. 'You mustn't be too hard on yourself. Lottie's not the only one who's been through the mill. Now if there's anything I can do, like baby - sitting in the evenings or weekends, all you have to do is ask.'

'Thank you.' Matthew felt overwhelmed and not a little ashamed of himself. Karen was being so kind! In fact, he now recalled, she was always the first to organise an office collection for anyone who was getting married or having a baby or leaving for another job. It was women like Karen who spread goodwill in life. How awful that it had taken Sozzy's death for him to realise that.

'Actually,' he added, 'I think we're sorted at the moment. One of Sally's friends has lent me her au pair while she's on holiday. Besides, I only need help when I'm at work. I don't want to go out at the evenings or weekends: that's Lottie time.'

Karen nodded again. 'You're a good father.'

He gave another short laugh. 'I don't think so.'

'Well, I do and so do a lot of others around here.'

She got up from the chair next to him and he couldn't help noticing her thick hourglass legs. Sally had had beautiful legs, long and shapely; she'd been justly proud of them.

'Better be getting on.' She gave him another warm smile. 'But remember my offer. If you need me to babysit any time, all you have to do is call. You've got my mobile number, haven't you?'

One thing was for certain, Matthew told himself the following week as he came home – later than he'd meant to, thanks to a meeting – he was going to make sure that nothing went wrong with Antoinette.

She seemed pleasant enough, although a little quiet, thought Matthew as he put his keys on the hall table. Her English wasn't great, it was true, and it was quite funny the way she spoke about a table being a 'her', but so far, she hadn't done anything awful like storming out or ransacking his wife's wardrobe. True, he'd found a few dirty plates that had been put back in the cupboard unwashed but that wasn't too awful in the scheme of things.

But the one thing he just couldn't get used to was the lack of privacy! There was nowhere to hide in your own home. At least, not in a house this size. Matthew slipped off his jacket and then paused. How odd! There was the sound of laughter from the sitting room as though there were several people there.

Wonderingly, he opened the door. There were two girls sitting on the sofa munching dry cereal from the packet and two more on the floor in front of the DVD player, watching some American comedy with extremely ripe language! Lottie was on a beanbag also with a cereal bowl and laughing with that cute little gap in her front teeth (that new tooth was taking ages to come through!).

He sniffed. There was definitely the lingering smell of cigarettes although he couldn't actually see anyone smoking. Over there, by Sally's grandmother's walnut sewing table, was Antoinette, lying down on the carpet, talking to someone on the phone. *His* phone.

His initial reaction was to demand why she had all her mates over, why they were watching an adult film in front of Lottie and what she was doing on his landline, but then he stopped. He couldn't upset a *third* au pair! Besides, this was Paula's girl. He had to tread carefully.

'Monsieur Evans.' Antoinette had quickly put down the phone and was walking towards him, hips swaying in a provocative manner that made him feel really awkward. 'I hope you do not mind but I have some friends here. They help me with Lottie.'

It was on the tip of his tongue to ask how many aides she needed to help with one small girl but Lottie was now flying towards him. 'Daddy, you're home!'

There was an 'ahh' from one of the girls on the sofa. 'She is so sweet. Look, we have been doing her hair!'

He'd thought there was something different about her. Lottie's long plaits had been redone and were now in little Swiss miss coils round her ears. 'Do you like them, Daddy?'

'Very nice.' He narrowed his eyes at the television. 'What are you watching?'

'*Friends*, Daddy. It's really cool.'

Friends? Then maybe he was over-reacting. 'Have you had supper?'

She nodded. 'Coco Pops.'

'But that's what you have for breakfast!'

Another solemn nod. 'Antoinette says it's easier.'

Did she now? He'd see about that. Or would he? Oh dear. On the one hand, this was his house and he was paying this girl to look after his daughter, not to have her friends round and dish out cereal as a main meal. On the other hand, Lottie was safe, wasn't she, and she seemed quite happy!

Maybe, thought Matthew as he went into the kitchen to rustle up some supper, leaving Antoinette and her friends to laugh in front of the television and make their calls, he needed to make some compromises. After all, this was only for a fortnight and then the new agency had promised to find him full-time help of his own.

*

'I think you did the right thing.'

Matthew looked across at Christina in surprise. He couldn't remember her ever expressing a definite opinion like that. Usually it was along the lines of 'How did you feel when you made that decision?' or 'What would you think of someone else who did such and such?'

But now, after he'd described the ensuing conversation with Antoinette (during which he'd agreed she could have friends round but that there was to be no smoking in the house and all programmes had to be suitable for an eight-year-old), his counsellor was nodding and expressing approval.

'And how are you getting on generally?' she asked solicitously.

Christina was slightly tanned, he noticed. Maybe she'd been away in the short time since he'd last seen her. Perhaps her husband had whisked her off for a romantic weekend. Or she'd just been sitting in the garden. They'd been having some glorious weather and Antoinette had taken Lottie for several picnics in the local park, no doubt with her friends.

In fact, they were probably there right now but he'd taken the afternoon off work for his appointment with Christina. He'd make up by working late tonight at home.

Matthew suddenly became aware that Christina was looking at him in a way that suggested he hadn't replied to her question. He was always doing that; going off in a world of his own and wondering, even though it wasn't any of his business, about Christina's background.

But he couldn't help it. He felt jealous, ridiculously

jealous of her at times for having a proper family that hadn't been torn apart by a disease which could have been treated if he or Sally had been more aware of the symptoms.

'Sorry?' he repeated.

'I was wondering how you were managing generally.' She leaned forward slightly, revealing a slight V-shape between her breasts under the coral silky top she was wearing. 'It must be a big change going back to work after so long.'

He felt relief at getting back on to safer ground. 'It should be but the weird thing is that it feels right. It means I can distract myself and think of something completely different. Then something will happen during the day that makes me feel guilty for forgetting Sally for a few hours.'

She nodded. 'I can understand that.'

Could she, he wanted to ask. Could she really? Frankly, no one could – not unless they'd been through this.

'And I still feel awful about poor Sozzy.'

She nodded again. 'Do the police know any more?'

'I'm not sure that they would tell me if they did. But I'm beginning to hope that they don't regard me as a suspect as I haven't heard from them for a while.'

She looked shocked. 'That must be rather worrying for you.'

Yes it was. Suddenly all the feel-good stuff he'd experienced from work that day was beginning to drain. 'There's something else too.' He hesitated. 'Is it normal for someone whose wife has only been dead for a year to think about...to think about someone else?'

Her eyes registered a quick shot of surprise. Too late, Matthew wished he'd kept his mouth shut.

'It's more common than we might expect.' Her tone was guardedly neutral. 'Some men – and women too – actually plunge straight into another relationship. It can be for all kinds of reasons. Security. The need to prove that they are still alive themselves or to make the most of every minute.' She paused, her cool eyes fixed on him as though it was his turn now.

Now they'd started, they had to finish. Besides, he needed to know and she was his counsellor, wasn't she? 'And is it necessarily a bad thing?'

Christina shrugged. 'I've had clients who have married other people within a very short time of being widowed and are still married. I've had others who've done the same and realised it was a mistake. And I have some who say they wouldn't ever feel right in even thinking about it.' Her voice sounded calm and reassuring. 'Has something happened that's made you ask this, Matthew?'

His skin began to prickle with embarrassment. 'There's a woman at work,' he began.

She nodded reassuringly.

'She always used to annoy me, to be honest, because she's rather over the top. But recently I've started seeing her in a different light. She's very kind,' he added lamely.

'And maybe,' said Christina softly, 'that's what you need right now.'

'Nothing's happened,' he added hastily. 'And I'm not sure I'd want it to because it would seem unfaithful somehow to Sally.'

Christina's head tilted slightly to the right as though considering this. 'Why do you feel that?'

Here we go again, he thought. Back to the little games of making him reveal his emotions rather than her telling him if it was OK or not.

'It's obvious, isn't it?' Anger made him stand up. 'I was married to Sally for nine years. Surely there's something wrong with me if I can start thinking about someone else when my wife's only been dead and buried for nine months?'

He could hear himself shouting except that it didn't feel like him. It was as though someone inside him was yelling things which his mouth then translated.

'Do you think it might help if you put yourself in other people's shoes? Thought about how *they* felt instead of you? Like Sally, for instance.'

'Are you saying I'm self-centred?'

'Do *you* think you are?'

'Yes. No. I don't know.'

She looked straight at him. 'It's natural after a bereavement. And I think you're angry too.'

'OF COURSE I'M BLOODY ANGRY.' He sat down again and then jumped up. 'I'm sorry, Christina, but I don't think these sessions are doing me any good.'

She looked surprised. 'Would you like a break for a bit?'

'Yes. No. I don't know,' he repeated. He gathered up his jacket and briefcase from the side of the chair. 'I'll ring and make an appointment if I want one. OK?'

He drove home feeling like an absolute heel. What had come over him? How on earth could he have behaved so badly to Christina, shouting at her like that? And why had he come out with that stuff about Karen?

Come on, said a little voice inside his head. You know perfectly well why. You should have told her. Told her the truth about Sally.

No, he told himself as he parked outside the house. That was one thing he couldn't tell anyone. Never. He'd made a promise, hadn't he? A promise that couldn't be broken.

'Hello?' he called out, opening the door. 'I'm back.'

There was no answer. Maybe Antoinette was still out with Lottie. No. There was the sound of giggling upstairs. Perhaps she was getting his daughter ready for bed although it wasn't even five o'clock yet.

'Hi,' he called out, going up the stairs. 'Lottie?'

Suddenly the bathroom door swung open and a stout lad with tattoos down his chest stood there with a towel round his waist, looking at him as though *he* was the intruder.

'What the...' he began and then stopped as Antoinette, also with a towel around her, water dripping from the tips of her hair down her brown shoulders, peered out from behind.

'Where is my daughter?' he thundered.

Antoinette looked nervous. 'She is in the park with my friends. Do not worry. They take care of her.'

This was outrageous! Utterly outrageous! If it were not for the fact that Paula was on holiday, he'd chuck her out right now. But then a picture of Sozzy came into his head. Poor dead Sozzy who might still be alive if she had stayed here.

'*You*,' he spat at the youth, 'get dressed and out of

here.' He threw a withering look at Antoinette. 'You get dressed too. I'm going to collect my daughter. When I come back, we will discuss this.'

Tears were rolling down her face. 'I am sorry. Please do not tell Madame Paula or I will get the sack and I do not want to go home yet. It will not happen *encore*. I promise you.'

Chapter 13

It was a small world in Corrywood! So it wasn't surprising, Jilly told herself ruefully, that the Parks family had heard about Heidi going to the Banks family even though Penny Parks had had first refusal. It was the au pair equivalent of two-timing.

But it wasn't just the stupidity of her actions that rankled. It was the fact that she had, unusually for her, done something that was morally wrong.

'It's just as bad as gazumping someone over a house,' David had said, shocked when she'd told him the full story. 'How could you have?'

'Because we needed to pay the bills,' she had flashed back.

'So it's my fault, is it?' He'd jerked away from her. 'I'm *trying to* get a better-paid job, Jilly, and I appreciate that you're trying to help financially.' His eyes looked sad and, for a minute, she wanted to put her arms around him. 'But this agency has changed you and it's not great for the children. The other day when I got back, they were still in their pyjamas, eating crisps for supper.'

Jilly felt as though she'd just been slapped in the face. 'Are you saying I'm not a good mother?'

David came back towards her, trying to give her a cuddle. 'Of course not. I just think you need to spend more time with the kids in the holidays and leave the financial side to me.'

This time, she turned away from him. 'Then I'll just sit at home and play mother hen until the bailiffs knock on the door with a repossession order, shall I?'

'It hasn't reached that stage yet, Jilly, and you know it hasn't. I'll be late tonight, by the way, and every other night this week and for the rest of the month too.' He gave her a strange look. 'Meanwhile, you'd better sort out this mess you've got yourself into.'

How dare he treat her like a child! But at the same time, he had a point. She needed to limit the damage caused by that awful notice on the internet.

Quickly.

The Parks family whom Jilly had so shamefully 'gazumped' lived on the other side of town where houses were one price bracket down from hers and probably four or five from Dawn's. It didn't, thought Jilly, as she knocked on the door of the terraced house, seem the most likely home for an au pair. This group of houses, unless she was mistaken, had only two bedrooms. But as she glanced through the window, she could see an immaculately tidy sitting room with plumped-up cushions on a beige chair and two children playing a board game on the floor. Very different from the chaos at her own home!

The door was opened by a tall, angular woman with wire glasses who glared at Jilly with naked hostility. Perhaps this wasn't such a great idea after all.

'Jilly from the agency, I presume?'

She gulped, remembering that Mrs Parks was a policewoman. Now as she shuffled from one foot to another on the doorstep, Jilly began to feel very stupid, just as she had during algebra lessons back in her school days. 'Thank you for seeing me.'

The woman held the door open. 'I haven't got long. You'd better come in.'

She led the way to a table in the corner of the sitting room bearing neat piles of books. The children stood up and introduced themselves politely. Jilly's mind went back to the twins whom she'd left at home, watching a video while Nick 'babysat'.

'You said you wanted to explain why you placed our au pair with someone else.'

This felt worse than she'd imagined it would! 'Strictly speaking, Heidi wasn't exactly *your* au pair—'

'We had an interview booked and you said we could have first refusal.'

Jilly had been going to tell a white lie. Something about making 'a mistake' with her paperwork. But now as she looked around this tiny but immaculate house with the beautifully behaved children and the ordered heaps of paperwork which were so different from her own untidy kitchen-table files, she found herself unable to add another moral mistake to the first.

'An electricity bill?' The frown lines above those wire-rimmed glasses, deepened. 'Why are you giving me this?'

'It's why I gazumped you,' said Jilly quietly. Then, in a low voice, so the children didn't hear, she explained about her husband's job and the bills which weren't being paid and how she knew it had been wrong to take the higher offer but hadn't been able to resist.

'I'm so sorry,' Jilly ended, wishing Mrs Parks would say something. 'But I have another girl who's just come on to my books and might be suitable. I will, of course, refund your fee whether you take her or not.'

There was a long silence, punctuated only by the polite 'your go's' from the kids round the Monopoly board. Then the face in front of her softened and Jilly felt a flicker of hope. 'It was quite brave of you to tell me this.'

'I'd rather you didn't mention it to anyone else.'

She seemed to hesitate. 'All right. I accept your apology and the refund. Do you have details of this new au pair?'

'I can email them to you.' Jilly bit her lip. 'Would you in turn take down those comments on the net about my business?'

There was a short silence broken only by the soft call of 'I've won!' from one of the children. Then finally Mrs Parks nodded. 'Very well.'

Thank heavens! 'Did you really complain to the trading standards people?'

'Not yet. I wanted us to speak first. You were still wrong, you know.'

Jilly nodded, feeling as though she was in the head - master's study. 'I'm sorry. It's been a lesson for me. Honestly.'

Light-headed with relief, Jilly returned home via Paula's after first ringing Nick to check that everything was all right at home. He was fifteen, she told herself. Her own mother had often left her in charge of her brother at that age. Besides it was good for him to have some responsibility.

'Hello, stranger.' A tanned Paula in her leotard opened the door. There was a catch in her voice that gave Jilly an odd feeling.

'Thought I'd pop round quickly after a meeting to see if you had a good holiday.

'A *meeting*,' Paula repeated, saying the word in a slightly acidic way. 'Sounds very grand.'

'Not really.' Jilly had been going to confide in Paula about the whole horrid gazumping business but decided now that this wasn't the time.

Was it her imagination or was her friend acting rather coolly? She hadn't even invited Jilly into the kitchen as usual. They were just standing there in the hall next to the art deco umbrella stand Paula had bought from the Affordable Crafts Show at Kensington the other month. 'Actually, there's something you ought to know.'

Paula looked irritated. 'Can't it wait? I'm just going to a meditation class. You ought to try it. Might calm you down.'

What was up with her? Recently, she'd been incredibly tetchy. Hurt, Jilly tried again. 'Did you get the message I left on your answerphone when you were away?'

'I had lots of messages. I'm still working my way through them.'

'The thing is...' Jilly stopped, wondering how to put this. 'Well, Marie-France – you know, the au pair I placed with Dawn – knows your Antoinette through language school. She says Antoinette has been leaving Immy completely alone at home while she goes out.'

Paula's face wrinkled in disbelief. 'That's ridiculous! If she did that, I'd know about it.'

'Apparently Antoinette told Immy that if she split, something bad would happen to her.'

Her friend's lips tightened. 'Your girl is making trouble.' She paused as though she'd just thought of something. 'Or you could be making it up so I'll get rid of Antoinette and take one of your girls so you can charge me a placement fee.'

Jilly took a step backwards. Right into the art deco umbrella stand, banging her heel. Ouch. 'How could you say such a thing?'

'Well, we all know how you're finding it hard to make ends meet. And, frankly, I was shocked when I heard you gazumped the Parkses for the Banks family.'

Did *everyone* know about it? 'I've sorted that one out,' began Jilly weakly.

'Yes, well, I don't need you to sort *me* out. I'm sorry but I don't appreciate your interference in my family when you can't even sort out your own stuff. Now if you don't mind, I've got a class to get to. And an umbrella stand to tidy up.'

Jilly drove home in a state of shock. How could her so-called 'best friend' treat her like that? Or was it her fault? Had David been right when he said that the business had changed her?

After all, before starting her agency, she wouldn't have dreamed of letting people down or leaving her son in charge of the twins for longer than she'd meant…

oh my God. Going into the house, Jilly stared around her, feeling her spirits sink even more.

The place was a mess! Food was strewn all over the sitting-room carpet and the twins were still in their pyjamas, glued to the shared computer. Fat Eema, back from an antenatal appointment, was squatting next to them, knitting some shapeless object and stuffing herself every now and then with huge handfuls of popcorn, some of which reached her mouth and some of which fell on to the carpet. Nick was nowhere to be seen.

'Harry? Alfie?'

Neither moved. No wonder they'd already exceeded their internet allowance that month. Unless it was Fat Eema downloading Turkish films…

Striding across the room towards the router, she yanked the plug out of the socket. Instant reaction! Even Fat Eema paused mid-mouthful to see what was going on.

'Where is Nick?' she repeated.

'Gone out.' Harry was grabbing the plug from her hand and pushing it back in the wall. 'He left you a message.'

What? Jilly read it disbelievingly. *Someone rang and cancelled their oh pear. Said something about comments on website.*

No! Even if Penny Parks took down her warning, the damage had already been done.

There was another message too, written in Nick's uneven capital letter handwriting. That was the trouble with this computer age. It meant kids couldn't write by hand. Not very well, anyway.

UNCLE GEREMY SAYS HE CAN COME TO TWINS' BIRTHDAY ON SATURDAY.

Their birthday! She'd almost forgotten. Well, not exactly. It had just got buried on her list. They had planned to go roller-skating and Jeremy, dedicated uncle that he was, had offered to come all the way down to help.

But she'd been so busy with work that she hadn't got round to ringing the boys' friends. Which meant that if she didn't do something right now, there wouldn't be any party because there wouldn't be any guests!

'Uncle Jeremy, Uncle Jeremy!'

The children were almost falling over themselves with excitement. Her younger brother was always popular with her kids. Good-looking, single and with a rather nice rectory in Suffolk, he was also a child at heart.

Indeed, he liked nothing better than to turn up every now and then (usually at bedtime) laden with unsuit - able treats like sticky sweets and DVDs with Parental Guidance warnings on them. Not exactly what you expected from a vicar but then again, Jeremy had always gone against the grain when they were growing up.

Now he was here, as promised, to help her take the twins roller-skating. That meant there would be three adults to supervise, including David and – amazingly, since she'd only issued last-minute invitations – fifteen ten-year-olds.

'Wonderful,' one mother had gasped down the

phone gratefully. 'Two whole hours all to myself! I can tell you, I'm counting down the days to the end of these school holidays. They seem to have gone on for ever!'

'Right!' Jeremy was already holding court. 'Who wants to come in my car!'

'ME, ME, ME!' yelled the twins.

'NO, ME.'

'NO, ME!'

It was a wonder they hadn't shredded her womb to bits in the competition to get out first.

'You can't take them all,' pointed out David, who always worried about Jeremy's driving and passion for fast sports cars. Her brother had made quite a lot of money in the stock market before discovering God but no one could say he wasn't generous to others. Taking elderly parishioners for rides in his latest car was one way. So too was spoiling his nephews. 'I can get two in the back of this one. Don't worry.'

'Is that your phone, Jilly?' David shot her a sharp look. 'You said you'd turn it off. It *is* the boys' birthday.'

'I know.' Jilly was fumbling in her bag to find the mobile, which as usual had sunk to the bottom. 'But I've got a new girl arriving and her family is meant to be picking her up at Gatwick so I have to have it on just in case there's a problem.'

He turned away. David had been doing a lot of that recently, both out of bed and in it. It wasn't fair. She'd always understood when he'd been stressed at work.

'Hello. What? Are you sure? That's awful. Yes, of course I will.'

She turned off the mobile aware that both her

brother and husband were watching her. 'Something up, Sis?'

'Yes.' She couldn't even bring herself to look at David. 'Heidi, one of my new au pairs, has been rushed into hospital. It turns out that she's asthmatic but the hospital wants confirmation that she disclosed this on her medical insurance form.' She felt her mouth go dry. 'I'll need to check my copy, back in the kitchen.'

Jeremy patted her arm. 'Don't worry. We'll wait.'

'I'll be as quick as I can.' Jilly raced back to the house, rifling through the folders for Heidi's file. Yes! There it was. *Occasionally asthmatic.* Phew! That was all right then.

Hang on. What was this? Jilly's eye fell on Heidi's original application form. It had been typed and above each 'a' was a rather odd splodge as though there was something wrong with the printer. Next to it, in the same file, was the reference letter from one of Heidi's former teachers. *Heidi is the best student I have ever had! I cannot recommend her highly enough.* And so on.

But something wasn't right. All the 'a's in the 'teacher's' letter had the same splodge on top, which, for some reason, she hadn't noticed before.

It looked as though Heidi might just have written her own glowing reference…

JILLY'S AU PAIR AGENCY:
GUIDELINES FOR FAMILIES

Please remember to pay your au pairs on time, every week. Preferably in cash!

Chapter 14

John Smith! Marie-France stared at the note for several minutes, hardly daring to believe it. Her father had rung! Well, not for sure. But the fact remained that despite all the odds – after all, it had been nineteen years – a Mr John Smith still lived in Corrywood. And he might just be the man whom Maman had fallen in love with!

As she sat on the edge of her beautiful new bed, all kinds of thoughts spun round her head. When Maman had tearfully told her the full story of her parentage, Marie-France's initial reaction had been pity for her poor mother who had returned to France, pregnant, only to be thrown out of the house by her stepmother. But she also felt furious with her English father who hadn't offered any support, either emotionally or financially.

'I will find my father to tell him what I think of him!' she had raged.

Yet now that anger had somehow diminished. Instead, she just wanted to find that missing part of her which every other child at school had had – and which she had been bullied for not possessing. A father.

As soon as she had finished her morning work, she dialled the number on her mobile, shaking with excitement.

'Hello?'

She tried to speak but her voice came out cracked in her nervousness. 'Meester Smith?'

'Who wants him?'

He sounded defensive. Use some psychology here, she told herself.

'I am sorry to disturb you.' She spoke clearly but was aware that her French accent might intrigue him. It certainly had an effect on Phillip! 'My name is Marie-France and I am an au pair in Corrywood. I am trying to excavate a long-lost family friend called John Smith who inhabited this town nineteen years ago. I place a note through your door and you rang when I was out.'

There was a short pause during which Marie-France felt she might be sick. Maybe she shouldn't have said so much; the information would be enough for him to put down the phone if he was her father and didn't want to see her.

Then, to her surprise, there was a chuckle. 'A long-lost friend, eh? Well, I've lived all my life in this town so I thought I might be able to help you. Why don't you come over here this afternoon for a cup of tea and we can talk about it!'

Marie-France's heart leaped. 'Thank you. That is fantastic! À bientiot!'

'Come again, love?'

'It means I will see you soon!'

There was another chuckle. 'Can't wait.'

What should she wear? Clothes, as Maman was always saying, sent out clear messages. She needed something that said she meant business but, at the same time, might make this man come clean with the truth.

Eventually, Marie-France slipped on a cool blue and lilac cotton dress she had bought in Oxford Road and placed two photographs of Maman in her bag: one that was recent, showing her in her high-heeled boots and faux fur jacket, and another in a shortish polka-dot dress from when she'd been Marie-France's age.

Stopping for a moment, she looked at the older photograph. It was true. They looked so alike! Poor Maman. She had had such a difficult life but now there was a chance to put things right. Not that she wanted money – that wouldn't do anything at this late stage – just recognition.

Monsieur John Smith lived on the far side of town but she had allowed plenty of time to get there in case she got lost. From his directions, it looked as though she took a left here and a right there and then…

'Hi! Marie-France!'

A woman was waving at her from a house she'd just passed. Jilly! She was surrounded by a horde of children and an older man plus a rather good-looking younger one at the wheel of a fabulous sports car. Even though it would make her late, it seemed rude not to get off her bike and say hello.

'It's the twins' birthday party.' Jilly looked rather frantic. 'I don't suppose you're free, are you? I've got a work crisis and I could really do with another pair of hands.'

'For goodness' sake,' interrupted the older man, frowning. 'You can't not go to your children's birthday party. I thought you'd sorted out the insurance problem.'

'Yes but now I've got a reference crisis and another bunch of urgent emails to reply to, so I might have to join you later.' She turned back to Marie-France. 'Sorry. You're probably busy anyway.'

'I regret I have an appointment.' She smiled at the good-looking man who was now getting out of the car. 'Such a shame.'

Jilly looked disappointed. 'I understand.'

'Aren't you going to introduce me?' said the sports-car man, holding out his hand with a smile. She knew that kind of smile. It meant he was interested. Marie-France felt a flush of pleasure.

'This is one of my girls,' said Jilly. 'Marie-France, this is my brother Jeremy.'

'Your *girls*?' He grinned wolfishly.

'I am au pair,' explained Marie-France, still taking in the fact that this amazingly good-looking man was Jilly's brother. Was he married? she wondered. 'Your sister discovered work for me with a family near here. She is very fantastic at her job.'

There was a noise from the older man – Jilly's husband? – who looked as though he disagreed.

'Thank you,' retorted Jilly with a 'See?' look.

'Well, I must be off now.' Marie-France got back on her bike. 'Have a great birthday, boys.' Then she stopped. *Mon Dieu!* Had Jilly seen that they had both climbed into the driving seat and had started the engine?

'HARRYANDALFIE!' yelled the father. 'GET OUT OF UNCLE JEREMY'S CAR NOW!'

Marie-France propped her bike up against the gate outside an odd-looking house with a bedroom that looked as though it had been added on the first floor in the middle. The rest was all on the ground floor. A bungalow, Monsieur Smith had said on the phone, although she hadn't understood what he had meant until she'd looked it up. The English language was a law unto itself!

There was a bell on the side of the glass door that led into a porch. Through it, she could see a pair of men's brown lace-up shoes. There were some plants too on the ledge; the kind with prickly leaves and small pink flowers.

Marie-France felt a thud of disappointment. Some - how she hadn't expected her father to live somewhere so...well, so ordinary. Maman had always been such a flamboyant person: surely she would not have fallen madly in love with a man whose shoes sat polished in a porch with pot plants? Then again, that would be his wife's influence, would it not?

She rang the bell again, her mouth feeling increasingly dry. There was the sound of someone coming! How she had waited for this moment! From the minute her mother had told her about her English father, she had pictured him in her head and he...he was not like this.

Marie-France felt crushed with disappointment as a small, round-backed old man staggered towards her with a broad grin on his face and – oh no, his flies were undone! 'Come in, come in, my dear.'

He was grasping her hands with his own cold, bony, veined ones as though he knew her. 'Sorry about the delay. Had to go to the lavatory, you know!' He gave her a conspiratorial wink. 'At my age, you need to go more often.'

Marie-France understood enough to be shocked. How rude! How coarse!

'This way, my dear.' His hand grazed her bottom as he steered her along a narrow corridor and into a room on the right. 'Now take a seat and make yourself at home. I'll put the kettle on.'

She gazed with undisguised horror at the maroon-patterned carpet with yellow swirls. In front of her was a brick fireplace with a gas heater inside, instead of a real fire like those you saw in picture books about England. There was a shiny gold-coloured trolley with tea cups already laid out and a cake still in its plastic supermarket wrapping. But what really caught her eye were the rows of dolls, sitting on the mantelpiece and in the display cupboards lining the room.

'Ah, I see you're admiring Lillian's collection,' said her host, coming back into the room with a large brown teapot. 'Very keen on her dolls, she was.'

'Lillian?' asked Marie-France faintly.

He crossed himself. 'My wife. Died twelve years ago tomorrow, she did.'

Bon! So there wasn't a wife around to ask awkward questions.

'And do you own children?'

'Just the one. Darren, who's twenty-four now.' He shook his head. 'I'd have liked more but Lillian wasn't keen on that side of marriage if you know what I mean. Sugar, ducks?'

'No thanks.' She took the tea and forced herself to drink it, trying to work out the maths in her head. If Darren was twenty-four, that meant he'd have been six when her mother had been an au pair. The age fitted but Maman had said that her family had had *two* boys.

The disappointment made her feel slightly sick but then again that might have been the tea. How she would love a decent bowl of coffee! 'I expect,' she said, taking another reluctant swallow, 'that you are wondering why I am arriving.'

He nodded, still grinning. 'Frankly, my dear, I don't care. It's just nice to have such charming company.'

'My mother was an au pair here nineteen years ago,' she began.

'Was she now, love? What was her name?'

'Collette.' She forced herself to take another sip. 'You are hearing of her?'

He shook his head regretfully. 'Sadly not. Mind you, we weren't the kind of family to have au pairs. My wife did everything, she did.'

Marie-France felt a mixture of disappointment and also relief. If this old man was her father, she didn't want any of his genes, thank you very much. 'He is called John Smith like you. Are you acquainted with anyone of that name?'

He made an unpleasant sucking sound as though he'd lost his teeth at the back of his throat and was trying to vacuum them up again. 'Not that I know of, ducks. Mind you, now you come to mention it, the postman was always muddling us up with a Jonathan Smith who lived round the corner.'

Jonathan Smith? No. Her mother had definitely said *John Smith*.

'Then I am regretful to bother you.' Putting her cup down, she wished she'd sorted out these facts on the phone, instead of thinking that a face-to-face conversation would be easier. Now she just wanted to get out of here fast.

'Don't go.' He leaped up. 'You haven't even finished your tea yet.'

'I am just thinking of something I need to get back for.'

'Well I've got your number so if I suddenly think of something, I'll give you a bell. It would be nice to see you again! Old men like me get very lonely!'

Gulping with relief at her near-escape, Marie-France cycled as fast as she could back 'home'. Dawn was at the door when she went in as though she'd been lying in wait. 'There you are! You're late!'

'I do not think so.' Marie-France showed her watch and smiled sweetly. 'I am not obliged to commence work for five more minutes.'

Dawn's eyes narrowed. She was wearing a floaty pair of white trousers with a slightly transparent top which made her look as though she was going to some kind of Far Eastern ceremony. 'How dare you question me. Look at that if you don't believe me.'

She pointed to an ornate gold-leafed clock on the hall table. There was so much gold and ostentation in the house that it wasn't surprising Marie-France hadn't noticed it before. The hands showed that it was five minutes ahead.

'It is fast.'

Dawn's eyes narrowed even more. 'It is not. Do you know how much that clock is worth? Thousands! Phillip has just bought it from a dealer as an investment.'

If she'd been back in France, Marie-France would have made a stand. If there was one thing Maman had taught her, it was to stand up for herself. But the last thing she wanted was for Dawn to dismiss her from Corrywood. It would only delay her search.

'I am sorry, *madame*,' she replied softly. 'I will start work immediately. What would you like me to do? The cooking? The washing? The children? The garden?' Or your husband?

She added the last one silently in her head although judging from Dawn's narrowing eyes – rather like those little slits in the Norman tower back home from where the French had fired arrows at the English – she might as well have said it out loud.

'Are you being sarcastic?'

Marie-France made her eyes widen the way she used to at school. '*Non, madame*. I am happy to make French *cuisine* for you. And I am happy to help with the washing now your housekeeper has departed. You want me to help in the garden too, now the gardener is despatched?'

Dawn looked unsettled. 'How did you know that?'

Because, Marie-France wanted to say, the cook had told her. She'd also informed her that both the housekeeper and the gardener had left because they could not cope with Dawn's erratic behaviour and her habit of paying their wages long after they were due.

Marie-France shrugged knowingly. 'I am part of your family now, madame. It is not easy to hide these things.'

Dawn's unsettled face showed that she had got her 'mistress' exactly where she wanted her. She'd said enough to show that she understood certain things. But she'd done so in a way that suggested she was ready to 'toe the line' as the English said. It was one of the phrases they'd learned in class that week.

'Well, perhaps you could mow the lawn tomorrow.' Dawn hesitated. 'Thank you. But first I need you to look after the kids. I've got a guest coming and I don't want to be disturbed. We will be in the conservatory. Got it? Oh, and don't forget we need two sweets for dinner tonight.'

Sweets? Instead of a proper pudding? That would be easy.

'Certainly. And please, it is possible for you to pay me last week's money now?'

'Yes, yes.' Dawn was batting her away as though she was an annoying fly. 'But not now. I'm busy.'

Marie-France was about to point out that this contradicted the agency guidelines when there was the sound of shouting. 'Mary-Frunch! Mary-Frunch!'

Tatty Arna – who simply couldn't pronounce her name properly – was running down the stairs now just as her mother disappeared out of sight. 'Quickly. Come upstairs. Tom is in your room!'

That could not be so! Racing up the stairs and along the corridor, she felt her breath catch in her throat. Gasping with horror, she saw that the entire contents of her drawers and wardrobe were all over the floor! Her clothes. Her school work. Her precious photographs.

NO! Tom had a pair of scissors in his hand and was about to slice through the picture she had of herself and Thierry which she kept by the side of her bed.

She rushed towards him but it was too late. Thierry's head and shoulders fluttered down on to the ground and smiled up at her helplessly.

'*Méchant! Tu es méchant!* You bad, bad boy!' How she would like to fly at him and smack him across the face. That would teach him. These kids were allowed to get away with murder.

'Go on. Hit me!' he taunted. 'Then Mum will have to send you away like she did the others before you.'

Marie-France stopped. He was right. If she gave him the punishment he deserved, he would win. 'Get downstairs,' she thundered. 'Now. Just wait until I tell your mother!'

But Dawn was nowhere to be seen. Carefully slipping the torn photograph halves into her pocket to show her boss later, she marched Tom into their playroom.

'No. You are not going to watch television. You are going to do your French verbs.'

'But—'

'No but's.' It was all she could do not to shake the boy. 'Do as I command you or there will be enormous trouble.'

'Je swizz...'

'*Non. Je suis!*'

'Je swizz. Tu swizz...'

It was nearly two hours later and Marie-France's nerves were on edge as she and the children sat in the playroom, known as the 'den', where the kids were allowed to make as much mess as they liked.

She'd calmed down a bit after the photograph

incident – perhaps it could be taped back together or copied so the two halves looked like one again. But she still needed to think of other ways to track down her father.

Facebook was the obvious one but it would attract too much attention from her friends and she had promised Maman that she would conduct her investigation quietly. But maybe she could put a message in the local paper. She'd see.

French girl seeks information about family friend called John Smith. Last heard of nineteen years ago.

That might do. But how would one go about placing such an ad? Maybe she could ask Phillip. There was a noise of a door opening outside. Was that him coming back from work?

'I want you to finish that exercise,' she instructed Tom. He scowled. Tatty Arna, meanwhile, was neatly colouring in a picture of the Eiffel Tower.

Slipping out of the room, she stopped. The noise had not come from the front door but from the door leading to the conservatory. Dawn was standing with her back to her in the arms of a tall, very good-looking Indian man who was rocking her back and forwards, making a crooning sound.

'Love,' he was murmuring almost as though he was chanting, 'love conquers all. Remember that, my beautiful Dawn, and you will not go wrong.'

Mon Dieu! Madame was having an affair in her own house! Scuttling back to the den before she was seen, Marie-France found Tom glued to his computer, his French exercises on the floor. What was the point! Suddenly, Marie-France felt a huge wave of pity for these poor kids whose mother had the morals of an alley cat and yet bit their heads off if they dared to do something wrong. Was it any wonder that Tom was such a handful?

'OK,' she said softly. 'I think we've had enough for now.'

'Really?'

A deep voice sounded from the French windows on the other side of the den. It was Phillip! She felt herself flush.

'Looks as though someone's been working hard!' He strode across the room towards the neglected exercise books, giving her a conspiratorial wink.

'Tom's been learning the "swizz" verb,' piped up Tatty Arna.

He gave her a questioning look.

'Don't ask,' groaned Marie-France.

'You look as though you've had a bit of a rough day.'

She nodded. The unexpected kindness made her eyes prick with tears. 'Want to tell me about it?' he whispered, indicating that they should go out to the patio for some privacy. She glanced back at the children. Tom was still glued to Facebook and Tatty Arna to her picture. They should be all right for a bit on their own.

'Tom went into my room and cut up a picture of my boyfriend. Look.' She pulled out the two halves ruefully.

'That's just not on.' He made as though to go back to the house. 'I'll have a word with him!'

'No.' Without thinking, she pulled at his sleeve and

he paused at the intimacy, as though amused. 'Please don't say anything. It will make it worse.'

'We will put a lock on the outside of your door to make sure they cannot get in.'

'Thank you. And...' she stopped.

'And what?' he asked gently. He moved towards her, pushing aside one of the extremely expensive Swedish patio chairs Dawn had just had imported. His proximity made her feel both nervous and excited.

'Your wife is having an affair,' she whispered urgently. There. She had said it!

'Really?' He didn't seem ruffled although maybe that was the shock.

'I saw her kissing a tall, dark man. I think he was Indian.'

'And they were definitely kissing?'

'Well...' she tried to recall exactly what she had seen. 'They were in an embrace. Right outside the conservatory a few minutes ago. In fact, I'm not sure we ought to be talking here.' She looked nervously round the corner. 'They might still be around.'

He made a strange noise which almost sounded like a laugh except that it couldn't possibly be. It had to be a cry of anguish. Poor Phillip! Unable to help herself, she reached out her hand and gave his a little comfort squeeze. Immediately, he bent down towards her and took her in his arms in the most wonderful warm hug. Then he looked at her straight in the eyes. He was going to kiss her! Yes! No! This was a married man!

Marie-France stepped back just in time but as she did so, there was a roar. Not just the roar in her ears which surely came from the thudding of the blood round her body at the opportunity she had just turned down, but the roar of a motorbike!

'Thierry?' She stared, unable to believe her eyes.

'Who on earth is that?' Phillip pulled back as the tall, dark youth with the silver and maroon helmet strode towards them across the lawn, scattering bits of turf with his biker boots.

Had he seen them? Marie-France's chest was pounding with apprehension. Then again, she told herself, trying to stay calm, what had there been to see? Just a hug. Just a kiss that hadn't even happened. He might not even have noticed!

'Thierry!' She flew towards him. 'What are you doing here?' Then she had a terrible thought. 'Is something wrong with Maman?'

He pulled off his helmet, revealing his long unruly black hair and gave her a strange look. 'No. I came because I wanted to surprise you. Instead, it is you who have surprised me.'

Marie-France felt a flutter of uncertainty. 'What do you mean?'

Thierry jerked his head in Phillip's direction. His eyes were blazing. 'It did not take you long to find someone else.'

'No! You've got it wrong. Phillip, tell him! Please! Explain you are my boss.'

Dawn's husband cleared his throat. 'I think I had better give you two some time together.' He placed a protective hand on her shoulders, a gesture that did not go unnoticed by their unexpected visitor. 'Call if you need me.'

Thierry's eyebrows drew together in fury. Then his

eyes fell on the two halves of the photograph that Marie-France still held in her hand. The photograph of the two of them, taken in happier times before her father and Phillip had muddled her mind. 'Now,' he said slowly, 'now I understand why you really wanted to come to *Angleterre*. To break up with me.'

'No!'

Suddenly desperate, Marie-France tried to grab the sleeve of his leather jacket. 'Please don't. I can explain.'

'I see for myself,' said Thierry, looking from the photograph to the handsome Englishman who was striding back to the house. 'This is why you do not return my texts!'

'But I haven't had any from you. Not for ages, anyway!'

'You lie! And when we speak on the phone, you just talk about your life here!'

'That's not true...'

'Yes!' He pointed to his eyes. 'These do not lie. I see you and that boss of yours kissing when I arrive...'

'We weren't kissing! He was just giving me a hug.'

'*Assez d'hypocrisie!* I do not want to know any more!' Thierry made a pah' sound, waving her away as though she disgusted him. 'You are more like your mother than either of you realise. Goodbye, Marie-France.'

And then he was gone, leaving a plume of grey motorbike smoke behind him. Marie-France stared after him. Part of her was furious. What an idiot for getting it all wrong about her and Phillip – and for saying she was like her mother. But the other half of her felt as though she had just missed out on something. Something that she couldn't now retrieve.

Before she could gather her thoughts properly, there was the sound of a door slamming and urgent, furious stiletto footsteps across the patio.

'MARY-FRANCE!' Dawn was virtually wagging a finger in front of her as though she was a two-year-old. Then she realised her employer was waving a packet of truffles. 'What kind of joke is this? I asked you to make two sweets for our dinner party tonight. So what do you mean by putting two chocolate buttons on each dessert plate? You'd better come up with something else. And fast!'

JILLY'S AU PAIR AGENCY:
GUIDELINES FOR AU PAIRS

Please remember that you are staying in a private home. It is not a hotel!

Chapter 15

'So what happened next?' asked Karen, wide-eyed. She was wearing a navy-blue dress that he hadn't seen before – one of those wrap-around flimsy affairs which revealed rather too many curves – and was sitting on the chair next to his desk, still holding the coffee she'd brought in for him.

Somehow, because he needed to talk to someone about what had happened, Matthew found himself telling her all about the au pair and the boyfriend coming out of his bathroom with one of Sally's towels, can you believe it, draped around his waist and Lottie apparently in the park with Antoinette's friends.

'Well, I raced down the road towards the rec to find her and there she was, happy as Larry, sitting in a circle on the grass with about four au pairs and being made a great fuss of!'

'Ah!' Karen's slightly podgy soft-looking face with too much blue eyeshadow looked as though it might melt.

'But Lottie then admitted that she'd given Antoinette permission to have a boyfriend over. She said she didn't want her to be lonely.'

'Ah,' repeated Karen along with a little what-can-you-do? shrug. 'How sweet.'

'I'm not sure.' Matthew felt an uncomfortable pang in the pit of his stomach. 'Actually, I've got a feeling that my little Lottie is cleverer than I thought. She's done everything she could to get rid of every au pair who's arrived.' He gulped. 'Poor Sozzy.'

Karen touched him lightly on the shoulder. 'You mustn't blame yourself for that.'

'I can't help it. There's something else too. I'm beginning to learn much more about my daughter than I did before Sally...before Sally died. She can be much more manipulative than I thought, just like her mother.'

Karen frowned. 'Like her mother?'

Matthew suddenly realised he'd gone too far. When you were on your own, it was so easy to voice thoughts that normally you kept inside your own head. That's why it had been good to have Christina as a sounding board, but he could hardly go back to her now.

'So what's going to happen now, Matt? I can call you that, can't I?' Actually, only Sally had abbreviated his name but she was babbling on, without waiting. 'You said that Antoinette is going to her other family this week now they're back from holiday.'

'Yes.' He gave a short laugh. 'And I've got yet another au pair arriving, this time from a different agency in London. She's Italian and a bit older this time: twenty-three. So hopefully she'll be more responsible.'

Karen's face tightened. 'A twenty-three-year-old Italian girl?' She stood up from her chair. 'Sounds like every man's dream!'

Suddenly he wanted to be alone. He hadn't meant to spill all this out to Karen even though at the time it had felt very cathartic. Now he was painfully aware that he had broken that privacy line between employer and employee. And unless he was mistaken, Karen seemed rather disapproving. Maybe she, like the nosy neighbour, considered it inappropriate for a single man to have a young girl in the house. Perhaps she was right.

'Actually I need to prepare for that conference this afternoon. Can you hold all my calls – unless it's about Lottie, of course.'

'Of course,' she repeated in a slightly stiff tone before walking out of the office. Great. Now he'd somehow managed to piss off his secretary as well as his counsellor.

'Now, Lottie,' said Matthew carefully a few days later. 'We've got another au pair coming tonight and this time I want you to be very nice to her.'

Her small face squinted up at him. They were having breakfast – a rather rushed bowl of cornflakes – because he had to get into the office. Paula (bless her) had agreed that Lottie could go over for the day until Genevieve arrived at Heathrow. This time, he was determined to be on time. Memories of having been late for Sozzy still haunted him.

'But, Daddy, I'm nice to Antoinette.'

'Yes, that's true.' Nicer than the girl deserved, he added to himself. 'But what about Berenice and poor Sozzy?'

'Why is Sozzy poor?' Lottie's eyes, so like her mother's, grew suspicious. 'Doesn't she have any money?'

Too late he remembered he hadn't told his daughter about the murder, feeling that it was too much for her to take in.

'I said "poor Sozzy" because you were unkind to her,' he said carefully. 'Remember what you did to her room? I don't want you to do the same to Genevieve's. I've spent quite a lot of time getting it ready.'

'But, Daddy' – Lottie's eyes filled with tears – 'I don't want another oh pear. I just want you at home.' She began to whimper and buried her face in his shirt so that he could feel the damp tears seeping through. 'If you go to work, you might not come back just like Mummy didn't come back from the hospital.'

This was awful! 'Listen, Lottie.' He held her to him, feeling her little heart beating against his. 'I promise that nothing will ever happen to me. I will always be there for you.'

Even as he said the words, he realised how foolish they were. Lottie was right. Something might happen to him one day and then where would she be? Between them, he and Sally only had one surviving parent and that was Sally's divorced mother who lived in Sydney. If he died before Lottie grew up – God forbid – she'd have to go out there or else to his childless sister in Scotland whom he'd never been that close to.

'Look, we've got to get ready now.' They were already running late, which meant he wouldn't be on time for his first meeting with a new client. 'Have you been to the loo?'

She gave him a do-you-think-I'm-daft-Daddy look. 'Course I have.'

That was one of the other things about being a single dad to a little girl. Checking that she'd been to the loo and making sure that she was dry after her bath was just about acceptable at the moment. But what would happen when she needed a bra and began her periods? 'One step at a time,' Christina had said, but that was all very well. Lottie needed a womanly touch. He couldn't afford a full-time nanny. So an au pair it had to be.

Somehow Matthew got there just in time for his meeting. 'We were about to start without you,' said James in a slightly clipped tone. During the last few weeks, he'd seemed increasingly irritated by the extra time Matthew had had to take off to sort out the various au pair crises.

Luckily, the client – a large commercial developer – approved the designs and they all went out to lunch to celebrate. 'Relax,' said James quietly when he noticed Matthew glancing at his watch.

'I'm afraid I need to get back soon.' He gave an apologetic shrug at the client. 'I was hoping to leave early.'

'Again?' asked James sharply.

'I'm picking up the new au pair from Heathrow.'

'Au pair?' The client looked impressed. 'Lucky you. I'd love one but the wife won't let me. What nationality is she? I hear the French are the best.' He winked. 'Very open about certain things if you get my meaning.'

Matthew, who hadn't particularly liked the client in the first place, felt a wave of revulsion. 'Actually I don't think it's very respectful to talk about "*them*", as you put it. Most are young girls who've never been away from home before and we should look after them. I need one because my wife died last year.' He stood up, ignoring the danger signals on James's face. 'Now, if you don't mind, I'll leave you to it and get back to work.'

Striding back through the square outside, Matthew began to feel embarrassed about letting James down like that. Yet he wasn't sorry for making a stand. What he'd said was true. It wasn't easy for young girls. Once more, a picture of Sozzy floated into his head. On impulse, he stopped and bought a large bunch of Stargazer lilies from a stall.

'Oooh, they're beautiful,' said a wide-eyed Karen when he returned. She waited expectantly and Matthew suddenly realised she thought they were for her. Maybe to celebrate the new deal that the whole office was talking about.

'Actually, they're a welcome present for the new au pair,' he said, blushing. Opening the drawer, he pulled out a packet of digestives which he'd had for ages and somehow never got round to opening. 'I wondered if you'd like these.' There was a silence. 'To say thank you for your part in the deal.'

There was another silence during which she took the packet and turned it over. 'The expiry date was last month,' she said quietly, turning back to her screen.

Matthew could have kicked himself for being so insensitive. His mind went back to that conversation with Christina. Was that what came of being self-centred? Of thinking about his *own* problems instead of others'? Still, he'd try to make it up to Karen tomorrow – get a box of chocolates or something like that. But right now, he had to crack on if he was going to get to the airport on time.

It was like waiting for a blind date! All these young women streaming down the slight slope into Arrivals, each looking for someone in the crowds behind the tape at the side and at the bottom. Matthew, with his sign *Genevieve*, felt as though he was a sleazy old man in lascivious expectation of a Thai bride.

'Waiting for your girl, are you?' asked an old boy next to him, glancing at the lilies – which now seemed too big – and the sign.

'Not exactly.' He was about to explain when the old man cut in.

'I'm waiting for my son. Haven't seen him for three years. Went to New Zealand, he did.'

Matthew fervently hoped Lottie wouldn't do that. Some of his friends had emigrated after university and at the time he hadn't thought about the impact on their parents. 'Make the most of each stage,' Christina had said at some point during their counselling. Wise words, he was beginning to realise. How he missed those chats...Oh my goodness, was this *her*?

A very tall, almost Amazonian girl in dark sunglasses headed towards him with long dark, glossy tresses. She was massive! Well, not all of her – just the top bit! Not sure where to look, he tried to concentrate instead on the very expensive-looking red leather suitcase by her side.

'Bloody hell,' breathed the old man.

'Meester Evans?'

He nodded.

She flashed him a smile that revealed teeth as perfect as Berenice's had been. Where did these au pairs get them from? Some dental warehouse for continental young things? 'I am very thrilled to greet you.'

'Me too.' Matthew's voice came out squeaky as he took in her burnt sienna suit with a shiny gold belt. 'Er, these are for you.'

She glanced at the lilies as though amused. 'Thank you.'

'Let me take this.' He tried to pick up the huge case but it weighed a ton. Unwilling to look like a wimp, he had another go. 'This way,' he managed to say between puffs. 'The car is over here.'

She talked non-stop all the way home! It wouldn't be so bad if she could speak proper English but every now and then she used inappropriate words that she didn't really understand the meaning of.

'The agency dictates that I preserve your daughter after class,' she boomed from the passenger seat.

He glanced across at her while waiting at the traffic lights. She had taken off her sunglasses now and he could see that she was wearing very heavy eye make-up that made her look a bit like a cat.

'Yes. Yes, that's right.' He was repeating himself like a schoolboy out of embarrassment. 'I'd like you to look after Lottie when I'm at work and then you can have every weekend off. She starts school next week so you will also have part of the day free.'

'You have enlisted me at the English class, yes?'

He'd learned his lesson on this one. 'That's correct.

They're twice a week in the morning. I've left the details in your room.'

Her heavy perfume was making him feel slightly sick. 'You will commence my salary immediately, yes?'

Hang on. 'The agency says that it is normal to pay at the end of the first week.'

Her eyes grew hard and he felt a sense of foreboding. 'But if you wish, I can pay you in advance.'

'*Grazie*.' She nodded as though he had, only just, appeased her. 'I have plans to visit, how do you say, Harvey Nicholas in Knights' Bridge.' She withdrew a pamphlet from a soft leather handbag that matched the suitcase (which he had only just managed to get in his boot). It was called *Serious Retail Therapy in Cities throughout the World*. She leafed through the pages reverently. 'I like shopping. I like it very much.'

'And do you like children too?' he couldn't help asking.

'Children?' Genevieve appeared to be considering the question as though it had never occurred to her before. 'They are OK.'

This had to work, he told himself after they'd picked up her daughter from Paula's. And this time, it might! Lottie, chattering away to Genevieve in the car, seemed quite taken by their new arrival; she couldn't stop looking at her hair. Matthew was beginning to cotton on to all this girly stuff.

This time, he went up the stairs before they did, just to make sure his daughter hadn't sabotaged Genevieve's room on the quiet. But it seemed exactly as he had left it with the bed rather nicely made, if he said so himself. There was also a vase on the table for the lilies.

'Shall I put your flowers in it?' he asked.

'My flowers?' She seemed to take ages to consider each question before replying. Then she put a well-manicured hand in front of her mouth, showing beautifully shaped red nails. 'I regret that I must have deposited them in the airport. I recall now. It was when you were positioning my case in the car.'

'Never mind.' He paused. It was like this every time he brought an au pair home; this awkward what-shall-we-do-next bit. You'd think he'd have got used to it by now. 'I thought we would have alphabet letters for dinner tonight.'

'Actually, Dad,' Lottie reminded him. 'We opened the last tin on Wednesday.'

'Tin?' Genevieve frowned. Then she caught sight of herself in the mirror on the other side of the room and instantly put one hand on her waist as though posing for an unseen photographer. Lottie was open-mouthed in admiration. 'I have special diet! Did the agency not tell you?' She flashed a smile showing those perfect, expensive teeth again. 'I only eat salmon. Smoked salmon. And my favourite drink is champagne. You have a bottle to celebrate my arrival. Yes?'

The following day, Matthew woke with an uneasy feeling in his stomach. He'd had to knock twice on Genevieve's door at eight o'clock in order to wake her before he left. Eventually, she had opened it, bleary-eyed, in a pale blue silk dressing gown. 'I am going to work now,' he said. 'Lottie is already up and watching

233

television downstairs. Please can you keep an eye on her.'

Another blank stare. 'Keep an eye on her? What does this mean?'

'It means please take care of her.'

'*Allora*, I take her to Knights' Bridge, yes?'

'No. I don't want you taking her to London. She might get lost. I want you to stay here.'

Genevieve looked disappointed. 'We go for a drive instead?'

'No.' He definitely didn't want her driving his daughter until he could see what her driving was like. Besides, his insurance company had quoted a ridiculous price for the extra insurance cover. 'Just play with her. I don't know. Take her for a walk. Watch television. That sort of thing. I have to go now. You've got my number at work, haven't you?'

'Got your number?' she repeated. 'I do not understand. Please speak more slowly.'

This was hopeless. For two pins, he would take the day off but James specifically wanted him to go to a meeting in London today. There was no getting out of it.

Matthew switched his phone off in the train as he always did, in order to concentrate on his files for the meeting. Then it occurred to him that if there was an emergency with Lottie, no one could get hold of him so he turned it on again.

It was then that he noticed her sitting a few seats along in the carriage on the other side. At least he *thought* it was her, although she wasn't wearing the kind of conservative skirts and trousers that Christina usually wore for their sessions. This woman had her hair down, instead of up in a tight knot at the back, and she was wearing skinny jeans with little purple summer boots that matched the colour of her glasses. She had long dangly earrings and was reading a book.

Matthew was tempted to rush up and apologise for his outburst in her office but something stopped him. A train carriage was hardly the most private place to talk. Besides, the more he thought about it, the more embarrassed he felt. This woman, this virtual stranger, knew more about his private life than…well, than anyone. If it wasn't for the fact that it would probably draw attention to himself, he would change carriages. His only hope was to sit tight and hope she didn't see him.

As the train drew closer to Marylebone, Christina began to put away her book and look around. Immediately, he glanced down at his files. He'd wait for her to get off and then hang back in the crowd.

'Matthew?'

Too late. She'd seen him.

'Hi.' He tried to look surprised.

'I saw you earlier but didn't want to disturb you.' She gave him an almost shy smile and he noticed that she seemed far less confident than she did in her counsulting room.

This was no good. He had to come clean. 'I'm sorry I stormed out the other day.'

She gave him a quick sideways look as they walked along and he noticed that she was wearing glossy stuff on her lips. It suited her. 'That's OK. It's part of the healing process sometimes.'

'No, it's not OK. In fact' – he glanced at his watch – 'I wondered if you had time for a quick coffee.'

She shot him another sideways glance. 'I'm meeting my daughter shortly.'

Christina had a daughter? Matthew was intrigued.

'But I've got half an hour or so if you have,' she added.

Half an hour? If he got a cab, he'd still be on time. Besides, something told him that this was a conversation he needed to have if he was really going to move on.

They found a small coffee bar and ordered lattes. She took hers with sugar, which surprised him somehow. He waited until the waitress put them on the table before launching straight in. 'Am I allowed to tell you something? I know this isn't a counselling session but I need to explain why I got so upset.'

Christina stirred her coffee without looking at him. 'Strictly speaking we shouldn't but I've noticed that you haven't signed up for any more sessions. So if you're no longer a client, it would be all right for us to talk as friends.'

He toyed with the small packet of sugar in the bowl in front of him. When did a promise cease to be a promise? When someone had died? He hoped so. For something inside told him that he needed to get this off his chest. Otherwise he was never going to be able to move on.

'The thing is,' he said slowly, 'just before Sally was taken ill, I found out she was having an affair.'

Christina raised her eyebrows.

'You don't usually do that!' he blurted out.

'What?'

'Raise your eyebrows or express emotion.'

She laughed. A nice warm laugh. 'That's because usually when you see me I'm in work mode. Counsellors are meant to empathise but only up to a point. They can't get too involved. But I *am* surprised at what you've just told me. It doesn't seem to fit.'

'I know.' He began to shred the sugar packet out of nerves. 'That's what I thought. It didn't last long. A one-night stand. Or so she said.'

'How did you find out?'

'A text message. Not very original, is it? She said the affair was a cry for help because I'm not very good at showing my emotions.'

Another wry smile. 'You seem quite good at that to me.'

'But I wasn't before she died.' The sachet was in shreds now. 'Don't you see? I only learned to do that afterwards but it was too late. She was right. Before, I was one of those men who wasn't good at showing their feelings. Sally and I met quite late – in our early thirties. She got pregnant with Lottie almost immediately and we found ourselves getting married. It wasn't the greatest of starts.'

She shrugged. 'I did the same except that I was very young.'

He was fascinated. 'Really?'

'Yes.' She looked as though she was going to say something but then decided against it.

'What happened?' he asked, unable to stop himself.

She coloured slightly. 'Let's just say that I know what it's like to be betrayed. I then brought up my daughter on my own from the age of four. She's now seventeen and hoping to go to university.'

He was still trying to take all this in. 'But you wear a wedding ring.'

'It makes life simpler. Especially my job. It's easy for clients to fall in love with a counsellor – after all, they know more about them than anyone else.'

He nodded. 'I can see that.'

'Let's go back to you.' It was as though she was in counsellor mode again. 'Is that why you felt guilty, as you said in our sessions? Because you feel responsible for Sally's death?'

'I know it's daft but if she hadn't been so unhappy, she might not have had an affair. If she hadn't got so stressed as a result, she might not have fallen ill.'

'So many ifs!' She took off her glasses and stared directly at him. Although he wanted to look away, Matthew was unable to. 'Do you know what I think? You're taking Sally's guilt on to your own back. It's a classic response. But you've got a double whammy because you're coping with betrayal and bereavement at the same time.'

'But why do I still wear her cologne if I'm angry with her?'

'Because part of you will always love her, even if you weren't suited and even if she betrayed you.' Christina smiled warmly. 'You had a child together. That binds you for life. If you want my advice, as a friend rather than a counsellor, it's to put the past behind you. Put it all in an imaginary box and lock it up or else you'll get stuck in the old pattern of *"what ifs"*. Then you can concentrate on what life has got to offer. Not what you've lost.'

She paused, and then gave him a curious look. 'How's your admirer at work, by the way?'

He flushed. 'She's started calling me Matt. Only really close people do that. And I didn't even invite her to do so.'

'If it makes you uncomfortable, remember what we said before about boundaries.' She pushed back her chair abruptly. 'Now I'm sorry but I've really got to go. Take care, Matthew.'

And before he could thank her, she was gone.

Somehow Matthew managed to keep going through the meeting with the client although he had to work hard to concentrate. Christina's voice kept floating in and out of his head. Yet her calm reassuring words had miraculously taken a huge weight off his chest.

He needed to thank her, properly, he thought, taking a free evening paper on his way back. Maybe a bunch of flowers and ... what was this?

There was a big headline: *SECOND AU PAIR FOUND DEAD IN PARK.* Below, was a picture of a stunning Brazilian girl from Kent who had been found strangled. Then there was a picture of Sozzy with a caption underneath:

Did this girl come to England to meet her Facebook lover?

Stunned, Matthew read on.

It is now believed that Sozzy Psuzki came to the UK to join a man she met on the internet. She got a job as an au pair in order to obtain a visa but then left her job immediately. Police are working on a connection between the two murders.

So it hadn't been his fault, or indeed Lottie's for messing up her room. He felt a flush of relief, but at the same time, an urgent need to check that both his daughter and the new au pair were all right. He had to warn Genevieve, thought Matthew as he raced along the platform just in time to catch the 6.07 back, about going up to London alone.

If no one spelt out the dangers to these au pairs, he told himself, walking briskly up the hill from the station towards home, they wouldn't know. On the other hand, he didn't want to scare her off. It was such a fine line!

'Hello?' Wow. There was an amazing smell from the kitchen.

'I am performing Bolognese,' announced Genevieve brightly. She was wearing a tea towel around her waist like a sarong and wielding a bright red plastic stirrer thing that he didn't recall seeing before. 'Lottie is my assistant.'

'Wonderful!' Matthew hugged his daughter with relief. Not only were the two getting on but the girl could also cook! Maybe the safety conversation could wait until after dinner. 'I'll just go upstairs and change.'

As he went through the hall, he opened the bureau drawer to get the money he'd taken out to pay Genevieve. What? It had gone. Perhaps it was at the back. He pushed his hand in and wiggled around. Nothing apart from some dust.

'Lottie!' he said uncertainly, going back into the

kitchen again. 'I put some money here yesterday. Have you seen it?'

'No, Daddy.' Lottie was shaking her head, tomato sauce around her mouth. He could tell from her eyes that she wasn't lying.

'What did you do today, by the way?' Matthew asked faintly.

'We proceeded to shopping,' trilled Genevieve. 'We enjoyed a fantastic time, did we not, Lottie?'

Lottie nodded, her plaits flying vigorously. 'Yes we did. We bought loads of stuff. It's really fun having Genevieve around. Thank you for asking her here, Daddy!'

EVEN MORE USEFUL PHRASES FOR AU PAIRS

I think you need a new washing machine

I cannot work today

Your car has been in an accident

I let the gas man in

I forgot to lock the front door

Please can you lend me some money?

I am twelve weeks late

Chapter 16

'It's just not on, Jilly! Birgitta lies in bed until gone nine o'clock. And she never gets her work done before going off to her language class. She won't use deodorant even though I bought her one. Just as a subtle hint, you know. *Then* I caught her using the landline to ring her boyfriend in Berlin without asking permission!'

Oh dear. This was exactly why she didn't have an au pair herself. Fat Eema, who was getting bigger by the hour, didn't really count. It was *they* who were looking after *her*, rather than the other way round.

But Jilly had supplied Birgitta to the Miller family and it was her job to sort it out. Just as she'd sorted out Heidi and the dodgy reference. In the end, she had gone directly to the girl and asked her for the truth. Heidi had burst into tears.

'*Ja*, it is true. I am so sorry. But my reference did not arrive in time from my teacher. So I make it up myself. My family, they is very pleased with me. Please do not inform them.'

Unsure, Jilly had rung Heidi's host family, explain - ing this was a courtesy call to check all was well. 'She's brilliant,' enthused Bill Banks, who picked up the phone. 'We're more than happy with her.' So Jilly made the rather dubious decision to let sleeping dogs lie, hoping she was doing the right thing.

The Miller family, however, was a different story.

'These sound like the sort of issues that can be sorted out calmly,' she began.

'Are you saying I'm making a fuss?' The voice rose indignantly. This could be awkward. Joanna Miller was chairman of the PTA and not someone to get on the wrong side of.

'Not at all. HarryandAlfie, don't do that!' She glared at the boys who had come tearing in from the kitchen, hitting each other with remote controls from the PlayStation sets that Jeremy had given them for their birthday.

'I beg your pardon?'

Phew! They'd gone out again. 'Sorry.' She put on her *you-know-what-it's-like* voice. 'Roll on the new term.'

'Actually,' came the icy reply, 'I *enjoy* spending time with my children in the holidays, which is exactly why I got an au pair from you so she could do the housework and allow me to concentrate on them. Presumably you have help too?'

'Yes,' blurted out Jilly. Just at that point, her mother's dog took a leap from his basket straight on to her lap and began licking her madly as though sympathising with her situation. 'I have...er...Bruno. Look, I think the best thing to do – Bruno, please, not now – is for me to have a word with Birgitta myself.'

'Very well. But frankly, Jilly, if you can't sort this out, I will have to let Birgitta go. I have to say that this won't really help your reputation. And it goes without saying that I expect a full refund.'

Her reputation? Was Mrs Miller threatening her? As for a refund...well, she couldn't afford one! The agency was only just breaking even – the business insurance had cost much more than she'd bargained for. And even though she'd always considered herself a 'people' person, it was impossible to please all her clients.

If only she could pick out the good bits from each au pair (and their families) and roll them into one! Life would be so much easier. You could do the same to husbands too while you were at it! If only Paula wasn't being so prickly. It would be comforting to talk this over with her. At some point, she'd have to find the time – and the courage – to talk to her about it.

'Jee-lee. I am hungry.' Fat Eema was waddling in, her hands clasped over her stomach. 'It is time for dinner yes?'

Fat Eema was always hungry! It was costing them a fortune. But however hard she tried to persuade the girl to contact her family, it was no good. 'My father, he will keel me,' she kept saying over and over again. 'I can never return to my homeland.'

'But maybe he will understand,' Jilly had tried.

The girl's eyes had fixed on her mournfully. 'No. I think it is you who do not understand. I am too ashamed.' Her eyes had filled with tears again. 'So very ashamed.'

Jilly hadn't been able to press her further. Of course, David was right. They couldn't afford to take on another mouth to feed. Yet she couldn't, in all con - science, allow Fatima to end up in some lonely bedsit or be taken in by social services.

'But what will happen to her after the baby is born?' questioned her husband, not unreasonably.

'We'll sort that one out when it happens,' Jilly had

replied vaguely before pointing out that although she was eating them out of house and home, Fat Eema had proved herself to be a godsend in other areas.

Not only was she a whizz at the twins' maths holiday homework but the other day, she had also pointed out that the supermarket's bill was incorrect, which meant Jilly had been able to get a refund. Just as valuable was Fat Eema's ability to deal with the boys – clearly it was just full-grown men she was allergic to – and could magically calm them down with what David called 'the Look', which she also directed at him from time to time.

'Your man is not good husband to you,' she had proclaimed the other morning after David had stomped off for work in a rather grumpy mood. 'You find new one, I think.'

'He's not that bad,' Jilly had said, both astounded and bemused. But the words had niggled at the back of her mind. In the past, she'd considered that she and David had a good marriage. But since starting the agency, it was as though someone had turned on a pair of taps allowing hidden niggles and irritations to come flooding out on both sides.

It was the same with Paula, who hadn't returned any of her calls since that horrible disagreement about Antoinette. If only they could make up! Tell each other that maybe both had spoken out of turn. Get together for a coffee like the old times. Maybe take the kids to a film while they had a good gossip in the back row.

Still, there was no time to fret about any of this stuff. Not when she had a difficult phone call to make.

'Birgitta?' Jilly steeled herself as the girl answered. 'I gather there have been a few teething problems with Mrs Miller.'

There was a sniff at the other end of the phone. Oh dear.

'My family, she says I can only have ten minutes in the bathroom before brake fast,' the voice rang out in indignation. 'I am permitted only to drink the cheap instant coffee while she retains the best for herself. And she insists I perform a time sheet before I am paid. If she is not content with it, my money is reductioned.'

That didn't sound very fair. 'Tell you what, Birgitta. Perhaps we ought to meet up for a little chat. How about the coffee shop down the road? The one next to the library. Yes. Library. It's where you borrow books. You don't read much? Well, do you know the other coffee shop next to the pub? You do? Great. See you in about an hour. OK?'

An hour! That should just about give her time to sort out the boys, take Bruno for a walk and...not the phone again!

'Hello? Yes, I remember. Oh dear. Actually, Mrs Thomas, Margit is right. Au pairs *shouldn't* have to work on bank holidays. Yes and au pairs *should* be given adequate time off for religious services. She says she's a Christian *and* a Buddhist? Bruno, not on my *knee*. Sorry. Bad line. She won't wash windows? Well, I'm afraid she is right on this one as you'll see if you check my guidelines. Yes of course I will have a word with her if you like...'

AAAArgh! One more job to do! Jilly surveyed the mess around her in the kitchen: dirty footprints and paw marks and a dishwasher which hadn't been put on even though it had been loaded for two days. Bruno was still clawing at her ankles. She'd have to take him with her. 'Boys!' she called out. There was the sound of the PlayStation roaring from the top of the stairs. 'I'll be back in about half an hour. OK?'

Such a relief to get out of the house! She actually envied David for being able to drive away and go into an office. It would be a doddle just to deal with work and not three children and a dog on top.

It was only when she reached the coffee shop that she realised Bruno wouldn't be allowed in. Birgitta, she could see through the window, was lounging at one of the tables, iPod in her ears, texting and talking to some other girls at the same time. They were probably all having a good old moan about their agencies and families!

Jilly motioned through the window to tell Birgitta that she was outside but the girl merely beckoned back – what a cheek! – to signify that *she* should come in to *her*.

'I can't,' she tried to say, pointing down to Bruno who was pawing away at the glass, able to sniff out a biscuit from miles away. One of the other girls was getting up now and walking towards her with a broad smile. It was Marie-France!

'*Bonjour*, Madame Jilly!'

The girl was kissing her on both cheeks and Jilly felt a rush of relief. At least she'd managed to place *one* girl who didn't give any trouble.

'Birgitta says you are here to talk to her!'

'Yes but I had to bring the dog with me and we can't come in. Could you ask her to come here?'

'I will look after him outside if you like.' Marie-France was sitting on her haunches, stroking Bruno, who seemed to remember her from the airport.

Jilly hesitated. 'He's very strong.'

'I am used to dogs. My mother's boyfriend, he has one.' Her face dropped and her eyes grew watery. 'I miss him although he makes me sneeze sometimes.'

Oh dear. Not another case of homesickness! 'That would be very kind of you.'

What a nice girl, reflected Jilly, bracing herself for the pep talk with Birgitta who was now looking at her sullenly through the window. If they could all be like that, her life would be so much easier!

Gratefully she handed over a black bag. 'You might need to pick up, I'm afraid.'

'*Pick up?*' Marie-France's eyes widened. 'I do not pick up boys. I am not that kind of girl.'

'I didn't mean that! The bag is in case Bruno does his business.'

'Ah! I see!' Marie-France giggled. 'English, she is a very strange language.'

Just like German and French and any other which wasn't your own, thought Jilly, heading through the door. In fact it was incredible how a country's border could create such enormous divisions in culture. And confidence too. Jilly began to feel rather awkward as she approached the table of loud au pairs, all of whom swivelled round to glare at her as though she was the enemy. Margit was there too so maybe she could kill two birds with one stone.

'Hi, Birgitta!' She made herself put on a bright voice. 'How are you getting on?'

Mrs Miller's au pair said nothing, glancing instead at the small fiery-looking dark-haired girl in a glossy pink coat who was sitting next to her. Scowling, the girl said, 'Her family is not treating her right.'

Her heart sank. It was Antoinette. 'Hello!' Jilly forced herself to smile. 'I'm Paula's friend. I didn't realise you and Birgitta knew each other.'

'We meet at school.' Antoinette hammered her fist on the table. 'Birgitta's family is no good. I tell her. She must leave.'

This girl was acting like a one-woman au pair union! 'Perhaps she might like to tell me herself about some of her problems,' said Jilly firmly, looking her straight in the eye. 'I believe you find it difficult to get up on time.'

'I am tired because she makes me work too hard.'

'Do you have a list of your jobs?'

The girl pushed across her iPad. On it was a spread - sheet outlining the chores which she was expected to do. This really did seem rather a lot! She'd need to talk to Joanna about that, head of the PTA or not.

'Margit has problem too,' thundered Antoinette with another bang on the table. 'Her family say she has to work on bank holiday!'

'Thank you but let's allow her to speak for herself, shall we? I have already spoken to your family and explained that you are entitled to have the day off.'

'Entitled?' Margit frowned. 'What is this?'

'It means "allowed".'

Her face brightened. 'Good. Thank you.'

'However, I hear that you need time to go to two church services every day and an extra hour for meditation.'

The girl flushed and looked across to Antoinette as though seeking confirmation. The other girl gave a Gallic shrug. 'She is Catholic *and* Buddhist – like me.'

'Nothing to do with getting extra time off then, for worship?'

'No.' Antoinette's dark eyes were boring into her. The girl was scary! She wouldn't be in Paula's shoes for anything.

'Perhaps,' suggested Jilly, eyeballing her back, 'it might be reasonable to go to church during your time off.'

Silence. She tried again. 'Are you enjoying yourself here, Margit?'

'It is OK.' She glanced across at Antoinette again. Clearly this girl was the ringleader.

'Right.' She stood up, noticing to her relief that Marie-France was back and Bruno was pawing at the door. 'I'd better be going but if there's anything else that upsets you, don't hesitate to get in touch.'

'Is that it?' Antoinette glared at her. 'Are you not going to tell off her family for arguing?'

What a cheek! 'I will talk to Mrs Miller and Mrs Thomas but I think it is best, Antoinette, if you leave this to me. You are not one of my girls, after all.'

'If I am not one of your girls, why do you tell tales of me to my family?'

Jilly felt a sickening thud. 'Paula is my friend. I heard something that I felt she ought to know. Goodbye, Antoinette.'

With that, she turned on her heel and walked towards the door. Honestly, these girls! They were so rude! Was it their nationality or their age? Either way, she was so relieved she didn't have one of those at home to go back to! Fat Eema, even with her fridge habit, was easier to deal with than all of that lot rolled together.

'Thank you, Marie-France.'

She took Bruno's lead from her and looked in her purse for some small change.

'No.' The girl waved her hand dismissively. 'I do not want paying. I am glad to help.'

'That's very kind of you.' She lowered her voice. 'Tell me. Is Antoinette still leaving Immy alone in the house?'

Marie-France's face tightened. 'I do not know. That girl is not good news. But unfortunately she is part of our group.'

'I see. Well, thank you anyway. See you around town, perhaps, and don't forget to ring me if you have any problems.'

If she was to get an au pair one day, thought Jilly, walking briskly back up the hill towards the house, that was exactly the kind she would like! Turning into her road, she heard music. It was coming from the other end of the street . . . from her end. No. Please no. Yes, it was from her house. Or to be more exact, from Nick's bedroom.

Rushing down the drive, she opened the front door. 'TURN THAT DOWN!' she yelled.

There was no response. Bruno raced up to Nick's room, while she followed. What? She stared, unable to believe her eyes. Two boys whom she'd never seen before were lying on the carpet, with their muddy shoes on, next to Nick. But what was worse – far worse – was that they were poring over her file marked AU PAIR PLACEMENTS. Nick must have taken it!

'Look at that one,' leered the taller boy with orange roots. 'Wouldn't mind banging her.'

'Do you mind?' Jilly snatched the folder away from them. 'You had no right to go through my paperwork like that, Nick. What do you think you're doing? And who are *you*?'

Nick flushed beetroot. 'They're my mates, Mum. Don't be so rude.'

'Well, I'd like you to leave. Now.'

The taller one actually pushed past her without one word of an apology, the other following him downstairs, both kicking the sides of the wall as they went. She marched behind them, slamming the front door after them before returning to her son's room where he was lying on the bed, just as he used to as a child when something was wrong.

'*Nick!* How could you! Especially after last time!'

Her son eyed her sullenly instead of apologising as she'd expected. What was going on? Nick had been fine until a few months ago. Was it just because he was finally becoming a teenager or was it because she hadn't spent enough time with him?

Whatever reason, she simply wasn't having it. 'Your behaviour was unforgivable,' she thundered. 'Where did you meet those boys anyway?'

He shrugged. 'They do a paper round with me.'

'Well, I don't want you hanging around with them

and I certainly don't want you getting your hormonal kicks from my clients. It's confidential information. I could get into a lot of trouble for that. Do you hear? Now where are the twins?'

Nick shot her another sullen glance that reminded her of the au pairs in the coffee shop. 'Out in the garden, playing French cricket.'

'I asked you to look after them!'

'I didn't need to.'

'Is Fatima with them, then?'

Nick got up and lay on the bed with his headphones on. He shouted something out but Jilly couldn't hear with the music.

Wrenching off his headphones, she yelled, 'What did you say?'

'I said there was no need cos Granny is downstairs with them. And stop shouting, Mum. It's giving me a headache.'

Her *mother* was downstairs with the twins? But she was meant to be safely tucked away on a Mediterranean cruise. Racing back down the stairs and into the kitchen, she stopped short. There, sitting at the table with its usual mix of files and cereal packets and the peanut butter jar with its lid off, was a tall, elegant woman – sometimes mistaken for Angela Rippon – smelling of Chanel and reading *The Economist*.

'Ah, there you are, dear,' said her mother smoothly, as though they'd only seen each other that morning instead of five months ago. She was looking, as usual, as though she had just stepped out of *Woman & Home*, with her impeccably swept-back white-blond hair and tailored beige trousers.

'How lovely to see you.' Jilly went to give her a hug. 'I thought you were away.'

'Just got back. Not too close, dear. I've just had my hair done.' Her mother offered her cheek, which had a healthy suntanned glow. 'I needed a break from your father. I can't seem to lose him at home as I could do on the boat.'

Oh dear! Sounded as if they were going through one of their rough patches again. For as long as Jilly could remember, her parents had either been at each other's throats or over-affectionate in public. It was exhausting – for both the participants and onlookers. Especially as it now meant rejigging bedrooms to make room for Mum. 'Why didn't you say you were coming?'

'Down, Bruno, down. You'll spoil my tights. Didn't you get my email?'

'I haven't managed to get through my inbox this week,' Jilly began to stutter. Her over-efficient, opinionated mother always made her feel inadequate, however much she loved her.

'I can see that there are several things you haven't got round to doing.' Her mother put down *The Economist* and surveyed the table in disdain.

'What do you mean?'

'Well it's clear, dear, that David was right to ring me. Sheila, he said to me, we need your help. Well, the one thing I can do is to organise a business. Now why don't I start with your accounts and you can get on with doing what you do best.' She flashed her a cold smile. 'Looking after your children. And by the way, you really need to keep tabs on your new cleaner.'

'New cleaner?'

'I found her – can you believe this? – sound asleep upstairs. Don't worry. I soon sorted her out. She's scouring the bath. A bit of exercise might help her shift some of that weight she's carrying. Right then. Let's get going, shall we?'

JILLY'S AU PAIR AGENCY:
GUIDELINES FOR FAMILIES

*An au pair should be treated as a member of the family.
However, it is not always wise to let her get too close.*

Chapter 17

At first, after Thierry had rushed off on his bike, Marie-France had been furious. Typical! He was so hot-headed and quick to draw the wrong conclusion.

Remember, she told herself, that time when his employer had accused him of fitting the wrong engine on to a bike? Thierry had insisted that he'd been following instructions but then had to backtrack when it became clear he was wrong. It had been the talk of the village – with its dependence on small bits of gossip for entertainment – for months.

Marie-France could not help smiling wistfully at the memory. She could see her little town so clearly. Thierry would be home by now, probably sitting in his usual spot in the café, nursing his cold beer. He'd be telling Monsieur Lèvre from the bakery that the English did not know how to make a decent croissant. He would throw in the reference to his visit to *Angleterre* in an offhand way with a shrug of his shoulder and a toss of his long hair that needed a trim.

Would he tell Monsieur Lèvre and maybe Pierre from the post office that he and Marie-France had had a blazing row? Maybe, she thought with a bit of a flutter in her chest, he would sink another cold beer and announce that he had decided to have a break because he did not want to be tied down at his age. Then he might give the barmaid a sultry wink – Thierry was very good at sultry winks – and offer to buy her a drink...

Meanwhile, Maman would be, right at this minute perhaps, coming back from work on the bus, looking more like an elegant customer than a shop assistant. She would be wearing a pair of high heels – maybe the blue pair with the little ribbon on the toes – and a trim skirt that flirted at her knees, showing off her silhouette to perfection. Then she'd go home and fry a steak from the butcher which tasted like real food instead of those awful chops Dawn bought in plastic boxes from the supermarket.

The image made Marie-France feel violently homesick as well as angry and hurt.

Plse rng so we can discuss this, she had said in her text to Thierry after his departure, but he hadn't bothered to reply. That wasn't really surprising. When they had fallen out last year over some triviality, he had ignored her for a week. Then he had turned up with an enormous bouquet of flowers and a sexy pair of red knickers, still with the market price on them, and they had made up in the woods on the outskirts of town.

'Is everything all right with your boyfriend now?' asked Phillip about a week after Thierry's dramatic exit. Her boss's husband had come into the kitchen so quietly that she hadn't heard him and she had jumped slightly. It was early – only just after 6 a.m. – but Dawn had asked her to make some chocolate mousses for a dinner party that night.

'Not really.' She gave a shrug while she melted the butter. 'He is a bit of a sulk, sometimes.'

Phillip made a too-bad face. 'I feel partly responsible.'

'Why?'

He scratched his chin, which bore a hint of a dark shadow in a very sexy cosmopolitan way. 'If I'd installed a lock on your door a bit earlier, Tom wouldn't have been able to get into your room.'

'He gets away with too much.' Marie-France stirred the egg yolks into the butter, aware that Phillip's eyes were on her.

'Yes. He does. But as I've said before, it is difficult for me to interfere.' He shook his head sadly. 'Dawn doesn't find it easy to take criticism, although, as you have experienced yourself, she doesn't mind dishing it out.'

Marie-France shot him a grateful look. 'That is true.'

He patted her on the shoulder lightly and his touch sent a little tingle down her back. 'Did you...' She hesitated, suddenly feeling that the question she had been about to ask was too familiar.

'Did I what?' he repeated.

'No.' She turned her attention to the chocolate, which was almost over-done, and poured it into the yolk mixture. 'It does not matter.'

'If you are wondering whether I spoke to Dawn about her "friend", as I shall call him, then the answer is no.' His eyes stopped twinkling and instead looked slightly wistful, which made her want to reach out and comfort him. 'Call me a coward if you like, but I can't rock the boat. Not yet.'

'Rock the boat?' she repeated questioningly. Her already-good English had improved vastly in just a few weeks – it was amazing how much you picked up when you had to speak a strange language every day – but there was still so much she couldn't understand.

Those handsome eyes fixed on hers as though she'd said something amusing. 'Rock the boat is a phrase we use to say that we can't disturb the situation. I would rather wait for...let's say certain developments to take place.'

'But how can you live with a woman who is so rude to you and takes lovers under your nose!'

She couldn't help the outburst. Phillip was too nice for his own good!

'It is sweet of you to worry about me.' He gave her hand a quick squeeze, almost making her drop the spoon. 'But I know what I am doing. Trust me. *Au revoir*. I will see you tonight along with your delicious chocolate mousses.'

'I don't think so!' Marie-France laughed. 'I don't get invited to your dinner parties.'

He frowned. 'Is that so? Dawn has always told me that you've turned down her invitations.'

What a liar! 'Au pairs are meant to eat with the family,' declared Marie-France, 'but I have to eat my meals with the children.'

Phillip's face hardened. 'We'll see about that.'

He'd only just closed the door behind him when Tom shot in, closely followed by Tatty Arna. 'You've got a letter, you've got a letter,' he chanted. 'But you can't have it!'

'The postman? She has arrived so early?'

'Mum gave it to me yesterday to give you. But I kept it!'

Marie-France dropped her chocolate spoon and lunged at the boy, who was indeed waving a postcard with a French stamp on it. She could recognise her mother's handwriting from here. '*Donne-la-moi.*'

Tom sniggered. 'Stupid Marie-France can't even speak English.'

'Don't you dare be so rude to me.' Grabbing the boy with one hand, she held the now-cool bowl of chocolate mousse over his head. 'If you don't give that to me, I will tip this all over you.'

The boy smirked. 'You wouldn't dare.'

'Yes I would. It's about time someone taught you a lesson.'

He made as though he was going to tear up the card. Right. She was careful to only dribble a bit on to his head but it was enough.

'There you are.' He flung the postcard on to the floor and shot her a look full of pure loathing. 'I'm going to tell Mum.'

'Then I inform her that you steal money from her bag yesterday. Yes. I see you! Now go back to your stupid PlayStation. When you are in a nice mood, we will enjoy breakfast together.'

Marie-France spent that morning making little cakes with Tatty Arna while Tom stayed sulking in his room. Dawn finally appeared at midday with puffy bags under her eyes and wearing a pink tracksuit.

'There was no need to make the mousses,' she said, waving dismissively at the row of perfect little pots on the side. 'Dinner's off. Phillip's just called. We're going out with his clients instead.'

'But I rise early to make them!'

Dawn shrugged. 'Then chuck them or give them to Tom. Not Tatiana. Girls can't afford to put on weight in this life. By the way, I need you to babysit tonight, OK?'

No it wasn't! She'd planned to go out with some of the girls from her language class. Too late. Dawn had already stomped off.

It was half an hour or so later, when she was helping Tatty Arna to lick out the bowl (poor kid deserved some fun!), that she heard the noise through the open window, coming from the direction of the pool. It sounded as though someone was crying. Leaving the little girl to carry on licking, she went out to investigate.

'Bonjour? Ça va?'

Dawn was sitting by the poolside, her head in her hands. 'What are you on about?' she whimpered. 'Go away.'

Marie-France shrugged. 'Very well.'

'No. Wait.' Dawn looked up. Her face was red and blotchy. Some people – like Heidi – looked attractively vulnerable when they cried. But not this one. 'I've got myself into a bit of a . . . Forget it. What am I doing, telling you anyway?'

'Suit yourself.' Marie-France had picked up this phrase from her English class. It felt rather nice, clipping off her tongue like that! But Dawn didn't seem very pleased by it.

'How dare you talk to me like that!'

'I am sorry.' Too late, Marie-France realised her mistake. She was still no closer to finding her father, despite having put an ad in the local paper with the help of one of the other French girls. The last thing she needed was to be sacked. She had to stay in the area. 'There is something I can do for you, to help?'

Dawn's eyes hardened. 'Yes. Stay out of other people's problems. Got it?'

What a difficult woman! Marie-France returned to her room, grateful to have a few hours to herself. It would give her a chance to read and reread Maman's postcard.

> *Chérie,*
>
> *We have had some new stock in this week which is très chic. I borrowed a beautiful skirt to wear to the dinner with Maurice and managed to return it without anyone finding out! Thierry has quit his job in the garage and gone travelling. Did you know? How are you getting on with your search? Please take care. Englishmen and French garage mechanics are not to be trusted.*
>
> *Love, Maman*

Marie-France's finger traced the outline of her mother's loopy handwriting and her eyes pricked with tears. How she wanted to see her! How she yearned to breathe French air again. But if she didn't seize the opportunity to find the missing link in her family, she would regret it for ever.

'I'm so sorry that our arrangements had to change for tonight,' whispered Phillip while he was waiting for

Dawn to get ready. 'I was looking forward to getting to talking to you at dinner.'

Marie-France had been sitting on the sofa in the den, cuddling Tatty Arna, who was watching a video. Tom, who had been sulky ever since this morning, was glued to his Xbox. He had so many toys! PlayStations, PSPs, mini-televisions. Enough to keep *all* the children happy in her village at home.

Now she looked up at Phillip, who was so handsome in his dinner jacket and red spotted tie, and flushed at the compliment. 'I understand.'

She broke off as Dawn marched in, scowling. She too would have looked nice had it not been for her face, which was pinched and mean-looking. Her dress, however, was a beautiful jade-green silk which sparkled as she moved and she wore long earrings in exactly the same shade. 'We won't be back until late,' she threw at Marie-France.

Phillip gave her an I'm-so-sorry look and a quick wink, which made her flush again.

Snuggling up to Tatty Arna in front of the Disney film, she allowed herself to daydream for the next half-hour or so. What if Phillip made a move on her? What if Thierry and she were over for good? What if...

The sound of the front-door knocker interrupted her thoughts. It must be Phillip or Dawn again, otherwise they couldn't have got through the security gate.

'Hello,' she began but then stopped. A man was standing on the doorstep, wearing a smart blue jacket over jeans. He had a pleasant smile on his face as though he knew her.

Mon Dieu! The advertisement! The advertisement

she'd put in the local paper for her father. He had arrived?

'Monsieur Smith?' she gasped. 'Monsieur John Smith?'

The smiling stranger seemed to consider the idea. 'Why not?'

'You saw my notice?'

'I might have done.'

'But how do you pass through the security gate?'

'What is this?' He narrowed his eyes at her. 'Twenty questions?'

Excitedly, Marie-France ran her eyes over him. He was about the right age: late sixties, sophisticated jacket, dark hair with a flick of distinguished silver and bluey-green eyes just like hers.

Slightly against her better judgement, she had put the address of the house in the paper as well as a phone number, in order to maximise the chances of finding her father. Well, there didn't seem to be any rules against it. And now he'd found *her*!

'Please.' She felt her heart beating excitedly. 'Come in.'

This was *him*. Her father. She just knew it!

'Thank you.' He looked over his shoulder. 'Mind if my friends come too?'

After that, it all seemed to happen so fast! Before she knew it, a strong hand had grabbed her and was pulling her up the stairs. What was happening?

'Marie-France!' cried out little Tatty Arna's voice.

'The children,' she yelled. 'Do not harm the children.'

'Put them in with the girl,' said another voice.

'Here's the door. The one with the lock on the outside,' said the man who was tugging her.

Furiously, she lashed out, scratching one of them, who yelled with fury. 'Bitch.' He pushed her into a room. 'In here.'

Thank God the kids were with her! She held them to her, comforting them as the door was locked outside. Then she heard more voices and heavy footsteps marching into Phillip and Dawn's room. 'There's some good stuff here,' she heard one growl.

'Bung it all in. Not that one – it's engraved. Don't take anything that's too easily traced. Now let's get out of this place. Quick.'

Thieves! Marie-France trembled. She had actually let thieves into the house, thinking the leader was her father! Dawn would kill her!

'I'm frightened,' whimpered Tatty Arna.

'Me too,' whimpered Tom.

Steeling herself, she drew them to her, wondering if she could climb out of the window to get help. No, it was too high.

'It's all right,' she said, sounding far braver than she felt. 'I will look after you and then your mother and Phillip will be back.'

'Mummy!' Little Tatty Arna began to cry. 'I want Mummy!'

She needed to distract the poor mite. But how? Then her eye fell on the guitar next to her bed and her mind went back to all those times in the woods back home, where she had sat on Thierry's knee and they had sung and played together.

'*Viens*,' she said encouragingly, holding out her arms

to the little girl. 'Sit here and Tom will play to us while we sing. Look, Tom. You put this finger on this string and the other on that one.'

To her amazement, he actually did as he was told.

'Bravo!' She clapped her hands. 'That sounds good, *n'est-ce pas*? You recognise the tune, yes? It is "Frère Jacques", the song I sing the other day.'

Tom's face lit up as his plump fingers fumbled with the strings. Yes! She'd done it. She'd managed to make them forget this terrible situation they were in. For the next half-hour or so, they carried on strumming. So much better for him than a PlayStation or an Xbox!

Then suddenly there was the sound of a car outside and a door opening downstairs. Marie-France's heart began to race. Had those bad men come back?

'Quick!' she said, pushing them under her bed. 'Hide there. Do not say a word and do not come out until I say!'

Then there was the scraping of the key being turned on the other side and her door was flung open. She picked up her guitar, ready to bring it down on the thief's head. He didn't scare her. Not any more. In fact she would do anything to protect the children.

'Go away,' she screamed. And then she stopped, taking in the familiar handsome face, the dinner jacket and the red bow tie.

'Phillip? It is *you*?'

'Where are the kids?' His handsome face was frowning. 'And why are you locked in here?'

It was all too much! Marie-France burst into tears. 'We have thieves! And it is all my fault!'

'Shhh.' Phillip drew her to him and stroked the back of her head comfortingly. 'It's all right. Now why don't you slow down and tell me exactly what happened.'

USEFUL PHRASES FOR SPANISH AU PAIRS

Would you like to be my boyfriend? (¿Quieres ser mi novio?)

You enchant me (Me encantas)

I don't understand (No entiendo)

Why? (Por qué)

I want to go home (Quiero irme a casa)

Chapter 18

He didn't have any proof! Matthew kept reminding himself of that when he was meant to be working. In fact, it was entirely possible that Genevieve might not have taken the money at all.

Since Sally had died, he'd been putting things in all the wrong places; so-called 'lost' keys turned up in drawers where he must have dumped them without thinking. He'd even once found Lottie's jumper in the fridge and a tub of marge in the linen cupboard.

'It's stress,' Christina had reassured him at the time. 'When people are under pressure, they often do this kind of thing. Try to get a routine going. As soon as you come into the house, put your keys where they normally go. I've got a hook for mine.'

What would she say now about money which might or might not have been pilfered by the new au pair? Not for the first time since he had bumped into Christina at the station, Matthew wished he hadn't ended their sessions so abruptly.

Then again, if he hadn't stopped being her client, she might not have confided in him. He'd been surprised when she'd told him about her marriage ending: somehow he hadn't put her down as another single parent. She was so composed and confident, and, well, capable. Would he be like that a few years down the line? He hoped so.

Part of him still felt guilty about revealing Sally's affair. 'Please don't tell anyone,' his wife had begged and he hadn't. That's why he hadn't mentioned it during his earlier sessions with Christina. So why had he gone and blurted it out in the coffee shop?

Yet his confession had also made him feel better. More able to move on. Capable of taking one step at a time, as Christina had advised.

But there was also nothing wrong with being one step ahead too! So maybe he'd lay Genevieve a little trap. Put out small sums of money in obvious places and see if they disappeared.

'Matthew?' Karen's worried face now appeared at his office door. 'Sorry to chase you but James wants to know if you've finished with the report.'

Was that the time already? A year of being at home with his daughter had slowed him down; made him less able to impose the same rigid deadlines on himself that he used to. 'I'm nearly there.'

It wasn't true. But if he blocked out thoughts of Genevieve stealing his money when she was meant to be looking after his daughter, he might just make it.

'Hi, I'm home,' he called out when he got back that evening, a little later than usual because of back-to-back meetings.

No answer. He hung his jacket on the hook by the door and called out again. 'Hello!'

Sometimes, as right now, he almost expected Sally's voice to answer. Instead, he could hear a foreign voice upstairs talking to Lottie. Quickly, he whipped out a twenty-pound note from his wallet and marked it with a small black cross on the corner. Then he placed it on the hall table just under a small bronze mermaid that he and Sally had bought on their honeymoon.

'Hi, Daddy!' Lottie flew down the stairs and leaped from the bottom steps straight into his arms.

He caught her, breathing her in. 'Careful, darling, you'll hurt yourself. Did you have a good day?'

She beamed. 'We went shopping. Genevieve bought a new dress. I saw this really cool top. Could I have it, Daddy? Please! Please!'

She'd never shown much interest in clothes before. Then he took in what she was wearing. It was her green school uniform but the jumper was tight and her skirt far too short. With a pang, he realised his little girl had grown during the summer.

'Good evening, Matthew!'

So familiar! But au pairs were meant to be part of the family so he could hardly expect her to call him Mr Evans all the time. Awkwardly, he watched Genevieve flouncing down the stairs with a wide grin, wearing a rather revealing red T-shirt.

'Dinner is relaxing in the oven. I hope you adore goulash. Yes?'

'Er, yes, thanks. Why is Lottie wearing her uniform?'

'I try it on to see if it is ready for school next week.' Big smile. 'My mother always do that to me, yes? I think we need to go shopping for bigger clothes. Do you want to donate me the money? Yes?'

Hah! She wasn't getting away that easily. 'It's all right. I'll take Lottie myself on Saturday.' He should have done so earlier, Matthew told himself guiltily, but

Lottie's recent growth spurt, coupled with lack of time now he was back at work, had thrown him.

Genevieve frowned. 'I am thinking the stocks will be smaller then. It is best to do it soon like the television adverts say. It is late-night shopping tomorrow. I could come with you if you please. Yes?'

No thanks, he was about to say, but then he suddenly thought how awkward it would be for him – a man – to go into the changing rooms with his daughter and check that something was the right size. It might be a good idea to have a woman with him.

'Thanks. I'll try and be back a bit earlier. By the way, in case I forget, could you please dust downstairs tomorrow and can you include the hall table?'

Genevieve nodded agreeably. 'That is no effort. Now, I think we will eat together. Yes?'

If his previous experiences hadn't taught him to be sceptical, Matthew would have thought that their new addition to the family was the perfect au pair despite that infuriating 'Yes?' at the end of almost every sentence. She was polite; she got on really well with Lottie, who was clearly besotted; and she was a great cook. ('My mother paid for me to go to a cookery school in Switzerland. Yes?)

On the other hand, she wasn't too hot at housework and he'd actually had to show her how the vacuum cleaner worked. Yet maybe that was because, as she said, 'My mother has people to do the cleaning at home.'

But *theft* was a different matter! Common sense told him that if she came from such a well-to-do family, surely she would have enough money of her own. But then again, there was no logic to au pairs. He would never have thought that Berenice was the type to try on a dead woman's clothes and as for Sozzy walking out like that and into the arms of a murderer, he just couldn't even think about that.

The following evening, he came back from work early. But before even announcing his arrival, he went to the hall table. The twenty-pound note underneath the mermaid was missing! Part of him felt a bizarre satisfaction at having caught her. But the other part was horrified. This meant another argument. Another au pair leaving...

'Daddy!' Lottie came running out of the kitchen, swinging on his arms, grinning with that cute little gap between her front teeth. 'We've been waiting. Genevieve and I want to go shopping!'

'Is that so?'

He turned to face Genevieve, who was ready with her smart suede jacket and matching handbag. 'What did you two do today?'

'Cooking.' Genevieve was nodding like a Dutch doll. 'I teach Lottie to make chocolate cakes. And then I buy presents for my family.'

With *my* money, he almost added grimly. He'd wait until Lottie had gone to bed that night and then tackle her on it. But right now, they needed to get a move on before the shops shut.

Wow! Two hours later, Matthew was more exhausted than he'd been after any day in the office. This school-uniform battle was a nightmare! Every other parent, or so it seemed, had decided to kit out their kids at the last minute and he'd had a near-tussle with another father who had his eye on the same green skirt suitable for eight- to nine-year-olds.

'I think this is ours, yes?' Genevieve had announced firmly and then, seizing the hanger before the rival could get there, marched towards the changing room where Lottie was waiting.

The other man had given Matthew a look that was somewhere between annoyance and admiration. 'Your wife is a very determined woman.'

'She's not my wife,' he said quickly.

But the man gave him another look. This time it was pure envy. 'Lucky bloke, that's all I can say.'

How embarrassing! It got worse at the cash till where Genevieve had stocked up a pile of crisp white shirts, socks, pants and PE stuff. 'Do we need anything else?' she asked as though they were a couple. Matthew flushed as the shop assistant looked from one to the other. This girl was almost young enough to be his daughter. What would everyone think?

She certainly didn't have any trouble spending money: the bill was staggering. He vaguely remembered Sally saying something about the cost of school uniform when Lottie had first started. Too late, he wished he'd taken more of an active interest instead of being buried in his work. Wasn't that, he recalled as Sally's words came back to him, one of the reasons why she'd had an affair in the first place? 'You're never there for us, Matthew. It's work, work, work.'

'We shall go for coffee, yes?' Genevieve was smiling with those perfect teeth again. 'My mother and I, we always have coffee after shopping in order to rest.'

Rest! It was he who needed to rest to get over the size of the bill.

'No. I need to get back.' He took a large bag of shopping in each hand and began walking towards the exit. 'Are you in tonight Genevieve?'

'I meet some of my new friends from school. Yes?'

Blast. He was going to have it out with her but maybe he'd wait until tomorrow evening. He'd give her one last chance. Just to be certain. 'That's fine. By the way, would it be possible for you to polish the bedrooms tomorrow?'

'Yes. Of course.'

'Thank you.'

That night, just as he was going to bed, Matthew put another twenty-pound note, also with a black cross, on the dressing table in his room, underneath his photograph of Sally.

His dead wife stared disapprovingly out of the silver frame. 'Well do you have any better suggestions?' he asked. 'If you hadn't died, none of this would have happened.'

That was unfair and he knew it. But as he tossed and turned, trying to go to sleep with Genevieve's music booming through the wall, he remembered something else that Christina had said. 'You have to get angry before you can move on.'

Well, he was angry all right. Not just about Sally. He was angry about Genevieve taking money. And he was angry at himself for ... well, for just about everything.

The following morning, the first thing he saw out of the kitchen window was Genevieve pegging out the washing. His boxers were fluttering in the wind next to a pair of scarlet knickers. That would give the neighbours something to talk about! Part of him wanted to laugh; the other part felt nervous about the money and whether it would still be there tonight.

'Penny for your thoughts,' said Karen when she brought in his milky coffee and biscuits at around eleven.

'More likely twenty quid,' he retorted without thinking.

Karen frowned. 'Come again?'

So somehow he found himself telling her all about it.

'My mother had a carer who stole things,' she said when he'd finished.

'Really?'

She nodded. 'We had to sack her. It was very difficult because I'd trusted her. It made me wonder how well she was looking after my mother if she wasn't trustworthy in other areas.'

'Exactly!' He felt a bond with Karen that he hadn't before as well as a stirring of curiosity. 'Was your mother in a home?'

'No.' Karen's eyes took on a far-away look. 'She was in her own place but it was when I was married and living in Yorkshire so I organised someone to come in and keep an eye on her. Soon after that, my marriage broke up and I moved down to look after her. Ironically, she died a year later and that was when I started here.'

First Christina's revelations and now Karen's! How was it that his PA had worked for him for over three years and he hadn't known any of this? 'I'm sorry.'

She seemed to snap out of her reverie. 'That's all right. I'm probably boring you anyway.'

'Not at all.' He struggled to make it right. 'Life does some really weird things to you, doesn't it? Take death.' He hesitated. 'I didn't know much about it until ...until Sally and it's put everything else into perspective.'

Karen smiled and it dawned on him that she was actually far more attractive than he'd given her credit for. 'I know what you mean. Now if you don't mind me saying, that report – the one that was due in yesterday – really does need to be finished. James is out at the moment but he's due back after lunch. If I work through my break, I could get it typed up for you.'

'That would be brilliant.' He'd forgotten all about it. 'Thanks, Karen. And not just for that. Thanks for listening.'

She flushed. 'Any time, Matt. All you have to do is ask.'

It wasn't until she'd bustled out of the door that he realised something. He'd learned more about her in the last ten minutes than he had since she'd first come to work for him. Didn't say much about him as a boss, did it?

When he got back that night, he gave Lottie a kiss and went straight up to his bedroom. The dresser was gleaming and Sally's photograph – along with the others, mainly of his daughter as a baby and then growing up in stages through six-by-four frames – was dust-free.

Matthew's heart thudded as he picked up one frame

and then another, just in case the twenty-pound note had been 'mislaid' somewhere else. But it hadn't. It had definitely gone. Yet instead of anger, he felt deep disappointment. He'd taken this girl into his house. Trusted her against his better judgement. And now look at what had happened.

'Genevieve!' he called out as he walked heavily down the stairs. 'Are you there?'

She bounced out of the kitchen, wearing another of Sally's pinnies; the one that showed a tipsy woman clutching a glass of wine with the words: *One more never hurt anyone*.

'Genevieve, may I have a word, please.' He glanced at the table where Lottie was icing some more chocolate cakes. 'Not here. In the other room.'

Her face looked apprehensive as she followed him in. 'Is everything OK? You are pleased with my work? Yes? I polish the silver, too, like you ask. Look!' She frowned slightly. 'There is only one problem.' She pointed at the cutlery which was lying on the kitchen table. 'It smells and everything has gone brown.'

For God's sake! She had used the tin of shoe-cleaning polish instead of the silver one under the sink! Still, compared with what was coming next, that was nothing.

Nervously, Matthew closed the door behind them so Lottie couldn't hear. 'Genevieve, I have to tell you something. Money has been disappearing in the house. I left some on the hall table and then some on my dressing table. Now it's all gone.'

Her cheeks grew small pink spots. 'You think I am thieving? Yes?'

'Well…' he paused. 'You do seem very fond of shopping.'

Her cheeks grew pinker still. 'I have my own money. My father give me my allowance.'

'Then why were you so keen to ask for your first week of pocket money?'

'Because I desire to go shopping.'

'Exactly. So I wondered if—'

'Do not say any more.' She whipped off Sally's pinny and flung it on the floor. 'You think I am thief so I will depart.'

'No. Don't.' He had a vision of her running off like Sozzy. 'Wait until you find somewhere else to live.'

'I do not spend another minute under your heads.'

'Roof,' he said automatically. 'I think you mean roof.'

'I book into a hotel and then I ring agency.' Her face was red with fury.

'But what about Lottie?' Too late he realised he'd made a mistake not waiting until the holidays were over. 'I've got a meeting with the school head tomorrow night.' His voice dropped. 'It's to discuss Lottie and how she's coping without her mother, before the new term starts.'

'I cannot help you.' Genevieve's eyes were flashing. 'You do not trust me. In my country, that is very bad.'

'Dad, Dad!' Lottie was at the door, taking in the scene with wide eyes. 'What's happened?'

'Your father says I am a thief!' Genevieve was crying now. 'I go now. Goodbye, little Lottie. I shall miss you.' She was hugging his daughter. 'You will miss me too, *piccolina*. Yes?'

'Dad!' Lottie's stricken face turned to him. 'Stop her.'

Too late. Genevieve had locked her door. On the other side, he could hear the sound of her opening drawers and slamming them before emerging with her suitcase. 'At least let me give you a lift to the hotel,' he pleaded, now wondering if he'd been too harsh.

'No.' Her eyes flashed. 'I have called a taxi on my mobile. And I will pay for it with my father's money. NOT yours!'

Yes, Paula said rather wearily. Lottie could come to them the next day and Antoinette would look after her although she'd have to take her shopping in the afternoon. She hadn't quite got round to buying school uniform for the new term.

'You don't seem to have much luck with au pairs,' she remarked tightly when Matthew dropped off Lottie the following morning.

'Don't,' he groaned, realising as he spoke that he'd forgotten to shave that morning *and* that he'd left his tie behind. 'I'm afraid I haven't had time to give Lottie breakfast.'

Paula gave him a worried look. 'Are you all right, Matthew?'

'Fine,' he said quickly. 'Just a bit pushed. I've rung the agency and they're going to see if they can find me someone else. I'm going to give it one last go and then … well, I don't know.'

He paused, half hoping that Paula would offer to let Lottie come back to her house until he returned from work.

'She could go to the after-school club, couldn't she?'

'Yes but it finishes at six and I'm not back until later. Anyway, thanks for today. See you later.'

By the time he got into the office, he was twenty minutes late for a meeting with the new client that Karen had organised. 'You look as though you've been through it,' she said, taking in his dishevelled appearance. 'Hang on. I think I've got a spare tie in here.' She opened one of her desk drawers and brought out an immaculately pressed blue and white spotted design. She blushed. 'It belonged to my ex-husband. I know it sounds silly but I still keep some of his things. It reminds me of what I used to have.'

That was so sad! His heart went out to this lonely woman whom he had clearly misjudged in the past. 'I don't suppose,' he said spontaneously, 'that you're free tonight?'

'Absolutely! Thank you so much, Matt!' She blushed.

Shit! She thought he was asking her out. 'Actually, I've got a parents' meeting at school to talk about the new term and I don't have a babysitter.'

Now she was blushing again, right up to her eyebrows which looked as though they had never seen a pair of tweezers. 'I'm sorry. Of course. Babysitting.' She was nodding vigorously. 'I'd be delighted. And do I gather that the twenty-pound note wasn't where it should have been?'

He nodded. 'I just don't trust the au pair any more.'

'Well, you can trust me!' She patted his arm rather too familiarly. 'Don't worry. I'll be there.'

'Thank you. I'll give you the address later.'

'I know where you live, Matt.'

'Really?'

For a minute he had this awful picture of her stalking him.

She blushed. 'It's on your file.'

Of course it was. Bloody hell. He was getting paranoid. If he wasn't careful, he'd lose his marbles. He really would.

A few hours later, he emerged feeling drained but exhilarated. The client had approved his plans – raved over them, even – which had restored his confidence. James had produced a bottle of champagne from a filing cabinet and they'd all had a glass, which had left him curiously light-headed and carefree.

'The agency rang,' announced Karen as he walked rather unsteadily back to his desk. 'You're in luck. They've found you a Dutch au pair who's already in this country and can start on Monday.'

'Brilliant!'

'The only thing is that the agency is shut now until then. The woman is taking a few days off. But she gave me all the details. I wrote them down. Here.'

'Jan Michaels.' Matthew glanced at his secretary's notes. Twenty-three years of age with a degree in literature. Non-smoker. That was all right then. No eating fads. Great. Experience with children. Good.

'They needed to know then and there,' added Karen nervously, 'so I'm afraid I said yes. I hope that's all right.'

He nodded. This time it had to work. It really did. 'Sure you don't mind babysitting tonight?'

Karen flushed again. 'It will be my pleasure. It really will.'

He got back as early as he could. The meeting hadn't taken long. It had merely been a short introduction to Lottie's year by Mr Balls who used to be head of Reception.

'How are you getting on?' he'd asked in a way that managed to be caring without being nosily sympathetic.

'We're managing. Childcare is a bit of an issue, though.'

Mr Balls had nodded sympathetically. 'We've got that one to come.'

Of course. He'd heard that he and his wife Gemma, who ran the Puddleducks playgroup, were expecting. 'Congratulations, by the way.'

'Thanks.' Mr Balls's face was shining and Matthew felt an unreasonable stab of envy at his good fortune.

When he got back, Karen was sitting on the sofa watching television. The sitting room had been dusted, he noticed, and the carpet vacuumed, which made him feel rather embarrassed. She'd think he was a slob.

'Everything OK?' she asked.

'More or less.' He glanced around the tidied-up room. 'I'm very grateful to you. Did Lottie go to bed all right?'

She nodded. 'Fell asleep while I was reading her a story, dear little lamb.' Yet there was something in her face that wasn't quite right.

'What's wrong, Karen?'

She flushed again. 'I wasn't sure whether to tell you

this but when I was tucking in Lottie's duvet, I found this under the mattress.' She held out her hand.

It was a wodge of crisp bank notes. Including two twenty-quid notes, each with a black cross in the corner.

'Looks like Genevieve might not have been your culprit after all,' she said quietly. 'I'm so sorry, Matt.'

JILLY'S AU PAIR AGENCY:
GUIDELINES FOR AU PAIRS AND FAMILIES

If you have an emergency, please feel free to ring me on my mobile! Day or night!

Chapter 19

Her mother hadn't been here long but already she had taken over the household. This wasn't unusual. Whenever her mother had stayed in the past, Jilly had had to grit her teeth.

Mum interfered with everything from the lack of alcohol in the house ('I can't believe you don't have any Bombay Sapphire, darling!') to her social life ('You'll get very dull, dear, if you don't go out more').

But this time was different.

Within a short space of time, her mother had somehow managed to clear the entire kitchen table so that you could see the scratched wood beneath again. 'You need to file everything properly,' she'd said briskly.

'I did, Mum. Look.' Jilly had pointed to the pile of folders stacked up against the wall.

Her mother had given her a withering look. 'What you need is an office. But there's not much room, is there? Not with your new arrival! I have to say, Jilly, that I'm very proud of you. Not everyone would take in a pregnant out-of-work au pair.'

The incredible thing was that her mother actually meant it. When Jilly had confessed that Fatima wasn't the cleaner but someone who needed help, her mother had been surprisingly sympathetic. 'It's dreadful the way some of these countries treat women. If she says she can't go home, she'll have her reasons.'

If only her mother's empathy extended to her own daughter!

'I could turn the twins' room into a study but they've had to move into Nick's to make room for you, Mum,' Jilly now said pointedly. 'How about the walk-in cupboard off the landing?'

It was meant to be a joke but her mother's eyes brightened. 'Perfect for storing your files. We'll take the door off. You can empty out the rubbish inside—'

'It's not rubbish.'

'Darling!' Her mother's eyes were fixed on her just as they had been all those years ago when Jilly had announced she was giving up her career in HR to be a full-time mum. 'Do you want to make a go of your little venture or not? I'm giving you the benefit of my business expertise. Frankly, people would normally pay me for this. Now, if you insist on staying in the kitchen, I need to work out a proper filing system. Where's your laptop? Please tell me you've got wireless.'

'Not exactly...' began Jilly.

Her mother let out an exasperated sigh. 'For goodness' sake, child. You're meant to be running a responsible service here. People are paying you to bring reliable helpers into their home, while naive young girls are coming to this country thinking they're going to have one long party with a bit of babysitting thrown in. Recipe for disaster!'

By the end of the week, Jilly had brokered an agreement between Margit and Birgitta and their respective families. She'd also, thanks to Mum, sorted out a 'proper filing system' with a back-up. 'Essential, dear, especially when it comes to husbands. Now talking of David, do I detect a note of tension there?'

Was there anything her mother didn't miss? 'He's just a bit fed up with the agency, that's all.'

'Hah!' Her mother leaned back against the sofa, as though pleased she had struck a nerve. 'That's men for you. Do you think your father liked me working?'

Jilly was taken aback. 'He seemed perfectly happy to me when we were growing up.'

Her mother's face assumed an odd expression which she had never seen before. It was a mixture of hurt and anger. 'That's because I fought tooth and nail to keep our marriage going. Don't look like that, Jilly. You know your father isn't an easy man to live with.'

Were they talking about the same person? Her father had always been the jolly, happy one of the pair. He had certainly been a real hit with her friends' mothers. A bit of a flirt, she could see with hindsight, but in a courteous, old-fashioned way with his trademark cravat and checked shirt.

'Your father has always been one for the ladies,' her mother now said tightly. 'I knew from the day I married him that I'd have to keep on my toes. That's one reason why I started my business, to be honest. Thought it would make me more interesting and distract me from wondering what he was doing during those long "meetings" after work. Don't you think I'd rather have stayed at home and played mother like you?'

Jilly was so shocked she could hardly speak. 'Really?'

'It would have been easier!' Her mother's cheeks were flushed with the drink – she'd had three tumblers already and it wasn't even eight o'clock. 'But my business brought in far more money than his salary as a lecturer and he got jealous. At the same time, he knew he couldn't afford not to stay married. We both liked our style of living. And that's not all...' She stopped. 'Isn't that the front door? Your husband's probably forgotten his keys again.'

Talk about timing, thought Jilly as she reluctantly got up. What on earth had Mum been about to say?

'David—' she began as she opened the door. And then stopped. Because it wasn't her husband at all. It was Kitty Banks, standing next to a very red-looking Heidi. Oh God. Don't say she'd discovered the made-up reference?

'Mrs Collins.' Kitty's tone was clipped and distant. 'I'm sorry to turn up unexpectedly but there's something we need to show you. Go on, Heidi.'

The girl thrust a mobile phone in front of her. On it was a picture of teenage boy who was – there was no other way of putting this – exposing himself. The spotty bottom looked vaguely familiar.

'I don't understand,' she began falteringly.

'Your son, Nick,' thundered Kitty, 'has been sending photographs of himself to my au pair and some of her friends. They've also been sending rude messages. What I want to know is how they got hold of their numbers.'

'I've no idea...' she began. Oh no. Please no. A picture of Nick and his friends, ogling her au pair file in his bedroom, flashed into her head.

'They must have got them from your records,' snapped Mrs Banks as though reading her mind. 'We only used your agency because you were local and I thought we'd support you. But you've let us down. Look at that poor girl who was murdered! And have you heard what happened to Marie-France?'

'No?' Jilly felt a chill go through her. 'What?'

'She let some burglars in and they locked her in her room. Luckily they're all right but—'

'That's awful. I need to ring her immediately.'

'Not until you've sorted this out first.'

'Is something wrong?' Her mother's cool voice, amazingly level after all those gins, came up behind them.

'It's all right, Mum.'

'I'm not just your mother, dear.' She flashed a challenging smile at Kitty Banks. 'I'm your business adviser. Now why don't you come inside, all of you, and we will discuss the matter. I am sure we can sort out some resolution.'

Jilly had to hand it to her mother. She was calm, firm and yet understanding at the same time. Yes, she agreed. Of course it was unfortunate but no harm had been done, especially if Mrs Banks was prepared to accept a free au pair placement when Heidi's stay ended. 'These teenage boys can be so difficult to bring up with their raging hormones,' she'd added with a sigh. 'Girls are so much easier.'

And Mrs Banks, who didn't have sons and looked as though she wouldn't know what to do with a stuck-in-the-zip problem, had nodded. 'I must say, I'm very glad I didn't have any myself. They seem, well, very boisterous.'

'Exactly,' her mother had replied and somehow, within half an hour and another couple of drinks (it turned out that Mrs-Banks-but-do-call-me-Kitty was quite partial to Bombay Sapphire too), the matter was resolved.

'Shouldn't we have made Nick come down and apologise?' Jilly asked afterwards.

Her mother had given her an are-you-daft look. 'And put him off sex for life? Don't be ridiculous. He was merely doing what any teenage boy would do if he found a list of women and their phone numbers. It was your fault, dear, for keeping your files in the kitchen. Goodness me! If you knew how hard I had to work at keeping our address book away from your father. He was always ringing up my friends to suggest "coffee".'

'Please, Mum,' she began. 'I don't want to hear—' but her mother was already calling up the stairs.

'Nick? Are you there? Come down, would you?'

'I thought we weren't going to tell him off?' said Jilly.

'I said we shouldn't reprimand him in front of some - one else. Giving him some firm guidelines is a different matter.'

Nick, who, from the look on his face, had heard the commotion, came skulking down with his headphones lying forlornly round his neck. Oh my God. He'd sprouted a spiky orange cockatoo hairstyle like his friend.

'Go on then,' he said challengingly. 'Tell me you don't like my hair.'

293

Jilly took a deep breath. 'Actually—'

'It's very nice dear.' Her mother flashed her a warning look. 'But what we really want to know is whether you are responsible for handing out your mother's au pair numbers to your friends?'

'No.' He tweaked the top of his gel hairstyle defiantly as he spoke.

'Come on, Nick. Don't lie to me. I'm your grandmother, not your mother.'

'I didn't *give* them, Gran. I *sold* them.'

'You what?' The crinkly lines around her mother's eyes deepened in amusement. 'Clever boy. A natural entrepreneur. I like it.'

'Nick, that was wrong!'

He shrugged. 'Your file was in the kitchen, Mum. Anyone could have looked at it.'

Her mother gave her a 'see' look.

'Well, I want you to tell your friends to destroy all those numbers and not make any more calls.'

Nick gave her a rueful look. 'That's a bit difficult.'

'Why?'

''Cos I've spent the money already and, 'sides, they've already contacted quite a few.' He grinned. 'One of my mates has actually got a date with some blonde from Scandinavia.'

Her mother looked impressed. 'Scantinavia. That's what your grandfather calls it. Well, Jilly. Looks like Nick's got more mettle than I'd given him credit for. You'll go far, my boy. Well done.'

Nick's face shone. 'Thanks, Gran. I really like having you here. It's cool.'

'Is that so.' Jilly felt disgruntled and, in a stupid way,

left out. 'Well, while you two congratulate each other on interfering in my business, I've got a phone call to make.'

Going into the kitchen, she rang Marie-France's number. 'I've just heard about the burglary. Are you all right?'

Marie-France's voice was small. 'I think so.'

'Can I come round and see you tomorrow?'

'Could you come tonight?' Marie-France's voice dropped. 'My family is out and it is easier to talk.'

Jilly glanced at her watch. It was already halfway through the evening and David still hadn't returned. Not even a *might be late* text. 'Sure. I'll be there as soon as I can.'

Mum would look after the kids. Marie-France's voice suggested this was more important.

'It was very frightening.'

Marie-France's face was pinched as they sat in Dawn's kitchen, which was bigger than the entire ground floor of her own house. The children had done their homework, she assured her solemnly, and were now in bed.

'The buggers lock us in the room for ages.'

'I think you mean burglars.'

Marie-France nodded. 'That's what I say. So I play my guitar with the children to make them forget. Then I give them big cuddles.'

Jilly could just picture it. Marie-France was a kind-hearted girl and brave too. Many girls of that age would have been freaked out!

'Then I hear another car and, thank God, it is Phillip.

He is come back because he forgets his phone. He calls the police and I tell them what is happening. The buggers, they take many things and now Dawn is angry with me because I let the first man in.' Her eyes swelled with tears. 'I make mistake. I think he is someone I know.'

What a nightmare! 'I can't believe Dawn didn't ring to tell me this.'

Marie-France shrugged. 'She is very busy with her "friend".'

'Her friend?'

Marie-France lowered her voice. 'She has a lover who comes here nearly every day. Phillip, he doesn't care.'

That was awful! 'Do you want to carry on living here? I have other families you could go to although they're outside the town and not so central.'

Marie-France bit her lip. 'I consider it but I wish to remain in Corrywood and besides, I make friendship with Tom now. He is nice to me since the buggers.'

'Burglars.'

'No.' Marie-France shrugged. 'I know what I mean. They are bad men.'

'You poor thing.' Jilly gave her a hug. 'You were so brave!'

'*Brave!*' Dawn's voice came from the front door. 'Is that what you call letting strangers into our home! I'm glad you're here, Jilly, even though you didn't have the courtesy to tell me you were coming. I want to com - plain about this girl you've set me up with. I've lost several pieces of jewellery as well as furniture, including a beautiful new gold clock in the hall—'

'Hey.' Phillip appeared behind her. 'We've been through this, Dawn. It wasn't Marie-France's fault. She thought she knew the intruder.'

Jilly noticed Marie-France shooting a grateful look at Dawn's husband. He was very good-looking, certainly, with a slightly Moroccan-looking swarthiness about his complexion, but there was something about his suave manner that made her feel uneasy. And unless she was mistaken, he seemed rather fond of Marie-France. Just look at the way he was casually draping his arm around her shoulder in supposed reassurance. Dawn's face was livid!

'I'm concerned about my girls' safety,' Jilly began. 'Marie-France has been through a very frightening experience. Most girls would have packed their bags by now. Frankly, I think you ought to be congratulating her, Dawn, instead of criticising her.'

Goodness! Where had that come from? Jilly had never heard herself sound so firm – it must have been watching her mother in action earlier on.

Phillip was nodding in keen agreement. 'We've suggested to Marie-France that she takes a couple of days off.'

'Have we?' Dawn's whiny voice sliced in. 'But I need her to cook for my dinner party on Friday.'

'Is it for children?'

'No, Jilly. Of course it's bloody not for kids.'

'Then she shouldn't be doing it! I gave you a list of an au pair's duties and it states quite clearly that she can be asked to make children's food but not cook just for adults.'

Marie-France reddened. 'I do not object.'

'See?' added Dawn sulkily. 'I can't help it if she offers, can I?'

'But we'll pay her extra,' cut in Phillip. 'Won't we, darling?'

By the time she got home, Jilly felt quite pleased with herself. It had been important to go round to show Dawn face to face that Marie-France had someone to look after her interests. She'd made the point about safety *and* she'd made sure that Marie-France was paid more money for those extra 'duties'.

'Where have you been?' David met her in the hall. 'I was worried stiff about you.'

'I told Mum I had to go out to deal with a problem with one of my girls.'

'But it's nearly ten o'clock, Jilly.'

'Where were *you* then? You didn't say you were going to be late.'

'I had a meeting.' He sounded evasive. 'I've got to go to bed soon or I won't be able to get up for work tomorrow.'

'Let me make you something to eat.'

'There's nothing left in the fridge. Fatima has hoovered it up.'

'There's no need to be sarcastic.'

'Isn't there? In a few months, I've lost my wife or as good as. One of our bedrooms has been taken over by a pregnant au pair who's always ravenous. And now your mother has come to stay. Anyone else I ought to know about?'

'My mother is *helping* me. And you asked her down.'

'My mistake. She's not helping our marriage. And nor,' he added, stomping up the stairs, 'is this bloody agency of yours!'

That night, Jilly couldn't sleep. David was acting like some Victorian husband. She had a right to a career, didn't she? Yet since she'd set up Jilly's Au Pair Agency, she'd lost her best friend, neglected her kids and was now on the verge of losing her husband too. Was it really worth it?

'Jee-lee!'

Now what? Reluctantly, Jilly got out of bed and fumbled her way through the dark to the landing where a heavily pregnant Fatima was clutching her stomach. 'I have pains. I see the doctor.' She sank down on the top of the stairs and gazed up at Jilly with calf-like eyes. 'Very bad pains. Plis. Help me.'

Chapter 20

It was so embarrassing, thought Marie-France. Everyone was talking about the burglary and now it was on the front page of the local paper. They had even managed to get hold of a picture of her – Dawn had apparently given one to the reporter without asking her permission. And rather than praising her for keeping the children calm during what was a very frightening time, Dawn kept bursting into tears because she had lost some 'priceless' rings and necklaces, not to mention that ornate gold clock.

But what really made Marie-France feel uncomfortable was that the couple had asked her to lie!

'I don't think you ought to tell the police that you let them in,' Phillip had said firmly on the night of the burglary. 'It might invalidate the insurance. We could just say that they got in through the downstairs cloakroom. The window was open, right?'

'But what about fingerprints?' she had asked. 'They won't find any.'

'Thieves often wear gloves.' Phillip brushed away her concerns as though they were irrelevant. 'And we'll pretend we forgot to lock the security gate. Please do this for us, Marie-France, otherwise we won't get any of our money back.' He gave her a disappointed look. 'After all, if you hadn't let them in, we wouldn't be in this mess.'

So she had done what he asked. Explained in shaky English – because she really did feel shaky – that she had been with the children in the TV den when the men had just burst in. Luckily, Tom and Tatty Arna didn't contradict her but even so, she felt very uneasy, especially when the policewoman was so understanding.

Meanwhile, instead of being grateful that she had lied for them, Dawn carried on moping around the house with a pinched, pained expression on her face and when she gave Marie-France her instructions for the day, she stood several feet away as though she didn't want anything to do with her.

'She's upset,' said Phillip softly when he came to find her in the library where she was dusting the false spines of the books as the cleaner wasn't there any more. 'Poor Dawn lost some stuff which had great senti-mental value for her.'

'What about the children?' Marie-France had demanded fiercely. 'She should be glad they is safe.'

'*Are* safe,' corrected Phillip kindly. 'You're right. She should. But Dawn's priorities aren't exactly the same as yours and mine.'

She liked the way he said that. '*Yours and mine.*' It suggested they had more in common than him and Dawn. And it made her feel appreciated and cared for.

He touched her arm. 'I think you were very brave. You must have been scared. Are you sure you didn't recognise the men from the photographs the police showed you?'

She nodded. '*Absolument!*'

Phillip shook his head ruefully. 'I'm sorry this has

302

happened to you. I have to say that I admire you for your courage! Most au pairs would have packed their bags by now and gone back to France.'

Marie-France dropped her voice. 'It is because I need to find a friend of my mother's.' She hesitated, wondering whether to tell him the truth. 'I think he is my father.'

His face registered surprise. 'Really?'

'She had a relationship here when she is au pair. That is why I ask for the telephone dictionary when I arrive.'

Phillip nodded. 'I'm beginning to understand now.'

Did he? But what would he say if he knew about the newspaper notice and the little note she'd put in the local newsagent?

'Marie-France,' murmured Phillip.

Mon Dieu! He was actually lifting her chin with his finger and forcing her to look at him! The familiarity of the gesture almost made her heart stop.

'Why do I think there is something you are not telling me?'

The way he was holding her chin made it impossible not to look straight at him. Her gaze wavered. She had to come clean. 'The bugger,' she began weakly. 'I let him in because I think I know him. I put an advert for my father in a shop that sells papers. And in the local paper too. You did not see it, no?'

Phillip's eyes hardened unexpectedly. 'Dawn and I don't read the local rag. In fact, she doesn't read, full stop. Please tell me you didn't put our *address* in it too?'

She nodded, suddenly feeling very stupid.

'But that was a crazy thing to do! No wonder we got done over.'

His harsh voice brought tears to her eyes.

'I am so sorry.'

He let go of her chin and walked up and down the room, head down and silent as though he was thinking. 'And you didn't tell the police about this advert?' he said at last.

She shook her head. 'I think they send me to prison.'

He gave a short laugh. 'They wouldn't do that but Dawn would go nuts.' He looked at her now in a kinder way as though she was forgiven and she was filled with gratitude. 'We've got to keep mum about this.'

'Mum? There is another mother here too?'

Phillip gave her another of his lovely smiles. 'It's an English expression. It means we've got to keep quiet. Or Dawn might sack you. It would also confuse the insurance form, which is complicated enough as it is. Do you agree?'

Of course she did! At the moment, she would have agreed – almost – to anything that the *gentil*, handsome Phillip suggested. He was her only protector apart from Jilly and besides he reminded her of the English teacher at school on whom she'd had a teenage crush.

After that, whenever she and Phillip passed in the kitchen or in the lounge, he would give her a conspiratorial wink as though to say 'We are in this together' and that sent tingles down her spine. Out of loyalty to her host, Marie-France mentioned none of this to Jilly when she came to see if she was all right. Nor did she mention it to Maman in her phone calls.

If Thierry had been there, she might have told him but according to Maman, he was still travelling.

The news made her feel jealous and abandoned. When she'd suggested travelling together, months ago, her boyfriend had declared it was impossible to take time off work. Well, he was doing that now, wasn't he? And if he was stupid enough to race off without letting her explain about the photograph, that was his problem.

Meanwhile, there was no hiding the theft from the other au pairs, who had all heard of it through their employers and fell on her when she arrived at class.

'*Mon Dieu*, Marie-France, are you all right?'

'Did they try to rape you?'

'How did you escape?'

'Did your employers give you a big reward?'

The questions were endless and continued through - out the class when their English teacher heard about it. 'I think,' she said, sitting on the desk with her legs crossed, 'that we should have a lesson on security. Marie-France, you were very brave but you were also very lucky.' Her face looked sad. 'You may have heard of the au pair who was murdered at the beginning of the summer. I know it was in London but she actually worked in Corrywood for a short time.'

Some of the other girls, who were new, made some shocked murmurs.

'And there have been more recent attacks on au pairs in London.'

Another ripple of concern ran through the class.

'There are some very important safety rules,' continued their teacher, getting up and walking to the blackboard. 'First, we must never give our families' address or phone number to strangers.'

Marie-France felt herself going red. Had someone said something about the advert?

'Secondly, we must never talk to strangers—'

'Then how are we going to get boyfriends?' one of the girls called out and the others laughed. It made the atmosphere slightly lighter but Marie-France still left the class feeling cross with herself. She had done something stupid in this quest to find her father yet she was still no nearer in tracking him down.

Maybe, Marie-France told herself crossly, she should have stuck to her original plan and gone to the Sorbonne.

'Coming up to London with us tomorrow?' asked Heidi running to catch her up as they walked down the road. 'We're going clubbing. *Ja?*'

'Is Antoinette coming too? I can't stand her. Such a tart. And she really neglects her little girl.'

Heidi made a face. 'Difficult to stop her joining in. But we don't have to have anything to do with her. There's a whole crowd of us. Come on! It will be fun and you need something to distract you.'

It was tempting after everything that had happened. 'OK. Yes. Thank you. I will come.'

'Mary-Frunch! You look beautiful!'

Little Tatty Arna was tugging at Marie-France's black sparkly skirt which she had teamed up with black leggings.

'Thank you, *ma chérie*.'

'Do you *have* to leave us?' Tom gave her a sulky

306

look. 'I want you to give me another guitar lesson.'

Incroyable! Since the burglary, the boy had been so much nicer to her. He'd also become really interested in learning to play; thank heavens she'd had the guitar in her room when they'd been locked in. Goodness knows how they would have managed without the distraction.

'I promise that I will give you a lesson tomorrow.'

He crinkled his face. 'Can't you do it tonight?' He looked up at her beseechingly. 'We want *you* to babysit, not horrible Mrs Pooface down the road. She makes us go to bed at nine o'clock and she takes away our iPads.'

'Quite right too!' Her heart gave a little flutter as Phillip came into the room. She could feel his eyes taking in her outfit approvingly. How good he looked in that crisp pink and white striped shirt over jeans and that nice pine smell which grew stronger as he came up to her.

'Stunning,' he murmured so only she could hear. Then he raised his voice. 'Marie-France deserves her evening off, kids. She's worked very hard. Now you can go and watch television while Mum gets ready and I'll run Marie-France to the station to meet her friends.'

'It's all right,' she began.

'No. I insist. I need to go out anyway to get some - thing. Come on or you will be late!' He gave her an apologetic shrug. 'I'm sorry. I couldn't help over-hearing you talking on the phone to one of your friends about your arrangements.'

She was both flattered and taken aback that he'd

been eavesdropping. 'You really *did* learn to speak good French, when you were working in Paris.'

He gave a small shrug as though he was pleased with the compliment. 'I also had a girlfriend from Nantes, long before Dawn, of course. Better not talk about that – she's terribly jealous.' He gestured that they ought to leave. 'Dawn is still getting ready and if I don't nip out for some fags, I'll never make it through the evening.'

It felt so good to be in the car with him! So right! As she stretched out luxuriously in the front of his car, she took a little sideways peep at him. Phillip was so handsome and he seemed to really care about her happiness, much more than Dawn.

'Are you sure you feel all right to go out after your terrible experience?'

'*Bien sûr*. I was not hurt.'

'No, but it must have been frightening. You must be careful in London, you know.' His hand accidentally brushed her thigh as he changed gears. 'Sorry. Just make sure you don't give out your address again.' He laughed but in a way that suggested he was serious.

'I won't.' She gestured at the group of girls who were already waiting. 'Just here will be great. Thanks very much.'

Without thinking, she leaned forward and kissed him lightly on both cheeks as she would have done a neighbour at home if he had given her a lift. Too late, she remembered this wasn't common in England. He seemed slightly taken aback but also pleased. 'Have a good time, Marie-France.' He pressed a twenty-pound note into her hand. 'That is for some drinks. No, I insist. *Au revoir*.'

She watched him drive off, wishing for a minute that *she* was Dawn going out with him that night. No. That was terrible! He was a married man. She and Maman might be alike in many respects but not in that one.

'Was that your family?' asked Antoinette excitedly, tottering towards her in a ridiculous short skirt and high spangled heels.

Marie-France nodded.

'You were very familiar, *ja*?' twinkled Heidi.

Marie-France shrugged. 'He is a good man. And do not look like that, you lot. I am not that kind of girl.'

Heidi shrugged. 'My mother's friend came to England and married the father of her family. I would not say no if I had a father like that but mine is old and wrinkly. I see it when he comes out of the bathroom wearing nothing. I think he hopes I fall for him but he makes me feel sick even though he is immensely rich!'

She made a face and everyone laughed.

'Right,' announced Antoinette. 'Let's go. We want to make the most of our night in London, don't we?'

Marie-France had heard of London clubs before but she hadn't realised they could be so loud and so busy. She enjoyed the looks that she was attracting from boys pretending to be men with their spotty faces and pointed shirt collars. None of them attracted her in the same way that Thierry did but it was nice to be admired, especially when she was getting more attention than Antoinette.

'You want to dance?' asked one youth, who didn't seem to have as many spots as the others. So she did. Whirling and twirling to the throbbing music helped to put the last few ghastly weeks behind her. Then there was a slow dance and he held her to him, tracing her back with his finger. It was not completely unpleasant if she closed her eyes and pretended it was Thierry.

Yet somehow a picture of Phillip kept coming into her head instead and she found herself wondering what it would be like if the two of them were close like this. When she came back to find the others, they were hanging together with a group watching the room with narrow eyes. Something smelt funny.

'You are smoking?' she asked Antoinette angrily. How stupid. They could get caught!

'Of course.' The girl offered her a roll-up. 'You want some?'

'No thanks.' Marie-France had never done drugs. Nor did she drink heavily like her friends were doing right now. She'd seen her own mother get out of control often enough and she didn't want to do the same.

'I am bored,' said Antoinette suddenly. 'We will go, yes?'

'I'm enjoying myself,' protested Marie-France. It would serve Thierry right, she thought to herself, if one of these boys asked her on a date. That would show him not to leave in a huff before she could explain and then go travelling without her.

'Then you can stay on your own.'

'*Nein doch*, Antoinette,' said Heidi crossly. 'That's not fair. Remember what the teacher said about sticking together.'

Antoinette shrugged. 'It's up to her.'

Not wanting to stay on her own, Marie-France

310

filtered out with the others into the night. There were so many lights! So many people! So much going on compared with Corrywood.

'I want to go shopping.' Antoinette had a gleam in her eye.

'Thought you said you were broke,' pointed out one of the others, Vivienne.

'So what? I can look, can't I?'

Amazingly, some of the shops were still open, including a clothes shop with rails of jeans and tops hanging outside. *Qu'est-ce qu se passe?* To her horror, Marie-France saw that Antoinette had slipped a blue silk T-shirt into her bag and started running off down the street. The sharp-eyed shop assistant had noticed!

'Stop,' yelled the girl but Antoinette was a fast runner. Marie-France looked round in panic for the others but they too had scarpered. 'No you don't,' said the shop girl as she made to run off too. 'You're coming this way.'

'It is not me.' Marie-France furiously tore at the girl's jacket.

'Stop it. You're hurting me.'

'I try to explain…'

'You can explain to the police. Now shut up and come into the back.'

It was awful having to be interviewed by the police *again*!

'I do not take anything,' Marie-France explained over and over to the policewoman, who looked more like her mother's boyfriend's dog with that face. Why did Englishwomen not wear lipstick?

311

'But you knew the other girls involved?'

Marie-France hesitated. If she admitted as much, then Antoinette would be charged. Much as she disliked the girl, they were both French after all.

'I do not understand,' she lied.

The policewoman rolled her eyes. 'Let me repeat it then in clear simple terms. Were those girls friends of yours?'

'No. I met them tonight.' It was so easy to lie that she believed herself!

The policewoman hesitated. 'If there was more evidence, I'd charge you. But I'll be kind and let you go on condition that you're more careful about the company you keep. Got it?'

Gratefully, Marie-France escaped out into the night air, hoping that the others would be waiting. But they were nowhere to be seen! Now she regretted standing up for Antoinette. Furiously, she made her way to the *metro*, which the English confusingly called the 'tube'.

'Please.' She tried to attract the attention of a woman walking past with a baby in her arms, even though it was nearly midnight. 'Can you tell me how to find Maril Bone?'

The woman walked on as though she hadn't heard but a nice man in uniform at the barrier told her to change at one station and then follow the signs to somewhere else up one escalator and then down another. It was all so confusing. By the time she got there, Maril Bone was deserted.

'Please. When is the next train to Corrywood?' she asked a man in an orange uniform. He consulted his chart. 'Five forty a.m., ducks.'

Tomorrow morning? Her heart did a little nauseous flip. That meant she would have to crash down here on the ground for the night. Marie-France's eyes filled with tears.

'Haven't you anywhere to kip, love?' It was a tramp shuffling up to her with brown baggy trousers held together at his waist. She could smell the urine from here! 'You can stay with me if you like at my place. Look.' He gesticulated towards a sheet of cardboard on the ground. Then he leered. 'Come on. Don't be shy. I know what you girls really want.'

Mon Dieu! He was undoing his trousers! Marie-France's skin goose-pimpled with terror as she backed away. You need to be street-wise in London, her English teacher had said. Remember that poor au pair who was murdered.

Gasping, she ran out of the station and on to the street by the taxi rank. What was she to do now? Marie-France prided herself on being strong but now she was scared. Really scared. The other girls – even Heidi – had abandoned her. She didn't have enough money for a cab let alone a room for the night. There wasn't a train until the next morning. And she was freezing. Absolutely freezing.

If you run into trouble, just give me a bell. Phillip's words came back to her.

Of course! She could ring the family. It was late, certainly, and Dawn would be furious but even she, surely, would see that it was better than sleeping on the streets. Her fingers shaking with cold and fear, Marie-France searched for her phone in her bag and dialled the personal mobile number he had given her.

313

'Not a problem,' he said in a wonderfully calm and reassuring voice when she explained the situation. 'Just sit tight.'

But where? She didn't want to go back into the station where the tramp was lurking. And there wasn't anywhere to sit outside.

'*Ing*-land, *Ing*-land!'

Marie-France stood in the shadows as a big group of football supporters lurched their way past, singing and roaring.

'*Ing*-land, I*ng*-land.'

Angleterre! Pah! At the moment, the last place Marie-France wanted to be was this wet windy country where her boss was a complete cow, a rude shopkeeper had accused her of stealing and her own father seemed to have vanished into thin air. For two pins – to use this ridiculous language! – she'd go straight home now.

'Want to come with us, love?' one of the louts yelled out. Another blew her a kiss – ugh! – but she ignored them and thankfully they passed on.

This was so horrible! She shivered, wrapping her pink pashmina around her. And it was beginning to drizzle too. Still, there was nothing for it but to wait. In the meantime, she felt tempted to ring Thierry. Just to hear his voice. To feel comforted.

'*Salut, c'est moi…*'

It had gone straight through to answerphone. Well, he would see the missed call and, if he cared, might ring back. Putting her mobile back in her bag, Marie-France's fingers closed around the little French/English dictionary she carried everywhere. Might as well use

314

the time to brush up on those impossible verbs and tenses.

I love.

I did love.

I would have loved.

I should love.

Finally, after nearly an hour, she spotted a little red sports car with the number place PHIL 1. Marie-France felt a flood of relief as she ran towards the passenger door, this time remembering to get in on the left. '*Merci! Merci mille fois!*' Leaning towards her rescuer, she planted a big kiss on each of his cheeks.

Phillip, so sexy in his leather jacket, looked flushed but pleased. 'Sounds as though you had a bad time. What happened exactly?'

So she told him about being pulled in by the shopkeeper even though it wasn't her fault and then his face seemed to flicker slightly. 'Better not tell Dawn this,' he said. 'She might not see it your way.'

Another secret!

He patted her leg reassuringly. 'It's all right. I believe you but not everyone would. Now I'll turn on the radio and you can have a nap if you like. You look all in.'

All in? What did that mean? Too tired to ask, she found herself sinking into a deep sleep, only waking when his voice said, 'We're here.' With a start, she woke up, taking in the house that was still partly lit up. Thank goodness. For the first time since she'd arrived, Dawn and Phillip's house felt like home.

'*Merci, encore.*'

'Not at all.' Phillip's face moved towards her and for a minute she thought he was going to kiss her. Part of her knew she ought to push him away but another part of her wanted to feel his mouth.

'What the fuck do you think you're doing!'

She jumped.

Dawn's face was at the side of the car. 'Seducing my husband like that, you dirty little slut. You're sacked, Marie-France. Get out. Get out of my house! Now!'

A 25-year-old Lithuanian au pair was attacked in Bow last night. Her phone and bag were stolen but she was not seriously harmed. Police are investigating a possible link with the murder of a Bulgarian au pair in Hyde Park in July.

Chapter 21

How could she have done this? Matthew asked himself over and over again that night. How could his sweet little Lottie have systematically stolen the clutch of twenty-pound notes that he had hidden in his various traps for Genevieve and then declared with a face that would melt butter that of course, Daddy, she didn't know where the money had gone.

His daughter had wilfully allowed the poor girl to take the blame! Even worse, she had done the same to all the previous au pairs that summer, getting them into trouble in different ways.

Some of it could just have been seen as childish japes but the consequence for Sozzy had been so grave that Matthew could hardly bear to think about it.

It was time for a firm talk with Lottie. So the morning after Karen's discovery, he tackled the subject over breakfast. 'Lottie. Do you remember all that money that's gone missing recently?'

Her eyes widened. She didn't even look embarrassed. Matthew felt a hollow beat of apprehension in his chest. 'Karen found it hidden under your mattress last night when she went to tuck you in after you'd fallen asleep.'

Immediately her cheeks developed two small red spots just as her mother's had done when he'd told her about the text. If Sally hadn't left her phone behind before going to work on the day he'd found out about her affair, he might never have been any the wiser. Maybe that would have been best...

'You don't think I put the money there, Daddy?'

He had to hand it to her. She was a good actress. Frighteningly so for her age. 'Well, who else might have done, Lottie?'

She shrugged. 'The tooth fairy?'

'I don't think she carries that much cash.'

'What about Karen? She might have found it and—'

This was too much! 'Karen had never been in the house before. She did me a big favour by babysitting last night and it's naughty of you to try and get her into trouble. It was *you*, wasn't it, Lottie? You stole the money to try and get Genevieve the sack just like you left an unkind note for Sozzy so she wouldn't stay and just like you told Berenice it was all right to try on Mummy's clothes.'

Lottie's blue eyes filled with tears. 'You're being horrid to me, Daddy. I'm going to tell my teacher when I get to school.'

He had a sudden vision of some more made-up stories which, this time, might be directed at him. Christina had warned him of this. What was it she'd said again? Something about bereaved children entering a fantasy world in order to escape.

'Why don't we tell Bryony about this,' he suggested, trying to put his arms around her. Bryony was the child bereavement counsellor whom Lottie was still seeing on and off. However, Matthew was beginning to think that she wasn't really helping. He'd had his doubts right from the beginning; she was only in her early twenties, which was surely too young to understand half of the things that he and Lottie had gone through.

She pushed him away. 'I don't want to.'

'Then how about someone else?' The idea came to him in a flash. Christina had already mentioned that she didn't specialise in children but maybe she would consider talking to Lottie.

Her whole body was now heaving with giant sobs. 'I want my mummy. I want my mummy back.'

Matthew's heart felt as though it was being shredded into tiny pieces and he felt sick at the same time. Had he been too hard on her? 'Come here, my little princess.' This time, she allowed him to give her a cuddle. 'Shhh, shhh.' Cupping her head with his hand, he rocked her to and fro on his chest. 'It's all right, Lottie. It's all right.'

'Don't go into work, Daddy.' Her voice was thick with tears. 'I don't want anyone else looking after me. That's why I made them go away. I just want you to stay at home and look after me like you did before.'

'But if I don't go out to work, who would pay the bills and make sure we had enough money to buy food?'

'We could just have alphabet spaghetti.' Lottie looked up at him, her face a bit brighter and more hopeful. 'Or we could move to a little house by the sea.'

It was laughable yet maybe she had a point. That might be the answer. Find a job with more flexible hours and downsize houses.

But not right now. He owed it to James to work out his notice. 'Maybe, princess.'

Her face was shining through the tears. 'Today? Can we move to the seaside today?'

How was it that a child of eight could be so guileless and yet so cunning at the same time? 'Not today but one day.'

Her face fell. 'You always say that and then it never happens.'

He'd remembered thinking the same himself at that age. 'I promise, Lottie. In fact, I'll ring up the office and say that I need to work from home today. Then I'll be able to collect you from school. OK?'

Lottie leaped off his lap and did a little dance. He had a vision of Sally buying her a pair of ballet shoes for her first class at the age of four. 'Thank you, Daddy.'

'But you must realise, Lottie,' he said in a graver voice, 'that stealing is wrong. You must never do that again.'

'I won't, I won't.' She was still dancing round the room, her eyes shining. He felt troubled. Had she just wound him round her little finger without him realising?

'I have to go on working for a few more months,' he continued firmly. 'And while I'm doing that, we're going to have another au pair. She's called Jan. And she's coming after school today.'

Lottie stopped dancing. 'Not *another*.'

'It's only for a short time, I promise.

There was a pout. 'Why?'

'Because. That's why.'

Her face grew sulky. 'That's what Mummy used to say.'

He felt a brief flash of compassion for his dead wife.

'I could go back to Paula's. I don't mind her oh pear. She doesn't have to live in our house with us, does she, Daddy? And she's always on the phone so we can do what we like.'

Matthew didn't like the sound of that but there was no time to argue. He needed to text James to say he wouldn't be able to make that meeting after all – it meant feigning sickness for the first time in his life – and then he had to get Lottie into school.

Right. Everything was ready for Jan. Her room was ready. Lottie had been told she had to behave this time.

Ding dong. The bell! She was here on time, exactly as she'd promised Karen. He felt rather bad that they hadn't even spoken on the phone but every time he'd called for a 'welcome' chat, it had just rung and rung without even an answerphone. Besides, Karen had said Jan sounded perfect and he trusted her judgement.

'Hi!'

A tall, blond youth stood on the doorstep with a large rucksack on his back. His handshake was firm. Very firm. 'It is very gud to meet your acquaintance.'

Jan? Jan was a man? A Dutchman?

'I'm sorry. I think there's been a mistake. I was expecting a girl.'

The youth's face dropped. 'You do not read my details?'

'Well yes, sort of. But I've been really busy and I must have missed something.'

Something rather important, clearly, Matthew added

silently to himself. 'I'm sorry but I have a little girl. It wouldn't be right. I mean…'

Oh God. Was this going to get him into trouble with the agency. Was there some kind of law against refusing male au pairs? Even if there was, he simply couldn't have a man looking after Lottie. How could he allow a bloke to wash her, make sure she'd cleaned her teeth, tuck her up in bed?

'I am always being rejected because of sex.' The youth was already picking up his rucksack and walking down the path, his head bowed.

Shit. This looked like another awkward call to the agency.

'Sure,' said Paula, checking her thick brown diary which seemed to have 'Pilates' and 'Course Circuits' scrawled on every page. 'I can have her this week. But then I'm going away on a yoga course and my husband is in Singapore. I don't really want my au pair to have another child to look after so I can't help you after that, I'm afraid.'

'Fair enough.' Matthew felt a stab of panic. Lottie would just have to go to the after-school club until 6 p.m. and then he'd leave work early. James would love that.

'Thanks,' he added. 'I'm really grateful.'

'Must dash.' Paula clearly didn't want to talk. 'I'm late for my spinning class.'

The call to the agency didn't go so well. 'Genevieve has been in floods of tears,' said the crisp woman at the other end of the phone. 'She says you accused her of being a thief.'

'I'm so sorry. There appears to have been a mistake.' Matthew felt his skin crawl with embarrassment. 'My daughter was playing a game with money, you see, and she hid it without me realising.'

'Do you know how serious this is? I have a duty of care towards my girls and now I need to find her a home.'

'She could come back here if she likes. In fact, I was going to ask if she'd consider that. Just for a few weeks.'

'I'm afraid not, Mr Evans. Genevieve says she never wants to see you or your daughter again and I can understand that. As for Jan, I told your secretary quite clearly that he was a man. All things considered, I'm afraid I am going to take you off our books. If you read our original contract, you will see that I am entitled to do this under "extenuating circumstances" and that your deposit will not be returned. Goodbye.'

Karen knew? How peculiar! But that still didn't take away the problem of what he was going to do now. Even if he did sign on with another agency, it was unlikely they'd find him a girl by Monday (he knew how these things worked now). And he'd already taken his full quota of holidays. Despite those brave words about handing in his notice, Matthew still hadn't got round to it. How would he pay the mortgage and bills without a salary? Maybe he'd wait another month or two...

The next few days were manic. It was back to the old routine of getting Lottie up early, finding every item of school uniform that seemed to have scattered themselves round the house (had she done that on purpose to try and get out of going?) and then dropping her off at Paula's by 7.30 a.m. so he could get to the office on time before explaining to James that yes, he was sorry but he did have to leave work early again as after-school club ended at 6 p.m.

'Not great, is it?'

No it wasn't. James had been more than generous with his compassionate leave. The condition had been that he would come back to work afterwards. And now he kept letting his friend and partner down.

'I'm so sorry.' He bit his lip. 'I thought that an au pair would solve all my problems – well, some of them. But they don't seem to have worked out.' He laughed nervously. 'I'm beginning to wonder if it's me and not them! All I want is to do the best for Lottie. It's not easy when you have kids.'

James's face, which had been sympathetic until the last sentence, moved away and stood by the window. His voice came out cracked and flat. 'And if you'd tried as long as we have to get pregnant, you'd understand how upsetting it is. Do you have any idea how frustrating it is when the parent brigade accuse you of not understanding this or not understanding that if you don't have kids?' He put his hand up as though wiping away a tear. 'You're lucky to have one. So quit moaning, will you?'

James and his wife had been trying to get pregnant? But he'd assumed they hadn't wanted any. His friend was right too. He *was* lucky to have Lottie. Incredibly lucky. Moving to James's side, he gave him a manly pat on the back. 'I'm so sorry. I had no idea.'

James stepped away, looking at Matthew coldly.

'That's just it. You think you're the only one with problems, don't you?'

Matthew felt as though James had stabbed him in the chest. But once more, his words struck a chord. Did his partner have a point? Was he, as Christina had already suggested, self-centred? Thinking only of his own problems instead of standing in other people's shoes?

He left James's office, deep in reflection and determined to rethink his attitude. As a result, he tried very hard to be understanding with Karen when she apologised effusively for the 'Jan' mix-up. 'I'm really sorry, Matt. I thought I'd explained he was a man.' She touched his arm briefly. 'I must admit that I also thought he might be easier than some of these silly girls you've been having.'

He gave a wry smile. 'You may be right. Perhaps I'm just old-fashioned, but I don't like the idea of a male au pair looking after my daughter.'

Not long after that, Matthew found himself next to a tall, blondish, kind-looking mother at the end of after-school club. He'd seen her before with twins and wondered how she'd managed.

'Hi. How are you doing?' She flashed him a sympathetic smile that he'd learned to recognise over the year. 'I'm Jilly. I knew Sally. Not very well but we used to chat.' She gave him another warm smile and Matthew found himself liking this woman.

'Thank you.'

'How are you getting on?'

Somehow he found himself telling her all about the au pairs who had been driven out of the house and how Lottie hated them, and then, with a deep breath, about Sozzy.

Her eyes filled with tears. 'I heard about that. It must have been awful for you. I run an au pair agency myself – we're still quite new actually – so it sent shivers all down me. It could happen to any of us. These girls come over here, most of them fairly naive, and then they can walk into all kinds of difficult situations. If you want, I'll put you on my list but, to be honest, I've got more families than girls. Still, you never know.'

'Thanks but I think we'll give up on the au pair front. We'll manage somehow.'

'Really?'

No, he wanted to say. Not really. Yet he had to face it. Au pairs weren't for him and Lottie.

He'd just have to think of something else. But what?

EMAIL FROM JILLY'S AU PAIR AGENCY

*Polite reminder to host families! Placement fees are now due two weeks **before** your au pair arrives.*

Chapter 22

Fortunately, Fat Eema's dramatic stomach pains had turned out to be a case of Braxton Hicks.

Her mother had snorted, the way she always did when irritated. 'More like over-eating pains, if you ask me! I'm beginning to agree with David. As soon as she's had this baby, we need to find her a job. And somewhere else to live.'

Perhaps, thought Jilly, it was time for another con-versation with their uninvited guest. The Turkish one, that was. Not Mum. Now where was she? Silly question. By the fridge, of course.

'Fat Eema,' she began. 'I mean Fatima.'

There was a chomping noise and then a large burp as their guest emerged into view with a breadstick in one hand and a pot of yoghurt in the other. 'Yes, Jee-lee.'

'Shall we sit down for a bit?'

The floor shook as Fatima heaved herself down with much groaning, her hands on her enormous stomach as though to protect it. 'Although we like having you here,' began Jilly, 'we feel it might be best if you went back to your family. Yes, I know you say your father would be cross but supposing I had a word with him on your behalf?'

Fatima's big brown eyes were huge with terror. 'You cannot do that. Or he will murder his brother. And my aunt and my cousins, they will be destitute.'

Jilly frowned. 'I don't understand.'

Fatima clutched her hand so tightly that it hurt. Then she looked around as though someone might be listening. 'My uncle,' she hissed in a stage whisper, 'he take advantage of me.'

Oh my God! Jilly felt sick. You heard about these things happening but it was hard to believe they really occurred in a so-called civilised country.

'My father too. He does the same. Since I am twelve years old.'

This was horrendous! No wonder she disliked men so much. 'Does your mother know?'

Fatima nodded. 'Naturally. But she cannot do anything. No one can. This is why I run away.' Her clutch on Jilly's arm tightened. 'Please. Do not make me leave you. I do not know where to go.'

Jilly's mouth was dry. 'Of course we won't. You can stay here. But we do need to make some enquiries.'

Fatima's forehead was beaded with perspiration. 'What kind of enquiries?'

'We need to find out what benefits you're entitled to, if any, and how long you're allowed to stay here.'

'Thank you.' Before she knew it, Jilly was being clasped in a heavy, sweaty embrace. 'You are angel, Jee-lee. I will never forget this.'

Mum came up trumps when she filled her in. 'Poor girl. Mind you, it's not the first time I've heard of stories like this. Leave it to me. I'll do the research. You've got enough on your plate. Now did you see that email I sent out about placement fees?'

She had! Thanks to Mum's business expertise, Jilly's

Au Pair Agency was actually beginning to make money! Anyone who was late with paying up front, received some stiff phone calls. 'I tell them I'm your PA. That is all right, isn't it, dear? It's easier for me to get heavy with them as I don't know them through school like you.'

It wasn't just the outstanding cheques that Jilly's mother sorted out. She was also an amazing networker. 'Your demand is exceeding your supply, isn't it? Now let's see.'

She whipped out her iPhone and began scrolling down her contacts. 'There's Helga who used to be my co-director. She lives in Switzerland now so she's bound to know some girls who need jobs in a boring little safe town like Corrywood. Then there's Erika, my German designer from the seventies. She knows everyone who's worth knowing in Berlin. And of course, there's Suzette in Paris. Remember her? She fed you Smarties to keep you quiet when you came into the office during school holidays. Now you go and pick up the boys from school and I'll email this lot. By the way, I'm going to use my own laptop instead of your computer – I can't think how you manage with yours. It's so slow.'

'Thanks.' Jilly hesitated. 'I'm really grateful for your help.'

Her mother was already typing away. 'What did you say?'

It was just like being a child again when she'd attempt to talk to her mother but not get a reply out of her because she was working. Yet now this was her own home, and Mum, though trying to help, was effectively ousting her from her own job!

'Mum, I'm very grateful for all this but I just wondered how long you're going to be staying.'

'For as long as you want.' The voice was dangerously crisp.

'Won't Dad want you back soon?'

There was a short laugh. 'Not if he's found other things to amuse him.'

Jilly felt a stab of alarm. 'Nothing's wrong, is it? I mean, I know Dad can be a bit...well, rather friendly with other women but he doesn't mean anything by it, does he? It's just part of him.'

'Is that so?' Her mother's voice had a slightly cracked edge to it now. If Jilly didn't know better, she would have thought Mum was about to cry. But her mother didn't do tears. Not even when Jeremy had gone away to school at the age of seven in short trousers and a puzzled look on his face.

'Actually, Jilly, I've decided to stay here for a little longer, if you don't mind. Give your father a bit of space and make him see what he's missing.'

Stay here? She felt another flash of alarm. Having your mother to stay for a few weeks to see the grandchildren and sort out your business was one thing but 'a little longer' sounded ominous.

'Ah, good. Helga has just instant messaged me. There's a girl in her town who's just finished her exams and wants to work near London as an au pair. Perfect. See! I've found you someone already. And by the way, I've put up our placement fee from a hundred and fifty to a hundred and ninety pounds. That should please your husband, shouldn't it?'

Hah! Nothing, it seemed, could please David at the moment. 'What do you mean your mother doesn't know when she's leaving?' he had demanded when she'd told him in a whisper that night in bed.

'I think she and Dad are having problems,' she had whispered back.

'Join the gang.'

'What do you mean?'

He turned to face her in the darkness. 'Well, let's face it, Jilly. Things aren't that great between us either, are they? I'm working my socks off to try and bring the bacon in but when I come back, I never see you any more because you're always on the phone sorting out some crisis or glued to your emails. And now your mother has virtually moved in.'

'You were the one who rang her in the first place!'

'Only because I thought she might make you see sense. I didn't expect her to take up residence. Then there's Fatima. I know it's a dreadful situation but it's not our problem...'

'David, we've been through this. She needs us!'

'So do the kids! You let Nick go out during a school night last week.'

'I didn't let him. He insisted and I couldn't stop him. You were still out.'

'Couldn't stop him? Who's the parent here? And what about the twins? You spent half their birthday party on the phone!'

'Aren't you ever going to let that one go?'

'All I'm saying, Jilly, is that this isn't working.'

There was a sound on the other side of the wall which suggested their row had woken up her mother. 'Are you jealous?' Jilly flashed back.

'Jealous!' David laughed. 'What of?'

'Of the fact that I might just be making a success out of my business, unlike you.'

'Thanks for the reminder.' He moved over to the edge of the bed and, too late, Jilly realised she'd struck a nerve which had been best left untouched.

'I'm sorry.' She reached her hand out towards him in the dark. 'I know you're doing your best. But can't you see I'm trying to do the same?'

'Yes but you shouldn't have to. It's *my* responsibility.'

'That's so old-fashioned...'

'Look, I don't want to talk about it any more. Goodnight.'

As Jilly tossed and turned all night, Fatima's words kept coming back to her. *Your man is not good husband to you.*

That wasn't true, of course. David was suffering from low self-esteem. The old David would never have said those things. But maybe she'd changed too. Running her own business had given her a confidence she'd never had before.

It wasn't just earning money. It was the surprising discovery that she enjoyed working. Loved making decisions that had nothing to do with school uniform or homework. Finding her own self-worth.

There was no way she was giving all that up! Eventually, when the neon light on the bedside alarm clock reached 2.07 a.m., Jilly turned over, with her back to David. Maybe it was time to make some tough decisions.

The following day, she made a huge effort to get the twins to school on time. But just as she was rounding them up and hunting for a piece of missing maths homework, her phone bleeped. It was Marie-France. *Hve been sacked. Pls ring.*

What? 'Hang on, kids,' she called out. 'I've just got to make a phone call. Get into the car and I'll be there in a sec.'

Hastily she returned Marie-France's call. 'It's me, Jilly. What's happened?'

Stunned, she listened to the girl's account.

'I do not have affair with Phillip,' she ended. 'But Dawn does not believe me. He is just friendly.'

Just friendly! She'd heard that before from her own father enough times when overhearing arguments between her parents. It was clear that Phillip's behaviour – she'd always found the man very smarmy on the few occasions they'd met! – had exceeded the boundaries and now Marie-France was paying the price.

'I will have to talk to Dawn,' she began. 'Then if you like, I'll find you another family. There are lots of people on my books who would be glad to have someone like you.'

Even as she spoke, she realised that might not be true. A new family would ask what had gone wrong with the old and there wouldn't be many women keen to take on a girl who had been accused of 'making a play' for the previous host husband.

'Thank you.' The girl ended the call sounding slightly brighter but now Jilly had to ring Dawn. The kids would just have to wait in the car for a few more moments.

'Dawn?' she began but before she could go any further, the woman began to yell in such a shrill, hostile way that Jilly had to hold the handset away from her ear. 'Absolutely disgusting...Mary-France has the hots for my husband...Want her out of the house...Are you kidding? Of course I won't give her a reference...'

All of a sudden, she found herself putting on her mother's voice. 'Actually, Dawn, I'm afraid I disagree. I have grounds to believe that your husband stepped out of line here. He has been rather "friendly", shall we say, towards a young girl who is meant to be living as part of your family instead of acting as an unpaid cook. In our agreement, we clearly state that girls should eat with the family wherever possible but Marie-France has been treated like a servant. So you might care to give her a good reference unless you wish me to take this further. I would like it emailed to me by lunchtime. Goodbye.'

There was the sound of clapping from behind her. Mum had been listening in! Just like she used to eavesdrop on her calls as a teenager.

'Well done, dear. I couldn't help overhearing. You *are* learning, aren't you? Goodness, what's that dreadful noise from your car?'

They both rushed to the window. 'Great,' said Jilly weakly, 'they've turned the radio up to maximum.'

'You go,' said her mother, 'and I'll get on with the

accounts together with Fatima. I've discovered that she's awfully good at figures, apart from her own. Now off you go and don't worry about our agency. I'll soon have it licked into shape.'

But it's *my* agency, Mum, she started to say. Too late. Mum was already on the phone and she had to get the boys to school.

'Mum,' said Harry nonchalantly as they were half-way there, 'I've left my PE kit behind.'

Shit. 'I'm not going back now.'

'But you've got to—'

'There isn't time—'

'Will you shut up, both of you,' said Nick wearily from the front seat. 'Fatima put your stuff in the boot. I saw her.'

Jilly should have been grateful. But it was one more signpost. Maybe she was more like her mother than she realised. More interested in doing her own thing than being a parent.

After dropping off the boys, together with the spotless PE kit that was indeed in the boot, she noticed a little red Mini in the car park that looked familiar. Of course! That had been poor Sally's and there was her nice husband Matthew to whom she'd been talking the other day.

'Hi.' She took in his baggy eyes and shirt that needed ironing. 'How are you doing?'

He shrugged. 'Still trying to work and be there at the end of the school day for Lottie.'

It was then that a big bell went off in her head. 'Actually, if you're desperate, I do happen to have a girl who is looking for work. I was going to offer her to the family at the top of my list, so can we keep this to ourselves? She's French. Very sensible and brilliant with children in my opinion but she's had a bit of a rough ride with another mother.' She glanced around in case Paula was hovering. 'A rather demanding one. You could call it a clash of personalities.'

He laughed shortly. 'That's very kind but I wouldn't subject an au pair to my daughter. She'd run her out of the house.' He sighed. 'Lottie wants me to be at home with her all the time but it's not possible at the moment.'

The poor man stopped as though he felt he'd said too much.

'Everything's possible with my agency!' Jilly found herself sounding like her mother again with that upbeat I-can-sort-you-out tone. 'We pride ourselves on a personal touch. Besides, Marie-France is very feisty so I'm sure she'll cope with your Lottie. You might have read about her in the newspapers. Her family was buggered – I mean burgled – and she was brilliant at keeping the kids calm. Why don't you try her out?'

Matthew hesitated. 'May I think about it?'

Jilly shook her head. 'Of course. But you'd be doing me a huge favour. I want Marie-France to go to a good home and I think she might be just the girl for you.'

It was almost like running an adoption agency! Still, one down and one to go. Going back to the car, she switched on her mobile. This was one call she needed to make in secret, outside the house. A deserted school car park was the perfect location.

'Dad? It's me, Jilly. Can you talk? Good. Now what on *earth* is going on with you and Mum?'

JILLY'S AU PAIR AGENCY:
GUIDELINES FOR FAMILIES

It is natural for au pairs to develop close bonds with the children in their care. Sometimes parents can feel jealous of this.

Chapter 23

Marie-France still felt a hot flush of anger at the memory of Dawn virtually dragging her out of Phillip's car after that terrible night out with Antoinette.

'Slut,' Dawn had hissed. 'How dare you try and make out with my husband?'

'I am not,' she had protested. 'Get off me. You're pulling my hair.'

'I do not care.' Dawn had pushed her into the hall. 'I want you out of my house tomorrow morning. Do you understand? And no, don't try and explain. I saw enough with my own eyes.'

She turned to Phillip, who was shaking his head as though Dawn was an angry child. 'As for you, I want a word. *Upstairs.*'

Marie-France had spent that night in her bedroom, packing and panicking; her usual resolve having deserted her. Where would she go? When she spoke to Jilly the next day, it was plain that it might not be easy to find another family, despite her kind words. Who would want a girl who'd been caught kissing another woman's husband?

This was exactly what had happened to her poor mother! And this was why she had to find her father. To make him pay. Not with money – that wouldn't do anything. But to make him realise how much damage he had caused by not facing up to his obligations all those years ago.

'Please don't go,' Tom had whined, screwing up his little podgy face. 'I'll really miss our guitar lessons.'

Who would have thought, a few weeks ago, that Tom could change so much? He was more interested in the guitar now than his computer or televisions. All he had needed was someone to give him some time.

'I will miss you too,' she said, hugging him. 'But you must ask your mother to find you another guitar teacher. You are very good at it.'

'I don't want you to leave either,' whispered little Tatty Arna. 'It was boring before you came. And you *promised* to put my hair in a chignon.'

'Then I shall do that before I leave today.' Marie-France took her hairbrush out and started to smooth Tatty Arna's long tresses. '*Regarde!* This is how it is done.'

In the end, Dawn did not throw her out that very day, partly because they had a dinner party that night and Cook had called in sick. 'You can stay on for a few more days,' her boss had announced coolly after breakfast as though she was doing her a favour. 'Meanwhile, I want you to make your apricot lamb dish for dinner tonight. We will be having eight to dinner. And tomorrow, if Cook is still ill, you can do your seafood linguini. We will be twenty then.' Her eyes narrowed. 'But on no account are you to talk to my husband!'

Marie-France shot her a cold stare. 'I do not feel like cooking.'

Dawn's face tightened. 'What did you say?'

'I do not cook for a woman who calls me a liar.'

Dawn's eyes were round with disbelief. Luckily, by this stage the children had left the table. That had been another of her small triumphs. When she'd first arrived, they'd munched toast in front of the telly. Now she had managed to get them to sit up, if only for a few minutes.

'How dare you talk to me like that! My husband has told me everything. He said that you rang him and begged him to pick you up and that he feared for your safety. So out of the goodness of his heart, he collected you. He also said that *you* tried to kiss *him* in the car.'

'The first part is true but not the second.' Marie-France's eyes flashed. 'We are *not* having an affair. It is you – with your bald-headed friend. No. Do not deny it. I have seen you. As for your dinner party, you can stuff yourself.'

Marie-France wasn't entirely sure what this meant but she had heard Tom saying it enough times so it must be rude. The effect on Dawn was impressive. Like most bullies, she caved in at the first sign of opposition.

'But I can't cook.'

'Then order in pizza!'

Marie-France spent the rest of the weekend in her room, trawling through various Find-a-Person websites. If only John Smith was not such a common name! Last week, she had tried to ring her mother to ask once more if she could remember anything else about him. Just a small detail might help! But her mobile had been switched off. So she'd called Maurice, who had explained her mother had been sent on a training course.

In fact, Maman had been strangely elusive for some weeks now! Every time she'd called her mobile, she was either 'unable to talk' or it went straight through to answerphone. If it wasn't for Maurice, who had explained her mother was very busy at work, she would have been worried.

Instead, she felt hurt. Clearly her mother wasn't missing her that much! Marie-France thought back guiltily to all the teenage arguments they'd had over the years. Maybe her mother was enjoying the peace and getting on with her own life now. It wasn't a very nice thought.

Today, however, Maurice had told her, her mother would definitely be in. Even though Marie-France still felt hurt, she couldn't wait to hear her mother's voice. Ah, yes! It was answering now. 'Maman? It is me.'

'*Chérie.*' Her mother's voice was sleepy as though she had just woken up. Of course! It was Sunday, wasn't it. The sun would be streaming in through her blue and yellow chintz bedroom curtains and Maman would be lying, no doubt, in Maurice's arms. There would be the smell of proper coffee floating up the stairs and the church bells would be ringing. Marie-France ached with homesickness.

'How are you, Maman?'

'*Très bien, ma chérie. Et toi?*'

'OK. It's been ages since we spoke.' She laughed, trying to make a joke of it. 'You haven't forgotten me, have you?'

'*Ma chère*, I could never do that.' Her mother sounded as though she had a heavy cold. 'You mean the world to me. I have just been busy at work, that is all.'

'You do sound run down. Take it easy, won't you? Listen, I was wondering: is there anything else about my father that you can recall? John Smith. It is such a common name.'

There was a sigh. 'Please do not do this, *chérie*. It is too difficult to find him now.'

'Are you sure you don't remember the address?'

There was a sigh. 'It was so long ago, *ma fille*. I cannot recall.'

Marie-France silently groaned with frustration. She was so near to her father and yet so far. 'Is there anything else about him that you can remember? Anything at all!'

Her mother's voice grew dreamy. 'He was musical, like you. He could play the guitar so that my very heart felt as though it was going to fly away. And he would sneeze. Big sneezes.' She giggled. 'It was very embarrassing sometimes.'

'Sneeze?'

'Yes. He suffered from allergies like you. *So* inconvenient.'

There was the sound of a man's voice in the background. Marie-France had been right when she had pictured her mother in bed with Maurice. 'I need to go, *ma chérie*. You are happy, yes?'

'Very happy, thank you, Maman.' She hesitated. 'Have you heard from Thierry?'

'*Non*. But he is not back. Maybe he is still travelling. Do not worry. You will find someone else. A more educated man. With cleaner hands. You meet someone in *Angleterre* yet? *Non*? That is a pity. *Au revoir, ma chérie*.'

345

Marie-France put the phone down feeling distinctly unsettled. Find someone else? She'd been convinced that Thierry would get in touch but there had been nothing. Maybe he really had gone for good this time. 'You are too young to be tied down,' she told herself sternly. But somehow that didn't ease the ache in her heart.

Then, that evening when she was getting the children's bags ready for school the next day, Jilly rang. 'I have found you a lovely family,' she had said excitedly. 'Not far from where you are now.'

'In Corrywood?' Marie-France's heart leaped.

'Yes. It is a father with a small daughter. But there is only one problem. His daughter does not really want anyone else to look after her. Her mother died nearly a year ago and her father has been at home, caring for her. Now he has gone back to work but she keeps driving away the au pairs.'

Marie-France nodded. 'I have heard through my school. The little girl, she is called Lottie, yes?'

'That's right.' There was a slight pause at the other end. 'There's one more thing too. You may find it a bit awkward living with a single man. People might talk and I am sure you don't want another situation like before.'

'This is not my fault.' Marie-France felt indignant. 'Dawn, she tells lies!'

'I'm just saying that you need to be aware of the circumstances. It wouldn't be a good idea, for instance, to walk around in a dressing gown.'

'I do not do so!' This was not fair! Jilly was sounding much tougher than usual. Did she consider her partly responsible for what happened with Phillip?

'You could start tomorrow if you like, in the evening.'

'Yes. That is good. Thank you.'

The next day, she bid a cold adieu to Dawn and hugged the children goodbye. How she would miss them – even little Tom! Phillip was nowhere to be seen. It hurt to go without saying goodbye…

Meanwhile, Jilly had kindly agreed to pick her up and drop her at the new family. 'You will like Matthew,' she said as they made the short drive to the other side of town. 'He's still suffering, poor man, from his wife's death. Mind you, their house isn't nearly as grand as Dawn's.'

'I do not care.' Marie-France was looking out of the window, watching the houses become smaller. 'I just require somewhere to stay where people do not accuse me of lying.'

Jilly gave her a funny look. 'Please don't mis-understand me, Marie-France. I have no reason to doubt you when you said that nothing happened between you and Phillip. But you are an attractive girl. Some men might be tempted to get the wrong end of the stick and Matthew…well, he's a widower. Probably vulnerable.'

'Wrong end of the stick? Is Meester Evans a violent man?'

'No.' Jilly looked horrified. 'It means getting the wrong idea.'

Marie-France frowned. 'I do not understand.' She drew herself up. 'But I do know that I am a good girl.'

'I'm sure you are.' Jilly stopped outside a modest

terraced house which didn't even have its own driveway. She smiled at Marie-France reassuringly. 'That's why I've kept you on my books. Now here we are. Let's go in, shall we?'

Hah! Even if Marie-France had been an Antoinette, she would not have fallen for Matthew Evans. He was only a little taller than her and rather plump. Yet he had a kind, boyish face etched with frown lines as though he was permanently worried about something. As for little Lottie, she looked as though butter wouldn't melt in her mouth. You would not think she was the *diable* that the others had talked about!

'Let me show you your room,' she announced gaily, skipping up the stairs after Jilly had left.

The door was slightly ajar. 'You go in first,' said Lottie her eyes dancing.

'Please, *you*.' Marie-France knew this game!

Lottie hesitated. 'Mummy always said that guests should go first.'

'*Vraiment?*' Marie-France gave the door a little push without going in. As she did so, something fell from the top of the door. It was a large black plastic spider. 'You want to terrify me, I think?'

Lottie went bright red. 'I didn't know it was there.'

Marie-France grinned. 'I do the same when I am your age. I liked to play jokes on people.' She thought back to the times when she had been small and had resented the attention Maurice had paid to her mother. 'Now you like to help me unpack my things?'

'Are you two all right up there?' called out Matthew in a concerned voice.

'Very fine. I shall descend and make supper, yes?'

Lottie shook her head so that her plaits whirled around. 'Daddy and I have already made you alphabet spaghetti.'

'Delicious!' Marie-France held out her hand. 'I'm starving. *Viens!*'

The table in the corner of the dining room had silver-framed photographs of a young woman smiling with a small baby in her arms. That must be the dead mother, she thought. How sad.

Meanwhile, Lottie was at the head of the table, dishing out the orange pasta which had burnt bits round the edges, watched by her adoring papa. 'It looks delicious, princess!' He beamed. 'Lottie made this on her own, you know.'

Marie-France felt a slight lurch of jealousy. If she'd had a father to grow up with, would he have called her his 'princess'?

'This is yours!' The little girl took care, Marie-France saw, to serve her food from the left side of the dish while she helped her father and herself to the other side.

'It is permitted to swap, yes?' She pushed her plate towards Matthew before touching it. 'My portion is a little too enormous.'

'Of course!'

'No, Daddy—' began Lottie, but it was too late. Matthew spat out the food on the plate in front of him.

'Ugh! Princess, how much salt did you put in this?'

Lottie's face crumpled.

'I am sorry, Daddy.' She shot Marie-France a fierce look.

'Do not worry.' She beamed at the little girl. 'Maybe I could make one of my special omelettes for us all! Come, Lottie. I will show you how it is done.'

Marie-France spent the next few days trying to outwit her small charge. Luckily, her own experiences in sabotaging Maman's boyfriends had taught her to be one step ahead.

Before using the washing machine, she removed a pink top which would most certainly have ruined her other clothes. Every night, before getting into bed, she looked under the duvet and invariably found a variety of odd items including a lizard which she carefully put back in its tank.

When the little girl offered to make her a cup of tea, she took a very small sip first. Just as she'd thought!

'I used to do the same to my mother's boyfriend,' she remarked.

'What?' Lottie's eyes were wide open with innocence.

'Did you use one squirt of washing up-liquid or two?'

'Three,' began Lottie before stopping herself. 'I mean, none.'

Marie-France giggled. 'Do not worry, I will not tell your papa!'

Lottie's face was a picture! Confusion was written all over it but there was something else too. A glimmer of amusement. Well, it was a start!

Meanwhile, Marie-France still wasn't getting any - where with the search for her father. Sometimes, she wondered if he had moved on. After all, Corrywood was a transient place; not like her village where most people stayed for ever. Her father might well have gone to London. Or America. Perhaps he was dead... Marie-France shivered. Still, it was something to breathe in the same air and to walk past shops that he might have gone into.

Then again, supposing, just supposing, that he was looking for her too? What if he had never stopped loving her, just as Matthew loved Lottie? It made her heart ache with what might have been...

The following Saturday, when Matthew had told her that he didn't need her help because he and Lottie were having some 'father/daughter time', Marie-France decided to catch the train into London on her own. She certainly wasn't going with the girls from language class! Antoinette hadn't even apologised since that terrible evening. And even her friend Heidi didn't seem to think she'd done anything wrong by running off. 'We have to look after ourselves, *ja*? But I knew you would be all right. You are strong like me.'

So instead of calling any of the others, Marie-France spent a lovely day doing the sights like the London Eye and a museum called the Vee and Ay. On the way back, she found herself walking through a lovely square in So Ho and then down a street with busy, lit-up wine bars. She was thirsty! Maybe she would have a quick drink before heading back. Threading her way through the crowd, she joined the queue at the bar.

'What can I get for you?' asked the handsome barman in a French accent. Then he did a double-take.

She gasped. 'Thierry?' She took in the mop of black hair, casually flicked over one eye: a style, she knew, that took several minutes to perfect. 'Is that you?'

His eyes were cold. 'Do we know each other?'

Marie-France stared at him. It was his voice. It was his face. He was leaning on the bar in the same casual way. And he still wore the little ring on his right hand that she had given him for his last birthday. 'Thierry Baccall,' she said in a low dangerous voice, 'do not play games with me!'

USEFUL PHRASES FOR GERMAN AU PAIRS

Ja	*(Yes)*
Nein	*(No)*
Vielleicht	*(Maybe)*
Stört es dich, wenn ich rauche?	*(Do you mind if I smoke?)*
Hast du einen Aschenbecher?	*(Have you got an ashtray?)*

Chapter 24

The first thing that Matthew noticed about the new au pair was her singing. Marie-France sang in the shower in the morning – which was, rather embarrassingly, right next to his bedroom so he could hear *every* movement – and she hummed happily while making breakfast. She also made up singsongs to get Lottie to do things she didn't particularly want to do, such as going to school.

'Time to get up,' he heard her chant in a way that lifted the 'up' so that it sounded like a song. Somehow it lightened the atmosphere in the house. In fact, if they'd had her in the first place, they might have been all right.

'I might be a little later tonight,' he told Marie-France. 'Do you mind cooking dinner again?'

Marie-France nodded. 'It will be my pleasure.'

His too, thought Matthew. He had to give it to her; this girl could cook. 'There's only one thing. Lottie is allergic to cheese and she hates the taste. Or at least she has since her mother died.' He stopped, not wanting to reveal personal details to a stranger but at the same time needing to explain something important. 'Sally didn't like cheese either, you see.'

Marie-France raised her eyebrows. 'So it is in her mind?'

'Maybe. But it definitely makes her sick so I'd rather

play safe. Talking of being safe, can you please make sure that you hold her hand when you come back from school? The cars here can go faster than they should.'

'*Bien sûr.*'

She thinks I'm fussing, thought Matthew. Well, so what? He'd already lost his wife; he couldn't lose his only child as well.

'Plis. I ask you something too?'

Here we go, he thought. There was always a catch with these girls. What was it this time? More time off? A pay rise? A contribution towards language school?

'Do you know of someone called John Smith who might live in the area? At least, he used to. He is an old man now. In his sixties, I think.'

What a strange request! 'No, I'm sorry I don't.' As he spoke, he saw disappointment in her face. 'But John Smith is a very common name,' he added. 'May I ask why you're trying to find him if that's not rude?'

Something flickered in the girl's eyes which were, he noticed, a rather striking greeny-blue. 'He is a friend of my mother's when she lives here many years ago.'

'Well, if I hear of him, I'll let you know. Now I must go.' He looked up as Lottie appeared at the door wearing – amazingly – her school uniform. How had Marie-France persuaded her to get ready this early!

He gave her a big hug. 'Goodbye, princess.'

Reluctantly, he went out to his car, aware that their curious neighbour was looking through the nets. She probably thought he was running a brothel with all these girls coming in and out! Unable to resist, he gave a sarcastic little wave. Why was it that some people simply couldn't keep their noses out of everyone else's business?

Karen was already waiting for him with a cup of coffee and a Danish pastry. 'I thought you might not have had time to eat,' she whispered conspiratorially.

He shot her a grateful smile. 'Thanks. What would I do without you?'

She flushed. 'How's the new au pair going?'

It was odd, he thought, how much he'd taken to confiding in Karen. But since she'd come to babysit and actually been in his house, he had felt closer to her. 'She seems pleasant enough and she's a great cook.'

Karen's face seemed to stiffen slightly. 'That's nice for you.'

'But she's quite bossy. She even questioned the fact that Lottie is allergic to cheese.'

Karen clicked her tongue. 'You're her father. You know her better than anyone.'

'Exactly.'

'Thanks. Look, I've got something to tell you, Karen. I'm going to hand in my notice.'

'You've been headhunted!' she gasped. 'I knew it. Your talents are wasted here.'

'No,' he cut in. 'I'm packing it all in. Lottie and I are going to move away. I'll take a lower-paid job somewhere and work hours that fit in with her. It's a gamble but we can't go on like this.'

Karen's face was aghast. 'But that means—'

'Matthew?' James was at the door. 'I believe you wanted to see me about something urgently.' He looked at his watch. 'I've got a three-and-a-half-minute window before my next appointment.'

Right. This was it. Crunch time! Nervously, Matthew followed him and sat down opposite. 'I'm afraid I'm going to hand in my notice.'

James nodded. 'I suspected as much. I've tried to be flexible, Matthew, but your heart hasn't been in it and, to be honest, I think it shows.' He pulled out a file. 'Actually I've been having a look at your contract. When we set up our partnership, we agreed on a three-month termination period. I'd be grateful if you could stick to that to give us time to find someone else. OK?'

Matthew was stunned. He knew he'd let James down but he hadn't expected this! Then again, maybe he ought to have. There had to be a limit on how many times you could let someone down at work. Then he remembered Christina's words.

'If I was in your shoes, James, I'd feel the same.' He held out his hand. 'No hard feelings. All right?'

James nodded. His handshake was firm. 'I'm glad you can see it my way but I'm sorry it had to end like this.' He handed over an official document. 'Under the agreement, you're entitled to the share you put in when you joined. Take a look at it and then sign it.'

So James had got it all ready. Part of Matthew felt hurt; the other part relieved. His share would pay the bills and mortgage for a few months. But supposing he couldn't find another job? It was a tricky market out there.

The rest of the day was spent in a haze. It didn't help that he had a project to finish by the end of next week:

a conservatory design which meant he had to work late.

'I think it's disgusting,' Karen kept repeating after he had told her, perhaps unwisely, about his conversation with James. 'Are you sure you don't want another doughnut? I always find that eating helps when you're under stress.'

Eventually he reached a stage where he could leave for the evening. By then the office was empty – even Karen had left – and he made his way to the car park, his head reeling with the events of the day.

On impulse, on the way home, he took a left turn to the cemetery. It had been at least a month since he'd been here and then Lottie had been with him. Every now and then, at her bereavement counsellor's suggestion, they had gone to lay a bunch of flowers on Sally's grave.

These, he noticed, now lay limply in the white urn he had bought. Crouching down at the side of the stone, he replaced them with a fresh spray of lilies, before pulling out the grass which had begun to grow over the words.

Much-loved wife and mother.

'That's not entirely true, is it, Sally?' he murmured.

His wife, mused Matthew, had been a peculiar mixture of brittleness and vulnerability. On the one hand, she adored Lottie, yet on the other, she had declared that she didn't know how to handle a baby and wanted to go back to work as soon as possible.

'Hello?'

A gentle voice – a familiar one – spoke from behind, making him jump. He looked up disbelievingly.

'Christina?' Getting to his feet, he hoped she hadn't heard him speaking out loud just now. 'What are you doing here?'

It was then that he noticed she was holding a small bunch of freesias in her hand and a pair of secateurs too.

'My husband is here,' she said simply.

'Your husband?' he repeated. 'But you got divorced!'

She smiled sadly. 'I actually told you that he betrayed me. Which he did. But then we talked about getting back together. Mike was on his way over when his car collided with a lorry.'

What an idiot he'd been! She was a bereavement counsellor, wasn't she? What could be more obvious than for someone like that to have experienced a similar situation?

'I'm really sorry.'

She bent her head graciously. 'It was a long time ago now.' Her eye flickered to Sally's stone. 'It appears that we are almost neighbours. Mike is over there.' She smiled and Matthew realised how much he had missed that warm smile.

'I tried to get hold of you,' he said, feeling like a foolish schoolboy.

'I took my daughter to Toronto to see her grand - mother. My husband was Canadian.'

Turning as if by mutual unspoken agreement to make their way back to the car park, they were now talking side by side.

'I'm so sorry,' he said again. 'How do you cope?'

'By concentrating on the present.' She stopped by her car and he realised he was closer to her now than he had ever been before. He could even smell her perfume, which was light and reminded him of roses. 'But it's not always easy. I was self-centred at first, only thinking about myself. And angry too. It took a while to work through it but I got there in the end. Just like you will.'

'You think so?'

'I'm certain of it.'

Her confidence made him suddenly feel a whole lot better.

Then she gave him another smile. It was surprisingly shy after her previous tone. 'How are you getting on with the au pairs?'

'We're on the fifth so far. Or is it the sixth? Hard to keep up!' Too late, he realised that his attempt to make light of the situation was rather sick when you thought of Sozzy. 'But I've decided to call it a day. I'm giving up work after Christmas so I can concentrate on Lottie.'

Her eyes looked worried. 'How will you cope financially?'

'We'll sell up. Move somewhere cheaper. And I'll do whatever it takes to put bread on the table.'

'How does Lottie feel about that?'

'She's keen. And besides, I don't trust anyone else to look after her. It makes me really nervous every time a new one starts, in case they don't watch her carefully enough when she crosses the road...Sorry. I didn't mean to upset you.'

'It doesn't. I've had to get over that myself. My daughter's taking driving lessons now and I hate it. It's not easy, Matthew. In fact...'

She stopped.

'Please go on.'

'Well, you don't think that Lottie has been trying to push away the au pairs because she's picked up on your worries, do you?'

'Maybe.' The idea unsettled him.

'Just a thought. Anyway, I must be going. Good to see you.'

'Me too.' Suddenly he didn't want her to leave. 'I've missed our chats. I don't suppose you're free for another coffee sometime, are you?'

'Perhaps.' Her voice didn't sound certain. 'Let's just see, shall we?'

Blast, he told himself as he drove home. You've really messed up there, haven't you, Matthew? All the time he was silently accusing Christina of not understanding, she'd been through it herself. And now she'd think he was making a pass at her. The sooner he and Lottie got out of here and started a new life, the better. Maybe they should go to Scotland. Even though he wasn't close to his sister, surely some family was better than none?

As he pulled up outside the house, he could see the front door opening. Was that his little Lottie coming out to greet him? No. It was a tall chap, about his age, with a darkish complexion. The kind of smooth man-about-town type you saw in Sunday supplements, advertising expensive male fragrances.

'*Au revoir!*' Marie-France was saying gaily. She was actually kissing this man on both cheeks! Was he a boyfriend? Crossly, Matthew increased his pace. She was meant to be looking after his daughter at this time of the day, not entertaining men!

361

They passed at the gate. The man was putting on his sunglasses and gave him a furtive look. 'Can I help you?' demanded Matthew.

'I was just dropping something off. For Marie-France.'

Then he was gone, heading towards an expensive-looking red sports car with the number plate PHIL 1 parked further down the road.

Dear Jilly,

Thank you so much for finding Martine for us. She has been a delightful au pair and we are thrilled with the service you provided. I will make sure that I spread the word about your wonderful agency.

Yours,
Mrs Gladman

Chapter 25

'You're planning to do what?' repeated Jilly.

'I told you,' her father replied in a voice that suggested he was extremely pleased with himself. 'I'm planning a surprise wedding anniversary party for your mother. That's why I encouraged her to come and stay with you, so I could get it all sorted. Well, that and have a bit of time to ourselves. It was a bit claustrophobic being together on the boat for all that time.'

There was a brief clink of a bottle at the other end as well as some jazz music in the background, indicating that he was making the most of her absence. Mum loathed jazz.

'You encouraged her to come and stay here?' repeated Jilly, checking that the kitchen door was shut. 'She told me it was the other way round.'

Dad guffawed. 'Well, you know what your mother is like. She always has to make out that she has the upper hand.'

That was true. 'But she thinks you're having an affair!'

'Ridiculous.' Her father gave a deep throaty chuckle. She could just picture him now. Dad was a bit of a Des O'Connor lookalike; he favoured navy-blue jackets and open-necked shirts, suggesting he was just of to an informal lunch at the golf club. His honey-coloured hair (tinted every now and then to hide the grey) would be impeccably smoothed back with a side parting. A real ladies' man who, despite everything, had remained married to her mother for nearly forty years.

'I'm very flattered but just because I've asked one of our oldest friends, Angela, to help out, doesn't mean there's anything going on. You know me, darling.'

'Angela? But Mum hasn't seen her for years.'

'Precisely. Far too easy to lose touch, don't you think? The party will be a good opportunity to get together. Anyway, I promise I'm behaving myself so don't worry about me.'

How could she not? He'd be lolling on the sofa, gin and tonic in hand. The *Daily Telegraph* would be open at the crossword page on the coffee table and Angela, who'd been widowed years ago, would be passing him a bowl of nibbles, possibly hoping for something more.

'Mum's really upset, you know.' She glanced again at the kitchen door, which might open at any minute. 'I think you ought to come clean about the party.'

'Nonsense. Now listen, darling. It's all planned for next month. We're going to have a marquee in the garden and the caterers are making your mother's favourite. Salmon en croûte.'

'But she's allergic to fish, Dad!'

'Ah. Silly me. Anyway, there's a meaty option. So whatever you do, make sure you keep her up with you until the party and then bring her down with the kids and Dick.'

'It's David, Dad. Not Dick.'

Jilly felt a wave of alarm. Dad was normally on the ball: how could he get his son-in-law's name wrong or forget his wife couldn't eat fish? She'd ended the conversation feeling extremely uncomfortable and wondering whether to tell Mum. But if she did, she'd ruin the surprise.

'What do you think I ought to do?' she asked David that night.

He turned over from her in bed. 'I could tell you what I think but you wouldn't pay any attention. You never do any more.'

'That's not fair.' Her words rang out in the dark. Why was it that conversations like this always sounded so chilling and scary when it was night?

'Take a good look at yourself, Jilly. Running a business has made you tough like your mother. It's all you care about.'

'That's not true. I'm worried about Dad.'

'But what about the rest of us? Look, Jilly, forget I said anything. I'm going to sleep because in the morning, I've got to get up at some ridiculous time and go into an office and do a proper job. Goodnight.'

A week later, they still hadn't really made up. Then, while she was visiting a prospective host family, Paula left a message.

'She wants you to come round for a coffee,' reported Mum. 'Friends just don't understand, do they? They assume that when you're self-employed you can take time off whenever you want.'

Paula had rung? That was a turn-up for the books! Her so-called friend hadn't been returning her calls for ages.

'What did she sound like?'

'A bit quiet, to be honest. She said she needed to see

you.' Her mother gave her a sharp look. 'Have you two fallen out?'

'She's being strange at the moment.' Jilly stopped, feeling awkward. It made her feel like a little girl at school, complaining about being left out.

Her mother gave her a surprisingly sympathetic glance. 'Probably jealous that you're working. I lost a few of my friends that way. I wouldn't worry about it. Oh and by the way, Heidi has rung in again, complaining that her host father is still walking round naked. We need to talk to Mr Banks first – no point in rocking the marital boat – and then if it continues, have a word with the wife. Make a note too, can you, that we will only place *ugly* au pairs with that family again.'

'Jee-lee. I am hungry.'

Not again! This baby was going to be huge! Jilly pulled out a chair for Fatima to plonk herself down on. She was wearing another of her enormous brown shift dresses which made up an entire load in the washing machine. She began to rub her ankles.

'Why don't you take Bruno out for a walk?' suggested Sheila tartly. 'It might do you good to have some exercise.'

Fatima eyed her reproachfully. 'But my legs! They hurt. And I am busy adding up your accounts.'

'*I'll* walk Bruno,' said Nick, who'd sauntered in, taken a piece of cheese out of the fridge, bitten into it and then put the rest back like a plaster impression at the dentist.

'Wonderful, darling,' said her mother before Jilly could tell Nick off. 'In fact, you get on so well with

367

Bruno that I was thinking of leaving him with you permanently.'

'Mum!' How could she? They hadn't even discussed this!

'Cool, Gran.' Nick was tickling the dog's tummy as he rolled over, leaving a trail of black hairs on the carpet.

'Your grandfather claims he's allergic to dogs although I think it's because he can't be bothered to walk him. Only wanted Bruno as an excuse to walk round and visit his lady friends.'

Enough was enough! 'Mum,' she began, 'much as we love having you here, Dad wants you to come back for something...something he's got planned for you.'

'Hah! I suppose he's organising a surprise anniver - sary party, is he? Well, he can forget that. I have no plans to leave here.'

Jilly didn't pursue the conversation. When her mother sounded like that, there was no point in trying to make her change her mind.

'I'm doing some networking after I drop off the boys,' announced Jilly the next day when she was trying to round up the twins for school. For God's sake, where was Harry's left shoe? And why was Alfie's maths homework in the vegetable rack?

'Networking?' Her mother was smearing natural yoghurt on her face straight from Fatima's tub in the fridge. 'I suppose you mean coffee with Paula. Well, don't be long, we've got work to do, like...'

The last part of the sentence was drowned by the noise of a stampede down the stairs.

'Mum, he's nicked my mouth guard.'

'It's mine, you idiot.'

'Well, I've spat in it so now it's mine.'

'Boys! Boys! Fight all you like over that mouth guard but you should know that it's been sharing a mug with my false teeth in the bathroom. Looked like it needed a good clean.'

'Gran, that's gross!'

'Precisely. Nick, are you walking Bruno *again*? You are a good boy. No, not you Bruno. Nick. Oh, and Jilly, if we're not in when you're back, it's because I've taken Fatima to her antenatal appointment.'

For someone who was so anti au pairs, her mother was surprisingly sympathetic towards Fatima, especially after her history had come out. It proved Mum had a heart after all! Meanwhile, as she rang Paula's doorbell, she felt nervous. Why did her friend want to see her? Was it to make up or tell her about some nasty piece of gossip? Someone else complaining about her agency?

Paula's unsmiling face at the door did nothing to allay her fears. Nor did the glass of wine in her hand. Paula had always liked her drink but in the last few months she seemed to be doing more of it than usual. 'Come on in.'

What was going on?

'Do sit down.'

Paula was speaking as though she hadn't been here before. Hadn't been in and out of this house so many times that it was almost her own. Perching on the end of her friend's cream sofa – the one that the kids weren't meant to sit on – she took a deep breath.

'What's wrong, Paula? Have I done something to upset you?'

To her surprise, Paula's face crumpled. 'Yes. No. Well, you and Nigel together.'

'Me and Nigel?'

'You're denying it then?'

'Denying what?'

'You're not having a thing together?'

'Are you crazy?'

Paula searched her face as though seeking the truth and then gave a little sigh, flopping back on the sofa. 'Sure?'

'Quite sure! First, I wouldn't look at anyone apart from David. And second – don't take this the wrong way – but Nigel simply isn't my type!'

Paula studied Jilly's face again and then nodded. 'OK. I believe you.'

Jilly leaned forward. 'Do you want to explain what this is all about?'

There was a small sigh. 'You know I told you ages ago that we weren't...well...doing much in the bedroom.'

Jilly's mind went back to the time before she'd started the agency. That was it. Something about Paula talking about a no-sex survey in the *Mail* and how she and Nigel were part of the statistics.

'Well, I had it out with him the other month.'

Jilly gasped. 'He's not having an affair?'

'He says he isn't.' Paula was pulling out a tissue from her sleeve. 'But he did say that I was getting boring.'

Jilly moved over and put an arm around her friend's shoulder. 'Boring? That's horrid.'

'I know. He said I ought to take a leaf out of your book and do something. Then I'd have something else to talk about instead of just children and the gym.'

'That's unfair.'

'But you can see why I got jealous of you. Nigel keeps saying how wonderful you are.' Her eyes glittered with envy. 'Jilly this and Jilly that.' She gave her a hard look. 'I know it sounds crazy but I began to wonder if you were having an affair with him.'

Smarmy Nigel? Ugh! Besides, even if he was the last man left in Corrywood, he was still her friend's husband. 'How could you even think that?'

But she didn't seem to be listening. 'And I even felt pleased when you messed up about double-booking that au pair!' Paula's eyes refused to meet hers.

That wasn't very nice. But at the same time, Jilly could sort of see why. 'Have you thought, perhaps,' she said carefully, 'of going back to work when Immy goes to school?'

Paula shook her head. 'What? I dropped out of uni – I've never told you before because I was too ashamed. And I'm not qualified for anything. Not even motherhood.' She lowered her voice. 'To be honest, I even find the children boring. All that answering stupid questions and having to explain why you shouldn't run across the road or why you have to do your home-work. It does my head in.'

'It's not easy,' conceded Jilly.

'That's why I'm always out at all those classes.' Paula smiled wanly. 'And I'm drinking more. Probably too much. But it takes me away from all this. Blocks out the feeling that I'm a failure.'

'You're not a failure!' Shocked, Jilly gave her friend a warm hug. 'If it makes you feel any better, my business is causing a real strain on my marriage. David says I'm a different person.'

'You *are*!' Envy filled Paula's eyes again. 'But in a good way. You're more confident. You've got lots of funny stories to tell.'

Jilly thought of the shoplifting scene which Marie-France had described to her in great detail. 'Some aren't so funny actually.'

'Well, you've got a bloom about you.'

Had she? 'I do like what I'm doing,' admitted Jilly. 'It's given me a sense of purpose.'

'*Exactly*. And that's what I want.'

Jilly gave her friend another hug. 'You'll find it. But maybe now's not the right time. If only men understood how hard it is for mothers to do everything.'

'Some men do,' pointed out Paula. 'Maybe I should have married someone else.'

'Don't say that.'

Paula stood up and looked through the window. 'Look, I don't want to talk about it any more. But thanks for listening. And I'm sorry I've been a bit of a bitch. It won't happen again.'

'It's OK.' But inside, Jilly still felt hurt that Paula thought she might be having an affair with Nigel. 'Look, I'd better be going. Mum will accuse me of skiving if I don't get back and Nick's got a day off school to finish some coursework so I want to keep tabs on him.'

They hugged each other goodbye, promising to meet up soon, and then Jilly took the short cut through the

372

park. Hang on. Wasn't that Bruno steaming towards her, his lead trailing behind him?

'Hello, boy. What's going on?'

Where on earth was Nick? Looking around, she heard a giggle from some bushes not far away. Striding towards them, she caught a glimpse of two boys and a sultry, dark-haired girl. The latter was hastily putting on a pink glossy coat but not before Jilly had spotted a flash of naked flesh underneath.

'Antoinette? Nick?'

'Mum!' Her son's terrified eyes looked back at her. 'I wasn't doing anything.' He scrambled to his feet, brushing dead leaves from his hoody. 'It was nothing.'

'I don't believe you.' Jilly caught Antoinette by the wrists as she tried to run off. 'What exactly is going on?'

The girl drew herself up like a wild animal about to enter the fray. 'Your boys, they say they pay me. It was their idea.'

'Pay you?' Jilly's blood ran cold.

The girl curled her lip. 'We do not do much. They are young and extra eager.'

Jilly felt sick. 'Go home, Antoinette. I don't want to see you. As for you, Nick, how could you?'

Her son hung his head. Clearly he was racked with embarrassment. Oh God! If she went mad, she might put him off sex for life as her mother had warned before, or he might even run away like an old school-friend of hers did when her parents caught her in bed with a boyfriend. She'd have to play this carefully.

'I think you'd better go home, Nick. We'll talk about this later when Dad's back.'

She turned to the other boy, now stumbling out from the bush looking defiant rather than awkward. He looked rather rough with a spiky haircut and filthy hoody and she didn't recognise him as one of her son's usual crowd. 'Haven't you got school to go to?'

There was a dismissive shrug. 'I've left, haven't I?'

'How old are you?'

'Sixteen.'

Sixteen! Still a child, almost. Why hadn't she known this was going on? Because she was working. That was why...

Her mother's lips had tightened when, on getting back, Jilly told her what had happened. 'Those girls are vixens. I told you, Jilly. Only after one thing. Well, two. Freedom and extortion.'

'That's a bit hard!'

'Is it? Supposing your Nick got her pregnant? She'd want money. Trust me on that one. And that would be just the beginning.'

Fatima, who was sitting so quietly in the sitting room that Jilly had forgotten she was there, shook her head. 'It isn't always the girl's fault,' she said pointing to her stomach, which rippled in agreement at exactly that moment like a giant whale.

Her mother took a slug of Bombay Sapphire. 'Very true, dear, but some of your au pair compatriots are knowing little hussies like Antoinette. Of course you can't tell Paula or word will get out.'

Jilly bit her lip. 'I'll see what David says.'

'Ha! Fat lot of good that will do.'

Fatima nodded. Since living here, her English had

improved no end although her understanding seemed better than her speaking. She'd also been teaching the children some Turkish phrases, much to their amusement.

'Your mother is right. I think Jee-lee needs new husband. A nicer one. I ask my cousin to find her one in Turkey.'

'Good idea, dear! And while you're at it, find *me* one too, can you?'

That evening, Jilly waited up for David. It was nearly eleven o'clock when she finally heard the key in the lock.

He threw a large brown envelope on to the table, looking flushed and excited. 'It's a job contract. I didn't want to tell you until it was certain but now it's sewn up after weeks of interview rounds and negotiations. That's why I've been working late and – I'm sorry – been a bit tetchy.' David pulled her towards him. 'The best news is that the money is twice what I earned before. So you won't need to work any more!'

Not work any more? 'I can't jack it all in just like that!'

His face frowned. 'But you're always stressed and complaining.'

'That's part of it. But I also get real satisfaction out of doing something.'

'At the expense of the children? They need a mother who's around more, Jilly, not someone who runs a half-baked business from the kitchen table with her senile mother.'

How dare he? 'She's not senile, just a bit forgetful.

And my agency is making money now! Don't be so bloody old-fashioned. I thought you were the kind of man who'd be pleased I'd finally found a job I loved!'

'And I thought you'd be pleased that I've turned my career round again!' David picked up his contract with a dramatic flourish. 'If you want to carry on, that's up to you. But I don't think that two people working crazy hours is fair on our children. Do you?'

There was the sound of someone heavy coming down the stairs. '*Jee-lee, Jee-lee.*'

David rolled his eyes.

'Yes, Fatima, what is it?'

Fatima's eyes were round with terror as she clutched her stomach. '*Tuvaletler nerededir.*'

'What does she mean?'

Alfie who'd wandered out on to the landing, sleepily clutching his PSP, piped up. 'She needs the loo, Mum. Quick!'

JILLY'S AU PAIR AGENCY:
GUIDELINES FOR FAMILIES

An au pair probably won't be used to the same customs or courtesies that we have in this country. This can lead to confusion! Here are some examples you might like to explain to your au pair:

Queuing

Morris men

Making toad in the hole

Apologising when things aren't our fault

The tooth fairy

Discussing the weather at every opportunity

Sunbathing on a cold, wet, windy beach in summer

Chapter 26

When Marie-France had spotted Thierry in that Soho bar, she'd thought she must have got it wrong. The tall, handsome, slightly arrogant-looking man with the hawk nose and floppy fringe, serving drinks to a crowd of besotted teenage girls who appeared to be hanging on his every word, simply *looked* like her boyfriend. It couldn't possibly *be* him.

Thierry was travelling across Europe on his motorbike. Her mother had told her that quite clearly. But when this look alike at the bar had caught her eye, he'd given a definite start of recognition. His face had grown cold and he'd turned away, leaving her to catch her breath and feel both sick and excited at the same time.

'What are you doing here?' she had tried to say above the noise of the bar around her but he had given her another cold stare.

'What is it to you?' he'd growled in English before turning away to serve more customers. She'd had to wait ages, watching his big hands – more used to tuning motorbikes – handle bottles and glasses with incredible ease.

'Can I help you?' asked someone else who was serving. Marie-France took in a petite brunette with a see-through white T-shirt.

'It's all right, thanks. I am waiting for Thierry.'

She rolled her eyes. 'Join the queue.'

So she had continued to stand there, feeling like an idiot, watching the two of them serve drinks to the crowd. Twice, she saw Thierry reach out and pat the girl's bottom as they dived in and out of the space under the bar or reached up for another glass. Were they together or was he putting on an act because he knew she was watching?

'What does a girl have to do to get a drink round here?' she called out eventually.

'Thierry!' called out someone else. 'You've got a fellow compatriot over there, judging from that sexy accent! Better not keep her waiting.'

Frowning, he turned to her. 'What is it that you want?' he growled again, this time in French.

'To explain.' She spoke rapidly, afraid he would turn away before she could make it clear to him. 'The boy in my family – Tom – he tore up the photograph of us. I was upset about it. You have to believe me.'

'I know what I see with my own eyes.' His lip curled in the way it did when he was angry or making love or both. 'I see also that the old Englishman watches you and that you are flattered.'

Phillip? 'No.' She flushed. 'You've got it wrong. There is nothing in it.'

'That is not what your friend Antoinette tells me.'

'Antoinette? What's she got to do with it?'

'She is a Facebook friend of Joel's nephew in the garage at home. She tells me you have been sacked for having an affair with the old man.'

'No. No that's not true.' Marie-France felt a flush of anger. What a bitch!

He spread his hands out. 'I do not care. Instead, I am having fun in London just like you.'

With that, he turned, taking care to sweep his hand lightly across the barmaid's bottom, making her giggle.

'You're making one big mistake,' spat Marie-France. Then, head held high, she stormed out of the pub. Just wait until she got hold of Antoinette. She'd kill her.

But to her fury, Antoinette wasn't in class that week. Off sick because it was 'the wrong time of the month' apparently. Hah! More importantly, she'd heard nothing from Thierry. Well, she certainly wasn't going to call *him*.

Then, totally out of the blue, Phillip had turned up with some sheets of guitar music she'd left behind. When she'd opened the door, she'd been so surprised that all her resolutions to ignore him flew out of the window.

'I am so sorry about Dawn,' he had said, taking her hands in his. 'She can be very jealous, I'm afraid, and she's really upset about the burglary.' He hesitated. 'On that point, the police have been in touch. They wanted to talk to you again about what happened so I gave them this address. I hope that's all right.'

'Of course.' She nodded, wondering whether she should remove her hand from his. It felt so warm and comforting yet it did not seem right, not with little Lottie in the other room. 'Do remember what we agreed, won't you?' he said quietly. 'It would be best, for your sake, if you did not say that you let the burglars in.'

'For my sake?' she repeated.

Phillip gave her hands a squeeze. 'The laws in this country are very different. You could be sent to prison for doing what you did.'

Prison? She was confused. 'But before, you say that would not happen!'

Phillip's hands gave hers one more squeeze. 'I've been looking into it and I think I may have been wrong. But do not worry. As long as you do what I say, I will protect you.' Then he reached across as though to give her a kiss on the side of her cheek but just as he did so, there was the sound of a car outside.

She froze. 'It is my family, Matthew.'

He had drawn away then and put on the dark sunglasses which he'd been wearing when he'd arrived. 'I must go. But please. Remember what we discussed.'

'Who was that man?' Matthew had asked.

'My old boss,' she'd replied quickly. 'He came to drop something off that I had left behind.'

Best not to mention the police, she told herself. With any luck, they would come when Matthew was out.

Meanwhile, her mission to keep one step ahead of little Lottie was going rather well!

'Guess what I find in my bed last night?' she said to Lottie one morning when she was getting her ready for school.

'What?' Lottie's eyes were round and innocent.

'A real live slug from the garden.'

'Ugh! That's horrible.' Lottie made a face. 'Didn't you want to scream?'

'No. I adore slugs. So I place it back into the garden again.'

The disappointment on Lottie's face was so sweet that it was all she could do not to laugh out loud.

On another occasion, she found a silver chain hidden in her underwear drawer. 'Lottie,' she asked when she collected her from school that day. 'Look what I find. This is yours, yes?'

Lottie nodded disappointedly.

'Good thing I discover it. Yes? Or your father might think I steal it!'

Not long after that, she found Lottie in the bathroom, pouring something into her bottle of shower gel. 'Vinegar! How kind of you, Lottie! In France, we often add vinegar to our baths to make them smell nice.'

Meanwhile, she continued trawling the internet for *more* find-a-person sites but as usual, they required vital information like a date of birth. Information that she just didn't have.

Her own sense of loss made her empathise with poor Matthew and also Lottie, whom she was really learning to love like a little sister. One way of keeping her happy was to teach her to cook!

'Look, Daddy, we've made you a proper French meal,' she called out delightedly to her father when he got back one evening. 'It has lots of garlics.'

'Garlic,' corrected Matthew, smiling.

'That's what I said. Marie-France says that the French eat snails but we didn't put any in this time.'

They all laughed and, for the first time since she'd arrived, Marie-France felt as though she was part of a proper family. Just look how they were all tucking in to her special recipe! Little did they know that her sauce had cheese in it but Lottie was wolfing it down. So good for her!

The following day, after school, she got out her guitar. 'You would like to learn some chords, yes?'

Lottie's eyes shone. 'Mummy used to play the piano when she was a little girl.'

Marie-France's heart skipped slightly with compassion.

'She's going to give me lessons when I am older.' The little girl's eyes held hers steadily. 'She's still alive, you know. Daddy thinks she's dead but I know she'll come back one day. Maybe she's just playing with her friend.'

Marie-France frowned. 'I do not understand.'

Lottie flushed. 'I shouldn't have said anything. Mummy said it had to be our secret when her friend came round to play upstairs in her bedroom.'

Mon Dieu! So Matthew's wife had had a lover! 'You must miss your mummy very much,' she said quietly.

Lottie nodded, her eyes filling with tears.

'I miss my daddy,' said Marie-France without meaning to. 'He went away too and I am trying to find him.'

'Really?' Lottie took her hand in his. 'Maybe he's gone to meet my mummy.' Her face brightened. 'I know. Let's look for them together!'

Marie-France swallowed the big lump in her throat. 'It's a deal.' Laughingly, they did a high five with little Lottie's small palm reaching up for hers. 'But you are to promise me something! You must cease playing little tricks on me. Otherwise your daddy might send me away and then we won't be able to help each other.'

Lottie frowned as though considering this proposition. 'OK. Now can we play the guitar again? Please.'

Marie-France decided not to mention this conversation to Matthew. If Lottie wanted to believe her mother was still alive, what was wrong with that? As for the 'friend', that was definitely better left unsaid. It would devastate the poor man if he knew his dead wife had had a lover.

Meanwhile, she'd got over her cool period with Heidi and sometimes they went to one of the local pubs in the evening. One night, she spotted a dark blowsy girl, propped up against the bar, talking to a man who was old enough to be her grandfather. Antoinette! At last. She hadn't been coming to the class recently and Marie-France was convinced it was because she was avoiding her.

'I want to talk to you,' she snarled in French, grabbing the girl's jacket and forcing her to turn round at the bar. 'What do you mean by Facebooking my boyfriend and telling him I had an affair with Phillip?'

Antoinette's eyes gleamed with hatred. 'Well you *did*, didn't you?'

'No. I didn't.' Marie-France flew at her again but Antoinette pushed her hard – bruising her bosom – so she fell back into a group of men. 'I am so sorry.'

'Any time, love. Having a fight with your mate, are you?' He grinned. 'We love a girl fight, don't we, boys, especially if it's with a French accent.'

She straightened herself but Antoinette, the coward, had already run away. 'Oy,' called out the bartender. 'Put a stop to that right now or I'll call the police.'

'Marie-France, let us go, *ja*?' Heidi shuffled from one heel to the other worriedly.

'Not so fast!' It was one of the men at the table that Marie-France had fallen into. 'Let's buy you a drink first. My name's John, by the way.' He grinned. 'John Smith.'

'*Nein*, thanks,' began Heidi but Marie-France stared at the man. Could this be Papa? He had a similar nose to hers – although a bit larger – and he kept blowing it on a large spotted maroon handkerchief.

'Plis.' She hesitated, flushing. 'Can you tell me. I am trying to find a friend of my mother's who lives here nineteen years ago. His name was John Smith too.'

'Was it now? To tell you the truth, love, I only moved here this week from Dublin but I can fiddle a few facts if you let me buy you a drink.'

He moved towards her, slipping his arm around her waist.

'How dare you!' Quickly, as Thierry had taught her, she bent his arm in a judo tackle.

'Oy. That hurts!'

'Serve you right!'

'Quick,' hissed Heidi. 'Let's go. *Ja*?' Hand in hand, they flew down the road towards Matthew's house. *Mon Dieu!* There was a police car outside!

'*Scheisse*,' whispered Heidi, appalled. 'That barman has found us already! You want me to come in with you?'

'No point in both of us getting into trouble. Besides,

I'm the one at fault.' Marie-France knew she sounded braver than she felt. Unlocking the front door, she steeled herself.

'There you are!' Matthew's face was creased with disappointment. Anger she could have dealt with but not that cold look. 'The police are here to see you. It's about the burglary at your previous employer's. They're in the sitting room. Lottie is in bed, thank goodness. Otherwise this would be very unsettling for her.'

Trying not to tremble, she made herself walk into the room. A man and a woman in police uniform were waiting. Neither was smiling. 'Marie-France Dubonne? New information has come to light over the burglary at Mrs Green's house. In your statement at the time, you claimed you didn't know how the burglars got in.'

Marie-France willed herself not to flush. 'That is correct.'

'The problem is, Mademoiselle Dubonne, that the insurance company has uncovered further evidence.'

Marie-France began to sweat.

'It looks as though someone might have let them in.'

Do not tell the police, Phillip had said.

Merde! What should she do now?

'Marie-France,' said the policeman, using her first name in an over-familiar fashion as though he was trying to befriend her like those horrible men in the pub just now. 'Marie-France, in this country, you could go to prison for not telling the truth.'

Mon Dieu! God knows what a British prison might be like! A picture of jail bars and a bowl of water came into her head.

She felt herself getting even redder. 'It is not my fault. I thought the man was my father, so I allow him in, but Mr Green, he tell me not to say this.'

The policewoman's mouth tightened. 'We will need you to come down to the station and make a fresh statement.' As she spoke, there was a sound from the walkie-talkie thing around her neck. 'A disturbance at the pub?' she repeated. 'Involving two French girls, one with long dark hair?' Her eyes narrowed. 'I might have a lead on that one.'

Marie-France began to tremble. 'I can explain.'

Together they went out into the hall where Matthew was waiting. 'I have to go with them. But it is not my fault. I need you to call Dawn and Phillip and inform them that I have to tell the truth. They will understand what I mean. OK?'

JILLY'S AU PAIR AGENCY:
GUIDELINES FOR FAMILIES

Make sure that your new au pair knows your address and telephone number off by heart so she doesn't get lost when she goes out! Emergency numbers are different in each country. Please explain our 999 system.

Chapter 27

After Marie-France left, Matthew ran his hand through his hair in despair and confusion. Just when he'd thought he'd found the perfect au pair, she'd been arrested! Or as good as.

She'd implored him to ring Phillip as she was being led away, and explain she had to tell the truth.

Tell the truth? What did she mean? So he'd got Dawn's number from Paula.

'Er, my name is Matthew Evans. This is a bit awkward, I'm afraid. I've got your old au pair and—'

'The bitch who tried to make out with my husband?'

Matthew was taken aback. Jilly had told him that Marie-France had had a 'clash of personality' with her old bosses. Then he recalled Phillip leaving his house the other day. Marie-France had claimed he was 'dropping something off'. Was there something more to this?

'I didn't know . . .'

'Well, you should have done. If you don't believe me, ask my husband. He'll tell you how she came on to him. Phillip! Phone for you.'

Matthew was beginning to feel even more uneasy.

'Hi.' Phillip sounded guarded. 'My wife says you want to talk to me about Marie-France. Is everything all right?'

'Not really. The police have taken her away for

questioning over your burglary. She asked me to ring and say she had to tell them the truth. What did she mean by that exactly?'

'I've no idea.' His voice was sharp. 'But I do have to warn you that Marie-France is a fantasist! She makes up stories. She seems like a very pleasant girl but she's not what she seems.' He lowered his voice. 'It's not the first time she's been involved with the police, I'm afraid. There was some confusion over a shoplifting episode with the other au pairs. She said it was another girl so they let her go.'

Matthew groaned. Talk about appearances being deceptive! And to think he'd been telling Karen how fantastic Marie-France was, with her cheery open manner and kind way with Lottie.

'What are you going to do?' asked Phillip sympathetically.

'Not sure. But I expect the police will pay you a visit if they need anything else.'

'Why would they do that?' The man sounded edgy.

Matthew hesitated. 'Well, I couldn't help over-hearing them when they were talking to Marie-France. They seem to think there is a problem over your insurance claim for the burglary.'

'What's he talking about, Phillip?' A squeaky woman's voice cut in on the extension.

'No idea. Look, thanks, Matt.'

It's Matthew to you, mate, he wanted to say. But Phillip had already put down the phone. Something wasn't right! The man had sounded distinctly uneasy and, besides, he hadn't liked that shifty way he'd put on his sunglasses when they'd met at the gate the other week.

Was it too late to ring the agency? Matthew's hand hovered over the phone. Yes. No. Marie-France had been taken away by the police, hadn't she? It was surely an emergency!

The phone rang several times but just when he was about to put it down, a polite but tired voice answered. Briefly, Matthew explained the problem, apologising to the man for bothering him.

'I'm afraid that my wife is out.' There was a slight pause before the voice continued, in a rather more animated way. 'But actually, this happens to be my field. Did you know I worked in insurance?'

Embarrassed, in case Jilly's husband had thought he was after a free piece of advice, Matthew assured him that he hadn't known.

'That's all right. Happy to help. Informally, of course. You'd need to get it checked out. But my understanding is that if someone who isn't a family member willingly opens a house to a stranger, there may be a problem with the claim.'

Aha! Something was clicking into place now! 'So Phillip might have told her not to tell the police what she had done?'

'Exactly! Poor kid. Look, maybe both you and I ought to go down to the station and see if she needs some help.'

But Lottie! He couldn't leave Lottie. Matthew's hand hovered over the phone. Unless Karen, who didn't live far away, could possibly come round...

*

When he and David got to the police station, they found a very distressed Marie-France with a red nose and mascara-streaked eyes, waiting to go home. 'I tell the truth,' she protested. 'I tell them I let man in.' She blew her nose. 'I also remember that Dawn and Phillip were going to have guests round to dinner that night. But there is change of plan and they go out instead.'

'How very convenient for the burglars,' remarked David heavily.

Matthew threw him a look.

'Then Phillip returns early,' continued Marie-France. 'But the buggers, they go then so he releases us.'

'Buggers?' repeated David, raising his eyebrows at Matthew. 'Interesting that Phillip comes back unexpectedly to release the children. Don't you think?'

'There is something else too.' Marie-France began to cry. 'About the argument with another girl in the pub tonight. It was about a private matter but the police, they are not going to press charges.' Her eyes appealed to Matthew. 'I am very sorry.'

Great! What did she expect him to do now? Forget all about it?

David leaped up. 'Can you both wait there for a minute? I just want a word with the duty officer.'

Ten minutes later, he came out again. 'What did you say?' asked Matthew curiously while Marie-France got into the back of the car.

'I simply suggested that they might care to check the state of Phillip's bank balance,' said David quietly. 'These burglars – although I rather like the other name for them – threw Marie-France and the children into her bedroom which happened to have a lock on the outside. Phillip had only put the lock there a few weeks earlier to give her privacy. Suspicious, don't you think?'

'The police told you all this?'

'No.' David glanced in his driving mirror. 'Marie-France confided in my wife when it happened. I thought it was odd at the time although I've come across all kinds of people who've done things to claim on their insurance.' He jerked his head towards the back of the car where Marie-France had fallen asleep. 'I feel sorry for her. If you ask me, she's the pawn in all this.'

David's kindness made Matthew feel guilty. Their new French au pair might have let them down tonight but she got on so well with Lottie that he didn't want to lose her. Besides, he hadn't taken to Phillip with the dark shades. Hadn't taken to him at all.

'Lottie's still fast asleep,' Karen assured him when he got back. She glanced sharply at his subdued au pair. 'How did it go?'

He nodded. 'Getting sorted, I think. Marie-France, this is Karen who works for me. Karen, this is Marie-France.'

The two women nodded at each other but he detected a hint of coolness in Karen's face. 'I go to bed,' said Marie-France quietly. 'I regret the problems I have caused.'

'It's all right.' He touched her arm lightly in reassurance. 'Will you be able to take Lottie to school in the morning?'

Her eyes widened. 'You still desire me to work for you?'

393

'Of course! Lottie has only just started to learn the guitar. How can I put an end to her lessons now?'

It was meant to be a joke but the girl just nodded sadly and went up the stairs. Karen meanwhile showed no signs of going and remained sitting on the sofa, so he had no option but to take the chair opposite.

Only now did he notice that she was wearing a slightly transparent blouse and had doused herself with perfume, the kind that made his nose tickle. 'Thank you so much for stepping in at short notice, Karen.'

She flushed. 'I enjoyed it, Matt. Really enjoyed it.' Then her eyes followed Marie-France as she went up the stairs. 'She's very pretty, isn't she, your French girl? It must be rather weird sharing a house with a woman whom you don't really know.'

'It is, but to be honest, I'm getting used to it. Marie-France is very easy to have around.'

'Even when she's hauled off to the police station?'

'Point taken.' He sighed. 'Still, it won't be that long until I've worked out my notice.'

She nodded. 'I'll miss you, Matt.' Suddenly she leaned across and kissed his cheek. 'Goodnight. See you tomorrow . And don't worry – I'll see myself out.' She laughed gaily. 'I'm getting used to your house now.'

Had he been incredibly naive? Did Karen fancy him? And – this was the bad bit – why was it that at times it felt frighteningly easy to go one stage further? It was so nice to be looked after. So comforting to be admired. Even though she wasn't his type, whatever that was. And even though he wasn't really ready for another relationship.

Matthew spent the next few days in the office trying to keep a low profile and ignoring all the little signs that his PA gave, such as brushing against him when she walked past his desk or asking if he was sure he wouldn't like a 'quick bite at lunchtime' because there was this 'lovely little café which had opened up round the corner' and served great mozzarella and tomato paninis?

Looking on the bright side, Marie-France hadn't had any more visits from the police as far as he knew *and* – thank goodness – she and Lottie seemed to be getting on really well.

Meanwhile, he had his 'date' with Christina! Of course it wasn't a proper date. Just a Saturday morning coffee in town when Lottie was at her gym class. But he was looking forward to it! Christina was such an easy person to talk to, especially now he knew that she had been through the same thing he had and was a single parent herself. Perhaps that was why, the following weekend, he found himself telling her about his evening at the police station.

'It's not easy for these girls,' she said, stirring her cappuccino. She'd arrived at the coffee shop looking rather chic. Her hair was shorter and cut in one of those styles which seemed to graduate down the back. It suited her, as did those long silver earrings. 'They arrive, these poor things, expecting a year's holiday, and then find themselves thrown into situations that many of us would struggle to cope with.'

'I'm struggling with something myself at the

moment,' he found himself confessing. 'Remember me telling you about a woman at work who seemed rather friendly?'

Her eyes took on a bemused but wary look. 'Yes, I do.'

'Well, I'm concerned that I may have encouraged her to think that I might be interested.' He was aware of blushing furiously as he spoke.

'And are you?'

'No. But it's like being a teenager again. I was never good at dumping girls. I didn't like hurting them.'

She laughed but in a kind way. 'I can imagine that. It's because you're a nice man.' Then her expression changed. 'The thing is, Matthew – and I'm speaking as a friend here – that it's not fair to allow someone to get the wrong idea. Don't you think?'

She was right! For the rest of the weekend, Matthew kept going over what he needed to say to Karen to get himself out of this sticky situation. By Monday morning, he'd decided. As soon as he got in, he'd have a frank, open discussion with Karen. He'd tell her that he was very grateful to her for stepping in but—

'Heard about Karen?' asked one of the other secretaries excitedly before he'd even hung up his jacket.

'No.' Apprehension shot through him. She'd had a car crash. She'd had a heart attack. She—

'She slipped on the frost in her garden at the week - end when she was feeding the birds! Broken her arm in two places, apparently – our Karen never does things by halves, does she? So she won't be in for at least four weeks.'

'That's awful.' To his shame, Matthew found himself feeling a flood of relief that she wouldn't be around for a bit. 'We must send her some flowers.'

'Already done.' The girl beamed at him. 'I'm going to be her replacement. James said so. He wants to see you now, by the way.'

Really? James had been virtually ignoring him since their last conversation, clearly pissed off by what he saw as Matthew's 'lack of commitment' to the partnership. *He* ought to try being a single dad. No, that wasn't fair. Poor James, not being able to have kids. Lottie made up for everything. Even Sally.

Not sure what to expect, he knocked on James's door. His friend looked up with a cool face. 'Ah, Matthew. There you are. May I introduce Duncan Greathew?' He gesticulated towards a short, zappily dressed man with a keen expression who jumped up immediately from his chair and pumped his hand.

'Duncan is a designer for a children's bedroom company. He is very keen to work with us but—'

'But I need someone who has children,' the man interrupted him. He spoke with a soft, chummy American accent. 'I was surprised to find that no one else in this company has kids apart from you, Matthew.'

'That's exactly why I'm leaving. James has told you that, hasn't he?' He gave his partner a pointed look. 'I'm a single parent and, as I'm finding out, it's not easy doing both.'

'That's a shame.' Duncan did indeed look dis - appointed. 'In that case, I'm afraid that I'm going to have to look elsewhere.'

'Unless' – James cut in swiftly – 'Matthew would like to reconsider his decision?'

Hadn't his friend understood *anything* he'd just been saying about Lottie?

Duncan looked awkward. 'Look, I don't want to cause any trouble between you two but I've heard great things about your work, Matthew. If you change your mind, please give me a ring.'

He shook his head. 'Sorry, but my mind's made up. I've got to put my daughter first.'

Duncan nodded. 'I appreciate that.' He held out his hand. 'Good to meet someone with integrity in today's world. Don't you think, James?'

HOW TO GET YOUR AU PAIR TO DO
WHAT YOU WANT

Having an au pair is a bit like suddenly having a teenager in the house. You need to use emotional intelligence!

Try using the 'I' word if you are criticising her, so you don't give offence.

For example, instead of saying, 'You haven't washed that cup up properly,' use the following phrase: 'I feel that the cup needs to be washed again.'

Extract from How To Cope With Help *by*
Maggie Giveup

Chapter 28

How many false alarms could a pregnant Turkish au pair have? When Fatima had announced she needed the loo, Jilly had thought her waters had broken. But no. She'd simply peed herself!

'When you're a little bit big,' the nurse had said delicately at the hospital, 'there's rather a lot of pressure on the bladder. Yes, you're fine to go home now. But take it easy, dear, won't you?'

No fear about that!

'What you need is proper help,' said her mother crisply. They were sitting side by side at their respective laptops at the kitchen table. Next door, Fat Eema was squatting on the carpet, doing the twins' maths homework while the boys were watching television. Sometimes it was easier to give in.

'You can't carry on a proper business unless you have someone who can run the house or help with your work.' Her mother allowed herself a rueful smile. 'It would certainly ease things between you and David. Don't think I haven't noticed! The two of you are hardly speaking.'

Jilly looked up from an email which had just popped into her inbox, confirming another placement with a German au pair just north of Corrywood. Great! 'What kind of help do you suggest?'

'Someone like me, of course, darling.'

Uh-oh. 'Mum, you know you're welcome to stay as long as you like but—'

'Thank you, darling.' Her mother bent her head graciously as though receiving a round of applause. 'I was hoping you might say that.'

'But what about Dad?'

'What *about* your father, dear?'

'Look, you know he's got this big party planned for your anniversary that you're pretending not to know about.'

Her mother shrugged like a petulant small child.

'Please don't say you're going to boycott it?'

'Of course not, darling.' Her mother gave a slow smile. 'I've even bought the most gorgeous aquamarine outfit from one of your little shops down the road.'

Thank goodness for that!

'But I'm *not* telling your father I'm going and nor are you. I want to keep him on his toes.' She stroked the side of Jilly's face in a rare tender moment. 'Now shall we go upstairs and I'll show you my dress?'

It was afterwards, on her way to meet Paula for coffee in town, that Jilly had another idea. Why not ring Marie-France and ask if she'd like to come with them to the anniversary party! She could keep an eye on the boys while she, Jilly, helped entertain with Mum and Dad.

'I also wondered if you'd like to earn a little bit of extra pocket money by coming in every now and then to help with agency admin work,' she suggested.

'*Mais oui!*' Marie-France declared enthusiastically on the phone.

Great! One more thing she could tick off on her

Done spreadsheet! Jilly felt a wave of satisfaction. If it wasn't for David, things would really be looking up.

'Heard about Dawn and Phillip?' asked her friend excitedly before she'd even had a chance to order a latte. 'She's chucked him out of the house!'

'No! Why?'

Paula bore the look of someone who was enjoying being the deliverer of juicy gossip. 'Surprised you don't know. It involves your girl, that French one. Marie what-not.'

'Marie-France? I've just asked her to help me out, part-time.' Jilly thought back to the coffee shop when Marie-France had taken the dog for a walk and all the other occasions when she had been so pleasant. 'She seems like one of the most reliable au pairs around.'

'You might want to reconsider that.' Paula's eyes sparkled. 'Apparently Dawn caught your Marie-France and Phillip having a snog in the car a few weeks ago. And one of the neighbours saw them from his balcony.'

'No!' Jilly felt seriously let down. Marie-France had *sworn* she hadn't had an affair with Phillip!

'Mind you,' chirped Paula. 'I can't really see Dawn as a single mum for long, can you? She'll be looking for husband number four soon. Certainly doesn't have any problem finding them. Suppose it's because of her money. She inherited it, you know, from her father. He built up a massive building company.'

Jilly was so troubled by the conversation that she mentioned it to David over Saturday breakfast the next day. After all, he'd been surprisingly good at helping Marie-France when she'd nearly been arrested.

'Sounds fishy, I agree. Still at least—' He broke off at the thunder of trainers down the stairs.

'MUM, DAD, HE'S HIT ME.'

'NO I DIDN'T. ALFIE HIT *ME*!'

Uh-oh. They were rowing in capital letters again. David gave a rueful smile. 'Don't worry. I'll sort it out. Want me to take them out for the day? It would give you a chance to catch up with all your paperwork.'

Jilly stared at him disbelievingly. 'Has Mum had a word with you?'

'What about?'

'Nothing.'

'Look, Jilly, I'm only trying to help.' He got up from the table abruptly. 'You might at least be gracious about it.'

Peace at last! True to his promise, David had taken the twins out and Nick was – she hoped – doing an essay in the local library.

'I need some space, Mum,' said her son as though *she* was the difficult one in the house.

'You mean you want to try your luck with some girl,' snorted his grandmother. 'I'm just nipping into town myself to see if I can find some shoes for your father's party if I decide to go. I'm having second thoughts, to be honest.'

Sometimes her mother drove her mad!

While they were all out, Jilly forced herself to update the monthly accounts on the spreadsheet. Then, just as she was getting into it, the phone rang. Again!

''Ello? My name is Madame Dubonne. My daughter Marie-France, she is one of your girls.'

Over the last few months, Jilly had become accustomed to all kinds of strange au pair accents. Occasionally she received overseas calls from a parent wanting to know more about her agency before their daughter signed up. As a mother herself, Jilly could understand it.

But now she felt a flush of foreboding. 'Of course,' she replied. Had Marie-France's mother heard about her daughter and Phillip already? Some au pairs' parents could be very controlling. Only last week, she'd had a phone call from a German father complaining because his daughter's English family hadn't taken her away for a weekend. She'd had to explain that the weekend in question had in fact been the couple's wedding anniversary and that they had asked the au pair to stay at home to look after the children. Some families expected far too much!

'I 'ave worries about my daughter,' continued Marie-France's mother. 'Her texts. They are not very enormous.'

The woman had a very strong French accent and it wasn't easy to follow her broken English.

'I miss my daughter and I need to know she is OK.'

Ah! Now that was something Jilly could relate to. The thought of HarryandAlfie or even Nick – difficult as he was being at the moment – being away for nearly a year made her feel physically ill.

'I do understand. I really do. I have children myself although they are younger. But I can assure you that Marie-France's new family is very kind to her. I know them personally.'

'Her *new* family?' The alarm in the voice rose to a high pitch. 'What happened to the old?'

Whoops. Sounded like Marie-France's mother hadn't known she'd changed jobs. 'There was a bit of a trouble over the burglary,' she said carefully. 'But please do not worry. Your daughter is now living with a very nice widower and his daughter.'

There was a gasp at the other end. 'Buggery? What is buggery?'

'Burglary, actually. It's when thieves get in and—'

'*Les voleurs?*'

Oh oh. Clearly Marie-France had kept that one quiet too and now she'd put her foot in it. 'Unfortunately, someone broke in when she was babysitting and, well, they locked her and the children up in a room. But they got out and no one was hurt.'

'This is terreeble! Why did you not tell me?'

'Your daughter is eighteen, Madame Dubonne. She is an adult.'

'I do not like this situation. I do not like it at all. And now my daughter is living with a *window*? I do not understand?'

'No. He's a widower. It means his wife is dead.'

'So there is no other woman in the house?'

'Well, no, but it's not as bad as it sounds. Matthew Evans is a respectable man and he is very pleased with the way Marie-France is settling in.'

She only hoped this was the truth. Even as she spoke, she had a vision of Marie-France making a play for Matthew Evans in the same way she seemed to have done to Phillip.

'Well, I am not happy about it. I do not like it one

leetle bit. You are a mother and you are running an agency *pour les jeunes filles*. You should tell me about this.'

'I'm sorry,' Jilly found herself saying but the furious Madame Dubonne had cut her off. Oh dear. In theory, she was under no obligation to update the parents on their daughters' progress. But if the roles were reversed, wouldn't she feel just as angry and worried as Marie-France's mother had sounded just now?

USEFUL TURKISH PHRASES

Merhaba (Hello)

Nasılısınız (How are you?)

Hadi, dans edelim (Let's go and dance!)

Evet (Yes)

Gule alerjim var (I'm allergic to roses)

Hayır (No)

Chapter 29

Was this a trick? Marie-France reread the text which had popped up on her phone. *Plse cme to house 2 talk. Dawn.*

'Maybe she wants to put a knife in you, *ja*?' suggested Heidi. They were sitting in the park at the time, after school, watching Lottie and Heidi's Amy play on the swings. It was so nice to speak to someone who was fluent in French. Heidi could speak three languages; she was very bright. 'The English, they are like that. They are rude about their men and then they get mad when someone else makes a pass at them.'

Marie-France began to wish she hadn't confided quite so much in Heidi, who wouldn't stop asking her questions about 'that good-looking Philippe'.

'You have seen him recently, yes?'

'No.' Marie-France was aware of a sad note creeping into her voice. 'He has not tried to make contact.' She shrugged, trying to show she didn't care. 'I should not have listened to him when he told me to lie about the insurance.'

Heidi shrugged. 'Have you heard any more from the police?'

Marie-France flicked her hand in the air as though she wasn't bothered. 'Nothing.'

Heidi laughed. 'Like I said, the English are weird. My family's husband, he still walks around naked when his wife is out. But I pretend I do not notice now. By the way, have you seen this?' She pulled out a piece of paper from her shoulder bag.

This is a reminder that the whole school will be putting on a talent show next Tuesday. Please let us know what your child will be doing by tomorrow.

'Reminder?' Marie-France did a double-take. 'I haven't seen this note before.'

'Nor me,' sighed Heidi. 'Maybe it went directly to our parents. I don't know about yours but my host mother is as bad as the kids for not passing on notes. It goes straight to the bottom of her Lulu Guinesss handbag like that swimming party invitation from Antoinette's family. Are you going to that too?'

'Lottie mentioned a swimming party but I didn't realise it was Antoinette's kids. I can't stand that girl.'

'Nor me. She told Margit in class that her family wants her to bring some of us to help out. I think it's a real cheek getting free help, but a whole lot of us are going so it could be fun. Not like this talent show.' Her eyes rolled. 'What's Lottie going to do? Is she gifted at anything?'

'She's got a great imagination!' Marie-France looked at the little girl, who had shot off from the swings to play hide and seek in the woody bit on the side of the park. She knew why. It was a game that Lottie played in the garden, convinced that her mother was hiding there. Poor thing.

'My child, she has no talent.' Heidi waved her hand dismissively in Amy's direction. 'All she is interested in is nicking my make-up and clothes. Says she wants to be the next Lady Gaga.'

Marie-France smiled. She could remember doing the same with her mother's things.

'So what are you going to do about Dawn's text?' persisted Heidi.

Marie-France shrugged. 'Go and see her, I suppose. But if she thinks I'm apologising for something, she's wrong. It's *her* who should be apologising to me.'

'*Ja!*' Heidi nodded, whipping out her compact mirror and reapplying her lip gloss just as a rather good-looking man with his black Labrador walked past. 'Quite right. You show them.'

Marie-France waited until she and Lottie had made tea together: fish pie (with cheese in it for protein!) followed by chocolate tart.

'Yummy!' grinned Lottie, her mouth smeared with cream, and Matthew had smiled approvingly. He seemed to have got over that awful business with the police. Now as they chatted round the table it felt really natural. Rather nice, in fact.

'Did you know that Lottie's teacher is running a talent show?' she asked.

Matthew groaned. 'Sorry. I forgot to mention it. It was in the class notes. Have you thought of anything you want to do, princess?'

'Play the guitar!' Her voice piped up assuredly and her little face shone, making Marie-France's heart sink.

'You can play a few chords but I don't know if it's enough for a talent show.'

Lottie's eyes filled with tears. 'Please, please. Mummy would like it, wouldn't she, Daddy? She loves dancing and music.'

Loves? That is the present tense, isn't it? Matthew threw a helpless look across the table at her and she could tell that he had noticed too. 'We can do our best,' said Marie-France, sounding bolder than she felt.

Lottie was jumping up and down. 'Can we practise this evening?'

'Darling, it's Marie-France's evening off.'

'I'm going out, I'm afraid.' Her mouth went dry at the thought of the appointment she had arranged with Dawn. Would Phillip be there? Part of her hoped so, despite everything. She missed seeing him every day, just as she missed Thierry. Was it possible to be attracted to two men at the same time?

'Please. Please. Pretty please!'

A vision of her mother not having time for her, thanks to Maurice, came into Marie-France's head. 'OK. Just a quick lesson.'

'That's fantastic.' Matthew gave her a grateful smile. 'I'll clear the dishes while you two go and strum your stuff.'

By the time she'd pedalled madly up to Dawn's, she was nearly half an hour late. Ringing the bell at the security gate, she fully expected a mouthful of abuse. Instead, there was a subdued voice inviting her to make her way down the drive. *Prends garde*, she told herself. A quiet Dawn was, in her experience, far more dangerous than a noisy one.

To her surprise, Dawn opened the door herself instead of the housekeeper. Her face was pale and devoid of make-up. She was even thinner than usual and her hip bones protruded through her white designer jeans. She also had a glass of red wine in her hand and, from her slurred voice, Marie-France suspected it wasn't her first that evening. 'Come in.'

Shocked, Marie-France stared around. Every room on the ground floor was piled high with packing cases. 'You are moving?'

Her words echoed eerily, the way sounds do when a place is empty of furniture. Dawn nodded. 'We have to. Phillip has cleaned me out.'

'I do not understand.'

Dawn gestured that she should follow her through to the conservatory. 'Please, in here. I need to talk to you before the children finish their computer game.' Her eyes wavered. 'I have to apologise to you.'

This had to be a trick! Dawn never apologised to *anyone*.

'Why?'

'Phillip has treated both of us very badly. He has confessed everything now to the police. We were losing money, you see. Or rather he was losing *my* money. He's a gambler as well as a cheater. So when he realised how things bad were, he arranged for the house to be done over ...'

'Done over?'

'Burgled. That's why he made us go out that night instead of having people round. He got one of his shady mates to pretend to break in and take things like the new gold clock in the hall which he hadn't even paid for in full. Then he claimed on the insurance. Except that it went wrong because you let them in without a struggle ...'

'I think he is someone else.'

Dawn waved her hand in dismissal. 'The point is

that because you let them in without putting up a fight, it means the insurance claim might be invalid. That's why he asked you to lie.' She smiled sadly. 'I almost feel sorry for him. Crazy, isn't it?' She looked at Marie-France as though seeking confirmation. 'I suppose it's because part of me is still in love with him just as you were.'

Marie-France felt herself going red. 'I do not love your husband.'

Dawn's thin pencilled eyebrows rose as though to disagree.

'I might...' Marie-France began slowly '... admire him but that is nothing. He try to kiss *me*. Not the other way round.'

Dawn smiled sadly. 'Just what the others used to say.'

'What others?'

'All our previous au pairs fell for Phillip and a lot of women around here, too.' Dawn sighed. 'Not surprising, is it? He has a way of making you feel really special; as though you are the only girl worth looking at. I left my second marriage for him, you know. How stupid was that? But I wasn't the first. That poor woman Sally who died young – whose kid you're looking after now – she was crazy about him although he'd never have left me. He had too much to lose.'

'Lottie's mother had an affair with Phillip?' Marie-France was stunned.

'They knew each other through the gym. One day, I came back early from a retreat and caught them upstairs. She begged me not to say anything.' Dawn's eyes narrowed. 'Of course I was going to. But then she got ill and I couldn't do it to her husband. Whatever everyone thinks of me, I *do* have some heart.'

Marie-France's head was reeling. How could little Lottie's mother have betrayed her family like that? 'So that is why you have affair yourself,' she said coldly. 'To get back at Phillip.'

Dawn's eyes narrowed. 'What are you talking about, you silly girl?'

"I see you! I see you snogging that man with no hair.'

Dawn burst out laughing. 'Yogi? He's my spiritual adviser. He's helping me to meditate my way through this. If it wasn't for him, I don't know how I'd cope. Tell me, Marie-France.' Dawn laid a hand on her arm; she could smell wine. 'Do you know what it is like to be poor. Really poor?'

She nodded. 'Certainly. My mother and I, we are not well off.'

'Pah! I'm not talking about money. We had plenty of that. I'm talking about *love*. My parents didn't love me because I wasn't a boy. They didn't bother with me. Never made me do my homework or go to school if I didn't fancy it. So even at my age, my own kids are better readers than me. That's right! Embarrassing, isn't it? So I decided that if someone fell in love with me, I would not love them back in case they hurt me.'

Her voice dropped. 'That's why my first two marriages broke up and that's why I haven't been able to show my feelings to the children.' Her eyes filled with tears. 'I couldn't cope if they rejected me too.'

Suddenly Marie-France began to feel terribly sorry for this messed-up woman. She was only spilling her soul because she'd hit such a low point. She was drunk too, if she wasn't mistaken. Drunk and tearful just like Maman used to be.

'Do you know what you must do, *madame*?'

Dawn was looking at her as though she was really listening for a change.

'You must tell your children what you have told me. No, they are not too young. They might understand. But at the moment, they are afraid of you. It is not a good thing to be scared of your own mother.'

Dawn put up her hand. 'Shh. They are coming.'

'Mary-Frunch, Mary-Frunch!' Little Tatty Arna threw herself into her arms. 'We've missed you.'

Dawn's face had reverted back to the pinched expression she usually wore.

'Me too.' Tom held out his guitar. 'Mum bought me this cos I broke the last one when I threw it at the wall but I can't play it without you. Can you give me lessons?'

'Maybe one day,' said Marie-France gently. 'But I'm afraid I need to go now.'

'Please,' begged Tom. 'I promise I'll be good. There's nothing else I can do and I don't want to be the odd one out in the talent show at school.'

Odd one out! How well Marie-France could remember that horrible feeling! Hadn't she been the odd one out at school because she hadn't had a father?

'Let me think about it,' she promised. 'I have an idea but I need to check with someone first.'

Meanwhile, little Tatty Arna was tugging her sleeve. 'Will you come and see us in our new home? We've got to move somewhere smaller – to a house that's only

415

got five bedrooms.' She made a face. 'Mum says she doesn't know how we're going to manage.'

Five bedrooms? Hah! Dawn's plea that she was being 'cleaned out' wasn't exactly accurate then. Marie-France knelt down and took Tatty Arna's hand in hers. 'You have your mum and you have your brother. You are very lucky, I think.'

Dawn nodded. 'Thank you.' She bit her lip. 'I don't suppose you would consider coming back to us, would you?'

'Sorry.' Marie-France shook her head. 'I have another family now.'

A family, she almost added, who really appreciated her. In fact, she couldn't wait to get back now to poor little Lottie whose mother had behaved so badly. Poor, poor, unsuspecting Matthew.

'Just one more thing. Someone rang for you the other day. Said his name was Terry.'

Her heart leaped! 'Do you mean Thierry?'

She'd been hoping he might ring her mobile but there hadn't been anything. Not even a missed call.

'I don't know.' Dawn seemed snappy now as though keen to be rid of her. 'Sounded French. Certainly couldn't speak much English. Still, if it's important, he'll call again, won't he? Pity we won't be here now we're moving.'

USEFUL FRENCH/ENGLISH PHRASES

Je ne veux pas travailler (I do not want to work)

J'aime ton mari (I fancy your husband)

Tes enfants sont terribles (Your kids are awful)

J'ai perdu le chien (I have lost the dog)

For homework, translate the following from English into French:

I have borrowed your credit card

Someone rang but I did not take a message

I am three weeks late

Extract from *Easy English for Challenging Au Pairs*

Chapter 30

Matthew felt as though he was going to choke with pride. Just look at the two of them, heads bent over the guitar! Marie-France was showing his daughter how to pluck various strings ('See? This one is A, *chérie!*') and as he picked out the strain of 'Lavender's Blue', he found himself wishing with all his heart that Sally was here to see this.

In the long months after her death, he had convinced himself that they could have got over his wife's stupid affair. It had been, as she had told him, a 'one-night thing with someone who meant nothing'.

'I had too much to drink,' she'd explained. 'I'm sorry, Matthew. So very very sorry.'

But instead, he'd yelled at her. Accused her of being a slut and every other word under the sun. Told her that he'd fight for custody every inch of the way. Refused to sleep in the same bed as her and then – this was the worst bit – ignored her when she went very pale over the next few weeks and said she didn't feel well.

'Go to the doctor then,' he'd snapped. 'And get yourself checked out in case you've picked something up from that lover of yours.'

And that's when they'd diagnosed something far worse: a rare, fast-growing cancer for which there was, at that stage, little hope. Now, infidelity seemed far less of an obstacle than death.

'That sounds amazing,' he said as they finished, giving a little mock bow. 'Your mother would have been so proud of you.'

'Mum can see us now, silly.' Lottie jumped up and down in excitement, trying to touch Marie-France's shoulders and pointing upwards at the same time. 'Can't she?'

Matthew felt uncomfortable for their au pair. Lottie's insistence that her mother was either hovering on the ceiling or hiding in the garden was unnerving at times.

'You are doing very well, *ma chérie*.'

'What about me?' demanded the squat, plump little kid who'd been sitting next to Lottie.

'You too,' smiled Marie-France warmly, looking at him pointedly.

Rather too slowly, Matthew picked up his cue. 'Great, Tom. Great!' When Marie-France had first suggested that they invited the boy from her previous family to do a duet, he'd been impressed by her initiative.

'Lottie isn't ready yet to do it on her own,' she had told him quietly. 'Tom is a starter too and he wants lessons. If he comes here, they play together. That is all right, yes?'

It had been a really good idea. One of his worries had always been that Lottie was an only child. It would do her good to have a friend round on a regular basis like this. As for poor little Tom, he felt sorry for him. There were all kinds of wild rumours flying around school, or so he'd heard, courtesy of Paula who had rung the other day to see if Lottie was going to the swimming party.

Some people seemed to know Phillip was being investigated by the police for fraud. Others apparently claimed Dawn had thrown him out because he'd had another affair. But, as always, it was the kids who suffered.

The following week, he told James he had to leave early. 'What is it this time?' his partner had demanded. 'A dental appointment?'

Their relationship had deteriorated even more since Matthew had refused to reconsider James's plea to stay on. Consequently, they'd lost the Kiddy Bedroom Range client which the firm could have done with and Matthew couldn't help feeling guilty.

'Actually, it's my daughter's school talent show.'

'Talent show!' James raised his hands in despair, which made Matthew feel awful. 'How about some talent in *this* place? Go if you have to, but make sure that the plan for the Coopers' place is ready by the morning. By the way, you might like to know that Karen rang when you were in a meeting. She says she's been signed off for a bit longer. Some staff don't have any sense of responsibility.'

James had to run a tight ship – especially with Matthew having been away for so long – but that comment about Karen wasn't very fair. Then again, he himself hadn't behaved very well towards his PA. Sure, he'd sent her some flowers after the accident but he hadn't called round, which was unforgivable considering she only lived at the other end of town. Maybe, if he was leaving early anyway for the talent show, he'd drop in on Karen just to make sure she was all right. After all, the poor woman was completely on her own. And she'd helped him out when he needed it.

Karen lived in one of those modern apartments at the top of the hill. The car park was at the bottom. Matthew, who'd always thought he was reasonably healthy, began to puff slightly. It couldn't be easy for a woman with a badly broken arm to make her way up and down to the shops.

She was at the door before he'd had a chance to ring the bell: a much thinner Karen with her eyes done up in exaggerated blue make-up and her right arm in a bright green plaster cast. There was an overpowering smell of her usual heavy perfume.

'Thank you so much for coming round,' she gushed, glancing appreciatively at the large box of mint chocolates he'd bought from the garage when filling up. 'How lovely. Thank you! Please. Come in.'

He followed her through the narrow hall and into a small sitting room where there was a pot of tea ready waiting on the table, complete with a home-knitted brown and beige tea cosy.

'I don't have anything to offer you to eat, I'm afraid, Matt. It's difficult to get out to the shops. I do have a neighbour who brings things in every now and then but I don't like to bother her. I suppose I could do one of those drop-off supermarket services but the last time I did that, they brought me the wrong kind of butter. Besides, my appetite's quite gone since the accident.' Karen ran her hands down the sides of her hips. 'I've lost quite a lot of weight, don't you think?'

She was gabbling fast in the way that people do

when they're nervous, realised Matthew. 'You look wonderful.'

She flushed. 'You're just being kind. Now, please sit down.'

He glanced at his watch. It had taken him longer to get here than he'd banked on, forgetting the lunchtime traffic always got busy, especially near Puddleducks nursery.

'Actually, Karen, I don't have much time, I'm afraid. I've left work early to watch Lottie in her school talent show.'

Her face fell. 'Of course.'

It was then that the idea occurred to him. 'Why don't you come with me? I'm sure Lottie would like to see you.'

Karen lit up as though she was a child who'd just been invited on an unexpected treat. 'That would be wonderful. Oh, Matthew. You don't know how happy you've made me. I feel like a prisoner in this place. It would be wonderful, really wonderful to go out for a few hours!'

It wasn't easy helping her down the slope, particularly with the frost that was already forming in preparation for what looked like a very cold afternoon. He had to hold her good hand, which was embarrassing, and then, when they got to the car, almost lift her in. 'I twisted my ankle as well as breaking my arm,' she explained, panting. 'A little less pressure to the right. Thanks. That's better.'

Feeling awkward and also concerned because all this was taking much longer than he'd thought, he leaped into his own seat. But before he could start the engine, he felt Karen reaching out for his hand. 'Matthew, just before we go, I want to say how much I appreciate this.'

'You already have,' he began, feeling slightly suffocated by her over-effusiveness. Maybe he'd made a mistake in offering to take her. Oh God. Maybe the other parents might even assume he'd brought a date! He'd have to make it clear that she was a sort of informal aunt to Lottie. The last thing he wanted was for others to get the wrong idea.

Matthew hadn't realised how nervous he would feel on Lottie's behalf until Mr Balls came out on to the school stage and introduced the event. 'We believe that every child has a talent inside,' he said in a warm but no-nonsense voice. 'Sometimes these gifts aren't obvious and that is where you, the parent or carer, and we, the teachers, come in. It is our job to bring out the best in our kids and, in so doing, to increase their confidence. Confidence is one of the greatest gifts we can give the next generation and it comes from encouraging someone to do the best that they can. That doesn't mean that they have to do it perfectly. In fact, I will be very disappointed if all our stars this afternoon put on a flawless performance.'

There was a nervous ripple of laughter among the audience. 'It is by getting through their so-called mistakes, without being made to feel silly,' continued Mr Balls firmly, 'that they will gain the strength to do the same in life.'

Matthew thought back to last night's practice when Lottie had made a complete hash of her piece. He'd been on the verge of suggesting that she did something else for the show but Marie-France had been wonderfully calm. 'If you make a false note, *ma chérie*, just go on to the next one. I tell Tom to do the same.'

Lottie had seemed reassured enough but Matthew still felt sick with apprehension as he wondered how his little girl was doing behind the curtain. Was she nervous? Was she wishing that her mother was here instead of him?

'You're shaking,' said Karen. 'Poor you.' She slipped her good arm into his for a couple of seconds, giving a quick squeeze of reassurance. 'Don't worry. I'm sure she'll be fine.'

And then the curtains drew back and William, Paula's eldest, edged out nervously before proceeding to sing a rather tuneless version of 'Wish Upon a Star'. It was awful! Real toe-curling stuff! But everyone gave him a huge clap at the end and the kid's face lit up. It was true, what Mr Balls had said, really true. That boy was going to go backstage, now, feeling good about himself.

The next act were a pair of girls who juggled two balls but kept dropping one. Again they were cheered as though they were a brilliant circus act. And then his own little Lottie came on together with podgy little Tom. They sat side by side on stools. Tom looked uncertainly at his daughter as though waiting for an instruction to begin and then she plucked the string.

Matthew wanted to put his head in his hands as she continued to play. It wasn't that she was off-key or playing the wrong notes. It was simply that the agony of watching made him want to curl up in a ball until it was all over. In short, it was far, far worse than doing any exam.

He felt so relieved that he started clapping almost before the final note had been played. '*Fantastique*,' yelled Marie-France, who was sitting on the other side of him. To his embarrassment, she wolf-whistled loudly, slapping her thighs with enthusiasm, and a couple of people turned round.

'Er, Marie-France, we don't usually do that here.'

'Why not?' Her eyes shone. 'She does very well, yes?'

'She was wonderful, Matthew,' said Karen with a catch in her throat. 'You must be so proud.' She slipped her arm in his again for another squeeze although it lasted a bit longer this time. To his surprise, he found himself returning it. 'I am,' he croaked. 'Very.'

They'd been asked to collect the children about half an hour after the show had finished to give the kids and teachers time to tidy up. 'I'll run you home,' he offered, thinking that this was better than making small talk with Karen with everyone watching and getting the wrong idea. 'Marie-France, do you mind waiting here just in case Lottie comes out early and then I'll come back to get you.'

It was just as well that Karen did all the nattering while he drove her home. He was unable to speak, still choked by pride and also sadness.

'Wasn't she wonderful, Matt? I think you've struck lucky with this last au pair of yours. Fancy being able to play the guitar like that! Oh, Matthew, please don't get yourself so upset.'

The last bit was said just after he had drawn up

outside her flat. 'I can't help it,' he managed to blurt out. 'I just wish that Lottie had had Sally there.'

'But she has you as a dad, Matthew! You're a wonderful father and such a good, kind man.' Now it was *her* eyes that were filling with tears. To his surprise, she leaned towards him and kissed him lightly on the cheek, even closer to his lips than last time. Without meaning to, he found himself hugging her back. It was so comforting to be comforted!

But as she released him, a tall elegant woman with blond hair tied up at the back and purple-framed glasses drew up in her car and parked next to them.

'That's my neighbour.' Karen made no effort to draw away. 'The one who does my shopping every now and then.'

Her *neighbour*? Matthew watched the woman glance across as though acknowledging them briefly and then walk up towards the block of maisonettes. So that's where Christina lived! Oh God. She must have seen him hugging Karen!

Hot with embarrassment, he recalled the conversation he'd had with her about the 'woman at work who seemed rather friendly.' What was it Christina had said in reply? Something about it not being kind to 'allow someone to get the wrong idea'.

Well, that's exactly what he'd gone and done, looking at Karen's rapt expression. And now Christina had the wrong idea too.

Idiot, idiot, idiot! Matthew mentally kicked himself all the way back to school where Lottie and Marie-France were waiting for him. But he had to put his own feelings on one side in order to tell his daughter how amazing she'd been.

'I was so proud of you!' He put his arm around her. 'You didn't get a note wrong! Not, of course, that it would have mattered if you had.' He turned to Marie-France. 'Thank you so much. You're a brilliant teacher.'

She beamed. 'Tom was very good too, I think.' Then her face darkened. 'It is a sham his mother could not be here to see him.'

'Don't you mean "a *shame*"?' he suggested.

She'd shaken her head. 'I do not think so. Dawn, she is not genuine.'

No point in arguing. Marie-France was a great improvement on all the others but he'd noticed that she could be quite bossy when she thought she was right.

That night, after supper, Lottie went straight to bed. 'She is exhausting,' announced Marie-France when Matthew came downstairs after kissing his daughter goodnight.

Exhausting and exhausted! He nodded. 'It's been a long day for her.'

'And for you too, I think.' Marie-France sat next to him on the sofa. It was the first time she'd ever done that! Au pairs were meant to share the sitting room with you. The guidelines said that. But usually Lottie was here at the same time and Marie-France had always sat on one of the chairs. Her proximity felt rather awkward.

'You are upset after the show, yes?'

Matthew nodded, edging slightly away from her. He wasn't going to make the same mistake he had with

Karen this afternoon. 'I wished her mother could have seen her.'

Marie-France's lips tightened. 'I was not going to tell you this, Matthew, but I do not like to see you so upset.' She lowered her voice. 'I do not think your wife is an angel.'

'I beg your pardon?'

'I have discovered she is having affair.'

'What?' He stared at her, stunned. 'Who told you this?'

'Dawn. She say her husband Phillip has affair with your wife. They meet at the gym.'

The gym? She'd said it was a man at work!

He leaped to his feet. It was all making sense now. The familiar way that Phillip had called him Matt on the phone. Sally had been the only person who had called him that. He'd picked it up from her! And Sally's sudden interest in the gym, and the text message with the initial P at the end.

'Where are you going, Matthew?'

'To find the bastard.'

'Ssh, Lottie might hear you.' Marie-France looked scared.

He felt so mad that he almost didn't care. 'Stay here, please. Look after her. I'll be back as soon as I can.'

Later, Matthew would say that he hardly remembered roaring up the drive to Dawn's house and making her tell him where Phillip was. Could hardly recall driving blindly through the streets to knock furiously at the door of the flat at the other end of town.

But what he did remember was the suave, smooth

428

face which answered: the face of the bastard who had gone off with his wife.

'Is it true?' he yelled.

'Calm down, Matt.'

'Don't call me that!' Throwing himself into the small hall, he tried to grab the man by his collar but Phillip side-stepped him deftly, almost falling over a suitcase. Clearly he'd had plans to go somewhere. Well, not now, he wasn't.

'Is it true? Did you have an affair with my wife?'

'Sally?' Phillip appeared to consider the idea. 'Actually, it is.'

'She told me it was a one-night stand with a business colleague.'

'Did she now? Well, in a way, we were doing business but it lasted a bit more than one night. Now come on, Matthew, there's no need to get upset about it, is there? She was lonely – you didn't really *do* it for her in that department, if you know what I mean. We had a lot in common. Try and see it my way, man to man, can you? Dawn and I simply weren't right for each other. But Sally is dead so there is really no point in—'

And that was the other bit that Matthew clearly remembered, because he'd never hit a man before. Not like this. Phillip slumped to the ground, clutching his jaw and whimpering like a baby.

'If you're going to mess with other men's wives,' said Matthew through gritted teeth and nursing his own hand which was searing with pain, 'that's what you're going to get. Be grateful it's not worse.'

Then he drove home, hardly knowing where he was

going, conscious only of an agonising pain in his right hand. When he opened the door, an ashen-faced Marie-France was waiting for him. 'You kill him, yes?'

'No, but I would have liked to have done. He might go to the police but I don't care.'

'The police?' She laughed. 'It is *them* he needs to be afraid of.'

'Why?'

'Dawn, she tells me that he tricks the insurance company.'

'I had a feeling that might be the case,' he said slowly. 'But I wasn't quite sure of the details...'

So Marie-France filled in the gaps. And then Matthew realised that now he *really* knew how to get back at Phillip.

USEFUL (BUT SOMETIMES UNRELIABLE)
LITHUANIAN PHRASES

Įveikatą(Cheers/good health)

Šis vyras užmokės uz viską (This gentleman will pay for everything)

Mano laivas su oro pagalve pilnas unguriu (My hovercraft is full of eels)

Chapter 31

Braxton Hicks *again*, the midwife had sighed after Fatima's latest false alarm. And if that wasn't enough, Jilly now had another irate mum on the phone: Brigid, with whom she'd placed an Italian au pair the other week.

'So within half an hour of getting here from the airport, Maria told me she was "going to explore the area". But by eleven o'clock in the evening, she hadn't come back! My husband went out to look – you can imagine how worried we were – and then found her in the local pub with a complete stranger. She was absolutely plastered *and* all over him like a rash. When my husband suggested that she came back, Maria announced it was her free time and that she could do what she wanted.'

There was a brief pause for breath at the other end during which Jilly leaped in quickly before her client could continue. 'I'm afraid she was right—'

'Hang on. I haven't finished.' Brigid – whose son Bruce had been a friend of the twins since Puddleducks days – was obviously determined to give her the whole story, word for word. 'The next day, she did some half-hearted dusting and vacuuming and then went out for the afternoon. When she got back, she asked if she could take a cup of tea up to her bedroom. Fair enough, I thought. But then within a few minutes, she came back down and asked if she could make herself *another* cup of tea. I thought it was funny she'd drunk that one so fast. So I followed her back upstairs and listened through the door. There was a man's voice on the other side!'

Brigid paused dramatically for effect. 'So we knocked on the door and there was all this scuffling on the other side. When she finally opened it, the curtains were closed even though it was the afternoon – and my husband could see a pair of male feet underneath.'

Jilly made what she hoped were sympathetic sounds.

'You wouldn't believe the sort of man standing behind my lovely curtains! He was really rough; the kind you'd cross over the road to avoid. And there he is, in my house with his nose – covered in studs – pressed against my lovely Designer Guild drapes from the Curtain Exchange.'

'So what did you do?'

'Yelled at him to get out, of course, and then I told Maria that I was calling you. She's meant to be a Catholic! Got all these religious pictures everywhere in her room but she seems to think it's fine picking up strangers in the street.'

'Oh dear.' Jilly sighed. 'I'm so sorry but maybe it's just a question of letting her settle in. It's her first time away from home and she's probably tasting a bit of freedom—'

'Well she can bloody well taste it in another house,' cut in Brigid crossly. 'I want to swap her for another!'

Not again! This had happened twice in the last month. First there'd been the au pair who had ticked the box for 'Driver' on the application form but didn't actually have a licence. (It turned out she'd banked on passing her test before arriving but had failed the week before.) And then there'd been another au pair who refused to cook meat. She'd stated she was a vegetarian but hadn't said that she couldn't physically touch the stuff.

'Brigid, do you remember what it was like when you were a teenager?'

There was an audible bristle at the other end. 'What's that got to do with it?'

'Didn't you ever try to do something that was, well, a bit risky?'

'Maybe. So?'

'Well I certainly did.' Jilly winced at the memory. 'One summer when I was about sixteen, my mother packed me off to spend a few weeks with a friend of hers, not far from here, actually. It was very boring compared with London so I shimmied out of the window and went to this dance round the corner in the village hall.' She laughed at the memory. 'I wasn't bad. Just desperate to find a boyfriend.'

'What's that got to do with this?'

'I just thought you might be generous enough to give this girl a second chance. I'll have a word with her if you like and explain she can't bring in strangers off the street. If at the end of this month, you're still unhappy, then of course we'll find you someone else.'

There was a grudging noise. 'All right. But only until the end of the month, mind.'

'Thank you for being so understanding. I'll call Maria on her mobile now and make an appointment for an informal chat.'

As she put down the phone, there was a strange click on the line. 'Mum? You were listening?'

'Of course I was, dear. It's like when those people record your call for training purposes. You did very well. I'm proud of you. I couldn't have handled it better myself. Well, I *could*, obviously, but you know what I mean. You've really come on in leaps and bounds. Now, did you find a PA as I suggested?'

Jilly groaned. 'Yes. A French girl who's working as an au pair for one of my clients. But I'm not sure about her now. She might have had a thing with someone's husband.'

'Listen, darling. Delegating is an art. Take her on; try to train her up; make sure she doesn't make a play for David; and if there are any signs of trouble, fire her. Simple. Your father was always ogling my personal assistants but I made sure it didn't go any further.'

'Please, Mum, I don't want to know all this stuff about Dad. What I would like to know, however, is if you're going to this party or not. Dad keeps ringing me about it. And remember, you don't know anything about it.'

'Of course I don't, dear. I'm upstairs in your bedroom trying on my outfit in front of the mirror. Did I tell you I bought a second one? Much nicer than the first. Come on up and tell me what you think.'

Mum looked incredible. She certainly didn't look her age. That Mrs Middleton coat-dress showed off her legs to perfection, spelling out 'elegance' with a capital 'E'.

'Amazing!'

435

Her mother gave a satisfied smile as though she thought exactly the same herself. 'Thank you, darling.'

'And your hair looks fabulous too.'

'Your little man down the road did it. Now tell me, what are *you* going to wear?'

As if she'd had time to think! 'I've no idea.'

'Thought as much. Tell you what. Why don't you go round to your friend Paula's and get her to go shopping with you. I'll hold the fort at this end. There are a few more spreadsheets I want to set up on the agency system before I leave you to it. Now do try to find something reasonably sexy, won't you, dear? It might bring David to heel again.'

Only her mother could use that kind of expression! 'David just doesn't like me working, that's all.'

'Sure?' Her mother gave her a pitying look. 'Because I caught him making a rather furtive phone call on his mobile in the car outside the other night. As soon as he realised I was watching, he quickly ended the call and shoved the phone in his pocket. Now if *that* isn't suspicious, what is?'

Jilly wasn't sure whether to confide in Paula or not. After all, her husband Nigel might tell David. On the other hand, she needed to talk to *someone*. It was also good to get out of the house! Ever since she'd started the agency, she'd felt tied to the house, never feeling able to turn off her mobile or be away from her files in case there was an emergency or a placement to be made. Even now, she had her phone on in the back pocket of her jeans, just in case.

'Sorry to turn up without ringing first,' she said

when Paula opened the door. As usual, her friend was in her jeggings. Behind her, in the den, Jilly could see the television blaring with one of Paula's favourite fitness instructors fiercely ordering her to squeeze her abs NOW. There was the sound of kids yelling from the garden and William ran past clutching a Halloween pumpkin and a water pistol.

'Not inside,' yelled Paula.

'But it's raining,' he screamed back.

'Then you're going to get wet anyway!'

'Where's Antoinette?' enquired Jilly as they went back inside, almost trampled by the small horde following with their plastic shotguns, leaving muddy footprints everywhere.

'It's her day off. God, how I hate half-term.'

'But it's not until next week – isn't it?'

'I know but I've got pre-half term stress. Did you get the invitation to William's party?'

'Yes, but—'

'And you are going to come along and help, aren't you? It's a swimming party at the leisure centre so I need as many eyes and hands as I can get.' Paula rolled her eyes. 'Nigel can't get along until later, apparently.'

'I suppose so but—'

'MUM, MUM...'

'Shit. Immy's stuck again. Listen, Jilly, I'm sorry but can we chat another time? Unless it's really urgent, that is.'

Jilly bit her lip. 'I'm worried that David is going off me.'

'They all do. It's called living with MAK. Marriage after kids.'

'No, but really. Nigel hasn't said anything, has he?'

'Not that I know of but he's shot off to Egypt again on business which is why I'm so grateful you're coming to help. Listen, Jilly, you're probably feeling insecure after Mark and Suzy. They're definitely getting a divorce and he wants to marry that nineteen-year-old, silly old fool. But David would be mad if he did anything stupid. And so would you.'

'I know, but—'

'MUM, MUM...'

'Was there anything else?'

'I wondered if you fancied coming shopping with me actually. I've got to get an outfit for Mum's party.'

'Shopping? With this lot going mad around me? Wish I could. Why don't you just go upstairs and take a look through my-used-to-be-a-size-twelve section. It's on the left.' She shot a glance at Jilly. 'You've lost weight, haven't you? Probably the stress of working again, lucky you. Anyway, you might fit one or two things.'

Halfway up the stairs, Jilly almost collided with a tall, dark-haired girl dressed in a black leather jacket, sporting what appeared to be two terrible cold sores. Then she realised they were two small pale pink lip studs. How revolting!

'*Au revoir*,' Antoinette muttered. 'I go out now.'

She was certainly dressed to kill, thought Jilly turning her attention to Paula's huge walk-in closet. Wow! Paula had the most amazing wardrobe collection. This purple shift dress was nice. And it fitted. Jilly surveyed her reflection in the mirror. Maybe a bit short? Then again, why not? She'd always been quite proud of her legs and here was a sweet little black cardigan to go with it.

If she teamed it with sheer black tights and high heels, she would look... what? Striking? Different. Not like the usual Jilly. She could see that from the image which was now smiling hesitantly back at her from Paula's lovely wardrobe mirror. And that was exactly what she wanted.

Of course David wasn't having an affair! She knew him better than that. But she definitely needed to do something to help their marriage get back on track.

Not long now until the anniversary party and if she was going to take a whole weekend off work, Jilly needed to get organised. If only she hadn't offered to help out with Paula's party today. Talking of which, she hadn't even got a present. Oh God. Jilly rifled through her present drawer trying to find something that Paula hadn't given her in the past. A play dough set. Too young? A cowboy outfit aged 5–6. Too small. A packet of Christmas chocolates in the shape of a stocking past its sell-by date. Tempting.

Instead, Jilly thought guiltily as she swallowed Santa's yummy bottom, she'd just have to buy something on the way to the party itself. Paula had asked her to take three kids in her car but she had to drop Nick off on the way to his Duke of Edinburgh practice and after that—

What was that commotion? It sounded like someone yelling downstairs. And Bruno was making the most peculiar noise!

'Jilly, Jilly.' Her mother was hammering at the door.

'That bloody dog. You'll never believe what he's gone and eaten now? My HRT tablets. The whole packet including the foil. It's going to set me back weeks. There's no way I can go to my own party if I look old and grumpy.'

'Your HRT tablets?' So that's how she did it! It wasn't drinking lots of water or taking weird supplements. But that wasn't important. Not compared with Bruno who was suddenly looking rather sprightly.

'Look, Mum, I'll take him to the vet if you do the D of E run. I'll have to ask Marie-France if she could take the twins to the party. And—'

'—Jee-lee.' It was Fatima, her nose in the fridge. 'I theenk I 'ave Braxton Hiccups again. Or maybe I eat too much *ekmek*.'

What the hell was *ekmek*?

'Bread,' piped up Harry helpfully.

'You'll have to come with me then,' she snapped unsympathetically. Scooping up the dog, she belted out towards the car, impatiently waiting for Fatima to waddle into the front seat before heading off towards the vet at the other end of town.

'HRT tablets?' repeated the receptionist, looking from her to the dog and then Fatima.

'Not for me.' Jilly was conscious of everyone looking at her. 'They're my mother's.'

'That's what they all say,' chuckled a jolly-looking man hanging on to a Great Dane.

'He will be all right, won't he?'

The receptionist looked grave. 'I can't say. Take a seat and I'll squeeze you in as soon as I can.'

'Mee-sis Jee-lee. I am hungry still.'

Everyone's eyes in reception swivelled to her as though Jilly was somehow responsible. 'I do feed her, honestly,' she said lightly, trying to make a joke. No one laughed. Not surprising. This was no laughing matter. In fact it was a complete bloody nightmare. The dog might die – although it had to be said that at this very moment, he was leaping all over the place, putting his nose into every crotch in sight.

Oh no. Not her mobile again.

'Madame Jilly?'

It was a deep-voiced man with a heavy French accent.

'My name is Thierry. I am a friend of Marie-France. You are the agency that give her a job, yes?'

'Well, yes but—'

'It is very urgent that I grab her.'

'Sorry. She's taking some children to a swimming party.'

'Where is partee?'

Jilly hesitated. Marie-France might not want to see this boy, but on the other hand, this sounded urgent.

'Plis,' he was repeating. 'I have a ferry to catch and I must tell her something before I go.'

'Mrs Collins?'

The vet was at the door now signalling she should go in.

'Plis,' the boy was still saying. 'I must talk to her.'

'Mrs Collins.' The vet was looking impatient. 'I was told you were an emergency. Would you like this appointment or not?'

Email from Susan Manners to
Jilly's Au Pair Agency

Thank you very much for teaming us up with Natascha. She is very nice but we have one small but hugely irritating and unsightly problem. Natascha eats with her mouth open at mealtimes and it is setting a bad example to the children. I have tried explaining it's bad manners but she won't stop. Any suggestions?

Chapter 32

She'd left her mobile behind, realised Marie-France as she drove to Antoinette's family's swimming party with the twins and Lottie. The excited babble in the back made it hard to concentrate!

'Can we go on that chute thing that makes you go so fast that your stomach spews out of your mouth?'

'Don't be stupid, dumbo. It's the other way round. It goes so fast that your mouth spews out of your stomach! Tom told me. His dad took him last Saturday.'

'But how does your stomach get back again?' This was little Lottie's worried voice in the back of the car. 'I don't like going fast, Marie-France.'

Originally, Jilly had been going to give them both a lift but then there'd been some panic over the dog and Marie-France had called Matthew at work to explain she was doing the party run after all.

'I don't know,' he had said and she had heard the worry in his voice. 'You've never done that route before and it's a tricky road.'

'But Lottie will be so disappointed if she cannot go,' pointed out Marie-France.

He'd reluctantly agreed and now here she was in the car with two noisy boys who were teasing Lottie but in a kind, brotherly way. It reminded her of her own childhood in France when she'd been so jealous of friends who had brothers – or indeed sisters.

'You're going to go right down to the bottom of the pool and lose your stomach in the deep end!'

'You're going to lose your mouth!

'You won't be able to eat again!'

'You won't be able to talk again!'

'BOYS! Stop.' She paused at a particularly busy stretch of road where they had to merge into a stream of traffic coming from the right. Why did the English have to drive on the wrong side?

There was a space! Quick! Right. Or was it left? Right. She'd go for right.

'Alfie, please stop kicking the back of my seat. Yes? And Harry, ascend your window.'

'But I'm waving at Heidi! Look she's behind us!'

Marie-France glanced in the mirror. It was true. Her friend was flashing her lights and waving. This swimming party might be good fun. Pity that the tarty Antoinette was going to be there too.

'I'm hungry!'

'I need a pee!'

'Too bad.' Marie-France certainly wasn't getting off the road now she was on it.

'I've left my birthday present behind.'

'Your mother can give it to Paula another day.'

Merde! The boys were such a handful compared with Lottie, who was sitting as good as gold in the back. Still, at least the journey was taking her mind off Phillip. Now she knew the truth about the burglary, she was furious! How dare he put his own stepchildren through such a terrifying ordeal?

Yes, Marie-France told herself as she overtook a car that was going too slowly in front, she'd definitely done the right thing in telling Matthew about the insurance scam. With any luck, Phillip would be punished. Yet she still couldn't get rid of that funny feeling in her heart for him.

The back-seat arguments distracted her so much that she made a wrong turn. Consequently they were nearly half an hour late and then it took ages to find a parking space. The pool was in a vast modern steel complex with a cinema and a bowling rink as well. *Mon Dieu*, the noise was deafening! It was like being in a human zoo, observed Marie-France, with all those kids rushing in and out followed by bored-looking parents. Some were clutching streamers and balloons, indicating that theirs wasn't the only birthday party today.

As they went in – 'Boys, not so fast!' – there was the overpowering smell of chlorine and she could see kids splashing in a huge pool on the other side of the glass wall. Her mind went back to when she and Thierry used to swim in the lake. It had been there that they had made love for the first time just after her seventeenth birthday. He had undone the strap under her top and . . .

'Marie-France, Marie France?' Little Lottie was jumping up and down next to her. 'I don't *really* have to wear my water wings, do I? The boys will say I'm a baby if I do.'

'Let me see how strong a swimmer you are,' she suggested. 'Then I'll decide.'

It was amazing to think how far they had come since

she'd arrived! It had taken time and perseverance but now Lottie really did seem to trust her. Finally as they made their way towards Paula at the ticket office, Marie-France felt even more protective towards this little girl who had been through too much.

Meanwhile, she had to keep her wits about her. This was a busy place. 'HarryandAlfie, stay with *me*. Like Lottie.'

Paula was frowning. 'Where's Jilly?'

'She had an emergency,' Marie-France began to explain but Paula's face grew stern.

'I should have known it. Toby's dad couldn't make it either. You'd think his dog could give birth on another day, wouldn't you? Right. Here are your tickets and your identity badges. Marie-France, you're in charge of these three. Antoinette and Heidi and the other au pairs have gone in to change. Shit. I forgot. You won't be able to go into the Men's, will you? Look, you boys. Go in on your own but meet us on the other side by the shallow end. Got it? Try and stick together, for pity's sake. I'll be in the Spectator's Gallery.'

So she was going to sit back while they did all the hard work? Paula would get on well with her mother! Maman had once, she recalled, taken her to an amuse - ment centre in the holidays. But instead of playing with her, she'd distractedly pressed some euros into her palm and said, 'See you in the bar later, *chérie*!' When she'd got there, her mother had been gaily knocking back a glass of Beaujolais, smoking a cigarette and chatting up one of the waiters.

'Hi! You made it!' Heidi was waving gaily from the

queue outside the Ladies Changing Room. 'Come and join us!'

Antoinette was there too, worse luck, wearing her Goth look: tight black leather jacket and leggings to match. She was eyeing up every skinny spotty youth around them.

'Oy!' snapped a large woman with bulges of fat over the top of her skirt waistband. 'Get to the back of the queue like the rest of us. And put out that fag!'

'Antoinette,' growled Marie-France warningly. Scowling, the girl dropped the cigarette and deliberately ground it into the floor with her heel.

'Bloody foreigners,' hissed the woman.

'See?' Heidi hissed at Antoinette. 'You give us all a bad name.'

'Right, next group!' called out the attendant and in they went.

Lottie took ages to get changed and by the time she was ready, the others had all gone in. 'Quick,' Marie-France said, grabbing the little girl's cold thin arm. 'Watch out for the spray!'

They laughed as the automatic jets in the wall by the footbowl switched on, spraying them both. Marie-France scoured the pool for the boys. Just as she'd thought, they hadn't waited at all but were just about to go into that huge blue chute. It was part of a spaghetti-like complex. It was really hard to keep your eye on all the kids!

'Marie-France, watch me swim!' Lottie jumped into the deep end before she could stop her. 'See. I don't need my water wings, do I?'

Clearly not. Just as the little girl wasn't allergic to

cheese after all! Sometimes parents really *didn't* know best! She looked across the pool to the spectator's gallery where someone was waving. It was Paula with her camera and what looked like a bottle of wine.

Heidi nudged her. 'Crazy, *ja*? She organises a swimming party when her husband is away working and she gets *us* to look after her guests. I'm so glad I don't work for her. She and Antoinette deserve each other, don't you think? By the way, have you seen her over there?'

Incroyable! Antoinette was just idly chatting to a group of boys, stretching this way and that in her skimpy red bikini and totally ignoring the group of children she was in charge of. Looked as if it was down to her and the other girls. This was impossible! There was Harry whizzing out from the bottom of the chute and there was Alfie scampering into it – or was that the other way round?

Marie-France's heart quickened. *Mon Dieu*. Little Lottie had somehow raced off towards the enormous closed chute and was now disappearing into it. Rushing past a group of boys who were gazing at her own figure admiringly, she pushed them to one side in her bid to catch her.

The noise was deafening! You couldn't hear anything unless you were right close up to each other shouting in each other's ear. Paula's waving intensified. If she was that excited, she should be down here with them!

She glanced up the entrance to the chute but couldn't see anyone. 'Lottie! Lottie! Come down. It's too high for you.'

Had she already come out the other end? Marie-France scanned the sea of bodies bobbing up and down in the water. No wonder the lifeguards sitting on either side of the pool in their chairs were concentrating so hard on the water. It was like being at a tennis match but – she realised now – far more dangerous. An uneasy feeling crept into her chest. Maybe she shouldn't have been so blasé about allowing Lottie to go in without water wings. The little girl would build up speed going down the tunnel and she'd hit the water with terrible force like that child just now. It didn't look safe!

'You going up or not?' It was the woman who had objected to her joining the queue behind Heidi.

Marie-France eyed the steps in front of her warily. She'd always been a strong swimmer. But being enclosed in a tunnel was different. It was one of the few things that terrified her. Once, she and Thierry had been visiting some ancient caves not far from home. Never before had she felt so frightened; so hemmed in. Sweat had trickled down her back and she'd been unable to breathe. 'It's OK,' Thierry had reassured her. 'I'll take you back.'

Right now, she was getting the same feeling but there was no Thierry to hold her hand. Yet Lottie still hadn't come down the chute. She *had* to go up to find her! She owed it to Matthew and to Lottie. And, she thought with a lump in her throat, to Sally too.

'I'm going,' she snapped at the woman behind her. 'Lottie? Where are you?'

Her voice sang out hollowly. Behind her, people

449

were shoving each other in the queue, desperate to get to the top. Up and up she went. *Mon Dieu* it was high. She could hear the sound of crying now. A high-pitched whine that set her nerves on edge. Up and up. Round a corner and... ah there she was!

'Marie-France!' Lottie was standing behind someone sitting at the top. 'Immy won't move. She's stuck.'

Immy? What was she doing here. Surely she was too young?

Marie-France knelt down beside the little girl whose face was blotchy from crying. 'I'm scared. I can't move.'

'Not you again,' snarled the woman behind her. 'You're causing a pile-up. There'll be an accident if you don't shift it.'

There was a strange thudding noise in Marie-France's ears as the blue walls of the tunnel seemed to be closing in on her. She felt faint. Sick. Immy began to cry again. The drumming in her ears reverberated so she didn't know if it was the sobbing she could hear or the general screams of the swimming pool.

'I said MOVE IT,' roared the woman. 'I'm being pushed from behind and so are my kids.'

Desperately, Marie-France forced herself to kneel down and take Immy on her knee. 'Don't leave me behind,' whimpered Lottie in her ear. 'I don't want to go down there on my own. I want you to take me on your knee too.'

'There isn't room, *ma chérie*.' It was true. Immy was like a plump little chicken. There was no way she could carry both of them.

'I can't move,' wailed Immy. 'And I need a wee wee.'

'I'm scared,' whimpered Lottie.

'MARIE-FRANCE. MARIE-FRANCE!'

She was hallucinating now. Imagining that Thierry was here, just as he had been in those caves. But wait a minute! There was a stir behind her. Someone was trying to climb up to rescue them. A lifeguard perhaps? Either way, the crowd behind was reluctantly parting as a tall, lithe skinny youth in boxers raced up the stairs towards them. Disbelievingly, she took in the soft brown eyes and flop of hair over that right eye along with the silver St Christopher round his neck that she had given him last Christmas.

'Thierry,' she gasped as he took her in his arms. *Mon Dieu!* She'd forgotten how his touch could make her melt.

'Thierry,' she repeated. 'Is it you? Or am I dreaming?'

'For God's sake,' snarled the woman. 'If you don't move, I swear I'll push you myself.'

'I've got something to tell you.' His eyes searched her face. 'About your father.'

'FOR CRYING OUT LOUD,' roared the large woman behind them. 'It's not *EastEnders* by the sea, you know.'

'*Pardon, madame.*' He flashed her a smile which melted most women and, miraculously, appeared to have a similar effect on this one. 'I apologise for holding you in.'

'Up,' Marie-France wanted to say. 'Holding you up.' But Thierry was now looking around, taking in the situation at a glance. She felt a bolt of relief. After all, Thierry was a volunteer lifeguard at the pool in the town near their home. If anyone could get them out of this mess, it was him.

'You take the little one and I'll take the bigger child,' he ordered.

'But I can't. I don't like—'

'Tunnels. I know. Sit down there, in front of me.' He splayed his legs on either side of her and lifted Lottie on to his lap behind her back. They made a tight unit of four. Ugh! She could feel a horrible damp warmth seep through, suggesting that Immy hadn't been able to hang on any more.

'OK, everyone,' announced Thierry. 'We're off!'

They spun down and down, round and round. The screams were so loud that they hurt her ears but she wasn't sure if they were hers or the kids'. With a terrific splash, they shot out of the bottom of the shute like peas coming out of a pod. Down. Down. Under the water, she thought she caught a glimpse of Lottie's red swimming costume. Up again! Yes! Gasping as she emerged out of the water, she could see – *Mon Dieu!* – Paula floundering in the deep end, sinking down to the bottom. She must have seen Immy shoot out and jumped into the pool after her.

'I can't swim!' the woman was screaming. 'I can't swim!'

Merde! There was one of the lifeguards shooting through the water towards Paula. The other had already scooped out little Immy and was making his way with her to the side of the pool where Antoinette was standing, waving her arms and no doubt claiming that Immy had just run off and that none of this was her fault.

Thierry was nowhere to be seen. Had he been a figment of her imagination?

Lottie? *Mon Dieu*. Lottie! Heart thudding, Marie-France flicked her wet hair away from her eyes and, urgently treading water, scanned the pool. *Merde*. Mother of God.

Where was little Lottie?

JILLY'S AU PAIR AGENCY: GUIDELINES FOR FAMILIES

Make sure the au pair knows where the first-aid box is. If she has not got a first-aid qualification, try to explain basic safety procedures.

Chapter 33

Matthew wasn't having the best of days. For a start, he couldn't stop worrying about Marie-France driving Lottie to that party. They'd had a few dry runs together and she'd seemed all right: steady and watchful when it came to other traffic. But you never knew.

That wasn't all, either. Ever since the talent show last week, he had had an uneasy heavy feeing at the pit of his stomach about Karen and Christina.

The first had sent him a card with a little red robin on the front. Inside, was a message in flowery writing. *I had such a wonderful time with you. Thank you for including me in your little family.* There had been a small kiss afterwards which had made his skin crawl.

He *hadn't* included her in his *little family*, as she'd put it. He'd simply felt sorry for the woman and now she'd misinterpreted that spontaneous hug he had so stupidly given her.

To make it worse, it appeared as though she had emailed several other people about it. Elaine, who worked in accounts, had made a point of mentioning it when she'd come up to give him some forms about his impending departure. 'I hear you took Karen out the other day.' Her eyes glittered with curiosity. 'That was really kind of you. She said she had a lovely time.'

'I didn't take her out,' he shot back. 'I invited her to

something at my daughter's school because she's been doing some babysitting for me.'

'Ah.' Elaine breathed in almost audibly. 'How sweet! It's really nice that you're able to help each other like that.'

She might as well have added the phrase 'two lonely hearts together'. It isn't like that, he wanted to say, but to deny it would simply have added fuel to the fire. Besides, they wouldn't have believed him. It was so easy to get the wrong idea just as Christina must have done.

Just as *he'd* done too. When Sally was meant to have been at the gym, she was really with that horrible swarthy grease bag. '*You didn't do it for her in that department.*' Wasn't that what Phillip had said before Matthew had socked him one?

Was that true? He had thought that his wife's reluctance to talk to him in bed, let alone do anything else, was because they were both exhausted. Neither of them had found it easy to have a small baby without any family help. But he'd never thought that she was having an affair.

'How could you have been so stupid as to risk it all, Sally,' he muttered under his breath as he sat at his desk now, poring over some plans for a supermarket car park. 'And how could you have done it with a man like *that*?'

'Hi, Matthew!' Belinda, who was James's new PA, swept in with another file. 'I heard you saw Karen last week! That was so sweet of you to take her out to dinner.'

Had everyone got the wrong idea? 'We actually went

to something at my daughter's school,' he retorted sharply.

Belinda raised her beautifully shaped arching eyebrows. 'Whatever! Anyway, when you see her again, perhaps you could give her this.' She put a bag in front of him. 'It's some of her personal stuff from her desk. We thought she might need it if she's not coming back for a while.'

'But I'm not going round to see her,' he began and then stopped. What was it Christina had said before. 'You need to set boundaries clearly.' He had to deliver these plans to the council planning department after lunch and that would take him past Karen. Maybe the bag would give him an excuse to put things straight.

This time he'd make it very clear, Matthew told himself, pulling into the car park by the flats. Explain that he valued her friendship but that...

Oh God. She was waiting for him at the door, wearing another of those too-clingy wrap-around dresses that revealed almost every curve. Desperately he tried to look somewhere else. The sling, for example, on her right arm.

'Thank you so much for coming, Matthew!' She glanced at the bag he was carrying. 'How kind! You shouldn't have brought me anything. You spoil me!'

'Not at all,' replied Matthew awkwardly as he followed her into her little flat and took in, with a sinking breath, the fruit cake on the trolley and the blue and pink floral china cups and saucers.

'It took me a while to get them ready,' she gushed. 'It takes so long to do anything one-handed! And I'm afraid

I've only got long-life because I'm out of the real sort until my neighbour comes round. But I thought—'

He cut in. 'Karen, I'm here to bring you your things from work, as I said. But I also wanted to explain something. The other day, when I brought you back from Lottie's concert, I'm afraid my emotions got the better of me.'

To his horror, she took his hand with her good one. Her eyes were sparkling with tears but they didn't look like the sad variety. 'Please, Matthew. You don't have to apologise. I feel the same way. I really do. It's not being unfaithful to your wife. I am sure she would want you to be happy. My brother's wife found someone a year after he died and—'

'No.' He heard his voice rise. 'That's just it, Karen. I don't feel anything for you. I'm sorry but I just felt... well... worried about you being here on your own.'

She moved backwards in her chair. 'But you *kissed* me!'

'No, you kissed *me*. I just gave you a hug and I didn't mean to do that. I was upset.'

God, he felt like a heel to watch her cow-like eyes fill with tears of hurt. 'It was all so emotional after the concert. I had wanted Sally to be there and—'

'I thought you cared for me!' Little red spots were beginning to appear on her cheeks.

'I do but not in that way,' he said helplessly.

She bit her lip. 'I see.'

Matthew's hands were sweating profusely. 'I don't want you to get the wrong idea or anyone else for that matter. Some of the girls at work... well, they seem to think that there's something going on between us.'

The spots on her cheeks grew brighter and she said nothing.

Matthew stood up. The sooner he could escape from here, the better. 'Of course, if you need something, just give me a ring. Shopping or that sort of thing,' he added hastily in case there should be any more misunderstandings.

She turned away in her chair. 'Please go, Matthew. I feel so embarrassed.'

'Don't be.' He reached out for her hand but she pushed him away.

'See what I mean? You're too kind for your own good, Matthew. You're nice to everyone and then other people misinterpret it. You ought to be careful with that au pair of yours. I hope she's not getting the wrong idea about you as well.'

Marie-France? His mind shot back to the other evening when they had cleared up the kitchen together after Lottie had gone to bed. It hadn't been her working time but she had insisted on helping. On one occasion – oh God – their hands had accidentally brushed when he had opened a kitchen cupboard and she had put something in. They'd both said sorry, the way you do when these things happen, and then he hadn't thought any more about it.

As he saw himself out of Karen's little flat, he felt stupid. Perhaps, out of courtesy, he *had* been too familiar. Well, now it would be different. He wouldn't call Christina after all in case she got the wrong idea too. But what exactly, he asked himself as he walked down a corridor of blue doors, wondering which one was Christina's, *was* the wrong idea? It was all so confusing.

Getting into his car, he turned on the radio, moving the dial from his usual frequency to the local station to find out about the traffic. 'There will be long delays out of Corrywood,' chirped the presenter, 'owing to an incident at a leisure centre in Hickvick. More details when we get them!'

Matthew's blood ran cold. A incident at a leisure centre in Hickvick? Wasn't that where Lottie's swimming party was? Fingers shaking, he dialled Marie-France's number. Her phone was off. Suddenly he began to shake.

Dear God, he began to pray, which was something he hadn't done for years. Not even when Sally had died. *Please let Lottie be all right. I'll do anything if you do this for me. Anything.*

Matthew glanced again at his watch, tetchily. Gone four. Damn. He was meant to be at a meeting with James right now but this was more important. For fuck's sake, where was the new leisure centre? Down this road? No. Maybe it was this turning. Yes! There was a sign at last.

Oh God. An ambulance was passing him, its lights flashing. Someone had been hurt. Not Lottie. Please!

'Sally, if you're up there, for pity's sake do something,' he found himself saying before pulling up to let it by. The traffic was stationary now. People were hooting; some were getting out of their cars to take a better look at what was causing the blockage. And now a youth in a neon orange uniform was coming towards them. 'The leisure centre's closed,' he heard him saying and there was a general groan from the car in front.

'But we've come specially for a half-term treat.'

'Sorry. There's been an accident.'

Matthew's chest did a flip. 'What kind of accident?' he yelled, leaping out of his car.

The youth shrugged. 'Can't say.'

It was then that he began to run. 'Oy,' yelled a voice behind him. 'You can't just leave your car there!'

Couldn't he? As he raced through the stationary traffic, Matthew could hear more people behind hooting him in protest. So what? He had to get to his daughter. Cradle her in his arms. He could see it all so clearly. She'd be slumped on the ground in pain. Or maybe she'd be trying to talk just as Sally had tried at the end. She'd be looking at him with her mother's large, sorrowful eyes...

'Daddy!'

'Lottie!'

His heart burst with relief as a small figure with long, wet plaits ran towards him, closely followed by a rather flushed-looking Marie-France. Behind was a youth he didn't recognise as well as two small identical boys.

'Daddy! We've had an *amazing* time! I went all the way up this big giant chute but there was this awful queue and there was a very rude woman and then Teary came up and he and Marie-France took us all down on their laps. But then I sank to the bottom of the pool – honestly! – but I came up and got out to look for Marie-France. But she couldn't see me for a bit cos there were all these people and then Teary found me and bought me a hot chocolate cos I was freezing and then Marie-France cried cos I hadn't drowned after all! It was cool, Dad. Really cool!'

Slow down, slow down! He didn't understand half of what she was saying but all he cared about was that she was safe and in his arms.

'I heard there was an accident,' he managed to say to Marie-France when he was able to compose himself. 'I saw the ambulance.'

'Someone fell over at the ice-skating rink in the centre,' piped up one of the small boys whose soaking wet hair was sticking to his scalp.

Relief washed over him. 'Where's Paula?'

'Inside, trying to count heads.' Marie-France gave him a meaningful look. 'This party, she is not organised. Paula has an enormous fright. She jumped in to get her daughter but she could not swim so the lifeguard, she pulls her out.'

'It's all my fault,' said Lottie, her eyes bright. 'I told Marie-France I didn't need my water wings.'

'You didn't wear your water wings?' he repeated slowly. He turned to Marie-France. 'Is that true?'

The girl flushed. 'Yes, but—'

'No buts.' He felt anger rising inside. 'I told you expressly she was to wear them. She's not a strong swimmer. I trusted you. And you've let me down.'

'I'm so sorry but—'

'And you.' He jerked his head at the lad, furious that Marie-France had brought a boyfriend along to a kids' party. 'Were you there just for the ride?'

'I do not understand.'

'Or did Marie-France just pick you up there?'

'Pick up?' His au pair's voice rose in indignation. 'I do not pick up like Antoinette. Thierry is my friend from home. I do not know he is coming. He help me at the top of the chute.' She clutched his arm and gazed up at him in undisguised admiration. 'I think he is angel to rescue us.'

Matthew put his arm around his small daughter's shoulders. 'If you'd looked after Lottie properly, you wouldn't have needed rescuing. I think we'd better go home now.'

'I've got to get these two back to Jilly,' said Marie-France, giving him a sullen look as though *he* was at fault and not her.

'Very well.' He could hardly bring himself to talk to her, he was so angry about the water wings business. 'You take them in Sally's... in the other car and I'll take Lottie.'

'You want me to work later, yes?' Marie-France's voice was shaking and he could see now that her lips were blue with cold. 'Because I like to talk to my friend before he goes again. I can fill up my hours tomorrow. Is that all right?'

'It will have to be, won't it?' said Matthew grumpily.

Just then, there was a loud shrill voice. 'Ten, eleven, twelve – shit, I can't see any more. Oh thank God. There they are! Look! There's Lottie and the twins. Thirteen, fourteen, fifteen – it's OK, Antoinette, I think we've got them all.'

It was Paula, rushing up with soaking wet hair and streaked mascara. He'd never seen her look so dishevelled before. 'Matthew! I'm so sorry. This whole thing has been a complete nightmare. Half the mothers who'd promised to help out cancelled on me – including your mum, boys. Oh dear. Does anyone know where I put my Rescue Remedy? Sorry I haven't got enough party bags everyone but I'll bring some into school next week.'

He left them to it, marching across the car park, feeling annoyed with himself for trusting a young girl with his precious daughter. 'Don't be cross with Marie-France about the water wings,' pleaded Lottie. 'It was my fault. Really!'

This time, he could tell, his daughter really meant it. For once, she hadn't intended to get the au pair into trouble. But how could he trust a girl who went against his wishes?

Damn. Not his mobile. Shit. It was James.

'Matthew? Where the f— are you?'

'I've had a bit of a problem—'

'DAD! Can we just go home now? I'm cold and I don't want to go swimming again.'

'Swimming? I don't believe it, Matthew. You've been swimming?'

'No, you don't understand.'

'I think I do.' James's voice was ice cold like the frost on the car windscreen that he had to clear before driving off. 'You leave early at lunchtime and then fail to get back for the meeting which, as you know, is vital. Instead, you've skived off when you know there's a deal to be sewn up. Look, Matthew. I know you've had a tough time and I've been as understanding as I can. But I'm terminating our partnership right now.

The accountant will be in touch about the financial side. And don't bother coming into the office to clear out your stuff. We'll send it on.'

JILLY'S AU PAIR AGENCY:
GUIDELINES FOR AU PAIRS

After a few weeks, ask your family if they are happy with you. Use this meeting as an opportunity to iron out problems on both sides.

Chapter 34

'*So* sorry to bother you on a Saturday – I didn't wake you up, did I? – but you do see my point, don't you, Jilly? I mean I know we're friends but this was always a business arrangement and I can't have a girl who walks around the house with a face like a poker and is surly to me when I ask her to get out the Hoover.'

'Yes, but—'

'And before you ask, I *have* spoken to her about it. She says she's upset because her parents split up last year so she came over as an au pair to get away. I feel really sorry for her but she's so miserable that she's making us depressed too.'

Jilly tried to cut in. Annie, a friend of a friend from Puddleducks days, was a nice woman but she could go on!

'And *another* thing. As soon as she's finished her "work" – which is basically moving the kitchen cloth around in slow motion – she starts cooking her own food because she doesn't like ours. She's *addicted* to fried chicken wings which reeks the house out...'

It was no good. She'd have to interrupt. 'Annie, I'm really sorry but I'm going to have to sort this out on Monday. I've got to get down to Sussex for my parents' wedding anniversary and I need to get the kids ready.'

There was a disappointed noise at the other end of

the phone. 'Sounds like *you're* the one who needs an au pair, Jilly.'

Exactly. Marie-France had promised to be here by now! 'Well I do. Sort of. Except that she's part-time and doesn't live in.'

'Hah! I don't blame you.'

The words 'so you don't practise what you preach' hung unspoken in the air between them.

'It's not exactly like that—'

'MUM. HARRY'S STOLEN MY IPHONE AGAIN.'

'NO I DIDN'T. IT'S MINE.'

She put the mobile down for a minute. 'HarryImeanAlfie, don't kick him like that and don't push him or he'll—'

CRASH.

Too late. That meant another twenty-minute delay while she cleared up the broken vase and Harry's bloody knee.

WOOF!

Now Bruno had entered the fray. What was that in his mouth? Not another pair of pants! Stolen from the laundry basket again, no doubt, although these were bright pink ones that she'd never seen before. Still, they'd do. Grabbing them, she held them against Harry's knee to stem the blood while still cradling the phone between her ear and shoulder.

'Annie, can we sort this out later? Thanks.'

She dropped the phone before Annie could disagree. 'Where did the dog get those knickers from?' she asked Nick as he sauntered into the kitchen, still wearing the jeans with cut-out knee holes even though she had told him ages ago to change for Mum's party.

'Dunno.'

'Maybe they're Granny's,' piped up Alfie, who now, out of guilt, was giving Harry a grubby bit of kitchen roll to mop up his tears. 'Nas ılsınız?'

'What are you talking about?'

'I'm asking Harry if he's all right in Turkish, Mum.'

Uneasily, Jilly began rifling through the kitchen odds and sods drawer in search of a plaster. The pink pants with the expensive designer label inside were too big for her mother, far too small for Fatima and they certainly weren't hers. Which only left David...

Feeling a chill pass through her, she sorted out Harry's cut, which fortunately was only superficial. So was *that* why her husband had been so cool and distant over the last few months? Not because of her job, but because he was having an affair? Had he brought this woman, whoever she was, here to the house when she'd been out? Had he simply put the pants in his pocket by mistake like a cheating husband in a film she'd seen once? Or was her imagination simply running wild because she was tired and had too much to do?

'Jilly! Ah, there you are!' Her mother tripped down the stairs wearing an elegant two-piece in blue silk. 'My case is in my room so maybe one of you boys could bring it down for me. Nick, you're not going like that are you, dear? And you *are* going to take off that fake tattoo, aren't you?'

Quickly she slipped the pink pants into her handbag. This wasn't a subject she wanted to discuss with Mum.

Not until she'd tackled David. '*What* tattoo?' she repeated faintly.

'The one on his arm, darling, which he's been hiding under his T-shirt. Haven't you seen it? Go on, Nick, show your mother.'

''Snot fake,' muttered Nick, reluctantly rolling up his sleeve to reveal a pink heart with some lacy writing below.

'It says "I love you" in French!' sniggered Harry.

'No it doesn't.' Jilly shook her head. Normally she'd have gone ballistic but compared with an adulterous husband, a tattoo was small beer. '*Je m'aime?*' Someone had got their 't's muddled with their 'm's.

'You're certainly maimed all right,' snorted her mother. 'Who did this?'

Nick looked slightly shamefaced. 'One of my friends, but it's OK. We sterilised one of your sewing needles by putting it in a flame.'

'How unhygienic! Aren't you going to tell him off, Jilly?'

'Later, Mum.' Her head was still spinning with pink pants and stupid thoughts that wouldn't go away.

'Well, I must say, you're being very laid-back about it. Now look, we need to go now or we're going to be late. Since David *still* isn't back, I'll drive myself with Nick.'

'Can we take Marie-France too?' suggested Nick, flushing furiously. 'She can help me with my French conversation.'

Her mother snorted. 'I bet she could. Where is she then? Honestly, these girls are so unreliable.'

Just as she spoke, Marie-France came cycling round

the corner, wearing a dress instead of her usual jeans. Oh no. Not the phone *again*.

'Maybe it's Jeremy!' Her mother grabbed the receiver. 'I do hope he's going to get there on time. He *said* he'd found someone to cover him for today. Hello? Hello? Bother. It's just rung off. I do hate it when that happens.'

There was the sound of a car on the gravel drive outside. It was David who'd gone, she recalled now from a terse conversation last night, to a so-called 'Saturday morning meeting' at work.

Jilly made to head upstairs. 'He can take you and Marie-France, Mum. I'll see him at your place.'

Her mother frowned. 'Don't you even want to say hello?'

'Not really.' If she did, she'd probably burst into tears or have a huge row with him and that wouldn't be fair on Mum. Not just before the party. She'd just have to be brave and wait until it was all over.

Right. Now they'd gone, she could concentrate on her list of things to do. Put pink pants out of head. Get dressed. Find mascara. Get twins dressed. ('Why can't we wear jeans, Mum?') Get dog in car. Put dog food in car. Find Mum and Dad's anniversary present (a picture of them on their wedding day in a rather nice frame). Wrap it up. Ignore the doorbell. Maybe not.

'Nigel!'

Jilly stared at the tall, self-assured man who was standing on the doorstep as though she should be expecting him. She'd never really cared for Nigel with his carefully combed-back dark hair and his penchant for black polo jumpers under jackets, whatever the weather. Yes, they had often gone out as a foursome to restaurants or school quizzes in the past. But that was because he had come as a package with Paula. Now, remembering what her friend had said about him earlier, she felt a distinct coolness.

'I'm sorry just to turn up like this but I wanted to apologise.' His voice sounded smoother than ever.

'What for?'

'The swimming party. It sounded like a complete mess to me. Typical Paula. She can't seem to organise anything, not even a children's party.'

'Actually, they're incredibly difficult to . . .' she began but he was already stepping inside the hall as though she'd asked him in.

'Anyone around?' He glanced behind her.

'The twins and my au pair.' She was beginning to feel uneasy now.

He touched her hand lightly, only for a few seconds but long enough for it to be more than a friendly gesture. 'I think you're incredible, Jilly. Setting up your own business. Doing something! Helping your husband when he's down on his luck.'

She stepped back as he got closer. Someone might see them and get the wrong idea. 'It's what any wife would do.'

'Hah! Not mine. She's always at the gym!'

'And do you know why?' Jilly felt angry now. 'It's because it's the only place where no one criticises her. Where she feels she can accomplish something.'

'Like you, you mean.' His hand touched hers again, but for longer this time. 'I don't know if I've ever told you this, Jilly, but you're a very attractive woman.'

'Have you been drinking?'

He made a rueful face. 'Only one or two before I have to go back and face my bad-tempered wife for a so-called family lunch.'

'Well, if I were you, I'd go back immediately and make Paula feel good about herself instead of coming round here. Now, if you don't mind, I have to go out.' She stared at him. 'To join my husband for a family party.'

The word 'husband' seemed to jolt him. Suddenly Nigel looked nervous. 'Of course. I see. Er, this conversation of ours. I'm sure you won't repeat it, will you?'

'Luckily for you, I won't. But only out of respect for Paula. Not you.'

Shutting the door firmly behind him, Jilly stood with her back to it for a minute, her heart pounding. So Paula had been right! If she wasn't mistaken, her husband had been trying it on with her. How awful. And – despite what she'd said earlier – should she tell Paula? Would it be kind to warn her friend that her husband had a roving eye. Or was it best to keep mum?

Even worse, should she tell David? Or was it possible – given the strange underwear – that he was making similar overtures to another woman? She felt sick with apprehension and disbelief. If Nigel could be like this, why not her husband too?

Oh no. Not the phone again! Jilly was gripped with a sudden panic. Supposing it was Paula? An angry Paula, who had somehow found out that her husband had come round . . .

'Jilly? It's Matthew.'

Thank goodness for that!

'Look, I'm sorry to ring at a bad time. I know you're dashing off for this family party but I've got a problem.'

Jilly felt a sense of foreboding. Matthew had kindly 'lent' Marie-France to her for the weekend. Had he changed his mind?

'Something rather unexpected has happened.' His voice dropped again as though he was trying to speak without anyone hearing him. 'Marie-France's mother has just turned up on the doorstep.'

'Her *mother*?'

'Yes. Says she wanted to pay a surprise visit. Rather weird, don't you think?'

'Very.' Jilly's mind went back to when she'd spoken to Madame Dubonne on the phone a few weeks ago. Definitely the pushy type!

'I don't know what to do with her. The boyfriend's gone off somewhere, thank goodness, but now I have this strange Frenchwoman.'

Jilly groaned. 'I suppose we'd better take her with us. It's going to put the tables out but we'll manage somehow.'

'Thanks.' Matthew sounded hugely relieved.

It took longer than she'd anticipated to get to Matthew's with the traffic, and she found it difficult to concentrate: a picture of those pants kept coming into her head. Maybe there was a simple explanation. But what?

Wow! Jilly stared at the very tall, pale, plump-faced woman (a bit like a hamster) with bright red hair and very high heels who was standing at Matthew's gate with a suitcase by her side. The curtains on the other side of the road were twitching and it wasn't surprising. The woman looked like a hooker.

'Is she from the circus?' demanded one of the twins. 'She's got really red lipstick.'

'Sssh, Harry. That's rude.'

'It's Alfie, Mum! Anyway, he's right. Her hair's weird!'

'Madame Dubonne?' asked Jilly, getting out of the car.

'Hah! You arrive at last.' The woman clipped her way to the car as though she was a taxi that was late. 'I am waiting.'

Jilly drew in her breath. No apology for turning up like this without notice.

Marie-France's mother handed her case to one of the boys in the back. 'You will take this, yes?' Then she slid into the front seat, showing more than just a flash of leg. 'We go to see my daughter now, yes?'

Jilly nodded. 'We're actually going to a family party. It's a bit of a drive. Er, are you sure you don't want to ring her and say you are coming?'

'Non.' The woman shook her head emphatically. 'I want it to be a surprise.'

'Is that a good idea?' began Jilly but the woman didn't appear to be listening. Instead, she was looking around keenly as they drove through town.

'*Mon Dieu, c'est différent*,' she mumbled under her breath.

'Of course! Marie-France said you were an au pair here some years ago. Quite a coincidence.'

The woman nodded. 'I work near here. Down that road. There!'

She pointed to a large house on the corner with a holly tree in the front garden.

Jilly gasped. 'That's was Aunty Angela's house until she moved! Well, actually, she's not a real aunt. She's a friend of Mum's from school.' She almost added the words 'until they had some kind of an argument' but then pulled herself up in time. 'Actually, she's going to be at the party.'

That reminded her. Mum still didn't know about Angela although she probably suspected. Please don't let there be a row...

'She will be at the party?' An amused look passed over Marie-France's mother's face. 'Then it will be a very big surprise, I think. A *very* big one.'

'Mum!' This was Alfie from the back. 'Where's Fat Eema?'

Oh my God. She knew she'd forgotten something. The last time she'd seen Fatima, the girl had been in the bathroom. There was no way she could risk leaving her at home – she'd only have another false alarm!

Hastily she did an eight-point turn in the road. 'I've forgotten someone. Sorry!'

JILLY'S AU PAIR AGENCY:
GUIDELINES FOR FAMILIES

*If you go out for the day, it is polite to ask your au pair
if she would like to come with you.*

Chapter 35

'So if my husband assumes that having a party is going to make up for everything, he's got another think coming.'

What does 'another think coming' mean, wondered Marie-France, listening to this chic older English-woman in front. You'd never think she was Jilly's mother! So confident. So put together. Her mother would definitely approve!

There was a jerk as the car went round the corner, pushing Marie-France, who was sitting in the back, towards Jilly's teenage son, who blushed furiously as he texted madly next to her. So sweet!

'He simply can't resist any female who flutters her eyelashes!' continued Jilly's mother. 'And now he's chummed up again with Angela even though he knows I can't stand her.'

Marie-France couldn't resist butting in. 'So why do you allow your husband to continue?'

The older woman turned round and glared. 'Did anyone ask you your opinion?'

'Sheila!' David threw Marie-France an apologetic look in the mirror.

'Don't "Sheila" me, David. This is meant to be a private family conversation. But if you really want to know, young lady, when you get to my age, a blind eye is better than half a pension. Now if you don't mind,

I'm going to have a little nap. I need to arrive bright and refreshed if *that* woman is going to be there.'

For the next hour or so, there was an uneasy peace in the car as Jilly's mother lapsed into a deep sleep, her head nodding in loud snores. Plugging her iPod in, Marie-France pretended to watch the fields outside that had replaced the suburbs. It gave her a chance to mentally replay the scene with Thierry, as she'd been doing again and again ever since it happened.

After the swimming party, she and Thierry had finally got some time to themselves in the pub round the corner from Matthew's. 'What do you mean you have something to tell me about my father?' she'd demanded, launching in without any small talk.

Thierry had taken a large gulp of red wine and tried to put his arm around her. Smartly, she pushed him away. He might have rescued Paula in the pool but she hadn't forgotten the way he'd flirted with that barmaid in London.

'Your mother confided in Maurice who then spoke to Henri at the bakery,' he began. 'He plays bowls with Pierre who is one of our regular customers at the garage. Your father isn't called John Smith at all. She made up the name because she doesn't want you to find him.'

Marie-France bit her lip. Why hadn't she thought of that before? 'Then what is he called?'

'She wouldn't say.' He stretched out his arm again and this time she allowed it to rest on the back of her chair. 'But it *is* true that he lived in Corrywood.'

That was something, at least. 'But why did my

mother tell me anything at all about my father, after all these years of refusing to discuss him?'

Something flickered in Thierry's eyes. 'I cannot tell you, Marie-France. Not yet. I made a promise.'

'Who to? My mother?'

He looked away. 'Maybe. Maybe not. But you will know soon enough. Honestly.'

'What do you mean?'

'I cannot say. But I need to ask you something.' He sounded sad. 'Why did you break up with me without talking it over? I was so hurt.'

'I didn't break up with you! I told you! Tom, the boy I was looking after, ripped up our photograph. I was trying to mend it.'

He shook his head, smiling as though she was telling a lie. 'I am not talking about the photograph. Or the texts which I sent.'

'And which I never received.' She was seized by a sudden thought. 'You did get my text about changing my sim card last month, didn't you? To get a better rate?'

He shrugged. 'I forget.'

Marie-France could have screamed. Thierry might be sexy and funny but he wasn't the brightest spark. 'So that's why I didn't get your messages, dumbo.'

He glared at her. 'Then how do you explain your Facebook?'

'What are you talking about?'

'It says your status is single.'

'I don't understand.' Marie-France tried to remem - ber when she'd last checked her profile. Not for ages. Matthew's internet connection had been down so she hadn't even been able to look at her Wall since moving in.

'See for yourself. Here.'

He pushed across his phone which was a smarter version of hers: the type that you could read your messages on. He was right!

'But *I* didn't change it.' Tears pricked her eyes. 'I kept it as "In a relationship" just in case.'

Thierry shook his head. 'I do not know whether to believe you, Marie-France. You have changed since you come here.' He stood up, tossing back his hair and sending hot shivers of desire through her. 'I'm going now.'

'Back to your little garage?' she snapped, furious that he wouldn't believe her.

'*Non!* To Ireland! And then wherever I feel like going.' His eyes glittered. 'I have you to thank for that, *chérie*. If you had not come here, I would not have followed you.' He paused. 'But now I'm moving on.'

His lips brushed the top of her head. '*Au revoir*, Marie-France. It was fun while it lasted. Yes?'

How could that have happened? How could her Facebook status suddenly say 'Single'?

'Maybe you were fraped, *ja*?' Heidi had suggested when she'd confided in her friend. 'You know. It's when someone hacks into your settings and changes stuff. It's Facebook rape.'

But who would have done that?

'Antoinette!' they both said to each other at the same time.

'She was mad at me for telling Jilly about Immy,' Marie-France remembered. 'Just wait until I get her.'

Heidi had put a hand on her arm. 'If I were you, I wouldn't make a fuss or she could do something else. Make up some horrible lie which would be far worse. The best thing to do with cyber bullies is ignore them.'

So she had. She'd cold-shouldered Antoinette, ignoring her as though she didn't exist. After all, the damage had been done. Thierry had gone. And if he really loved her, he'd have believed her.

'OK, everyone.' David's voice cut in on her thoughts. 'We're here.'

Marie-France looked out of the window as the car crunched down a horseshoe-shaped drive. Wow! What a beautiful house! Its white exterior was set off by that golden creeper climbing up the front. And just look at those huge bay windows in the front. Jilly's parents must be very rich!

At the door, dressed in a navy-blue jacket, beige trousers and a scarlet cravat, was a rather good-looking man in his sixties. He was coming towards them now and opening the passenger door.

'Darling, how lovely to have you home.'

'Hello, Hugh!'

Marie-France watched entranced as Jilly's mother coolly allowed her husband to help her out of the car. David was now shaking his father-in-law's hand and Nick was morosely nodding from a distance.

'This is Marie-France,' said David, encouraging her to come forward. 'She's one of Jilly's agency girls and she's kindly helping us out this weekend.'

'French, eh?' The older man's face lit up.

What a handsome man for his age! Very tall and athletic-looking with striking blue-green eyes and a charming smile.

'Don't even think about it, Hugh,' said Sheila crisply. 'She's far too young for you. Now are we going inside or not?' Her eyes glittered. 'I've been looking forward to a quiet weekend. I do hope you don't have anything planned.'

He laughed loudly. 'Of course not.' Marie-France watched Jilly's handsome father put an arm around his wife. It made her wish now that she hadn't thrown off Thierry's arm when he'd tried to comfort her.

Feeling a little out of place (after all, it wasn't as though she was family), she followed them through into a beautiful hall, with a table studded with silver photographs. There was a teenage Jilly along with a slightly younger boy. Then there was a picture of Jilly and David on their wedding day. Gosh, they looked happy! David was glancing at that too as though he hadn't seen it for a while. And there was a black-and-white photograph of the much older couple – only just recognisable – on their wedding day.

'Happy anniversary, darling,' said Hugh as he flung open a pair of huge wooden doors. Inside were at least thirty people sitting round a beautiful oval table draped with a white tablecloth and fully laid with gleaming silver cutlery and pink napkins. Balloons hung from the ceiling and, as they went in, there was a burst of music from a group of cellists in the corner. She recognised one of them. Wasn't that Jilly's brother with the cool sports car? *Mon Dieu!* He had a priest's collar round his neck! Was it a fancy dress party? If so, she was wearing the wrong thing!

'Happy anniversary, Sheila and Hugh!' called out someone and there was a huge wave of clapping. Jilly's mother, noted Marie-France with amusement, was standing there almost regally with a slight bow.

'How wonderful! I adore surprises!'

As she spoke, there was the sound of another car drawing up outside followed by a stampede of feet. The twins raced in and threw themselves at Jilly's father.

'Hi, Grandad.'

'Did Granny tell you she knew all about your party?'

There was a roar of laughter from the table.

'No.' The older man's eyes were twinkling. 'But nothing about your grandmother would surprise me.'

'And nothing about your grandfather would surprise me!' retorted Sheila crisply. 'Including the way he pretends to forget things.'

The old couple really cared for each other, realised Marie-France enviously. They might snipe like this but there was genuine affection there.

'Where's my daughter?' demanded Hugh. 'Ah, there you are, darling. Brought some more guests with you, I see! The more the merrier.'

All eyes swivelled to the large Turkish girl who waddled in before sinking on to the nearest chair as though she had just completed a marathon. '*Tuvaletler nerededir?*' she gasped.

'Fat Eema needs the loo,' piped up Alfie.

'Goodness me, you were right, Sheila,' said Hugh, impressed. 'His Turkish really is coming on, isn't it?'

Just as he spoke, a very tall, round-faced woman with a mop of bright red curly hair strode into the room as though she owned it. '*Bonjour*,' she said gaily. Then she gave a mock curtsey to Sheila and Hugh. '*Joyeux anniversaire!* What is it? Do you not recognise your friend's old au pair?'

Old au pair? *Quoi?* Marie-France stared. This woman could be her mother's sister! A plumper version of Maman with different hair. And heavy make-up that made her look like, as the English would say, rather tarty.

'Maman,' she started to say, 'is that you?'

But even as she spoke, there was a groan. Jilly's mother had gone quite pale and was clutching the back of a chair. 'Collette? *Collette?*' Then she glared at her husband. 'For God's sake, Hugh. What kind of sick joke is this?'

MORE CONFUSING ENGLISH IDIOMS
FOR FOREIGNERS

Keep an eye on (To watch)

Half a tick (A short period of time. Not to be confused with fleas)

Not on your Nellie (No way. Not to be confused with elephants)

Bottoms up (An invitation to drink. Note: this is <u>not</u> a sexual invitation)

Egg on your face (Something that makes you look stupid)

Sixes and sevens (Confused? You will be)

Chapter 36

Collette? Collette?

'I do not understand.' Marie-France struggled to make herself heard over the indignant voices around them. 'Maman! What is going on? Why are you here?'

Her mother held her arms out for a hug. '*Chérie!* I need to tell you something that I should have done before.'

Marie-France's chest thudded with apprehension. 'Tell me what?'

At the same time, Jilly seemed to be having an equally heated discussion with her own mother. 'I refuse to talk about this in front of everyone,' Sheila spat. There were bright red spots on her cheeks. 'I am humiliated. Utterly humiliated.'

Her husband made to take her arm but she threw it off angrily. Shooting her a concerned look, he picked up a glass from one of the tables and tapped a teaspoon on its side to get everyone's attention.

'We appear to have a slight family crisis on our hands,' he announced without any of the confidence he had displayed just now. Someone tittered uncomfortably but everyone else sat still with shock.

'If you don't mind, we are going to retire to the library to sort it out. Jeremy, would you come too.' It sounded like an order rather than a request. 'And you too, Angela. In the meantime, everyone please top yourselves up with the bottles. We won't be long.'

Marie-France found herself being swept up in the exodus led by Jilly's father. She wanted to interrogate her mother (who had clearly put on weight during her absence) but Collette was striding on, her head tossed up defiantly as they trooped into a book-lined room with a leather-topped desk, a sofa and some easy chairs. Her mother immediately flopped into one, as though exhausted. Under any other circumstances, Marie-France would have examined the books, some of which were in French and Italian. She had never seen such a collection before in one room, apart from a public library!

'Sweetheart.' Jilly's father was putting his arm around his wife. This time Sheila didn't shake it off, noticed Marie-France. Instead, she seemed to be clutching her husband's hand for support. 'Do you want to explain the situation to our children or should I?'

'Mum!' Jilly's voice rang out. 'You're frightening me. What's going on?' She turned to her brother. 'Do *you* know, Jeremy?'

He bit his lip, went beetroot red and looked down at the ground. 'I think I might.'

Jilly's mother gave a short, hoarse laugh. 'I wondered if this day would ever come. Well, now it has.'

'Sheila,' said Angela timidly.

'No, Angela, we owe them the truth.'

'*Mon Dieu!*' Marie-France threw her hands up in the air in exasperation. 'This is mad house. Someone explain to me. Yes?'

'Very well.' Jilly's dad was giving her a strange look. 'After all, it affects you more than anyone else.'

What did he mean?

His voice was firm, rather like an actor's, and when he spoke, he looked straight at her in a way that made it hard to look anywhere else. It was mesmerising. Hypnotic even. 'I don't know how much your mother has told you but when she was your age, she worked as an au pair in Corrywood for our friend Angela Wright.'

Marie-France shot her mother an accusing glare. 'So much for John Smith!' she hissed in French. 'Do you know how much time I wasted?'

'I lied, *chérie*.' Her mother shrugged as though this was perfectly acceptable.

Jilly's mother gave her usual snort. 'So she *still* hasn't learned to tell the truth. And before you say things you might regret, Collette, you might recall that my French is rather good.'

'And I,' flashed back Maman, 'understand more English than you might think, even if I do not speak perfect!'

'Please, both of you!' cut in Hugh. 'Let me continue. Angela had two sons. The older one, from her first marriage, was called Adam. He was a great friend of Jeremy's.'

Was? Instinctively, Marie-France's skin began to prickle.

'Tragically,' continued Jilly's father, 'Adam died from an asthma attack at twenty-three. He was allergic to all kinds of things.'

'*Mon Dieu*,' said her mother, quietly crossing

489

herself. Marie-France's head was spinning. Adam was allergic? To all kinds of things? Including dogs, perhaps?

The older man was looking directly at her now. 'When the boys were only sixteen, Collette was baby-sitting Adam's younger brother in Corrywood. Jeremy was staying with them during the summer holidays and we were due to collect him that night. But when we arrived, we found him and Collette in, let's say, a "compromising position" upstairs.'

'Dad!' Jeremy was puce red.

'Let me continue, son. But it transpired that Collette had also been intimate with Adam.'

'*Non!*' Marie-France whipped round to face her mother. She still couldn't get used to the change in her appearance. What had happened to her mother's usual chic self? 'Please tell me this is not true?'

'They were just silly boys, experimenting,' added Angela quickly. She smoothed down her hair nervously. 'I wish now that we hadn't made such a fuss about it. In fact, we wouldn't have done if...'

Her voice tailed away but it was too late. 'If my mother hadn't got pregnant with *me*, you mean! That's what happened, wasn't it?'

Collette nodded slowly.

'A baby?' Jeremy gasped. 'You had a baby?'

'We kept it from you, son,' intercepted Hugh smoothly. 'No point in ruining your life. Or Adam's either.' He sighed. 'At least that's what we thought at the time. Anyway, when this girl wrote to us from France about her pregnancy, she admitted she didn't know *which* one of you was the father. For all we know, it could have been a third person!'

'*Non!*' Collette's eyes were flashing. 'I am no slut.'

Jilly's mother snorted. 'Really?'

'We paid her a sum of money every month.' Angela took over in a subdued voice. 'It wasn't easy for us because we weren't as well off as Sheila and Hugh. But the worst bit was that it destroyed our friendship. Sheila said I should have somehow stopped Collette from seducing a pair of teenagers under my roof.' She threw Hugh a grateful glance. 'Luckily not *everyone* blamed me.'

Jeremy, pink-faced, cut in. 'She *didn't* seduce us. We … we were just as willing.' He looked at Collette now as though seeing her for the first time. 'She was a real stunner and, well, we'd never been that close to a girl like her before.'

Collette pouted. 'So you do not think I am good-looking now?'

'Of course but—'

'Please!' Marie-France made to cover her ears. 'I don't want to hear any more.'

'But you must!' thundered Collette. 'You are all forgetting what happened to me! My parents, they said they would have nothing to do with me. I had to bring up my daughter on my own.' She pointed at Jilly's mother. 'That woman, she returned the pictures I send of you as a baby. Didn't even want to know your name. Not like Angela. She was much more *gentille*.'

She swayed as though she was going to faint and Marie-France held on to her arm. 'I had to move into a small village where no one knew me. At first I pretend I am a widow but then the rumours start. After that, many people, they would not talk to me. And their children, they would not play with my daughter.'

She gave Marie-France a scared look. 'I am sorry, *chérie*. You must be so ashamed of your mother.'

Yes she was! But she was also shocked by the way she had been treated by these people in front of her. 'My mother was barely eighteen!' Marie-France glared round the room. 'Not much more than a child. Yet you thought you could just pay her off like that and get rid of us. Well, you can't.'

'Can't we?' Jilly's mother's eyes flashed. 'From what my daughter has told me, you have inherited your mother's morals. Didn't you make a play for some woman's husband? Phillip, wasn't it?'

Marie-France shot Jilly a baleful how-could-you look. Then she realised they hadn't covered the most important point of all. 'But who is it? Who was my father? Was it Adam?'

Silence.

'Or is it' – she pointed a finger at Jeremy in his clerical collar and pink face – 'you?'

'That's exactly it.' Jilly's mother's voice rang out in a strangled cry. 'We still don't know. Your mother refused to have any tests, so she could collect two lots of money. If we didn't, she threatened to tell the boys about you. She blackmailed us!'

Collette shrugged. 'It is true. But my life was ruined. How else was I to survive?'

Marie-France wanted to shake Maman and Jilly's stupid mother and that man with the vicar's collar. 'You know what?' she yelled at them. 'I don't care. Because I never want to see any of you again.'

Rushing away from her mother, she dashed past the other room with all the guests and out into the road, narrowly avoiding a car. Shaken, she walked on and on, shivering in the cold but desperate to get as far away as possible from the horrible truth behind her. Finally, breathless and damp from the fine rain that had begun to fall, she reached a town with a station sign.

Thank God! She just had enough in her purse for the London train which was arriving right now! Leaping on before anyone could stop her, she took a seat next to a child who was scrambling over her mother's lap, uninterested in the colour book on the table.

'She's a real pain to keep still,' the mother said apologetically but Marie-France, who would normally have made a funny face to amuse the child, looked away, her head reeling and her feet aching as the train jolted its way further and further away from the terrible, embarrassing, toe-curling scene she had just witnessed.

Her mother had slept with two teenage boys! How awful was that? No wonder she'd made up a name – because she didn't know the real one! But as the train drew nearer to London and her thoughts became clearer, Marie-France realised something else. Her mother's arrogant behaviour all these years had hidden a terrible pain and shame.

Was it really right that she should be punished all this time later for something stupid she had done – with the encouragement, no doubt, of two randy teenage boys – at the age of eighteen?

But where did that leave her? Who was her father?

Was it Jeremy, the blond vicar with the pink face who now seemed a bit of a wimp instead of the hunk she'd originally thought he was. He should have stood up and explained the situation like a real man instead of stuttering and flushing and wringing his hands like that. Or was he Angela's dead son? Tears pricked her eyes. Neither seemed particularly appealing! Neither seemed like the image of the handsome strong courageous image of her father that she had carried in her head for so many years! Maybe now this Adam was dead, she might *never* know. Marie-France could have wept with frustration if it were not for all the people around her. How could she have come so near but still be so far from the truth?

At Waterloo, Marie-France stood for a while in the station, pushed in different directions by passengers who all – unlike her – had somewhere to go. She certainly didn't feel like making her way across the tube system and returning to Matthew's. Not yet anyway. She needed somewhere to think. Somewhere quiet.

Even though it was nearly dusk, there were still quite a few people in the park, including a large group of teenagers, sitting on the grass, swigging out of bottles. John Smith! *John Smith!* She eyed the label incredu-lously. Was that how her mother had thought up her so-called father's name? From a drink?

'Want to join us, gorgeous?' One of the boys was holding out a bottle. It smelt like beer. Thierry's favourite tipple. How often had she tasted it in his mouth when they kissed?

'*Merci*.' Marie-France never drank beer or lager. She didn't like the taste. But, *Mon Dieu*, she had to have something after the shock of what had just happened.

'Aren't you going to sit down with us?' called out the boy as she walked on, still clutching the bottle. But his invitation washed over her as the horrific implications whirled round and round her head. For all her defensive words, the fact remained that Maman had slept with two boys at the same time. She was no better than Antoinette.

A man in a leather jacket and a shock of black hair walked past, giving her a quick look. Her heart did a little flip. For a minute there, the stranger had reminded her of Thierry. What was it he had said in the pub after the swimming party? That there was something else he knew about her father. 'I cannot tell you, Marie-France. Not yet. I made a promise.'

Well now she knew too! Maybe she'd try and ring him right now. Out of everyone, Thierry was the only one who would understand how she felt. But where was her phone? Scrabbling in her bag, she couldn't find it. *Merde!* Don't say she'd dropped it somewhere? She'd need to go back. Retrace her steps.

But the ground in front of her seemed wobbly. Perhaps it was the drink on an empty stomach which was making her light-headed, combined with the shock of the afternoon's revelations. Walking back unsteadily the way she had come, still clutching the John Smith bottle, she could see fireworks in the sky. Pink and silver ones like giant arcs of light. *Bang!* A couple of kids suddenly chucked a banger on to the grass as she walked past which made her jump. It was getting really dark now. Scary. Cold.

Marie-France shivered. Lucky little Lottie would be at the school bonfire party by now with Matthew. He would be holding her hand; keeping her safe like any good father would. Not like her own. Whoever he was.

'Got any money to spare, love?'

The gravelly voice behind her made her jump. Looking up, she saw it was the man in the leather jacket she'd seen earlier.

'*Non...*'

Merde! A sudden pain shot through her shoulder. The leather jacket man was trying to pull her bag away! The bag with the taped-together photograph of Thierry inside that she hadn't been able to throw away, despite everything. 'Give that back!' she shouted furiously.

If her right arm had been free, she could have done one of the judo movements that Thierry had taught her. Instead, with her left, she brought the bottle down with all her might on to the man's head. But as she did so, a giant firework went off above them and in the light, she could see a glint of something metallic in her attacker's hand.

'Aaagh,' she screamed. *Mon Dieu!* Her stomach was on fire. Roaring with agony. Shooting with pain as though a firework was going off inside her body.

'Help!' she tried to shout but no words would come out. '*Au secours!*' And then everything went black.

JILLY'S AU PAIR AGENCY:
GUIDELINES FOR FAMILIES

Your au pair is entitled to stay out all night if she wishes. But she should be back for work the next morning. Ask her to let you know if she's going to be late, so you do not worry.

Chapter 37

Matthew and Lottie were at the fireworks party when his mobile rang. His daughter was oohing and aahing at the purple and silver and gold loops and circles in the sky above. He'd never been a great one for fireworks, not even as a child. So much noise! And now as a father, the potential for accidents seemed horrendous.

'Did you see that one, Daddy?'

'Yes,' he managed to reply, squeezing her hand, making sure she didn't go anywhere.

'Pretty, wasn't it?'

'Very.' Matthew tried to sound as though he was taking part in the fun but it was hard to concentrate. Not when he was worried sick about how he was going to support them, now he was out of a job.

Lottie was leaping up and down, her little hand in its woolly glove firmly in his. 'Can we get a burger now, Daddy! I'm starving.'

And that's when the phone had rung in his jeans pocket. At first, he'd felt like ignoring it but the screen ID had said it was Jilly.

'Hi! How's the French contingent? Sorry. Can you speak up?' He motioned to Lottie that they needed to move away from the noise of the fireworks.

'What? No, she's not here with us. Yes, of course I will. You will let me know, won't you?'

Lottie was standing there, both hands on her hips as though she was an adult. Since Sally had died, his daughter always needed to know what was going on, however small the detail. Maybe, as Christina had said sometimes, it was because she was afraid of more shocks.

'Let who know what, Daddy? 'What's happened?'

He put his hand round her shoulders and moved her towards the burger bar, hoping to divert her. There was no reason for her to get upset. Not yet.

'That was Jilly from the agency.' He tried to sound casual.

'I could tell that!'

'Marie-France is meant to be working for her today at a family party in Sussex.'

'Dad, I'm not a baby. I know that as well.'

He took a deep breath. 'She went for a walk.'

'Like Mummy did when she needed space?'

Sometimes her maturity made him want to laugh and weep at the same time. 'Exactly. And now... well she hasn't come back yet.'

Lottie stared up at him, her face bright in the glow of the bonfire. 'Maybe she's at *our* house!'

'That's what I'm hoping. Do you mind if we leave after we get your burger?'

Lottie was already yanking him towards the car park. 'I don't want it now. Come on, Dad. What are you waiting for? If we find her fast, we can bring her back to the display. Marie-France would love fireworks. I know she would.'

It took nearly half an hour to drive back through the traffic. There weren't any lights on, realised Matthew with a sinking heart as he pulled up outside the house.

'Marie-France!' called out Lottie, charging in through the front door. There was silence. 'She's not here.' Lottie's eyes filled with tears. 'I want my Marie-France!'

My Marie-France! Matthew couldn't help feeling a bit jealous.

'Find her,' she demanded bossily. 'Ring Paula to see if she's with Antoinette.'

So he did but no, she wasn't, Paula told him in a rather cheesed-off tone. Jilly had already called. She wasn't with her Swiss friend Heidi either.

'Lottie,' said Matthew, kneeling down quietly next to her, 'did Marie-France ever tell you where she went at weekends?'

His daughter raised her tear-stained face. 'She used to look for her daddy.'

'Her father?'

Lottie wiped her nose on the back of her hand. 'You mustn't tell anyone, Daddy. It's a secret.'

Was that so? 'Where exactly did she look for her daddy?'

Lottie looked scared. 'In a big park. In London. She said you could hide there.'

It wasn't much to go on but it was better than nothing. 'Tell you what, princess. Why don't you watch this DVD for a bit. I just need to make some phone calls.'

After he'd rung the police ('I don't know if the park detail is relevant, but I thought I ought to tell you about it') he went and sat down beside Lottie who was watching the cartoon he'd picked out for her. It was daft, but seemed to do the trick. His daughter appeared to have forgotten about Marie-France, for the time being at least.

Meanwhile, his own imagination was running riot. Jilly had explained there'd been some kind of family argument involving the French mother and Marie-France had run off. It was like Sozzy all over again.

Creeping out into the kitchen while Lottie was still laughing at the television – how could children forget so easily? – he rang Jilly's mobile. She picked it up immediately, answering it in the kind of tone that sounded as though she was hoping for news. 'Have you heard from her?' he asked.

'No.' Her voice sounded strangled. 'We're going to report her as missing.'

He could hear noises in the background. Arguments. Someone with a foreign voice. 'We're back home now,' said Jilly. 'Her mother is staying with us for the night and my Turkish au pair has had another false alarm. I'd better go but I'll ring if there's any news.'

It didn't feel good. Not good at all.

'Daddy,' called out Lottie. 'I'm hungry.'

Of course she was! They'd never got that burger, had they? What kind of father was he, forgetting to feed his child? It was nearly her bedtime, for goodness' sake!

'Can we get a pizza? Please. Pretty please! We might see Marie-France in town. She might be watching the fireworks *there*!'

It was a possibility, he supposed, and at least it would be a distraction. Tucking her little hand in his, they walked down the hill towards the takeaway shops. Outside was a crowd of foreign girls with their harsh continental accents and short skirts with leggings or jeans but he didn't recognise any of them. Then, while they were waiting for their order, he felt a tap on his shoulder.

'Marie-France!' he started to say, whirling round.

It was Christina.

'Sorry.' He flushed. 'I thought you were someone else.'

She gave him a slightly odd look. 'That's all right.' She looked down at his daughter, who was clasping his hand firmly. 'You must be Lottie!'

He'd spoken so much about her that it was weird to think Christina had never met her before.

'We thought you were our oh pear,' said Lottie stolidly. 'She's gone missing. Like the other one.'

Christina raised her eyebrows. 'Really?'

'Mum!' A tall thin teenager with a small silver nose ring sauntered over, ignoring Matthew and scowling at Christina. 'Why did you order pepperoni? I said I wanted veggie!'

Christina shot him a look that seemed to say: 'See? I have parenting problems too.'

'This is Emma. Emma, this is Mr Evans.'

'Matthew, please.'

'If you two go and sit down there, Matthew and I will sort out the food. You could tell Lottie about your band.'

'A band! Wow!'

Lottie's excited voice sounded as she'd completely forgotten the drama over Marie-France.

'Thanks,' said Matthew in a low voice.

Christina gave him a conspiratorial smile. 'I reckon we've bought ourselves a few minutes. Now what's this about your missing au pair?'

Briefly he filled Christina in.

She looked shocked. 'That's terrible.'

'I know.' He nodded glumly. 'I don't seem to have much luck with looking after people. First Sally. Then Sozzy. And now Marie-France.'

'Matthew!' Christina was shaking her head but in a kind way. 'Remember all that work we did about not blaming yourself?'

He nodded. 'I'm trying. But it's not easy after being married to someone who constantly blamed you for everything.'

'I know.' Her voice sounded as though she might just have had the same experience herself. Maybe that's why she was so understanding with him. 'It's a hard habit to break.'

'Exactly! And now you've probably heard from Karen about what an awful boss I am.'

'Actually' – Christina touched his arm – 'I know all about Karen. Poor thing has a bit of a reputation in the block for latching on to people.'

'Really? Then you don't think I acted badly?' He bit his lip. 'I did give her a hug . . .'

'She'd take that the wrong way!'

'She did.' He was about to say more but his phone began to reverberate in his back pocket. Unknown number? His heart leaped. 'Sorry. I must take this.'

He turned back to the phone. 'Yes, this *is* Matthew Evans. I see. So what do we do now? Right. You'll keep me informed? Thanks.'

Numbly he stared at her. 'That was the police. They've found Marie-France's phone. In Waterloo Station. It had my number on it.'

'But what about the girl?'

He shook his head. 'That's just it, Christina. They've no idea where she is.'

JILLY'S AU PAIR AGENCY:
GUIDELINES FOR AU PAIRS

Try not to walk alone on your own at night. You need to be streetwise in England – just as you do at home!

Chapter 38

So Marie-France hadn't gone back to Matthew's. Maybe, hoped Jilly desperately, she might have returned to *their* place after the party. But she hadn't.

'Where is my daughter!' Collette was virtually stamping her feet in those ridiculous high heels.

'I don't know!' Jilly could feel her temper fraying. 'If you hadn't upset everyone like that, she might still be here!'

'Jilly!' Jeremy put a hand on her arm but David cut in.

'My wife's right. You can't expect to play around, Collette, without any consequences.'

The Frenchwoman frowned. 'What he say? I do not understand.'

'Mum, Mum, I'm starving!'

'We couldn't eat Granny's food. It was sick!'

Great. So now she had to cook dinner again on top of everything else! Well, it would have to be pepperoni pizza from the freezer. Again.

By ten o'clock, after she'd finally got the kids to bed, they began to get really worried. 'I'm going to call the police,' said Jeremy firmly.

'I'll do it.' She wavered, not sure if they were making a fuss or not. After all, Marie-France was an adult. And she'd only been gone a few hours. On the other hand, she was one of her girls and Jilly couldn't help feeling responsible in the wake of the argument.

It took a while to explain the situation before she was put through to the right person who, understandably, wanted some personal details about herself for 'security reasons'. Then she listened with mounting disbelief to the voice at the other end.

'What is it?' demanded David, seeing her stricken face.

Her voice stuck in her throat so that it came out raw and raspy. 'Someone's handed in a phone near Waterloo. It's Marie-France's.'

'What?' Collette looked puzzled. 'You speak too fast. What is it you say?'

Jilly bit her lip. Her initial anger towards this woman who had ruined her parents' party was now dissipating into pity. 'Your daughter's phone has been found,' she said slowly.

There was an excited burst of French back. It was too fast for Jilly but not, it seemed for Jeremy. 'She says that if her phone is there, Marie-France will be too,' he translated slowly.

Jilly felt cold. 'Not necessarily.'

Collette's face crumpled. 'I want to go and search for my daughter!'

'That would be like looking for a needle in a haystack,' interjected David.

Marie-France's mother squinted at him and then back at Jeremy. 'What does he say?'

'He says that would be hopeless.' Jeremy reached for her hand and began stroking it in comforting circles as slow, silent tears slid down Collette's face. 'London is too big.'

Jilly nodded, feeling helpless. 'The police say we have to sit and wait.' She bit her lip. 'I'm afraid it could be a long night.'

Miraculously, not one of the children had woken up, demanding food or laptops. Even dear old Fat Eema had crashed out after pigging out on a cheddar cheese doorstopper that she had taken from the fridge. Now the rest of them were sitting in silence in the sitting room as the clock ticked on.

Ten o'clock. Then eleven. Every now and then, she and David took it in turns to bring in a tray of tea and biscuits but no one could eat.

Each one of them was on alert in case the phone went. But it was deadly silent for a change. Mum could have rung to see if there was any news, Jilly told herself. And Dad too. Didn't they care?

Then, when it was nearly midnight, Jeremy spoke. 'When you were putting the children to bed,' he said quietly, 'Collette and I began sorting a few things out.'

David made an awkward noise in his throat. 'That's between you two,' he said. 'Don't feel you have to do any explaining.'

'Actually, we do.' Jeremy was speaking in a very calm, mature manner in what their mother sometimes referred to as his 'clerical voice', and Jilly felt a flash of admiration for her brother. 'We *do* want to explain, don't we, Collette?'

The woman nodded. She was awfully pale, Jilly noted and shaking too. 'I was very young,' she began in a faltering a mixture of French and English. 'It was my first time away from home. England was very strange to me. I did not know any other au pairs and I was homesick. I had to look after a little boy. He was extremely spoilt.'

'Still is,' muttered David.

It was true! Angela's youngest son still relied on his mother's handouts despite the fact he was on his third marriage.

'But he had an older brother,' continued Collette, looking up at Jeremy with a catch in her voice. 'Adam. I thought he was very handsome.' There was a silence. 'And I think his friend Jeremy is handsome too.' She was smiling now into the distance as though recalling the memory.

This time it was Jilly who interrupted. 'But they were only sixteen.'

David made a snorting noise. 'Trust me. Sixteen-year-old boys feel much older.'

'So do middle-aged men in possession of pink pants,' she muttered.

David gave her a strange look. 'What are you talking about, Jilly?'

'We'll talk about it later. Sorry, Collette, do go on.'

'One evening, when I was babysitting, the boys came in with a bottle of wine.'

'I think I know where this one is going,' murmured David.

Jeremy took a deep breath. 'I'd like to take over here, if you don't mind, Collette.' He withdrew his hand and sat up straight, squaring his shoulders as though preparing for a confessional. 'Adam and I had already had too much to drink and I'm afraid we persuaded Collette to have most of the bottle.' He coloured. 'It's fair to say that we took advantage of *her*, rather than the other way round.'

David's face was a mixture of admiration and shock.

'You're just saying that,' began Jilly.

'NO.'

She'd never heard her brother shout before.

'No, I'm not. Then – this is the horrible part – before we knew it, the parents walked in.'

'You were all in the bed?' asked David.

'I'm afraid so.'

'Oh God,' breathed Jilly, thinking of how she had found Nick the other month with Antoinette. 'How awful for them.'

'And how embarrassing for you boys,' said David slowly, his face looking softer.

'Thank you, David.' Jeremy nodded. 'Mum, true to form, blamed Angela for leaving us alone in the house with what she called a "temptress" and I was dragged back home. I had no idea that Collette was pregnant. No idea at all.'

'But I *wrote* to you!'

A look of pain flashed across Jeremy's face. 'I didn't get any letters. But I wouldn't be surprised if Mum intercepted them. Meanwhile, as you all heard earlier on today, she and Angela both sent money to France every month.'

'Why didn't she tell you about the baby?' demanded Jilly.

David cut in. 'It's as they said. She didn't want to ruin a young boy's life. That's what they thought in those days.'

'But why didn't they tell *me*?' demanded Jilly, who

was trying to work out the dates in her head. If Jeremy had been sixteen, she would have been eighteen. That meant she would have been…

'Going off to university,' interjected Jeremy. 'Auntie Angela told me this afternoon that Mum didn't want you to be upset by anything.'

'I don't get it.' She swung round to face the red-headed woman. 'Let's just fast-forward a few years. You brought up Marie-France on your own, which couldn't have been easy.'

Collette shrugged. 'She was a stubborn child. Like both her fathers.'

'But why, after all this time, did you suddenly decide to tell her more about her parentage when you had refused to discuss it for years?' persisted Jilly.

There was a little cry. 'Because I am ill!' Collette put her hand up to her hair and tore it off with a flounce. Jilly gasped! There was a shiny bald pate underneath.

'I have cancer,' whispered Collette. 'But I do not tell my daughter because I must protect her.'

So that explained the weird hair and the heavy make-up, disguising, perhaps, the ravages of the drugs that had no doubt been used to treat her.

Collette's eyes seemed to be begging everyone to understand. Either that or, Jilly thought guiltily, she was piling on the dramatics.

'But then I think, supposing I die? She would not know who her father was. So I started to tell her. I tell her I fell in love with a boy.'

Jeremy started. 'You were in *love* with me?'

'Not *you*, stupid. The other one. The more amusing

511

one.' She dabbed her eyes. 'I still cannot believe he is dead.'

Jeremy looked away and Jilly winced as she saw the hurt in his face.

'And then... then I begin to lose my nerve so I tell her half the truth. I say her father is called John Smith after the beer. Yet I was stupid enough to give her the name of Corrywood.' She shrugged. 'When she go to England, I say to myself, this is good because I can have my operation and treatment without her knowing.'

Jilly could understand that. As a mother, you would do anything to protect your children from hurt.

'But then the cancer does not go away.' Collette's eyes filled with tears. 'The treatment, she is not working. So I come to *Angleterre* to tell my daughter the real truth. I tell her that her real father was *you*.' Here she jerked her head at Jeremy. '*Or* the dead one. I do not know which.'

Marie-France's mother was sobbing now. Tragic sobs that made David's face melt with compassion. She had to hand it to the Frenchwoman. She knew how to handle men! Jilly felt a touch of jealousy as her husband patted Collette's hand reassuringly. 'It can't be easy. I think you've been very brave.'

'Well, I think . . .' she began. And then stopped at the sound of a loud snort from the door. Fatima had waddled downstairs and was standing there, resplen-dent in a kingsize sheet which she had made into a shift dress, waggling her finger at David.

'You are bad husband,' she hissed. 'She work hard but you always criticise.' She shot a fiery look at

Collette. 'And now you hold hands with another woman in front of her eye! I find Jee-lee a better husband in Turkey.'

'Sounds promising,' Jilly couldn't resist saying, shooting David a filthy look.

'I theenk she should accept proposal from man on doorstep.'

'What?' David began to laugh.

'You not laugh. This man, he like your wife. I hear when I am in bathroom today.'

Oh my God. Fatima had been upstairs when Nigel had turned up. She must have heard everything!

Her husband was looking confused now. 'What is she talking about?'

'I'll tell you later.'

'Actually, everyone, I'd like to say something.' Jeremy was standing up now, gripping the back of his chair so that his knuckles were white. 'Despite what everyone thinks, I would have liked to have had a family one day.'

Jilly held her breath as she waited for the inevitable gay confession. Hadn't they had enough revelations for one day? Now, thanks to Fatima, she was going to have to tell David about Nigel and then it might get back to Paula. What a mess!

'But after Collette,' continued Jeremy, 'I felt so ashamed that... well, I went off the whole sex thing.' He went beetroot red. 'So I decided I couldn't hurt anyone again. It's why I've chosen my profession, I suppose, or rather, why my profession chose *me*.'

They were all silent for a moment. Apart from a little squeak from the biggest person in the room.

'Jee-lee!'

'Please, Fatima,' she whispered. 'Not now.'

But as she spoke, the phone rang. Jilly froze, unable to move. Was this it? Did someone finally know where Marie-France was and, more importantly, whether she was all right? Jilly began to shake and so too, she noticed, did Collette, who was now leaning against a white-faced Jeremy for support.

'I'll get it,' offered David tightly.

'Mee-sis Jee-lee!' Fatima stumbled off the chair and was crouching on the floor, puffing in great breaths.

'In a minute, Fatima.'

'They've found her,' said David quietly. Then he looked at Collette, clutching Jeremy's hand with a tell-me-now expression on her mascara-streaked face. 'I'm afraid you're going to need to be very brave.'

JILLY'S AU PAIR AGENCY:
GUIDELINES FOR FAMILIES

You may find that your au pair wishes to bring her parents over for a brief holiday. Do not feel obliged to put them up! Suggest they stay at a nearby hotel or B & B instead.

Chapter 39

'Mary-France! Mary-France!'

The voice seemed to be calling her from a great distance. Go away, she wanted to say. Go away. She had been having a lovely, deep dream in which she'd been ringing the bell at her old village church. Back and forth. Back and forth. Rather like a cradle.

'Mary-France! Can you hear me?'

This was an English voice, she found herself thinking dimly. Only the English pronounced it 'Mary' with an 'air' sound instead of the French way.

'You're coming round now, dear.'

Coming round from what? Slowly she opened her eyes to find herself in a white room with a nurse leaning over her. 'You're in Recovery, dear.'

Wasn't that what happened to alcoholics or cars? Curiously, she looked down at her body. There was a strange tight feeling round her chest and her throat felt dry and sore. 'What happened?' she rasped.

The nurse started to say something but stopped. 'You were involved in an incident but you were very lucky. You're going to be fine. Just rest now.'

What kind of an incident? But then the nurse had gone and someone else arrived to wheel her bed through the corridors and down into another room. 'How do you feel?' asked another voice.

'Sick,' she managed to say. *Merde*. Too late!

'That's all right, dear. Don't worry. We'll get you mopped up in no time.'

Mopped? What was mopped?

Just then, the door opened and another nurse marched in. 'The police are here,' she announced briskly. 'I've said they're to have five minutes and no more.'

Feeling totally fuddled now, she looked up and saw a man and woman, both in uniform, standing at the foot of the bed. A horrible panic swept through her. Maybe they'd linked her with Antoinette's shoplifting. Or perhaps it was because of Phillip's insurance scam!

'Mademoiselle Dubonne.' The woman, quite young, spoke first. 'I am sorry to bother you but we need to ask you some urgent questions about your attack.'

'My attack?' she repeated, looking down at her bandages.

'You don't remember?' This was the older, harder-faced policeman. 'You were stabbed.'

Mon Dieu! She would have crossed herself if she'd been able to move her arms. So that explained the nagging dull ache in her stomach!

'We believe he tried to steal your bag.'

A dim memory of a man who looked like Thierry was beginning to come back. She'd been in London. That was right! Hyde Park with its lovely trees and tranquil air. The only place where she felt at home in this strange country.

'It would be very helpful if you could take a quick look at these pictures and see if any of them resemble your attacker.'

She glanced down at the sheaf of photos in front of

her. Her stomach was really beginning to hurt now and her head ached. 'Thierry,' she said weakly, pointing to one picture. 'It's so like him,' she tried to add but the words wouldn't come out.

'Thierry?' demanded one of the policemen. 'Thierry who?'

Too late. She'd already slipped into a delicious, drowsy, painkiller-fuelled sleep where none of this mattered. None of this at all.

Marie-France had no idea what time it was when she woke to find yet another nurse taking her blood pressure.

'Morning,' the woman announced chirpily as though this was some kind of holiday. 'Can you drink this? Wonderful. You need as many fluids as possible at the moment. Now, are you up to visitors because your family have been waiting to see you for quite some time!'

The nurse's accent sounded different from Matthew's and also Jilly's, so it was hard to understand exactly what was saying. But there was one word Marie-France clearly recognised. Family! That must mean Maman! Marie-France struggled to get more comfortable as her mother tripped in, head held high and red heels clip-clopping across the floor as though she was on a catwalk. '*Ma chérie*, how are you?'

Marie-France felt a chill pass through her as she saw the others behind. 'Why are they here?' she demanded, pointing at Jeremy, Angela and Jilly.

'I *knew* we should have let you have some time together,' said Jilly quickly.

'No, Madame Jilly. You are my friend. But not *them*.'

'I'm sorry, dear.' Angela's voice was soft and kind. 'But we couldn't stay away.' She took Marie-France's hand. 'Not when we'd only just found you again. I'm so glad you're all right. We all are. You lost quite a lot of blood, you know.'

Merde!

'She said "blood", *chérie*.'

Hah! Struggling to get a better position on her pillows, Marie-France jerked her head at Jeremy. 'So now you're going to tell me that he was the only one whose blood matched mine and that, hey presto, he is my father. Welcome to fatherhood, dear Daddy, after eighteen years!'

Her mother gave a short shrill laugh. 'Don't be silly, dear. That sort of thing only happens in films or books.'

Angela made a funny little noise. 'I wish it had.' She took out a handkerchief from her bag and blew her nose. 'I've got to be honest, Mary-France. After my son Adam died, I really did hope you were *his*. Unlike Sheila, I asked for pictures of you as you grew up. Treasured them, I did, putting them in a special album. That's why I fell out so badly with Jilly and Jeremy's mother. She didn't want to know anything about you; not even if you were a boy or a girl.'

Jeremy shrugged apologetically. 'If Mum doesn't want to be troubled by something, she just blanks it out and pretends it never happened.'

'So I'd like to think, dear, that I could help you out now your mother isn't well—'

'What?' Marie-France stiffened. 'Maman? You are ill?'

Her mother glowered at Angela before making a dismissive wave in the air. 'It is not important, *chérie*.'

Really? Marie-France studied her mother sharply. She'd always been a bit of a drama queen, announcing she felt 'like death' when really she was just exhausted after work. Yet this time, Marie-France sensed she was underplaying something for a change. It was all making sense now! The thick red hair she could see, at close quarters, might well be a wig. The weight gain was possibly due to drugs. And her bosom, which she'd been so proud of in the past, just didn't look the same.

'Not *cancer*?' she whispered.

Her mother nodded tightly.

'*Mon Dieu*.' She leaned back on the pillow.

'It's all right.' Jeremy's smooth voice cut in. 'It's natural to be scared at times like this. But your mother is going on a new treatment when she gets back, isn't that right, Collette?'

'*Absolument*. We have to be positive.'

This was even worse. Her mother was usually so histrionic! She'd have expected her to burst into tears by now. This calm, mature woman scared her.

'They can do so much now in medicine,' continued Jeremy. 'And—'

'Go away!' Marie-France tried to shout but it came out as a hiss instead. 'How dare you try and comfort us? We don't know you. You're nothing to us. At least Angela here cared from the beginning.'

Jeremy's voice was laced with hurt but there was indignation too. 'I *would* have done if I had known.'

'I know that's true,' began Jilly.

'*Go away*!' Marie-France pressed the Call button. 'I want you to go. Not you, Maman. I need you to stay.' She tried to hug her mother but the damn machine at her side was in the way. 'It's all right. I promise. I will look after you now. I'll come straight home. I should never have come to this stupid country in the first place.'

'Hush, *chérie*.' This time it was her mother comforting her, the way she had done as a child. 'It is all right. I did not want to worry you. That is why I swore Thierry to secrecy.'

I cannot tell you, Marie-France. Not yet. I made a promise.

She'd assumed he knew something about her father when all the time it was something much more important. Her mother's health.

'We will leave as soon as we can,' whispered her mother, kissing her forehead. 'And then everything will be back to normal. I promise.'

Marie-France was doing well, the doctor said, repeating the nurse's words that she had been 'very lucky'. She could be discharged in three days or maybe even two.

'Isn't that great?' demanded another nurse whom she'd never seen before. The turnover was astonishing yet each one spoke as though they'd known her for ever. 'You're quite a heroine. Have you seen the papers, by the way? No? I'll bring one in for you after your visitors. You do want to see them, don't you? She's the cutest little thing I've ever seen.'

'*Marie-France!*'

Her heart soared as a small girl with blond plaits skidded across the ward towards her, closely followed by Matthew. She screeched to a halt and was about to take a leap on to the bed before her father stopped her. 'We were so worried about you!' She tossed her plaits back over her shoulder. 'Daddy said you might have died! How far did you get? Did you see my mummy?'

Mon Dieu! She looked up at Matthew who was shaking his head.

'Lottie,' he began, 'I told you. Marie-France is very tired. She can't cope with all these questions.'

'No. It's all right.' An idea had just come to her. 'Actually, Lottie, I *did* see your mother.'

Matthew visibly stiffened, sending her a 'What-do-you-think-you're-saying?' look.

'She said that she loves you very much,' went on Marie-France quickly. 'And she told me that she can see *everything* you do from where she is.'

Lottie's eyes widened. 'She can?'

'*Mais bien sûr.* She spotted you when you put salt in the sugar bowl when I arrived. But it's OK. She thought that was quite funny.'

Lottie giggled.

'She didn't think it was so funny when you stole some of Daddy's money and pretended that the other au pair had taken it.'

The little girl's face dropped. 'I promise not to do that again.'

'Mummy likes it when you do your spelling homework and your maths too.'

Lottie nodded solemnly.

'*And* she knows about the tooth fairy!'

Lottie blushed. 'Really.'

Matthew raised his eyebrows. 'I'm not with you on this one.'

Marie-France tried to smile but it hurt too much. 'It doesn't matter. But your wife also had a message for you.'

He gave her a quizzical look. 'Is that so?'

'*Absolument!* I was hoovering between life and death, you know.'

He gave a small smile. 'I think you mean "hover".'

Whatever. 'Your wife says you must start a new life.'

Matthew's face took on a sceptical look. 'I see.'

'Just one more thing.' Marie-France reached across for Lottie's little hand. 'Mummy doesn't want you to be sad any more. She says that although she can see you, you won't be able to see her for a very long time. So she just wants you to get on with your life too and be happy with Daddy.'

Lottie raised her head up to the ceiling. 'OK, Mummy,' she called out. 'I will.' She turned to Matthew. 'Can we have a pizza now? I'm starving.'

Marie-France felt exhausted after their visit. Had she done the right thing? 'I hope you approve, Sally,' she murmured. For pity's sake, what was she doing talking to a dead woman whom she didn't even know? She needed to pull herself together before her mother came to visit again this afternoon.

But first she had to make a phone call. The person at the other end was surprised to hear what she suggested. Possibly a little nervous too. But, as she explained, they might as well get it over and done with. After all, she was in the right place, wasn't she?

'Lunchtime, dear!'

Ugh. The food in this place was disgusting. Still, there was some post on the tray and a newspaper.

Curiously, Marie France opened the pink envelope. A Get Well card from Sheila? Wonders would never cease. But if she thought that was going to make up for everything, she was mistaken.

Flinging it on to her bedside table, she turned to the newspaper, which wasn't the same as the one which Matthew took. But as she leaned back against the cosy hospital pillows and took in the headline on the front page, every nerve in her body stiffened. *Qu'est-ce que c'est que ça?*

HYDE PARK SUSPECT ARRESTED

Following the shocking attack on French au pair Marie-France Dubonne last Saturday, a man has been arrested. He is thought to be a former boyfriend of the victim, with whom she had a recent disagreement. Several witnesses have come forward, including 18-year-old Antoinette Malfille who helped to identify the suspect.

'No,' yelled out Marie-France with a scream that sent an auxiliary nurse rushing to her bed. 'No. This is not true. *Ce n'est pas vrais!*'

524

JILLY'S AU PAIR AGENCY:
GUIDELINES FOR AU PAIRS AND FAMILIES

*Sometimes a family has to accept that their au pair is
not right for them. And vice versa...*

Chapter 40

What a mess! Matthew surveyed the pile of dishes left over from breakfast and the day before that. Upstairs, his own bed hadn't been made for days and Lottie's room was in a state too.

'We need to tidy up,' Lottie said solemnly, putting on a pair of the fur-trimmed washing-up gloves that Berenice had left behind. 'Mummy wouldn't like it. Remember what Marie-France said. She wants us to carry on life as normal.'

Matthew tried to smile. Carry on life as normal? He hadn't told Lottie about being 'let go', as James had put it. He'd merely told his daughter that he'd put the house on the market and when they sold, they'd move to 'somewhere by the sea'. He'd always rather liked that idea.

But it wasn't going to be easy. And although it was, of course, right that Marie-France should go back to France with her mother to recuperate, where did that leave them? Finding another au pair? Asking more favours from Paula?

The only person who had really helped was Christina but he could hardly ring her up. Not now. It had been great – really great – bumping into her like that in the pizza place but after that phone call from the police, telling him that Marie-France's mobile had been found, he'd been so shocked that he couldn't even remember saying goodbye. In fact, he seemed to recall, he'd just rushed out, dragging Lottie with him. She must think he was mad or at the least very rude.

'Daddy! The doorbell! I'll go!'

Lottie was there before he could stop her. On the doorstep stood a middle-aged couple with a young woman whom he vaguely recognised.

'Yes?'

He didn't mean to sound abrupt but really he could have done without this.

'Mr Evans.' The young woman was smiling brightly. 'Sorry we're a few minutes late. This is Mr and Mrs Woodbury.'

'Late?' he repeated. 'I'm sorry. I don't understand.'

The girl's smile dimmed slightly. 'Your three o'clock appointment, Mr Evans. I spoke to someone here yesterday who said it was fine.'

Lottie! 'I'm sorry. That was my daughter. She's only eight, well nearly nine actually, but I know she can sound grown up.' Wildly he looked around at the chaos. This was the very first viewer the estate agency had brought round. What would they think?

'Could you just give me a minute to clear up?'

The man frowned. 'We're on a tight schedule, I'm afraid.'

'We don't mind if it's a bit untidy. Honestly,' trilled the woman.

A *bit* untidy?

With a sinking heart, Matthew allowed them in, watching their faces as they moved swiftly from one messy room to another. When they got to his room, he put his hand across the door. He simply couldn't bear them to see his own unmade bed.

'This is *my* room next door,' trilled Lottie.

The man gave her a sharp look. 'Shouldn't you be at school?'

'I've got time off! We've been visiting our oh pear in hospital. She got stabbed but she's getting better now.'

Mrs Woodbury clutched her husband's arm. 'I think we'd better go, dear.'

'She didn't get stabbed *here*, if that helps,' called out Matthew, but they had gone, followed by the estate-agent girl with her smooth smile, saying she'd be in touch.

'You didn't tell me they were coming,' he said to his daughter as soon as the door had shut.

She shrugged. 'I forgot. Daddy, do we *have* to move?'

So that was it! She hadn't told him on purpose!

'I've changed my mind, Daddy. I like it here. I've got my friends and I don't want to leave my school.'

He knelt down beside her. 'Look, Lottie, I'm sorry but I can't afford to pay for this house any more. It's too expensive.'

'But that's why you go to work! To earn money.'

He took a deep breath. 'I'm not going back to work now, Lottie. Not for a bit anyway. I'm going to spend some time with you so we don't have to have another au pair.'

She made a face. 'But I like Marie-France. I want her to come back.'

'She can't. You know that.' Damn. Was that the

doorbell again? Maybe the estate-agent girl had forgotten something.

'Hello? Oh. Hi.'

It was the nosy neighbour who was always peering through her curtains. The one whose name he didn't even know. Now they were close up, he could see that she was slightly younger than he'd thought; rather jolly-looking and possibly in her mid-fifties.

'My name's Margaret.' Her handshake was warm and plump. 'Margaret Cross. We haven't met before so I hope you don't mind me turning up like this. It's just that I read about your poor French au pair in the paper and I wanted to say that if you ever need someone to babysit, I'd be very happy to help out.'

She held out a plate of chocolate cup cakes. 'And I thought you might like these. They're left over from when my grandchildren came to stay from the States.' Her face fell. 'They've gone back now.'

So she was lonely! No wonder she spent so much time looking out of the window. 'Thank you,' said Matthew, stunned. 'That's very kind.'

'Heard the news?' asked Paula when he dropped off William after school the following week. Now he was at home all day – bored stiff if he was to tell the truth – he was able to do his bit with the school run. 'The police questioned Marie-France's boyfriend by mistake! Nice boy, apparently, called Thierry. She mistakenly identified him from a picture when she was still woozy from the anaesthetic and they charged right in because Dawn had told them that her husband had declared Thierry to be 'rather aggressive' with 'blazing eyes' when he'd turned up at her place during the summer. I'm ashamed to say that my Antoinette added her pennyworth too, out of spite apparently.' She made a face. 'Terrible, isn't it?'

'So now they haven't got a suspect?'

'Oh yes. They have, thanks to Marie-France clonking him on the head with a bottle. That helped to pin him down. Spitting image of the French boyfriend apparently, but he's English. They've arrested him and – get this! – the paper says they're questioning him about other murders including your Bulgarian girl.' She shivered. 'Horrible, isn't it, when it's so close to home!'

Suddenly Matthew felt very sick. Even if they did find the right man, it wouldn't bring Sozzy back. He might not have known her very well or even liked her but it was weird to think he was one of the last people she'd seen before her death.

'Don't be sad, Daddy.' Lottie patted his back as he got back into the car to take them home. 'Remember what Mummy told Marie-France about being happy? Now, what's for supper? I'm starving!'

Again! Where did his skinny little girl put it all? And weren't kids amazing at being able to switch from really heavy stuff like death to something trivial?

If only adults could be the same.

Of course he didn't expect to find Christina there. What kind of parent got a takeaway pizza every night? But at the moment, it was the only thing that Lottie would eat. That and scrambled eggs with cheese which she'd suddenly developed a craving for.

'We'd like a family-sized margarita, please!' chirped Lottie at the counter.

Why was it that the phone always rang at the most inconvenient moments? Propping his mobile between his ear and shoulder, he tried to wrestle a tenner out of his wallet at the same time. 'Hello. Hello? Sorry. Thought I'd lost you there for a moment. Yes, this is Matthew Evans.'

'Matthew?' an amused American voice was at the other end. 'It's Duncan here. We met at your offices last month. Got a minute to talk?'

'Actually, I'm with my daughter. We're buying pizza.'

'Man after my own heart! What kind of parent buys his kids pizza on the way back from school? A hungry dad, that's what we say in our house. Listen, I know you've left James's practice but I still can't find the right architect for my kids' project. Would you like to come in tomorrow to my office and discuss this with me?'

'Sorry. Lottie, watch how you pick up that pizza box or it will fall out! Look, I don't have any childcare at the moment. I'm taking a sabbatical until we move house.'

'I don't think you get it, Matthew. I don't want you to work in our office. You can work from home. And I can assure you we're offering a very competitive fee structure. How about it?'

Wow! Matthew put his mobile away, stunned by the figure that Duncan had just offered and wondering if this was a practical joke. A commission which would pay more than he had got from James? Working from

531

home so he could still take Lottie to school and collect her?

'Two margaritas, please.'

'No, Mum, I said I wanted pepperoni. You never listen to me! I *said* I wasn't vegetarian this week.'

Swivelling round, he saw Christina and her moody daughter Emma at the counter. 'Hi.' Christina flushed. 'I was hoping no one else would see me here. I mean, what kind of parent buys their kid pizza on the way back from school instead of cooking a proper family meal?'

'A hungry parent?' he suggested.

Emma and Lottie rolled their eyes.

'Mum's so embarrassing.'

'So's my dad.'

'Listen,' he said quickly, 'why don't you come back to our place to eat? It's a bit of a mess but—'

'That would be great,' scowled the teenager who was wearing a small gold nose ring instead of the silver one she'd had before. 'Anything so we don't have to go home where Mum will nag me. That's all she does. Have you done your homework? Have you made your bed?'

'I think Matthew has got the picture, thank you,' said Christina, giving him an I-hope-you-understand look.

'We do it the other way round,' chirped Lottie. 'I nag *him*. But someone has to. Isn't that right, Dad? At least that's what Mummy told Marie-France when our oh pear nearly went to heaven.'

Christina raised her eyebrows.

'It's a long story,' whispered Matthew. 'Tell you

532

when they're safely tucked up in front of the television.' He stopped, realising he'd presumed too much. 'I mean, if that's all right with you?'

For one very long minute, she just stood there looking at him as though seeing him for the very first time. Then, to his huge relief, she nodded. 'I'd like that, Matt,' she said simply. Then she grinned. A rather mischievous grin with a twinkle that he hadn't seen before. 'I *can* call you that, can't I?'

'Absolutely.' He nodded, feeling a lovely warmth sweeping through him. 'Of course you can.'

HOW TO SAY 'HAPPY CHRISTMAS'
TO YOUR AU PAIR

Joyeux Noël! (French)

Bon Natale (Corsican)

Jwaye Nowel (Haitian Creole)

Buon Natale (Italian)

God Jul (Swedish)

Feliz Navidad (Spanish)

Noeliniz kutlu olsun (Turkish)

Chapter 41

Six weeks later

The last time Jilly had been to France was for a school trip when she'd been about the same age as Nick. But now, the cool, glassy terminal of the airport and signs in another language brought back memories of that teenage exchange. Everything had seemed so different! So scary! So new! And so far from her mother at that age.

Was that how Marie-France and the other au pairs had felt? Maybe she hadn't appreciated that fully enough.

'We're going to see our *tante*,' piped up Alfie at Passport Control.

'She's Mum's *niece*, stupid. Not our aunt.'

'Don't kick me! That's my French leg.'

The man at the desk raised a quizzical eyebrow at her.

'Sorry,' said Jilly apologetically. 'They've just discovered that they have a French relation and now this one here – that's Harry although I know he looks like Alfie on his passport – thinks his right-hand side is French and that Alfie's French side is on the left.' She made a please-understand-my-terrible-accent face. 'Sounds crazy, doesn't it?'

For one minute, she thought the passport control officer was going to refuse them entry – on grounds of insanity perhaps? – but then he waved them on. David was making a beeline for the luggage carousel with Nick who was actually talking earnestly to his father instead of to his iPhone.

'Let me get this right, Dad. Uncle Jeremy got Marie-France's mother pregnant when he was only a year older than me. But he only found when he and Marie-France had their Dee En Ay taken when she was in hospital.'

'Spot on.' David's voice sounded steady. That cold critical attitude had evaporated during the panic over Marie-France's stabbing and now he was back to his usual self.

Mind you, that might not have happened without a rather painful let's-thrash-it-out conversation which had taken place after Marie-France had been found.

'Of course I'm not having an affair,' he'd insisted when she'd tackled him about those pink pants which *still* no one had claimed. 'But I will admit that I felt inadequate when everything went wrong at work.'

He had given her a rueful I'm-sorry look. 'And to be honest, I felt threatened by your agency. I'm sure that's why my own parents' marriage broke up. Mum was much more successful than Dad, just like your mother was. And I was frightened the same would happen to us.'

She could understand that. But even so, she wasn't letting him off that lightly. 'I'd expected you to be supportive – not jealous or threatened.'

He nodded. 'I know. And do you know what made me change my mind? It was your parents' party. I looked at your mum and dad and I realised they're amazing.'

'Amazing?'

'Yes. They argue, I grant you, but when push comes to shove, they're a team. They couldn't exist without each other and that's how I feel about you. I'm sorry, Jilly. Really sorry. I can't imagine life without you.'

She'd leaned against his chest, feeling his warm arms around her. 'I can't imagine life without you either, David. But it hasn't changed the situation. Running an agency is stressful. And I need your support.'

He nodded. 'You have it.' He frowned. 'There's just one thing. It's about Fatima.'

Her heart sank. She could guess what was coming next!

'What was all that stuff about the man on the doorstep?'

'You mean Nigel.' She took a deep breath before explaining exactly what had happened. Rather flatteringly, he was furious.

'If it wasn't for you and Paula being such good friends, I'd have nothing to do with him. Smarmy bugger. I've seen him in the pub, chatting to other women. How dare he do the same to my wife? I'm going round to give him a piece of my mind.'

Somehow she had persuaded him not to, pointing out that it wouldn't help Paula. 'Frankly, I think it's best not to interfere. Things might get better between them. Like they have between Mum and Dad. You know, I can't help feeling that the reason Mum was so understanding about Fatima was that deep down she's always felt guilty about Collette and Marie-France.'

David, still clearly livid about Nigel, had nodded. 'You could be right.'

The repercussions and the questions were endless – and they were still continuing at the airport where her husband was, right now, engaged in a serious conversation with Nick.

'So Uncle Jeremy was irresponsible really, Dad. He should have used contraception.'

David didn't miss a beat. 'You could say that. If you want me to buy you some condoms, I'm happy to do so.'

'Gross, Dad. That's sick. Anyway, I've already got loads. We got them free at a school talk.'

She hadn't known that!

'But then if Uncle Jeremy had worn a raincoat, Collette wouldn't have given birth to Marie-France. So it's all worked out, hasn't it?'

'You could say that but—'

'Dad!' Alfie, who'd caught the tail end of the conversation, was looking puzzled. 'How do raincoats stop you having babies?'

'Let's just change the subject, shall we?' said Jilly hastily. 'Now here's Auntie Angela. Wait, you lot!'

'Thank you, dear. Ah, that looks like my bag coming round now. Oh, do be careful, dear, there are some breakables inside. Just little gifts, you know. I thought it would show them how grateful I am to be included.' She touched Jilly's arm. 'I do hope I'm not in the way.'

Jilly was about to say that of course she wasn't but Angela was still gabbling away nervously. 'Marie-France might not be my granddaughter but I still feel fond of her. Silly, isn't it?'

'Not at all . . .'

'Every year, when her mother used to send us pictures, I used to pore over them and convince myself I could see Adam in her.' She fumbled in her bag for a handkerchief. 'My way of keeping him alive, I suppose.'

Jilly gave her a quick cuddle. It would have been better if Marie-France had turned out to be Adam's. At least then she'd have had a grandmother who wanted her. Still, her own brother had come up trumps and, she had to admit it, Marie-France was an unexpected gift of a niece. In a way, she reminded her of her brother at that age: very charming but with a mind of his own and not afraid to tell others how to do it better.

'I do wish that Sheila had agreed to come.'

Jilly nodded, thinking back to her mother's tight-lipped expression when the DNA test, done on the quiet by Marie-France and her brother, had shown that Jeremy was the father after all. But Jilly knew that, deep down, her mother was hurting. Badly. She was all too aware that by not telling Jeremy that he had a child, she'd deprived a little girl of her father and vice versa. Nothing could ever make up for that.

Yet it could have happened to her! Just look at how Nick had sold off phone numbers for Antoinette and the other au pairs, as though he was some sort of pimp! It was so hard to control a teenager without a padded cell, an iPhone and a steady supply of Pot Noodles.

Pot Noodles! That reminded her. Would Fatima really be all right at home? Her mind went back to the evening when Marie-France was being rushed to intensive care at the same time as Fatima went into labour.

Eventually, after fifteen hours, she'd given birth to a ten-pound whopper although she'd caused huge consternation in the ward by refusing to allow any male doctor near her. Her son – Charlie, named after Prince Charles apparently – was incredibly good and Fat Eema herself had proved to be an amazing mother. During the day, she would knot the baby into a huge scarf behind her back and insisted on still helping the boys with their maths homework.

They could even count to ten in Turkish now. Bir, iki, üç . . . And so on.

There were still some visa issues to sort out but, to be honest, Fat Eema was part of their family now even though there were some things that would never be known.

When it came to putting the father's name on the birth certificate, Fat Eema's lips had merely tightened. 'I will not say,' she spat. 'I never want anything to do with him again.'

Poor thing. Yet it was hard to feel sorry for her: she was so much happier now. Always chanting Turkish nursery rhymes to her son whom she adored – how ironic that she should have had a boy!

They'd had to stop thinking of her as Fat Eema too. Amazingly, most of her baby weight fell off her within weeks so that Fatima actually developed hips and cheekbones. She began wearing clothes that were less shapeless including . . . guess what? Three pairs of pink pants, just like the ones she'd found before, suddenly turned up in the wash.

'They are mine,' she had said, blushing. 'Marie-France, she buy them for me when I was big with baby. She say they are my goal. She say that if I want to wear them, I must lose weight. I am trying hard. Yes?'

Was there anything that Marie-France hadn't tried to put her nose in?

'Jilly!' David's voice brought her back to the present. To the airport in France where they were about to meet Marie-France on her home ground. 'Come on. They'll be waiting in Arrivals.'

Jilly's heart began to beat wildly. Was this really a good idea? When Marie-France had rung from France and asked them all out to join her and her mother for Christmas, her immediate reaction had been to say no. Politely, of course. But then Jeremy had jumped at the idea, even though it meant taking time off at one of the most important times of the year for him.

'Did you tell your parishioners the truth?' she'd asked and he'd nodded.

'Of course I did. I'm not ashamed that I have a daughter. How could I be? She's a wonderful human being. But I do know that I have a lot of making up to do and... well, there may be a time when her mother isn't going to be around. Marie-France will need me even more then.'

Very true. Meanwhile, still feeling nervous about what lay ahead, Jilly took in the fresh French air – was it her imagination, or did it smell different from home? – and went through the green channel. There was a small crowd of people waiting expectantly in Arrivals. She swept her eyes over them, looking for a tall, dark-haired girl with a slightly Roman-shaped nose and flashing eyes.

There was Marie-France, waving madly! And there, next to her, standing proud with a spiky black urchin haircut, wearing a skirt that was surely a little short for her thirty-seven years, was Collette. With a distinctly hostile expression on her face.

JILLY'S AU PAIR AGENCY:
GUIDELINES FOR AU PAIRS AND FAMILIES

Many families and au pairs continue to keep in contact for years afterwards, often visiting each other!

Chapter 42

If it wasn't for Thierry, thought Marie-France when they were waiting for Jeremy's plane to land, none of this would be happening. Her mind went back to that terrible time in the hospital when she had read the newspaper article. It was all her fault – well, partly – for saying his name when the police had shown her the photographs.

'It is a mistake!' she had screamed to the police. And eventually, thank God, Thierry had been released and come straight to the hospital. She'd expected him to be mad at her but he'd been cool.

'Hey, it's OK,' he had shrugged, sitting on the side of her bed even though the nurse had instructed him firmly to stick to the visitor's chair. 'It's sorted now and the newspapers say they have someone else instead.'

He had kissed the top of her forehead then, rather unexpectedly, and it had sent the same old magic down her spine. Not that she was going to let him know that, of course.

'The main thing is that you're safe *and*, of course, that you've finally found your dad.'

She had scowled at that. 'A wimpy gay vicar, you mean?'

'C'mon, Marie-France. You don't know he's gay and even if he was, would that matter? We don't choose

544

our relatives. We just get them. And if you're lucky, they hang around.'

He had looked away but not before she had seen the hurt in his face. Thierry's mother had left home when he was six and his father had reluctantly brought him up until he was sixteen before kicking him out and telling him to make his own way in life. It was a subject he didn't care to raise very often.

'If I were you, Marie-France,' he'd said, furtively drawing an envelope of tobacco from his pocket, 'I'd get to know your father a bit better when they let you out of this place.'

'But I'm going straight home!'

'Then ask them over to France.' He grinned. 'That would get a few tongues wagging in the village.'

Invite them to her own home? Maybe! But not just yet. Instead, she needed to supervise Maman's recuperation after her treatment. She also had to work in the village's only café so they could put food on the table. Money was tight and she didn't like to ask about the handouts which had been coming from England all those years. Maybe they had now stopped? She certainly wasn't asking for any more!

Jeremy emailed her all the time and she usually replied. Yes, thank you. Her scar was healing nicely although it ached a bit from time to time, but it was nothing to worry about. Yes, she did have to testify at the trial, which would probably be in the spring. And yes, he was right. Although it would be painful, she needed to do this for Sozzy and the other au pairs.

Marie-France was warmer with Jilly who also sent

how-are-you-doing emails and photographs of the children. Naturally, there was nothing from Jilly's mother, the old witch.

As for Thierry, he was back from Ireland now and touring a place called North Umberland (and sending the occasional text). But the village was very quiet without him and her other friends who had all gone off to university. If it had not been for her mother's illness, she could have stayed in the UK with little Lottie. How she missed her!

Now her mother needed more treatment, she might even have to give up her place at the Sorbonne to look after her. After all, hadn't her mother put her own life on hold at eighteen, instead of having an abortion? So it was only right that she should reciprocate.

'What are you doing for Christmas, *ma petite*?' one of her elderly neighbours asked her in early December. That's when Thierry's words came back to her. Why not? Why not ask Jeremy – she still could not say the word '*father*' – and Jilly over to visit?

'I have family coming over,' she had replied on the spur of the moment.

The old woman's face had creased with curiosity. 'I did not know you had any!'

Marie-France had shrugged, enjoying the look on the neighbour's face. 'They are English,' she could not resist adding.

'*Anglais? Mon Dieu!* I shall look forward to seeing them.' And with that, she bustled off, no doubt to tell everyone.

Within a few hours, Marie-France was being approached by friends who wanted to know about these surprise relatives who had turned up out of the blue.

'What have you done now?' her mother had demanded when word reached her, as was inevitable around here. 'I do not want people to know our business.'

'Maman,' she'd said, 'it's nothing to be ashamed of. You were a young girl who had a baby. It's not a crime. Times have changed.'

Her mother had laughed mirthlessly. 'Not here, they haven't.'

Her words made Marie-France uneasy but it was too late. She'd already emailed Jeremy and Jilly and then Angela had called to ask if she could come as well. And now, here they all were, at the airport, waving and smiling!

'*Merde*,' muttered her mother under her breath. 'I only hope you know what you have let us in for.'

SURVEY BY *CHARISMA* MAGAZINE

One in eight people spend Christmas alone.

Chapter 43

'What are you going to do for Christmas?' asked Margaret wistfully back in Corrywood. Matthew had been trying not to think about it. The twenty-fifth of December was one of those really difficult times, like Mother's Day, when Sally's memory – never far away – loomed up in big print. Even though things had got so much better in the last few weeks with his new job, it was all still so raw.

'I'm not sure. It's not as though we've got any family to invite.'

'Nor me.' Her eye fell on the pile of Christmas cards he was opening in the kitchen where they were having a cup of tea. 'Got a lot, have you?'

There was a touch of envy in her voice. She was still lonely! Even though she was looking after them, Margaret also needed someone to take care of her. She'd only been in their lives for a short time but already it felt as though he had known her for ever. He couldn't thank her enough for that. She was the grandmotherly figure that Lottie so desperately needed.

Now he picked up one of the cards to show her. 'This one's from Sozzy's parents.'

'Your Bulgarian au pair? The one who...'

He nodded as her sentence tailed away. 'They say they are thinking of me at this time.'

'That's kind.'

'I should have sent them one.' He could have kicked himself. 'I'll have to see them at the trial. I'm being called as a witness because I was the last person known to have seen her before the attack.'

Margaret shot him a sympathetic look. 'Poor you. And poor them. Listen, I was thinking. Would you and Lottie like to come to me for Christmas lunch?'

Christmas lunch? A meal that was usually shared with close family or friends? Yet isn't that what the three of them had become? He couldn't imagine life now without Margaret popping in and out with a Victoria sponge she had just made or him going over to help her sort out her dodgy boiler.

'That would be lovely,' he began, but then stopped as Lottie tore into the room, plaits flapping.

'DAD! DAD! There's this really cool advert on television for Disneyland in Paris. Can we go. Please! Pretty please!'

'I don't think so,' began Matthew but then as he looked first at his daughter's face and then at Margaret's crestfallen one, he had an idea. Why not? He was earning enough from his new job, wasn't he? And hadn't Christina subtly suggested during one of their many coffees, that it was a good idea to start new traditions when you were coping with change?

'Margaret…' he said, hoping he was doing the right thing without talking to Lottie first. Then again, she really liked the older woman who had stepped in as a mother's help. He often found the two of them cuddling up or baking cakes. 'I was just wondering. Have you ever been to France?'

JILLY'S AU PAIR AGENCY:
GUIDELINES FOR FAMILIES

Christmas can be a strange time for au pairs who are away from home. Try to include them in your festivities. Be prepared for homesickness...

Chapter 44

Jilly had been pleasantly surprised when Marie-France rounded the corner in her little dented white Renault – slightly fast, it had to be said! – and screeched to a halt outside a gorgeous white cottage with a magnolia tree in front.

Just as well her mother hadn't come after all. She could almost hear her speaking now. 'So that's where our monthly payments went!'

They'd trooped in, feeling rather awkward. Where would they all sleep? But then Marie-France led the boys up a ladder to an enormous attic with three beds, beautifully made up in crisp white linen. 'You are here,' pronounced Collette, throwing open another door with a large double bed and heavy mahogany chest of drawers.

'And you' – her eyes flashed at Angela – 'are here.' She gesticulated to a makeshift bed next to her daughter's bed in Marie-France's room.

'Perfect,' breathed Angela who would no doubt talk all night to Marie-France about her son. Poor thing.

'As for you,' sniffed Collette, giving Jeremy a dismissive haughty glare, 'you are in the wood shed.' There was a brief pause, then she gave the glimmer of a smile. 'Do not look so worried. There is a bed and a heater there. Besides, it is fitting, *n'est-ce pas*? Was not your God born in a simple place?'

That was two days ago and the atmosphere was still tricky, thanks to Collette, who was being decidedly prickly. But Jeremy was amazing in the way he steered potentially awkward conversations on to safer waters.

Then again, Jeremy had always been a people person, which was partly why his parish drop-in centre was usually bursting. Marie-France, she couldn't help noticing, was slowly warming to him too. There had been long chats in the corner of Collette's sitting room with the two of them poring over photograph albums. Angela had been hovering on the fringe, clearly desperate to join in but not wanting to impose until Jeremy, who suddenly noticed, invited her to join them.

But Collette was a nightmare! 'May I help you?' Jilly offered every time their hostess started to prepare a meal. But she was met with a stony stare.

'You English, you do not know how to cook, let alone make love.' She waved her hand in the direction of the twins who were playing in the snow outside. 'You look after *them*. And do not let your big boy anywhere near the girls in the village. I do not want them to get pregnant too.'

Ouch! But she had a point. Nick, whose ideas about French girls had obviously been boosted by his experience back in Corrywood, kept going for walks on his own with his iPod, probably sussing out the local talent. David, meanwhile, had taken to going outside as well 'to get a better reception' and was constantly talking on the phone.

It made her feel uneasy. He might be off the hook

with those pink pants but, unless she was mistaken, *something* was going on.

After lunch on the third day, they all went round the village in an exploratory group led by their hosts. There wasn't much to see, to be honest. The church; the school where Marie-France had studied; a run-down chateau on the outskirts at which they could only gawp from a distant wire fence. And a post office cum general stores that was open for two hours a day, and the café with red gingham tablecloths and wine bottles streaked with candle wax where Marie-France had been working.

Corrywood must have seemed like a big city to Marie-France!

That night, when they'd all gone to bed, Jilly tossed and turned on the goose-feathered mattress, shivering as the wind blew through the shutters. Had it been a mistake for them all to come here? she wondered. Tomorrow was Christmas Eve! They should be at home – maybe sharing a glass or two with friends, instead of sitting it out in a house with a frosty hostess. Perhaps Jeremy should have come out here without them. And what about Mum and Dad who were all on their own?

Then she heard it. At first it sounded like a cat. 'David.' She pushed him slightly. 'Can you hear that?'

When her husband was asleep, very little could wake him. Pulling on her dressing gown, she creaked open the door and padded downstairs. There, by the range, sat Collette. Without her wig. Quietly, Jilly sat next to her and took her hand. The other woman instantly pulled it away as though it had been burned.

'What are you doing?'

'I'm sorry.' Jilly felt embarrassed. 'I heard you crying. I wondered if I could help.'

'Help!' Anger flashed in her eyes. 'Your family has done nothing to help me.'

'That's not quite true,' began Jilly.

'You think money is the answer? Does it stop people staring? They look at your brother and they see he looks like his daughter. Now they call me a liar.'

'But you invited us!'

'That was Marie-France's idea. She is very stubborn when she wants to be.'

Jilly nodded. 'It runs in the family. My boys are the same.'

Collette's eyes took on a dreamy look. 'I wanted boys. I wanted a big family when I was young.'

'Marie-France says you have a boyfriend.'

'Pah. Maurice? I turn him down.'

'He asked you to marry him?'

'Yes. But I refused him because I think he should ask twice. But then he doesn't.'

Jilly could see what Marie-France meant about her mother being a drama queen.

Suddenly Collette grabbed her arm. 'And now, because I need more treatment, my daughter says she will not go to the Sorbonne. It is such a waste!'

For some time, the two women sat, holding each other's hands, not speaking. She's virtually my age, thought Jilly. This woman could have been me. Wouldn't she too have felt bitter if, at the age of eighteen, taken in by the novelty of being in another country and perhaps throwing caution to the winds,

555

she had been seduced by two young boys?' And if so, how would she have felt, nineteen years down the line? Wouldn't she, too, have felt angry? Cheated of the life which had been denied her. A bitter-sweet feeling because she had a lovely daughter but at the cost of a marriage and more children?

Then a whirring sound cut into her thoughts. The clock was striking midnight. It was Christmas Eve!

Collette stood up and wiped her eyes. 'I have things to do. Food to prepare for tomorrow.'

'May I help you?' asked Jilly quietly.

The other woman appeared to consider her suggestion and then nodded. 'Very well.'

For the next half-hour or so, they stood next to each other, slicing carrots and potatoes and then smearing the chicken with fat before putting it into the range to cook slowly for the following day. Soothing, mechanical actions that seemed to calm them both.

'Thank you,' Collette said quietly as she took off her apron and hung it on the back of the door.

'No,' said Jilly, giving her a quick hug before padding up the stairs. 'Thank *you*.'

This time her husband was awake. 'I missed you. Everything OK?' Her husband's arm slid around her in that comfortable jigsaw lock they had developed over the years. 'She wasn't having a go at me as well, was she? Didn't suggest you found another husband like Fatima did?'

'No.' Jilly wriggled uncomfortably. 'But everything *is* all right between us, isn't it, David?'

'Course it is,' he mumbled before starting to snore.

So why didn't he sound convincing? Eventually, still

troubled, Jilly began to doze off but almost immediately – or so it seemed – her mobile bleeped. It was a long answerphone message from Paula.

Please let her be all right! For a horrid few seconds, Jilly felt sick in case Nigel had walked out. But no, Paula's excited voice soon put that fear to rest.

You're not going to believe this! Remember how Antoinette asked if she could have her money in advance so she could buy Christmas presents for the kids? Well, she's only gone and left in the middle of the night with all the money and taken one of our Harrods suitcases with her.

There's something else too! That au pair you placed with Kitty Banks from school – that really stunning Heidi girl – has run off with the husband who kept walking around half-naked in front on her! And wasn't she the one with the dodgy reference you told me about?

Don't worry! I won't say a thing. But I did hear through one of the other mothers that Heidi's also been hacking into people's Facebooks and changing their status details just to make trouble. Poor Kitty says she always seemed like such a nice girl. Friend of your Marie-France apparently…

THEME FOR THE CHRISTMAS SERMON AT CORRYWOOD PARISH CHURCH

Christmas is a time for forgiveness…

Chapter 45

It was weird! Before they had all arrived from England, Marie-France reminded herself, she'd been really worried. What if Maman was rude to her new family? What would everyone in the village say?

But now Jeremy had actually arrived and she could see people in the village clocking how obvious it was that they shared certain features. Funny! Marie-France had always thought she looked like her mother. But after meeting Jeremy, she could see they shared the same thin, distinctive nose. The same hands with long slender fingers. The same bluey-green eyes. Even the same joyous laugh! It was both scary and comforting.

But she still couldn't use the word 'Dad'. It wasn't just that Jeremy, with his boyish fair looks, looked more like an older brother. It was because a father was someone who had been there for you all through your childhood. Not a man whom she'd only discovered through chance.

Even so, they got on very well. During their walks, she discovered they shared similar passions. 'When did you learn to play the guitar?' he asked.

'At school. Someone donated one to the music class and when I picked it up, my fingers seemed to know what they were doing.'

He nodded. 'When I met your mother, Adam and I were in a band.' He laughed in a touchingly embarrassed way. 'I was bass. We used to put on concerts at the village hall.'

She could see that somehow: a tall blond teenager and all those teenage girls staring up at him with admiration.

Then the conversation had turned to her mother. 'You must be worried about her,' Jeremy had said in a kind but probing way.

'Of course.'

'Do you ever pray about it?'

She laughed out loud. 'If there was a God, my mother wouldn't be ill.'

'Maybe this is his way of helping. By bringing us all together.'

'Hah! Your mother wouldn't agree.'

'Ah, my mother.' He spoke in an amused but slightly sad way. 'I'm afraid that Mum is very stubborn. Rather like us.'

Us! That felt nice. 'But I changed my mind about you.'

He nodded. 'You did indeed. I still don't quite understand why you asked us over.'

They stopped by the old village pump for a minute while he read the sign above it. 'I think,' she said softly, aware that Maurice Sevronne from the shop, her mother's old flame, was walking his dog just the other side of the lane, 'that it was because I felt half of me was missing. I needed to know who my father was.'

'Finding your father and then knowing who he is are two different things,' pointed out Jeremy.

'Very true.'

'The getting-to-know bit takes time.'

560

She nodded.

'Do you want to give me that time? I would do anything for you and your mother.' He was blushing furiously now and speaking rather too loudly. 'I have a great deal of regard for her. She is a very brave and beautiful woman.'

Marie-France couldn't help giggling all the way home. Maurice Sevronne's eyes would be popping out of his head even now! Serve him right for not moving fast enough. Every woman – well every *French*woman anyway – knows you have to turn down a man at least once if you are serious about him.

After dinner – a magnificent roasted chicken from Monsieur Terron's farm – they opened their presents as was their custom. 'Can *we* be French too!' demanded Alfie. 'Then we wouldn't have to wait another whole night for Father Christmas!'

The boys were so excited! Even Collette seemed to like having young children in the house at Christmas though of course she wouldn't say so.

'Do you think Father Christmas will still remember our stockings in the night?' asked Harry wistfully. 'We did email him before we left. In French and English just to make sure.'

'And Turkish,' added Alfie.

'I'm sure he will,' soothed Marie-France, watching her mother open the beautiful beige silk nightdress she'd bought for her months ago, from a lovely shop in London called Liberty's. Maman gave her a pair of peacock-green dangly earrings which went well with her hair. So beautiful! It made her slightly embarrassed about the modest presents she had bought for the guests: a small locally made wooden picture frame for each one. For the boys, there was a large football to share which they started kicking round the kitchen immediately.

'Be careful,' said Collette sharply just as David was about to stop them. 'I do not want anything broken.'

'Boys, do you hear?' said Jilly, flushing. 'Now, Collette, I hope you don't mind, but we've clubbed together and given you a present for both you and Marie-France.'

Her mother immediately tore open the envelope. 'We'd like you to use it to buy an air fare so you can come back and see us in the spring,' said David quickly.

Collette gave him an 'are-you-joking? look. 'I think my daughter and I have seen enough of *Angleterre*, thank you very much.' Even so, she snatched the cheque, folded it neatly into four and tucked it into her pocket with a little pat of satisfaction.

'Thank you,' said Marie-France, deeply embarrassed by her mother's bad manners. 'It is very kind of you.'

That night, they all went to midnight mass where, just as Marie-France had feared, everyone stared at them. But she was beginning not to care any more. The only thing that really mattered, she thought, as her phone bleeped with a 'Happy Christmas' message from Thierry, was that Maman got better.

HOW TO GET THROUGH CHRISTMAS
AS A SINGLE PARENT!

Start by making your own new traditions… Do things you didn't do before, when you were part of a couple.

Extract from *Dads Alone* magazine

Chapter 46

Sally and Matthew had always intended to take Lottie to Disneyland in Paris. It had been one of the things on their list for 'when she got better'.

But after her death, it had lost its appeal. All those garish pictures in brochures with giant Mickey Mice splitting themselves with laughter and fairy towers in a world where, as Matthew had already learned, there was no magic wand to make everything better.

Yet what was the alternative? A long grey Christmas Day at home in front of the television with a ready-stuffed turkey and sweet sherry – he had a feeling that Margaret would like sweet sherry – pretending that they were a family who was doing a lonely neighbour a favour? No. After the difficult time they'd just had, surely he could do better than that for his daughter?

And he would! Maybe it was the commission from Duncan that had restored his self-esteem, not to mention his bank balance. Or perhaps it was the fact that, at long last, Matthew had now created some stability for his daughter (thanks to Margaret). But either way, he was beginning to feel stronger and more positive than he had for a long time.

Whenever he felt himself slipping back into those 'what ifs' and regrets about the past, he pictured the box Christina had told him to imagine and packed all the old doubts and worries inside, before mentally sealing the top. 'Crazy,' he told himself. Yet it worked. It was definitely helping him to move on.

Now he was going to face Christmas with a strong and positive attitude for the sake of his daughter. It was, Matthew told himself, going to be different from last year when he and Lottie had both been so raw and lost. So he'd start by setting new traditions – a rather good piece of advice in an article he had read at the dentist's. Disneyland, here we come!

The trip, he insisted, was part of Margaret's Christmas present for looking after Lottie. 'Matthew, that's so kind of you! I feel sick with excitement!'

And now, as they got off their Eurostar train and checked into their Disney-themed hotel, he also found himself being swept away by the spontaneity of his own actions and – it had to be admitted – by all the glitzy magic.

'Dad! Dad!' Lottie was jumping up and down in her bedroom, which had a pink palace of a bed. 'Can we go straight to the park?'

So they did, leaving Margaret behind in her room to relax ('You should see my bathroom, Matthew. I could spend all day there!') before heading for one of the tallest rides in the park. It made his stomach plummet just to look at it! Of course he knew *why* Lottie wanted to go there.

'What do you think is up there?' said his daughter after they'd queued up along with loads of other families, some of whom, he was heartened to see, were lone dads like himself.

'Mummy?' he said, preparing himself for questions about heaven. He knew it had been too good to be true. For the past few weeks, Lottie had been so distracted by the end-of-term play in which she'd played Dorothy in *The Wizard of Oz* (Margaret had turned out to be a great costume-maker) that there hadn't been any awkward questions about Sally.

'No, silly.' Lottie elbowed him in the ribs. 'Accumulative clouds. We're doing them at school.'

'Don't you mean cumulus?' asked Matthew, relieved that the subject hadn't turned to heaven. That was another thing. Lottie had become much more like her old self. She was concentrating at school. She'd stopped looking for her mother in the garden. And she didn't make up any false stories that got others into trouble.

It seemed as though they were both moving on. As he and Lottie went hurtling down the Minnie Mouse slide, Matthew thought about the dinner date he and Christina had arranged in the New Year. Who knew what it would lead to? But even if it came to nothing, at least he'd have proved that he'd been brave enough to take a chance.

Just as long as it didn't upset Lottie. That was another reason why he'd taken the house off the market now he had at two-year contract with Duncan. Stability for Lottie meant allowing her to live in an area where she had friends.

Meanwhile, there was still one more thing he needed to do. Something that Christina had suggested. Some - thing that sounded crazy but, well, was maybe worth a shot. Something that would have to wait until they got home.

'Dad! Dad! Look,' called out Lottie as they returned to the hotel and found Margaret. 'I've lost another tooth.' She held out her little hand. There, in her palm, was a small white lump.

'It's a real tooth!' she insisted, jumping up and down. 'Not a pretend stone like before.'

'What do you mean, love?' enquired Margaret, who had the mini-bar open and was looking a bit flushed.

Lottie looked awkward. 'When we had the oh pears, I used to pretend a tooth had fallen out but really I put a little stone under my pillow so the tooth fairy came. But I had to stop that when Mummy told Marie-France what I was doing.'

Matthew didn't know whether to laugh or cry. 'Lottie, that's lying!'

'No, it's not.' Margaret put her arm around his daughter. 'It's called having a fertile imagination. Maybe she'll be a writer one day, Matthew. Now that would be something, wouldn't it?'

A week later, Matthew stood by Sally's gravestone, the letter in his hand. He'd been going to put it by her stone but somehow it felt better to read it out loud. It wasn't long. And it had been easier to write than he'd thought.

'Hello, Sally.'

He glanced uneasily behind in case anyone else was there but the cemetery was deserted. 'It's me, Matthew.'

Well, maybe she'd thought it was that scumbag Phillip who was now in an open prison for fraud. Apparently he'd been planning to make a quick escape to the Cayman Islands when he was arrested.

'I just wanted to say that I forgive you. You

shouldn't have had an affair, but I can also see why you did it. I wasn't perfect. *We* weren't perfect.' He laughed out loud. 'In fact, we were all wrong. It was only Lottie who kept us together in the first place. But she's worth it, Sally. She really is. You'd be so proud of her if you could see her. She doesn't tell lies any more. But Mr Balls at school says she's really imaginative. You should read her stories!'

He stopped briefly to compose himself before continuing. 'I'm working from home now but Margaret, one of our neighbours, comes in when I can't collect Lottie from school. We had some au pairs for a while but it didn't work.'

He stopped, bracing himself. 'One got murdered and I still can't help feeling slightly responsible for that. She ran off, you see... and then someone strangled her.' He shivered. 'The trial's next year and it's going to be horrible, giving evidence, but then life isn't easy, is it? You know that.'

The words were pouring out now. He could imagine Sally standing there; not with an irritated expression on her face, but with the kind smile that had first attracted him to her. 'Go on,' she seemed to say. 'Go on.'

'We're all right, Lottie and I. We even went to Disneyland for Christmas. Remember how we always said we'd do that? Lottie still talks about you and she'll always love you.'

He hesitated. This was the difficult part. 'In a way, so will I. But I've met someone else, Sally. I don't know if she sees me in the same way but I'm going to give it my best shot. Wish me luck. Be happy. Wherever you are.'

Kneeling down, he put a single lily on her grave and then stood up again. Reaching into his pocket, he drew out an empty bottle of aftershave and placed it next to the stem.

Matthew glanced at his watch. If he was quick, there was just time to freshen up before meeting Christina for dinner.

ADVERT IN THE *CORRYWOOD ADVERTISER*

Looking for an au pair for the Easter holidays?

Then contact Jilly and Paula's Au Pair Agency, your local specialist!

Chapter 47

Spring

'It's awful, Jilly. It really is! Nadya refuses to sit with us for family meals and then raids the fridge when I'm out at work. Last week, she wolfed her way through an entire packet of Finest Scottish Salmon.'

Jilly took a deep silent breath on the other end of the phone. 'Leave it with me, Mrs Fisher,' she soothed. 'I'll have a talk with her and then if she still doesn't work out, we'll find you a replacement.'

'I gather that was Frieda Fisher again,' remarked Paula, looking up from her screen where she was compiling another of her amazing spreadsheets. 'I heard about the salmon theft at school. It's no big deal. When I think about the things that Antoinette got up to, I don't know how I managed.'

Jilly went back to her desk opposite Paula's and looked out across the garden where the daffodils were coming into bloom. 'It's a big deal to her and that's what matters.'

Paula shrugged. Jilly was still getting used to her friend wearing what she saw as office outfits: neat little cardigans over well-tailored trousers instead of jeggings. 'Still,' she said, getting up to make a cup of coffee from the machine in the corner. 'That's why we work, Jilly, you and me. You're good with people thanks to your HR experience and I'm not bad at admin. What do you think of this?' She passed over a timetable of suggested au pair activities. 'I thought it might be a blueprint!'

'Great idea.'

Paula flushed with pride. Everything between them had been so much better after David had suggested asking a few friends round for New Year. 'What about Paula and Nigel?' she'd suggested. 'You can't ignore him for ever.'

'Then I'll have to say something.' David gave her a look. 'Don't worry. I won't make a scene. I'll take him to the pub first.'

They had both returned in one piece with a slight coolness between them. And the first thing Nigel did was to go up to Paula and give her a kiss on the cheek.

'I told him not to be a fool any more, among other things,' said David in a low voice. 'Let's just hope that he listens this time.'

Then the others arrived and, before long, with the help of a lot of laughter and wine, they toasted in the new year.

'To Jilly's Agency!' said David, raising his glass.

'To Jilly's Agency!' everyone chorused.

Later, when she and David were clearing up, he had an unexpected suggestion. 'Why don't you ask Paula to be a partner? That way, you'd have more time for the kids and be less stressed.'

'And where do you think we're going to work? In the airing cupboard? As it is, I'm fighting for space on the kitchen table. And even though Mum's gone now, I don't want to move the twins back into one room. They'll keep each other up at night.'

'I'm aware of that,' said David, slightly shiftily, 'and that's why I've been busy organising a late Christmas surprise. It was a bit of a gamble and I probably should have consulted you first but it's arriving next week.' He handed her a brochure from his jeans pocket. 'What do you think?'

Jilly gawped at the picture. Above it was the headline: WORK FROM HOME IN YOUR OWN GARDEN OFFICE.

The price tag made her blanch.

'We can't afford this,' she gasped. 'And anyway, where would it fit?'

'We *can* afford it because things are much better at work now *and* I've done a deal with the suppliers. I've been looking into this for months – I'm surprised you haven't been suspicious about all my furtive phone calls – and I've got it down to a good price. I've had someone round to check on the positioning too and it could just about squeeze in between the fence and the kids' swing.' He took her hand. 'It's also a good idea to have a barrier between home and work, Jilly, so you can cut off.'

Cut off! Know when to stop work and spend time with the family instead! David was right. She did need to do that.

'It's also a sorry present,' added her husband, looking rather shamefaced. 'I know we've been through a rough patch and I also know it was mainly my fault for feeling so inadequate. No. Don't disagree. Fatima – and your mum – pointed out a few home truths before Christmas.' He took her hands in his. 'You wouldn't really take her up on her suggestion to find a Turkish replacement for me, would you?'

That wasn't the first time he'd mentioned it. Clearly, good old Fatima had struck a nerve.

'Maybe not.' She snuggled into him. 'But only if you understand that I've changed. I'm not going back to the old Jilly.'

He nodded. 'I can see that. In fact, I'm really proud of you.'

'Honestly?'

He nodded. 'But have a think about bringing Paula in. It might be just what you both need.'

Jilly wasn't sure. Would her friend really want to give up her exercise classes? After all, it wasn't as though she needed the money. But to her amazement Paula had jumped up and kissed her on the cheek when she broached the idea. 'That would be fabulous, now Immy's at pre-school! A proper part-time job! And not one that takes me away from the kids. Imagine! I can tell everyone now that I'm co-director of an agency!'

Co-director! They hadn't even got round to discussing titles but what the heck. If it worked out with Paula, she wasn't going to get precious. And to her surprise, it *was* working out. Two heads were better than one. Like right now.

'If Nadya doesn't quit her fridge-raiding, we could always place Katrina with Mrs Fisher instead,' suggested Paula, returning to her desk.

'Katrina? The German girl who rang yesterday because she isn't happy with her London agency?'

'Exactly. Now if you don't mind, I'd quite like to finish early. Immy has a ballet lesson.' She flushed. 'And Nigel is taking me out to dinner. He's been so much nicer since I started working with you.' She gave Jilly a nudge. 'Especially in the bedroom department. I think he respects me more. And you know what? I respect myself more too for doing something!'

Jilly felt awkward. She still wasn't sure if she should have warned Paula about her husband's roving eye. Then again, maybe it was none of her business. But if things *did* go belly up with Paula and Nigel's marriage, she'd be there to help her. After all, that's what friends were for.

'Think I'll call it a day too.' Jilly got up and stretched. How lovely to be able to lock the door and go back to the house without worrying about work. The children should be back from school soon and she'd need to start thinking about dinner.

She and Paula brushed cheeks at the back door and then she went inside. The house was immaculate! Surfaces gleaming and today's post neatly stacked on the kitchen table. Goodness! It looked as if there was no need to worry about tea. Something delicious was bubbling in the oven. What bliss!

'Hello! It is us!' There was the sound of the front door opening and the trampling of two pairs of small feet. 'We are returned!'

A tall, beaming, fantastically good-looking youth with a shock of blond wavy hair strode in, closely followed by the twins. 'Jan's going to take us to play football in the park after tea,' announced Alfie.

'And he's going to do my maths homework,' put in Harry.

'Brilliant. But maybe Jan would like a cup of tea first?'

'Earl Grey or Russian Caravan?' Jan grinned at her. 'How you English love your tea!'

And how the other mothers at school loved Jan! He had been another of David's ideas. 'Even if you two do set up in business with a proper office, you're still going to need some help,' he'd pointed out.

Then she'd had the phone call from a Dutch boy called Jan. He didn't want to work in London where male au pairs were more acceptable. He wanted to work just outside and Corrywood would suit him fine. But the women here, it seemed, were prejudiced. Their husbands wouldn't like it, they'd told other agencies who'd been unable to place him. So he was desperate. Could she help?

'I'll take you on to my books,' Jilly had said. 'In fact, I think I know just the family for you. My lot could do with a man around during the day.'

And that was how Jan had come to live with them! He was well behaved, didn't have BO, got on brilliantly with the boys and gave Nick some dating tips with the result that her eldest was now seeing a nice girl from school. Very occasionally she spotted David giving her a sharp look when Jan leaped up to pull back her chair for her at dinner. Great! If it kept her husband on his toes and made her feel good about herself, all well and good.

Meanwhile, Fatima had finally moved out. Somehow, Jilly hadn't been surprised when Jeremy had suggested that now Fatima's immigration papers were sorted, she should go to live with him in Suffolk. 'It would be nice to have a baby around the place,' he'd said rather wistfully. 'And we've got a great college on our doorstep. She wants to do an accountancy course. Did she tell you?'

But Fatima didn't like men! Or did she?

'Jeremy, he is different!' Was it Jilly's imagination or was that a dreamy look in the girl's lovely brown eyes? 'He is kind. Not like most men.'

There was another surprise too. One that had arrived in the post that morning. A white card with silver edging: *Collette Dubonne and Maurice Sevronne invite you to their wedding on 25 May.*

According to Marie-France, Maurice had got so jealous of Jeremy at Christmas that he'd finally proposed again. And this time, Collette had said yes.

'Shall we accept?' asked David when he saw the invitation later that evening.

She nodded. 'Definitely.'

'Is this one of those marriages because Collette is so ill?'

'Marie-France says the latest results are good so all we can do is hope, I suppose.'

He nodded. 'Why don't we go on our own? Jan can look after the boys and we could fit in a dirty weekend in Paris at the same time.'

'That,' she said, drawing her to him, 'sounds wonderful.'

Oh no. Not the phone again!

'Leave it,' murmured David.

'I can't. It's my turn for the evening shift.'

Reluctantly, she pulled away. 'Jilly and Paula's Au Pair agency!'

The voice at the other end was laced with a panic that Jilly recognised all too well. It was the voice of a stressed mother who had too much to do and not enough hours in the day.

'Hello? Kylie, please let me talk. Is that Jilly? Sorry it's rather late. I'm desperate and everyone says you're the best around here. Kylie, get down. I'm looking for some help but I've heard some real horror stories. My friends say that the French are moody and the Germans are bossy. And apparently you can't have Scandinavians because they run off with your husband. I suppose what I'm looking for is the perfect au pair. Can you help? *Kylie. I said no...!*'

PS

EMAIL FROM JILLY AND PAULA'S AU PAIR AGENCY

Come and help us celebrate our first birthday! Bring your au pair and a bottle!

ANSWERPHONE MESSAGE FROM JILLY'S MOTHER

Darling, it's me. Look, can you have your father for the weekend? And the cat too? She's expecting kittens but not until next weekend. I wouldn't ask but I've suddenly decided to go to Paris. Just a little trip. Thought I might just pop in on Marie-France. Angela keeps going on about how chic she is. You'd think she was *her* granddaughter, instead of mine…

EVERYTHING YOU NEED TO KNOW ABOUT BEING AN AU PAIR IN ANGLETERRE!

A 'spit and tell' bestseller by Antoinette Malfille.
Slash
Five-star review by Paris ~~Match~~

Dear Marie-France,

I'm so looking forward to your visit next month. I just wondered, could you bring your guitar? I'm putting on a charity concert and thought we might do a duet together. I'm a bit rusty on the bass, mind you, so I might need some help.

Love, Jeremy

Dear Jilly,

I have recently interviewed Heidi Jerman as an au pair and she has given me a reference which you wrote for her. However, I am concerned as the typing appears to be very similar to her own original application letter. Please can you verify that the reference – which is excellent! – is genuine.

Yours,
Caroline Concern

CORRYBANKS SCHOOL NEWSLETTER

Congratulations to Harry and Alfie Collins for winning the school prize on Culture. Their project on Turkish language was absolutely stunning and highly original.

We also congratulate Lottie Evans and Tom Green on winning the school talent competition. As I'm sure you'll agree, they are both very promising guitarists!

CORRYWOOD ADVERTISER

Matthew Evans and Christina Hill were married quietly last Saturday at Corrywood Registry. Their daughters Lottie and Emma were witnesses.

POSTCARD FROM LA MATERA, ITALY

Dear Matt and Lottie,

Thought I'd send you a postcard to say how much I enjoy living in Italy. Funnily enough, it was one of your au pairs who gave me the idea. I thought that if they can travel, why can't we? I've found a job as a personal assistant at a wonderful hotel and I love it! Do come and visit any time.

Karen x

Dear Dad,

Well, I've done it! I can't believe three years have gone so fast. I graduate on May 24th – and it wouldn't be the same if you weren't there. Can you ask the rest of the family if they can come too? I know Mum would have liked that. Thierry will be there as well. Did I tell you he's doing a foundation course in engineering at a school near Paris?

Love Marie-France

Dear Marie-France,

I'm so proud of you. Is it all right if Fatima and Charlie come too? He's just started pre-school – can you believe – and will be learning French! So it will be a great experience for him.

All my love,
Dad

ALSO AVAILABLE IN ARROW

The Playgroup

Janey Fraser

'A must-read for anyone who has children' Katie Fforde

It's the start of a new term at Puddleducks Playgroup

For Gemma Merryfield it'll be her first year in charge. Watching the new arrivals, she can already tell who the troublemakers will be, and not all of them are children!

What Gemma doesn't realise, though, is that former banker Joe Balls, now head of Reception at the neighbouring school, will be watching her every move. As far as he's concerned, Puddleducks puts too much emphasis on fun and games, and not enough on numbers (preferably squared).

But when one of the children falls dangerously ill and another disappears, Gemma and Joe have to set aside their differences and work together.

'A terrific story and enormous fun' Judy Astley